MW00980522

VOICES OF REVENGE

VOICES OF REVENGE

E. Bero

Copyright © 2008 by E. Bero.

ISBN: Hardcover   978-1-4363-0817-5
               Softcover   978-1-4363-0816-8

All rights reserved. No part of this book may be reproduced or transmitted in any form or by any means, electronic or mechanical, including photocopying, recording, or by any information storage and retrieval system, without permission in writing from the copyright owner.

This is a work of fiction. Names, characters, places and incidents either are the product of the author's imagination or are used fictitiously, and any resemblance to any actual persons, living or dead, events, or locales is entirely coincidental.

This book was printed in the United States of America.

To order additional copies of this book, contact:
Xlibris Corporation
1-888-795-4274
www.Xlibris.com
Orders@Xlibris.com
45086

For Marshall Mathers
AKA
Eminem

*"The closest I can give you
to experiencing the real thing"*

Thank You
Mom and Dad

CHAPTER 1

The first time was to test my inner strength for one who deserved it. And they did . . .

I had just come home from work on a late afternoon. It was hot with cool wind breezing through the air. My uncle was bitching at me for not cleaning up around the house like I always didn't.

I had my car and was old enough to leave. I wanted to treat myself to a movie and get away from uncle. A lot of things happen to a person when they catch themselves walking the streets late at night. I took with me my trusty switchblade. At seventeen years old, I was never too careful. Ever since I realized my friends weren't really my friends, I have to shield myself with something to keep them away. The mace was always attached to my keys and sometimes accidentally burned me with the spray. The knife was a lot more convenient. One thing you'll learn about me; I trust no one.

It was ten o'clock with a full moon out. I was utterly alone. I have no friends. It's a long story and I'm willing to give you the satisfaction it gave me. It's hard for me to tell the tale of my deepest darkest secrets. They do come back.

The movie theater was across town. I always went to the same theater because not that many people went there. I wouldn't feel so all-alone. It was just behind a shopping center in between a Chinese restaurant and a pool hall. I paid for my ticket and went into the dark theater. The seats were empty but a few that were filled with three other couples.

As I watched the flick about law and what happens behind closed doors like The Firm, A Few Good Men, The Client, Yadda! Yadda! I looked down passed my combat boots, which were kicked up on the seat in front of me. I saw two kids close to my age kissing in the dark. I looked away to ignore them and I saw another couple cuddling each other. I felt lonely.

At the time, I hadn't been with or spoken to a girl since I lost my girlfriend and my friends. I was made to look stupid and never once saw them or her again. People like them like to pin you down so you can't get up. You try to breathe but no air gets in. I was choking for two years.

She was great. She had short red hair, light blue eyes, and beautiful shaped lips. She was one of the most beautiful girls that hung around my kind. She hung around but she wasn't seen as one who belonged.

The first time I caught a glimpse of her was at school. She came down the office steps. She had a small black bag near her side and books in her hands. She sat down on the steps that led up to the doors of doom. She was only ten feet away from my friends and I. Her lips I wanted to kiss from far away without seeing anything else. I stood there talking to my skateboarder friends when I looked over at her. I saw her eyes glimmer from the morning sunshine reflecting on them like water. I waved for her to come over, but she just looked at me, eyes barely open because the sun was just behind me. I waved for her again. She was still questioned on what I was doing. She waved at me.

"Hey what's going on?" I asked, smiling like I was a goof.

"Oh," was the response I had in return. "I thought you were someone else."

I saw her up close without all the bright light. Nothing shinned on any other girl in the world as it did on her. Her eyes were still sparkling and glistened in the light. She had on ripped up blue jeans, a pair of combat boots, and a shirt that said GWAR. I knew she was like us. There have been some cute punk rock girls and goth girls but not like her. Not like this red headed girl who could make any man drop to his knees.

"Do you happen to know Terry?" She asked.

"Terry? The one with the rainbow bright red hair?" She nodded. "Yeah I know." I knew her all right. Everyone knew her. She was one of the dumbest girls that I have ever met. She thought that every man in the free world wanted her because she had a chest close to the size of Dolly Pardon. *And a reputation to match that chest!*

"Are you going to school here?"

"No."

"What school do you go to?"

"That stuck up school Alamo High. I met Terry at a show and we promised we'd hang out. I'm waiting for her. Do you know when she'll be here?"

Before I could try to stir her away from trouble, low and behold her chunky ass came walking up the path with her x-boyfriend, David. She was completely full of herself. She was wearing red ripped fishnets; red ripped shirt and her black leather skirt.

"Well you know me," I said to her as I put out my hand for her to shake it and get my name. She walked away with no goodbye. I watched the two smile at each other as they talked. The girls walked right passed me without saying a word and knocked into me a little as if I weren't there. She was precious and I knew her life was in danger. Doom was coming.

I saw the way David looked at the new girl. He looked at her as I looked at her. Amazed with her eyes, hair, and lips. But his expression was more of a, "I want to get into her pants," tone. I, on the other hand, saw her as something more than a girl to sleep with. She was something more.

Lila was a girl that everyone in the free world wanted. It was her hair, that bright red hair at shoulder length, which somewhat resembled a beatnik Betty.

She got into trouble with Terry as I did psychically saw. Terry got her into drugs and *boys*. Oh the boys. She didn't seem like a slut. Terry went around telling tales of her beautiful friend out of jealousy. Some people believed it and some didn't. I chose not to. My faith would always be that my one true crush was not a whore like Terry.

Lila didn't see me or notice me. I was a very nice guy when I wanted to be. She just didn't speak to guys like me. I was her age and she wanted the older popular type. Terry was so jealous she was spitting nails.

From what I heard, Terry told Lila to hit on David. Lila didn't want to because she knew they used to be together, but Terry pushed. So the two began to talk on the phone and at shows.

Show: A cross between heavy metal, to punk rock, to hard core, where a set of different bands play. People into this music like to hang out, drink, get into fights, whenever possible, start a Pit and get messed up.

Pit: (MTV term; mash pit) Group of people pushing, smashing, hitting, thrashing, and knocking down anyone in the circle of people, where they can throw out that young adult, teenage rage.

But she didn't get in the *Pit*. She just sat near the stage drinking a beer she sneaked in and let the band members smile and wink at her pretty face. When I saw her I tried to get her attention by getting into the Pit. But every time I tried to see if she was looking, she was never watching me. I felt like an idiot knowing she never remembered me nor asked for my name.

Speaking to her was not going to come for a while. She just didn't care for me.

Terry finally couldn't take it anymore. She cornered her in the bathroom at Lila's school. Fortunately I ran into a girl who attended Alamo High school. She told me what happened.

They were in the bathroom when Terry showed up with a few of her little punk rock followers. Lila had no idea Terry had a problem with her. But that was how Terry was. She liked to pretend to everyone that she was your friend and then she'd do or say things behind your back.

Lila turned to her and ended up with a punch to the face. She tried to push off Terry by pulling her hair but Terry went at her. All the while, Terrys' friends were cheering her on.

"Get her!"

"Kick her ass Terry!"

"Yeah, fuck that bitch!"

Lila ended up with a black eye, bloody nose, busted lip, and a broken ego. She was really embarrassed after that. After the whole incident, I never really saw her again. She had no idea that no one cared. We knew what Terry was like. I wish I told her what Terry was like when I met her but I guess I didn't really get the chance.

There are moments in our lives, when we look at a person or there's something that we don't have the courage to just go and grab. We fear what we don't know. I've looked at this girl and just kept on with my life like I never saw her. *But what if?* What if I took the chance to walk up to her and tell her how I fell when I laid my eyes upon her. What if? What if I saw someone stranded on the road and kept going. What if they could have been my soul mate but I never knew because I kept going. I had second thoughts.

What happens after that sometimes, or at least for me, is it plagues me. I think about regret. I regret not telling her about Terry. I regret not telling her I want her number. Hell, I regret not telling her my name.

During the summer I spoke about her off and on. People asked me sometimes why I wasted my breath on a girl I would never have. She was *too good* for me. I didn't mention her to my girlfriend Mary though. She was in love with me. Mary pushed the relationship on me.

Then I saw *her*. She was at a party. And so was I. I helped Lila out while she was drunk. She barely remembered me. But after that it was smooth sailing. Unfortunately, my girlfriend caught us kissing. She left crying. I blew it off. I was like, "whatever."

And Lila was a dream come true. I remembered the first time we made love. It was under the stars out in a field by a house I used to live at. I treated her like she was the number one priority in my life. I guess that was my fall. I took her out a lot. She avoided hanging out with the crowd that once loved her. She was embarrassed about what Terry had said and done to her. But not a one even remembered anything about that. People only remember that she was a very pretty girl. If Terry was around to challenge her again, she didn't want everyone to see what happened in the bathroom.

After I got jumped by all my friends I didn't care. I was just embarrassed that it happened. I thought Lila would be there to comfort me. She had been jumped by Terry so I figure she'd tell me it doesn't matter or everything is going to be all right, you still have me, *catch my drift?*

All it did was lower her opinion of me. After almost a year together she seemed to be acting different. Just after the fight with my friends, she suddenly had all these people she was hanging out with, *without me.* Every time I tried to be with her, she made up excuses.

One day, I skated to her house, taking the back entrance to her room. I don't even want to remember what I saw. Her on Nick. Nick Kind of laughed at me, while she covered herself up. He was like, "could you shut the door?"

I began to cry in that lonely dark theater. I turned away from my memories to focus on the movie but it was already over. Before I left the theater, I wanted to get something to drink so I stood in line with the other people. The couple next to me argued about something that I couldn't take my ears away from.

"I thought I meant something to you." Said the man who was angry with this carrot top voluptuous woman.

"Look, it just happened. I didn't plan it . . . I'm sorry. I thought I wanted to be with you but I think we're better off apart. So we can be free to"-

"Fuck anyone?" He said. And as he said those dirty words she smiled. "How could you do this to me? At the movies no less." He raised his arms at the theaters. "You're nothing but a fuck'n whore!" Everyone was staring.

I watched him storm out of the building cursing on his way out. When I looked back, she was in my view smiling at me like she was a beautiful guilty proud bitch. I stared at those evil green eyes. I noticed the way her red hair dangled down her face. She smiled at me but I was disgusted. Why are the redheads so conceited? They like to sleep around and hardly settle down to normal faithful lives.

I left the theater thinking about the man and how he felt. I knew what he felt in his heart. The desires to give all you have to that one beautiful girl and she throws it in the trash as if it were easy to come by.

I stirred my car towards the exit. The red head walked in front of my car then over to my window. I imagined rolling my tires over her head and the hot rubber of my tires is burning her *red hair*. She smiled at me.

"I know this is strange to ask, but could you give me a lift? I kind of lost my ride." She squeezed her breasts together as she spoke. They rubbed together like water balloons ready to pop.

I wanted her sluty hands off of my vehicle, even though my car didn't look as good as it would turn out. I *was* going to go home and eat. One of those comical light bulbs lit up inside of my head. I smiled at my own imaginations. She believed I wanted her. A lesson learned is a lesson that should be taught. She needed a good talking to. And I could talk *all night long*.

"Sure, I can give you a ride."

As I contemplated the whole idea in my head, she already came around to the passenger side of *my* car and got in. I looked at her strangely as if she had no right to invade me and or my car. I got a flash of Lila's face on hers. I closed my eyes and looked at her again. *Don't bring your fuck'n promiscuous drama in my automobile!*

"Where to?" I asked.

"Your place would be nice." She laughed. She must have thought I was older. I was probably eight to ten years younger than she was.

She let her hair down. She flashed her legs at me. Yeah, they were nice, but they were a weapon meant to use or hurt people. I can see how men would do anything to get into the pants of these women. These women of the Devil are good. He paints a nice portrait on the outside but inside they were black, empty, souless.

I pulled into *our spot*. She and I made love there. Lila and me. It was our special place. At the time I wanted to go there every time we had an anniversary.

"Here?" She asked.

"Yeah," I said as I laughed out loud.

I took her hand as I helped her out of the car. We walked down passed the creek where there was no one around for miles. I knew that only because I spent countless hours walking around that area thinking of Lila. I would picture us making love in our very special spot.

I could hear the bugs humming in the wind. The crickets were croaking loudly and strange animals called into the night. How would I scare this bimbo? I should make her get naked, take her clothes, and leave her out here with nothing. Or maybe I should tell her that I'm some crazy guy with a gun and I'll be watching her from abroad. We're getting there soon so I had better think of something.

I stopped at a tree near *my* special spot. I looked around. She smiled at me. She sat down in the grass giving me that *it's time* look. She took off her shirt. As I stood over her, looking at her breasts, I tried to imagine I were somewhere else. She grabbed me by my jacket and pulled me on top of her. We kissed with the moonlight shinning over my head. She started kissing my ear; sucking my neck. She pulled on my jeans wanting me to take them off. I was hesitant. I hated it. *Every moment of it.* Then she proceeded to unzip my jeans. I reached into my back pocket for my seven-inch blade. I wanted to rip apart her clothes and make her eat them.

Instead I began to hear whispers. "Kill her." It said. Then my heart began to pound hard. I was sweating and felt dizzy all over. I felt, as though I would faint right there on the breasts of a girl I didn't know. All I could hear were so many voices. Voices that did not have one familiar tone with each call.

I pulled the knife closer as I could barely breathe. I felt hands choking me and I thought she was doing it. But it was nothing but shadowed hands choking me to do it or I would die myself. I brought the blade down into her chest. She screamed and I didn't know what to do. I couldn't breathe myself; the hands didn't let go. The more I resisted, the more they screamed and choked. I tried to aim for her heart; still she screamed out loud. As I swung down the blade I felt and heard her breastplate crack. She sucked in her breath. I slammed into her throat. Her mouth dropped open as I backed away leaning against the tree. Her hands tried to grab the knife but her arms just fell to the side. She had this look on her face as if she couldn't believe that I stabbed her. The hands let go of my neck and the voices stopped whispering.

I watched her bleed to death. Her last sound did not come out. It was only a silent screech. She grabbed the knife and closed her eyes. A tear fell down her cheek. Oh god! Oh my god! What have I done? The voices were gone and left me all alone to explain to myself what I had done. I got down on my knees and pulled on my hair screaming. I pulled out the blade and as I did blood started squirting out of her body. So much blood! I wiped my forehead with my sleeve. Blood on my face. I looked down at my feet. Blood was spreading around the woman's' body as if someone had left a hose in the grass on full blast. I was afraid and shaking all over.

As I began to walk away, I couldn't take my eyes off of the mess I had made. I ran looking back as I leaped. I ran down near the dirty creek water to wash off my face. I watched the blood sink to the bottom of the clear water. As soon as I cleaned off, I rushed to my car. I kept trying to think of what to do. What if I got caught? I was panicking in my car. I looked around and it was back to that same insect humming as when we first made our way up the creek.

Sometimes when someone's watching you, you can feel it deep inside and you want shudder. But I didn't feel that. Instead, I screamed out loud in my car. I put in a CD. I turned the industrial music up loud to the point of busting out my speakers. At that moment, even though I knew some kind of being was there, making me do it, I was the happiest person alive. I headed down to my brothers' house.

"That stupid bitch!" I cried out loud.

Then I heard a sound I didn't want to hear at this moment in time. Red and blue flashing lights trailed behind me. I looked in the mirror to see if there was any blood on my face. There was none. I tossed my jacket on the floor as I stuck my blade in my glove compartment. I pulled over to the side of the road.

My heart began to pound as I saw the policeman in my rearview mirror. He was big, black, and tall. He had on a blue uniform and my head began to swell. He knocked on my window as I sat there thinking to myself, trying not to sweat. I rolled down my window.

"License and registration please." He said while looking at his pad of traffic tickets he could be distributing to some poor sucker out there whose license plate light went out.

"Sure," I said as I nervously smiled. I quivered and shook while I pulled out my license. I stuck my arm out the window and unfortunately I dropped it on the floor. "Whoops," I said as I opened the door. I accidentally smacked him in the head with the car door. The officer leaned down to pick up my wallet for me. He stood up tightly clenching my wallet. He looked at me for a moment as I had apologized then looked at my license.

"Insurance?"

Oh no! It was in the glove compartment with the blade. "Oh yeah!" I smiled. I reached over, opened it up, and pushed the blade aside. I grabbed the form and handed it to him. "There you go."

He looked at it, then returned it to me. "Mr. Alex Dugan, you were going seventy in a fifty-five speed zone."

That's what this was about? Some stupid petty speeding rampage! Maybe this was just a way to catch me without having to restrain me. In an act of murder you don't want to upset or let on that you know about what they had done.

"I didn't notice." I tried to look innocent but in this life and with his title he's probably heard it a million times.

"Well this is a moving violation which cannot be handled with just a quick payment." He signed the pink slip, then tore the tissue-like paper off. It echoed through the night loudly. He then handed me my wallet. "You ain't gonna hit me now are you?" He laughed, so what the hell . . . I laughed with him. "You have a good night. And watch that dial."

"Thank you officer." I said thanking the heavens above for my release.

He walked back to his black and white police car. He was shaking his head and laughing. I watched him drive onto the freeway. He turned off his lights and it was over. It went completely silent and hollow. My eyes watered in relief. I couldn't believe this was reality. I was afraid. And there was nothing to comfort me now but the silent sounds of a few cars whizzing by me as I sat there holding back the tears.

"Hey Alex!" Jumped my brother Anthony. "What's up bro?" He smacked my head a little and gave me a big bear hug. "How is it going?"

"Okay and yourself?" I asked trying to hide the difference in myself.

"Great. Now sit your weird ass down and have a little with Jennifer and me."

We walked over the front porch where my brothers' wife sat. They were snorting cocaine, which they did occasionally. It used to upset me that they took cocaine. Growing up, I only liked to take certain drugs that I knew I couldn't get addicted to.

My brother started taking cocaine and crank when he ran away. He was a bit hefty and couldn't find any way to get rid of the blubber that had collected around his belly over the years. When he noticed the change in his size after taking cocaine for a couple of weeks, he kept on. When he reached the point of his liking, he tried to quit but it was really hard. It took some doing but he cut back a lot. Now it is an occasional thing. I tried to help him as he was trying to get off of the stuff.

"You want a hit?" He asked while sticking the tray in my face. I didn't like powder too much, but I needed something to get my mind off of a lot of things I had done that day. I looked at my brother as he seriously held the tray up close. His brown hair was brushed back and looked blonde in the light that came from inside of the house. His skin was really pale as he was hardly ever in the sun with him working the graveyard shift.

"Sure, I'll take a little." I took hold of the tray.

"That's strange. I have never seen you take any of this shit. I just have the common courtesy to ask."

"So, does this mean I can't have any?"

He laughed then smacked me on the shoulder. I could see in his trembling hands that he was wired. He continuously tapped on his cigarette as he smoked. I hoped that the old habit was dying easy and not so hard.

Tony looked at me strangely. His eyebrows came together. "Say man, what are you doing here so late? Where were you?" He asked me.

I was not expecting to answer such easy questions with so much on my mind. I didn't know how I would answer that. What was I to say, 'Hey Tony, I was board and decided to kill some bimbo on a whim and I'm afraid I'm going to get caught.' But I had to think of something.

"I was at the movies."

"The movies?" Disapproving. "They're not open this late."

"There was one theater open late. After I watched a movie, I went to get something to eat at a twenty-four hour burger joint."

"The one close to here, Jimmy's burgers?" He asked me.

What was up with all of the questions? I looked at him. I think I must have scared him with my facial expression. "Yeah." I said sternly.

"Oh, cause that's funny . . . they closed down a long time ago."

I looked at him as he put a cigarette in his mouth. I closed my eyes not knowing what to say. I looked at him again. He smiled at me.

"What?" I asked.

"I didn't say anything."

I closed my eyes again. "How are the kids?" I asked trying to change the conversation. My brother had the most wonderful sons in the world. From a person like me, it seems strange that I would even think of children. But my one wish would be to have my one son named after me. It would always be him and me with no crazy wife/mother around to ruin him. I could be everything to that boy.

Tony went on to tell me the boys were doing well in school. John was four and David was five. He felt like he was getting on in age but he was only twenty-one at the time. To him it seemed like yesterday he was sixteen.

The cocaine was hitting my head pretty hard. I began to notice what it was doing as I spoke rapidly and tangled a weave into my tongue. I had enough. For a person like me who never took any cocaine, it sure was making me feel up and up. I looked at Jennifer who was quiet the whole night. She stood up.

"I'm going to check on the kids. Besides I'm tired." She said as she was walking inside. She didn't take much cocaine. She was a pothead and that didn't bother me so much because she was a good mother who never did it around the kids or while they were near. *And* she spent every waking moment with them.

We saw her giggling in the house. The two of us started laughing. We didn't know why. Maybe it was because she was messed up. Maybe it was because we were messed up. I stopped laughing. I began to wonder off into my own thoughts. I was thinking about the red headed girl. I didn't even know her name.

"What's wrong Alex? Coke fucking with your head?" Asked Tony.

I looked at him kind of sad. Then I tried to push all of my thoughts out of my head. "Nah. The coke is actually making me feel a little better."

"You look different tonight. You also look worried."

I looked up. "Tony, what's the craziest thing you ever did? And I don't mean things like bending backwards to fight for your rights. I mean bad . . . Fucked up. Like you did something you regret or you could've."

"If you're asking if I ever rapped . . . No. Something crazy? Let me think." He looked up at the sky, which was the blackest blue I had ever seen. I always remembered that night of horror. It was the darkest color I have ever thought it to be. There were only a few stars out that night. It seemed to be that way all night.

"Brother, something's you don't tell anyone. But I trust you." At that moment I thought maybe he was in the same constellation with me. He killed too. And if he did, then I could tell him about what I did.

"One night some friends and I got really messed up. And I mean completely off the wall. We were drinking, smoking, and we took some PCP." He took a drink of his beer. "I don't like to remember this night of stupidity. We ran out of money for weed and beer so I stole some from Uncle Mike. After that we went driving around. Keep in mind that I was in high school at the time. There was a party going on, on the upper side of town. You know, rich folks. We went in as if we owned the place. When they noticed us, they told us to leave. Instead we started drinking everything. One man was about to call the cops. But before he could, we beat him up pretty bad. The people started getting out of hand. One of my friends pulled out a knife. He told them to get in the walk-in closet. We locked them in there. They were yelling and screaming. We stole a lot of stuff then took some bats and busted up the house." He turned away from the sky. He looked at me.

I just had this expression on my face like, "What?"

"Pretty fucked up aye?" He took a drink of his beer.

"That's it?" I asked.

"Well what did you want, an axe murder or something?"

I made this face as if to say, yes. He looked at me funny. He didn't want to think I really meant it.

"Forget it."

"No Alex, what do you mean? Maybe I misunderstood."

"Tony, do you ever think about people who hurt you or revenge."

"Sure, like my teachers." He laughed.

"Would you ever do anything mean to them?"

"What can you do?"

"Did I ever tell you about a girl named Lila?"

"Not really."

"I was in love with her."

"That's great Alex."

"I caught her fucking another guy." I turned to him when I said that and gave him a look that must have put fear into him for years on in. He was worried about me at that very moment.

"You didn't do anything . . . Did you?" He was concerned.

I did a side smile as if I did. But then I made a sad face. Now he was really confused. I looked down. "No I didn't." He let out a relieved breath of air. "I wish I did. I wish I could've kicked her in the head or something. She crushed me. I never loved anyone so much in my life. She was beautiful. She had this dark red hair and these lips like no other girl. Now when I see women who screw with men's' heads, I want to slap them or hurt them. Is that wrong of me?"

"Fuck no. You're talking to a guy whose girl left him with the kids for another man. Usually you never hear about that. The man usually leaves. But that's not the point. She cheated on me. Did you know she doesn't even want to see the boys?"

"Yeah."

"What kind of a mother is that? You tell me, I mean, I have to be with my sons, they're apart of me. You don't think I'd like to cut her fuck'n throat for that? I mean, fuck my feelings for the moment, but what about my sons? They're the ones who have to suffer. But you can't just go around cutting their throats and beating people up for their actions." He took a drink of his beer. He smiled. "Unless you're crazy."

Poor guy. I looked at him. "I never thought about it that way. I just thought about other stuff. Like cheating stealing whores who have no self-respect. I never thought about mothers who abandoned their kids."

"Well, why would you? You're only seventeen. It should be years before you get into those situations. There's no reason to worry about that."

That night I woke up on my uncle's couch crying. I had a nightmare about what I had done. My uncle was getting a midnight snack when he heard me panting. He looked over at me while he had a sandwich in his hand.

The light from the icebox closed and it was dark once again. I didn't realize it was him until I heard his voice. "Alex, are you alright?" He asked.

I just looked at him and lay back, holding the covers close to my chest in the dark. I couldn't speak. No, I'm not all right uncle, and I never will be.

CHAPTER 2

After the first time, I could not live with the guilt. It was eating up my soul into nothingness. I was quieter than before, not wanting to tell the tale of my actions. I was afraid if I did speak out loud; my story would come out. I could never let my soul tell another what I had down.

What I realized then was that my life was nothing but bits and fragments of *nothing*. I had nothing to show for my life or childhood. I couldn't think of what to live for anymore. But I found something that gave *new* meaning to my life. I mean no one gave two shits about me so I was going to take all of that heartache back and onto another. I was going to make people remember my face onto their death. The Redhead was a *bitch*. She was a whore for cheating on her boyfriend and being so god damn proud of it. If people could stop the hurt before they commit their actions, I could forgive. But when you pretend to love while you're with others, then I *will* dig your grave for you.

To me it was just a way of getting back at Lila and people like her. I wish I did kill her when I caught her. I would have let her torture my soul for her faithful love. She took away everything I believed in life about love and passion. I have no one to love. And just like others, she fed me a love that just wasn't there. I was a blind fool hoping that the fairytales were true. But one thing was true; I had been kissed once and changed from a frog into a prince. *A demonic prince.*

My parents were nothing to me. They were *nobodies*. They hid from me like they wanted nothing to do with me, trying to avoid interaction with me as much as possible. They will pay. And I can remember every bit of pain I went through as a child.

When I was young, my father was in the Military and my mother took care of my brother and I. She was young and didn't know what to do so when worse came to worse, she pulled out my fathers' belt. At that time the Vietnam War was going on. Daniel Dugan died in combat. I only spent few times with him when I was too young to remember. I can only hope he was nothing like my stepfather. When I was five my mother married a man named Patrick Mchale. Her lost love was replaced with a man who treated her like a dog and she didn't care because he had a job that would take care of her and her two sons.

His favorite past time was to hit us with the belt. He grabbed my hand and wouldn't let go. He sometimes used the belt buckle on us. He hit my left hand so much I was lucky I didn't write with that hand or people would have noticed.

When they were having problems with money, they moved in with my stepfathers' grandparents in Dallas, Texas. They sent me with my Uncle Michael and his wife in Gilroy, California. Gilroy was great. I loved California. I wished my mother would have stayed here and dumped that awful husband of hers. My uncles' wife was real quiet. But I had a feeling that she didn't want anything to do with us.

When Michael went to work, my cousin would beat me up. We fought all the time. Or at least I was beat up. He was four years older than I was and three times bigger than I was. One can only assume that this is what life was like so live with it. The two of us didn't go to the same school because he was in middle school and I was in elementary school.

Tony ran away because he was tired of Uncle Mike telling him what to do. He lived at his friends' house with their parents. I was left alone with my uncle who barely even spoke to me. I don't even know if he got the money my mother was supposed to send me or if she just didn't send it.

Starting middle school was tougher than I thought it would be. I had no friends and this guy who was three hundred pounds and two feet taller than me, wanted to beat me up. He followed me to my next class, pushing me on the floor all the way there. I was afraid. I didn't know how to fight especially someone of that girth.

"I heard you were talking shit." He says.

Now at this point, I will freeze the whole story. For instance, let's say I was *talking shit*. What does that infamous line mean to kids these days? It's an excuse really. It's a way to pick the most awkward and ridiculous fights. I have never told anyone the line, but I have heard it on occasion. Now I've never spoken to this giant before in my life, let alone do I know the bastards' name. So how on earth, in this god forsaken universe was I able to *talk shit*. At this point I would like to run for my life.

I told him I didn't even know him. But he didn't care. So I called him a *fatass* who liked to pick on people smaller than them because anyone else would've kicked his ass by now. He got mad. Before I knew it, I was being punched in the head. With his weight on top of me, I couldn't breathe. The teachers were the only ones to save me from suffocation.

With everyone treating me in this fashion, after the childhood beatings from stepfather, mother, cousin, and now classmates, how would I make it out of life alive? I am what you call the one who would like to commit suicide or want to take action. Which do you think I was? From my judgment with the red head it's pretty clear where I might turn out to be.

There are a few kinds of ways that we teenagers use to get through hard times. Some of us just sit here and take it until one day we just blow up on someone worse than anyone could ever expect. Then there are those types who take all those horrible days to heart and end up killing themselves. *And then,* there are those vengeful people who let it eat away until they come back for revenge. Keep an eye out for those kids who seem to be scared to go to school and also those who like to bully around others.

I switched schools. I always switched schools. But this time I met a great bunch of guys. We didn't care what anyone thought of us or if they wanted to beat us up or shake our hand. All we wanted to do was listen to Industrial rock and go skateboarding. We would get stoned and practice some tricks on our skateboards. These guys taught me that life's too short to worry about what other people think about me. We stole from other people. My friend Gabriel would ride on his board next to some old ladies and steal their purses. They couldn't chase him as he skated away. They were too old.

One day we were hanging out at Burger King across the street from my house. We sat outside drinking soda and talking about sponsors that could support us. I watched this old lady get a tray of food through the window, and she sat down to eat. I looked at her purse. It was calling me. I kept imagining twenty dollar bills in her old lady wallet which probably looked like a beaded coin bag.

"Aye, you want to get some acid tonight?" I asked.

"What for? You got money?" Asked my friend Doug.

"Nope." I smiled as I looked at the old lady inside.

Everyone turned their heads to look at what I was looking at. They laughed and all at once they were caught up in conversation.

"All right Alex, you know the rules," said Gabriel. "The person who brings it up must want to do it themselves. We'll be waiting on our boards when you get it. I'll leave your board right here, so you can jump on it when you get out those doors. Just hurry."

I smiled at them. I wanted to impress them. I did as instructed leaving my skateboard with them. I thought nothing could get passed me. This was the Day of Judgment. This is one of those days that changes your life forever. And what could've been is now what you wouldn't want. Something you could have avoided *then* is now lost in imagination.

So I walked in. I went to the bathroom trying to find my moment in time. My friends were watching from outside. The old lady looked behind her and saw me. She smiled unpleasantly at me, then back to her food. I acted calm as I traveled passed her table. I just reached out and grabbed the *old bags'* purse. I saw my friends as I was running to the door. They jumped on their boards as planned. But what wasn't planned, was the two cops who had walked through the doors as I was about to escape. It just so happened they wanted to eat there. But in the car, they were arguing over Chinese or Mexican food. To end the fight, they pulled in *here* . . . where I was making my first attempt to juvenile delinquency.

My choices were limited to *one*. My uncle was through. His wife was on the verge of leaving. She didn't know how to handle us kids. My brother gave him a hard time and now I was. I wasn't ready to deal with the life I wish I avoided from the start. But it was my own doing, so I should take it like the boy I so eagerly did not want to be. My ending days in California were spent with my friends. They gave me a gift along the way. It was something I would never forget. My friends decided to throw me a little goodbye party. They knew a lot about me. They had me drunk and stoned.

As I sat in a recliner, my closest friends came hovering over me. I had a joint in my mouth and was laughing at some jokes that the others were telling from the couch next to me. I looked up at them with squinting eyes trying to gather all my thoughts.

"We have a gift for you."

What was this gift that had them so exited and serious. They grabbed me by my arms and threw me into one of the empty rooms. There was one light that came on. It was red, which reminded me of an old military movie. I stood there trying to figure out the riddle that they had left me concocting.

And there my riddle was, plain as day. She walked out behind me. She was *hot*. She was in high school no doubt. I was only in eighth grade. She was wearing this little tank top and a tight skirt. Her hair was long and a light brown color. She walked right up to me, not one word uttered, then grabbed my face giving me my first real tongue kiss.

You know, you'll always remember your first time. She tried to make me feel comfortable; and she did. I *was* nervous. My palms were sweating. I tried to hold her as we kissed but I was shivering too much to get a grip on reality. Sometimes I think back, not about the girl, but the friends who were cool enough to put that together. Never again would I meet friends who stood together and didn't stab each other in the back. The right friends are hard to find.

That was the last chapter of my childhood in California. I said my good-byes. I headed to Texas where troubles begin . . .

In the beginning you find yourself in bed with what was so appealing for the first time. I wanted to feel the joy that I had my first time. I couldn't let go. After rummaging through the high school sluts, I met my girlfriend Mary. She got attached and whether or not she wanted to be with me, I didn't care. She was pretty but anorexically skinny. It wasn't a turn on. My new friends and I were skating around downtown and she was shopping for new clothes there with her friends. She started to hang out with us on the weekends, watching us skateboard. I slept with her to kill time.

I had no feelings for the girl. I didn't care to know who she was or where she was coming from. That's probably why I bit it so hard in the end. She told me she liked me a lot and thought of me all the time. I couldn't reply in the same way she had wanted.

One night, I went to a party. My friends and I were drinking beer. This was around the time I was changing. I was growing into a skater-punk. As soon as I got there, my friend Nick, Steve, and Craig were sitting in the back porch, smoking weed. We were joking around all night long.

Then this girl walked outside drunk as hell. I didn't see her face because she was leaning over and her dark red hair covered her face. She leaned on the side of the house to let it all out. Her hair was silky soft and *red*. It was shoulder length and straight. Then she looked up . . . I saw her face. I know her. She had full lips that looked like they were pushed out ready to kiss. Her eyes were blue surrounded by an oriental curve. She was wearing this black and white stripped long sleeved shirt and a tight long black skirt. It was love all over again. I couldn't take my eyes off of her. I hadn't thought about or seen her in a very long time. She had curves in all the right places.

She looked up with this sick feeling expression on her face. Right away, before anyone could move, I flew to her for companionship. Oh Lila, dear Lila. I waited so long for the chance to speak with you again.

"Are you okay?" I asked.

She looked at me. The expression on her face made me think one of two things, either I disgusted her or she was completely sick. "I'm okay. I just hardly drink. My stomach can't handle too much."

I gave her this look waiting to see if I sparked anything within her to think of who I was. "Well, if you want, we can sit in the front and just relax for a little while. I could keep you company while you try to sick it out. And I like to listen."

She smiled shyly. "That would be really nice." She said after a short while of staring at me.

As we walked toward the front of the house, I stared at her and would not take my eyes off of her. As I looked back, my friends were staring at us. I smiled back at them, for some of them were the ones who told me I would never be within a few feet of Lila. I smiled at her like I was in love. I wanted her to really look at me and see the person whom she spoke to that one time.

We sat against one of the cars parked on the side of the house. She was looking down at the floor while holding onto her stomach. I just stared at her beautiful face. I wanted to make her think that I was a god. I was sweet and would do anything for her if she just said the *word*.

"Don't think about it." I said as I looked at her.

"I can't help it, it hurts."

"Well what can I do to take your mind off of it?" I can't believe I said that. She must think I'm a pervert. "I didn't mean it like it sounded." I put out my hands like I was innocent. "Let me just say that I know who you are."

"Oh you do, do you? And how is that?" She asked.

"Well, I can't believe you can't remember me." I turned away. Uncanny isn't it? I can sit here and hope that someone I'm in love with could remember at least the few minutes we spoke. I looked back at the girl. "We met one day at my school where you were waiting for Terry."

She closed her eyes trying to remember and get rid of the pain. She looked at me again. "Would you rather I lie and say I do when I don't?" She asked with a scared expression on her face.

I looked away as though I were angry. But if I could just sit here and take the time to realize that we only spoke for five minutes in time and since then, we had never spoken a word to each other. I only wished she would talk with me. I looked back at her then changed my frown upside down.

"Oh yeah, just lie to me. I want you to think I'm the most popular guy in the world." I said.

She started laughing at my jokes. We talked all night long. I found out that she was more than just a pretty face and a beautiful body. She was smart, she was cool, and she was the most precious thing next to a flower. And her name just made my heart sink. I wanted to kiss those pretty lips. Unfortunately,

I did not have the chance to. She did however, give me her phone number. And so it begins.

"Alex, where have you been?" Asked Mary.

Just hearing her voice made me sick. I had forgotten all about this skinny little girl. But what was I to do with her. Should I tell her the truth? I had fallen for a beautiful girl with a mind that drives me up the wall . . . Nah. You always have to have a back up plan. This beautiful girl will be calling my house to be with me. And if she doesn't, there will always be Mary.

"Sorry Mary. I was out practicing with my friends. There's some skating sponsors that are coming to town soon and I want to be prepared. That's all. What do you say, we meet up downtown and get something to eat?"

She was quiet for a minute. "Well okay. When do you want to go?" She was excited.

"Soon baby, soon."

I hardly held the girls' hand when I saw her. She was dressed real good; I'll give her that much credit. I didn't feel right. She wanted to make more plans but I told her we would wait and see. I took her to eat at some Chinese restaurant.

After that, I thought I was so slick. A week later, I went with Lila to the mall. The two of us went walking around and then got something to eat. I saw my friends there. I said hi, but I didn't want to hang out with them. All I wanted was Lila; I was focused on her the whole time. Nick sent me strange vibes. He looked at Lila with these puppy eyes. He looked at me with evil eyes. I hope he's not jealous. That would be fatal.

After we ate, we walked around the top floor. We sat down at a bench. I looked at her in those tight jeans and tank top. She was hot.

"Would it be too much if I asked for you to kiss me?" I pleaded.

She looked at me then smiled with those beautiful kiss lips. She stood up. She touched my cheeks with both hands. She pulled my face close to hers and she kissed me. I was like butter. That feeling would never exist *again*. I kissed her lips and her tongue softly and passionately. Just the way those lips should have been kissed.

"Alex!"

I jumped up in surprise. I turned my head around whilst Lila had her arms wrapped around my neck. And there was *Mary*. She was standing there with her little friends. She just looked at me with tear-filled eyes. And I didn't know what to do. So I shrugged, like I didn't care, as if to say, "Oh well, you caught me. Now be gone with you." What made me let her go was the fact that I had Lila in my hands. She was mine and I had no need for little skinny Mary. I saw tears streaming down her face. And that was that.

Sometime after that I went to a skate park where all the sponsors were choosing their pick of good solid skaters. I skated my tail off out there in the heat. I thought about Lila the whole time. She was my priority now.

I was so tired. I can remember everything down to the temperature of my forehead. As soon as I was done, I went to the urinals to release myself. I wasn't even sure if it were real cause I was light headed from the heat. The moment stays with me here in my mind, in my memories, in my broken heart.

I looked in the mirror and began to check my teeth. I splashed water on my face then slicked it through my hair. I saw the reflection of them all. In walked Steve my big fat punk rocker friend. I turned around with a smile.

"I didn't know you guys were going to the skateboarding competition." I said to them. He was with his fat friend Joe.

"I came to see you." Said Steve.

"Cool."

"I heard you've been talking shit." Said Steve.

Now we can pause . . . Okay what's up with the famous line from my *so-called* friend? But here we go . . .

"What are you talking about?"

"I know all the things you said. You told everyone that I couldn't get a girl as good as Lila. That I'm nothing but a big fat slob."

"Get off it man. I never said that. I'm outa here." I grabbed my board and headed towards the door.

He grabbed me by my shirt and threw me against the wall. He started punching me in the stomach and in the face. I didn't know what to do. I wanted to hit him with my board but it was on the ground. I kneed him between the legs. He grabbed my head and banged it against the wall. I fell to the floor. They walked out laughing at me. I sat up on the floor spitting up blood. Then I grabbed my board crying. What was I to do in this situation? I really wanted to stick up for myself and for once be strong enough to *not* be the kid who was beat up. But I was so small.

I picked my pride off of the floor and headed out the door. As soon as I walked out, I saw the crowd of punk rockers waiting for me. Nick and Steve were in the front. I stepped back. Then I ran. I ran as fast as I could but someone tripped me in my escape. They beat me. They beat me until I couldn't get up anymore.

I curled up into a little ball. How was I going to explain this to my chauvinistic stepfather? I would have to hide out or show him the truth.

Some people tried to help me up but my reaction was to tell them to, *fuck off!* I lay there like a vicious Chihuihua.

I have no pride, I have no strength, and I swear that one day it would be different. I found out what had been eagerly waiting for me. Nick and Steve were jealous that I was with Lila. For the longest time Nick had a crush on her and she would never give him the time of day because he always came off as perverted. She was with me. His friend got the beautiful girl. The only way to make him feel better was to make me look bad. And they did a good job of that. I wonder what she'll think of me now. She shouldn't have been with someone who was a loser. But her reaction was just to ignore it.

Now, when I think of my childhood, I wonder where I had gone wrong. My name is Alex Dugan. And I was a loser. My story to you is about revenge and what it takes to get there. I wonder what you will think of me. I tell my most inner humiliations to avoid the reoccurrence of the next murderer. I thought my words should be shared. Your children should think twice about picking on people. They pushed too much. I can't take all this life that society has to offer. I am the one who will be waiting thirty years till you forget about me and *then*, I come back into your life and onto your death. Remember me. I will *always* remember you.

I never went to a show after that, but just one time. I was afraid, as was Lila. I took a chance. My friend Tom, the only friend left, went with me. His friends' band was playing and we got in for free. I wasn't up to going but I didn't want to hide away. I had to show them, they couldn't break me.

My heart was sinking into my stomach when I saw Steve there with the same fat fuckers. I didn't go inside once I saw them. I sat in the front on one of the picnic benches. At the end of the show, Steve and his friends walked up to me. Oh god, another fight!

"Hey Alex, I never meant for all those punkers to jump you. They just didn't like you or something." He turned away. "I'm sorry." He said. Then under his breath he said, "Yeah right."

I just walked away. I didn't want to be there. How could he? My own friend. I wished I could kill him. Or told him off. But then, I still hold that beauty queen.

As time went on, more people ignored me. I was nothing but a sorry ass skater boy. When school was almost out, I made an effort to pass with good grades. I never tried so hard. I had high marks and for the first time, teachers told me I had potential. They used to think I was slow. But I never tried then.

Summer came around and my last friend moved away. He hardly talked to me. When he did, it felt like a sympathetic conversation. No one to get high with, no one to talk to. I had no one. I was completely and utterly alone. I decided to just finish high school and go to college.

That summer I spent it alone in the hot Dallas sun. It was after my birthday when I lost Lila. I told you her story. After losing Lila, I didn't even leave the house. The only time I left was to get weed.

In July I went back to California to visit with my uncle, then convinced him to let me stay. I couldn't stand being in Dallas anymore. I had no one in California either. I couldn't find my old friends. The only person I had was my brother. You never know how hard it is to be without anyone until they're all gone.

Hurt, pain, and regret. These are the only feelings I have left in me now. Ever since the first time, I have felt nothing. All I can think about is how scary it was to kill her. It wasn't who she was or her family or her life. It was about my family, my life, and me.

I think a lot about Lila. The girl, the one who broke my heart is making me feel pain in my chest. I wish it were never like this. I should've known something that sweet tasted so bad.

Being alone was a different story.

I was in love only one time during my life. I have never had another girlfriend since then. When I loved, I knew every detail about her. She was five feet three inches. Her father was well off, which meant, she usually got what she wanted. She looked like a model. At times, I had to pat myself on the back for landing a girl that good looking. Presently, I kick myself in the ass thinking of how blind I was. I should have just dropped her and that was it.

I could hardly remember my first time. *The surprise.* It was good and I can remember how it happened and what she was wearing, but I can't even remember her name. It was in me to hate these women of my nightmares. Of this earth. They use people and abuse people worse than a man can. It's a given that we're all heartless assholes. But they have the power to hold your child in her arms and tell you you're not the father. They can say a child is yours so you can support them, when really it was from the guy she slept with last week and might be the one she sleeps with next week.

I have a few pictures of some girls I was dating in school. Lila especially. What I miss was the companionship. I miss holding hands with a woman, knowing she was with me. It matters no more. I am part of the *Al Bundy* club, *No mame!*

It was quiet, dark. A solitude I was used to. Too late for anyone to be out on a work night. I had slept the whole day after work. I found myself roaming the streets of San Jose. Only bums were out now sleeping in the streets. I just walked out of the house not knowing why I was even there. Not going anywhere but walking in one direction.

"May I help you?" Asked the lady with an Eastside accent.

"Oh ah, can I have a burrito and a large sprite?" I pulled out my wallet and counted out my money.

"It'll be four sixty three please." She walked away to make the food. I liked eating burritos from little stands like this one. It was well worth the effort to come to this side of town.

"Here you go sir." She said as she handed me my food and drink. When I gave her money, I could smell something horrid. Then I felt hands on my shoulder. I turned around. An old man stood before me. He was short, dirty with rags covering his body, and his breath smelled worse than him. Through my eyes, no man or even *woman* for that matter, should live out in the streets.

"Do yah have any change?" Asked the dirty old man with a raspy voice.

I pulled out my wallet and gave ten dollars. That wasn't half as much as I could have given him. He happily took the money and left. I sat down at the table outside the stand. After I finished eating, I wanted to go home. I could see my car from where I was walking. My beautiful 58 Chevy, with a brand new paint job was staring at me from afar.

As I walked I could see out the corner of my eye. The bum was there in plain view. I gave him money to eat and he was buying drugs in the alley behind some old liquor store. Was this what my money was paying for? I want to know why he would do that, knowing I was near. If I were out here with nothing, I would not use what somebody gave me for drugs. He could have at least waited and pretended he had good intentions with my money.

"Take him." Voices whispered. "He's a liar."

Ah . . . No . . . I hit my head. Stop it. But it wouldn't stop. It could go on for as long as it wanted. They could last for days without ever dying down. Screaming in my head. Turning a migraine into a position to want to kill yourself. I had to go with it. I stood there with a stone cold look in my face. The voices showed me some of the future and most of my painful past.

All I could hear was my heart pounding a thrashing thump. It thumped rhythmically with the pain striking in my head as they whispered what they wanted me to do. I went straight to my car, got inside, and shut the door. I opened my glove compartment and stuck my knife into my back pocket. I got out of my car going down the alley as if in a trance.

Not a person around except the bum singing to himself in the dark. He barely made it to the other side then fell over behind a garbage can. As if I were the quiet, rotten, slick *Grinch,* I came towards him. As I came to him, he was on the ground laughing. He was high on whatever I paid for. I pulled out my knife. I slashed down. Blood squirted on the wall. I came down until my arm was soar.

"Is this what my money paid for?" I screamed.

I let go and wiped the blood on his ragged coat. I backed away and watched him shaking on the ground. His mouth and eyes wide open in surprise. No life. A puddle formed around him. I looked around but no one was there. The sound of my heart beating stopped in my head when his heart stopped. As I walked away, I lit a cigarette.

I sat in my car for a while thinking about life. I had no feelings for the redhead and this bum . . . I have no answers. I still have a long way to go in life. They whispered to me about giving me the gift of life. I'm still waiting.

CHAPTER 3

It wasn't a girl or a boy that I heard so many times in my head. It was both coming together in harmony. I believe it's the devil and if not him, himself, then it's one of his demon disciples. They speak to me often. When they whisper low and I can hear them clearly, I know it's because they just want to talk to me. When they scream and create pain in my head, they want it done. In that moment alone with the victim, if they call, I come. If I do not do as they yell, I will be punished unbearable pain until I do as they want. Hours, days, as long as I wait.

They seem to be all around me. I've learned to control them within myself. I've tried to fight the pain but they win. They *know*. Any person, who comes in contact with me, I am given a piece of the pain they have done onto others. I can see the evil they've done. If I see nothing, *they* whisper the awful things I don't want to hear.

I realize now, I heard them before. I didn't remember them. I must have, had an open heart. An open mind for deception. I close my eyes and try to make the fear go away. As a child I could not shut out the pain. I was afraid. They weren't closet monsters, but they were demons.

I sat down on the couch. There was a TV in the living room, which could only be on when my stepfather was around. He was coming home soon, so I had to turn it off. It was late. He worked until eleven at night. I feared seeing his dirty greasy face in mine for watching his TV. I was only grateful that Uncle Mike sent me here for the summer and not for *life*.

I had to sleep on the couch. My mother worked over night at a diner. She was the assistant manager and was the only manager willing to work over nights. That's why they gave her the position and pay.

Alone I was. It seemed as though I liked it that way. The only light on in the apartment was the one out in the patio. I closed my eyes. The wind was blowing and swaying the trees outside against the windowpane. I heard the whistling wind flow through the patio scurrying up leaves, which sounded like bottle caps tapping on the cement. I wanted to turn on the TV but if he caught me, I'd be in for it. The wind was going through these lapses of blowing and going completely quiet. It blew up really loud then trailed off with the sounds of clacking.

"Alex . . ." No wind. No bottle caps. Only, "Alex . . ." I sat up. I looked around to see if that sweet sounding voice was my mothers, though, she never sounded like that before. She had a kind of nonchalant tone to her words. "Alex . . ." What was that? I held the covers close to my chest. They gave me comfort as a child when my stepfather beckoned me to him for a beating and they sheltered me as an adult as I was covered in blood not believing what I did. Had my conflictions with my parents turned me into this? Had they slapped these demons in my head and made me crazy? If I told anyone, especially a psychiatrist, I'd be put away for good. If they were real and not a tumor in my head, then I would like doctors to leave me alone, for they could not help me now. Not even after the things I had seen or done. I'd rather these voices be demons, as I believe. If they're real, Satan can save me, though I fear what will become of me when I follow. If they were not real and I'm crazy, I would not want to live life like a maniac or psychotic, split personalities, whatever they want to diagnose me with. Do I really want to mope around on drugs for the rest of my life, or do I want to run around doing as they say and let life be life?

"Come with us . . . . don't be alone . . . don't be afraid." They whispered with no wind blowing and I knew what I heard was loud and clear. That is the moment I stood up to look around for the voice in my head. I rummaged through the whole house. I began to tear apart and empty out the closets. The house was beginning to look as though someone had tried to rob them.

With some nick knacks in both hands I yelled, "Where the fuck are you!" I threw the stuff the floor and pulled on my hair. I looked at the mess I had made worried that he would be home and see what I had done. That's when I began shoving everything back into the closets and under the beds. But it looked ridiculous.

I sat down on the couch rocking back and forth only my arms could comfort me now. I began to whimper, for if you knew my stepfather, you would be scared too. After shaking so much, I ran into the bathroom and let it all out; two hot dogs I cooked for dinner, some chili (which was the worst of it all), some ruffles (which ruffled no more), and the Big Red (made here in Texas). I felt tears swell up into my eyes. The memories of what he was capable of before was echoing in my head. And my head began to pound.

I lay back on the couch once more to calm my nerves. I wanted to run away. I felt crazy right then and there. I had always heard the same voices but they were only a dream. It seemed to be when I was a small boy, that they were dreams. Mother told me I was dreaming in the dark of the Goat who stood over my bed with his hands resting over my shoulder so I couldn't move. "That was just a dream son, go back to your room," she said. The old lying woman.

All my thoughts came back to me. The string that held the pages together was now beginning to sew a complete novel. I realized then I had to suffer the consequence of their actions which were not my own. So I sat there, with the light now off, alone again. The wind picked up. Sudden quietness fell into the house. Nothing ticked on the clock; no compressors of the air conditioner, nor the fridge were on. It was utterly quiet. And I began to feel a chill in my skin being so alone yet not feeling alone. Not even feeling like *just* one person was in the room with me. I felt many eyes on me.

"Come to us Alex." I opened my eyes. Within this room were many red eyes that I can't explain with just words. The shadows stood or sat all around the room just staring at me. And I could only wish that these eyes were my imagination. Instead they came closer to me. "Kill them . . . he will never hurt you again." They whispered as one. And my heart pounded faster than I could ever imagine a heart attack could feel. I couldn't breathe. My air was being sucked out of me. "Kill." They said as they came closer. I screamed and ran out the door. As I ran through the open field of the apartment complex, I felt something in my hands. I looked down to see what it was. A blade, one I had never seen before, right here in my hands.

I looked back even more fearful of what I would see. And still I wish I never had. At dramatic speed were all of the shadows with red glowing eyes chasing me. Two came close to me; their hands shook the hand with the knife. I screamed loudly. When I looked back, there was a large tree before me, which I ran right into, headfirst. I fell on the floor, the blade flying out into the grass into disappearance and I was out cold.

When I awoke, I was in the hospital. It was concluded that I was a sleepwalker. No evidence of the knife was found. The house was in rampage from a nightmare, and the only mark on me was a huge welt on my forehead. They gave my mother some pills to help me sleep more relaxed so I wouldn't get up through the night on another rampage. As it was, my stepfather was ready to kill me, but for the rest of the summer, at nights, they popped me full of pills. It was at the point where I couldn't move out of bed even though what I saw that night came to me on occasion. I was stuck there dreary staring at them as they spoke. They made me believe it was *nightmares*. Nightmares are not supposed to come out and chase you out of the house. And nightmares don't come while you're still awake.

I was glad to leave by the end of the summer. It seemed like I didn't even see any of the summer. Being on pills, all you do is sleep and daze. It was to the point where I wanted the pills. I knew what time they were ready to give them to me. Both of them worked late shifts. When my stepfather left for work I was okay. But before my mother left, she would make sure that I took one of the red ones and one of the white ones. She didn't want her husband to say anything to me because I hadn't taken any of the pills.

I didn't spend any time with them. They worked. When they were off two days out of the week, they would spend time with each other and leave me alone. I was able to get one moment where I was free. I had begged them not to leave me at home. I was afraid that the visions I had would be there once my parents left. It took two weeks of asking. My stepfather just got annoyed with me and said yes.

I watched one of the, "Friday the 13th's". I only wish I had his strength. The first person I'd go after was my stepfather. I'd use one of his mechanic tools too. I wish my father were here. I bet he wasn't so mean. He'd play ball with me, take me to the movies, and always ask what I was feeling.

As soon as the movie was over, I didn't want to go home. I wanted to run away, get on a plane to California, and then live with someone who sometimes paid attention to me. But not really. What I liked most about my uncle was he didn't beat me.

I had a few dollars. I saw how the arcade room was crowded with kids my age. I strolled on over and begin a game with monsters fighting monsters. I was beating everyone who tried to play against me. Those three-quarters lasted a long time. I was having a good time. When the game was over, I turned around to walk outside and the sweetest little girl was standing next to me smiling. She had a blue headband in her head, which pulled her blonde hair back. She was wearing a blue Jean jacket and skirt. I smiled at her.

"Hi." She said as she stood there. She was twelve like me.

"Hi." I smiled shyly at her. "What's your name?"

"Ashley."

"Well this here is Ass-hole." I looked behind her as I heard the deep raspy voice penetrating through my ears. "And you're get'n the fuck into the car yah little shit."

I looked at the girl embarrassed as I was and smiled. Patrick the stepfather grabbed me by the collar and yanked me to the car. I was so humiliated. Everyone was staring at us. As soon as we got home I knew what would happen. He shoved me in the house. Then he smacked me in the face a couple of times. One cheek was red and the other he landed right on the eye, which was a light purple when the next day came.

My mother just yelled at me and said what was I thinking. I couldn't say anything. After the beating, they made sure I wouldn't be sober until the bruise was gone. So I was zoned out for almost a week and a half. I didn't know how many times they came up to me and put more pills in my mouth. Sometimes, Patrick used to punch me in the arm while I was out, and then make fun of me. I could just see his ugly skinny face in mine. He had five o' clock shadow, he smelled of beer and old hot dogs. He would sit next to me on the couch while I drooled on myself and make fun of me.

There was always this hope within myself that this wouldn't always be so. During middle school, they were teaching us that we would leave our parents some day. "What would you like to do when you graduate from school?" People talked about going to college, getting a good job and their own apartments. I wanted to do the same. I would never again have to visit with these jerks.

One memorable occasion was my third attempt. I was walking along the local high school. I was going to Stanford University near by. The high school was not far from the dorms. It was around four thirty in the afternoon. Everywhere I went, I wasn't myself. I didn't like to show my face to many people. I had on my baseball cap and your average Joe T-shirt and jeans.

"You little fuck'n prick!" I heard the voices at a distance.

The voices were coming from the left side of the schoolyard. There were two boys beating on another. The picture I had seen with these boys walked across my eyes in slow motion so that I could see everything as it was.

I saw the boy on the ground. His eyes covered in glasses, his body small and fragile. In his arms he held a bag and he would not let go. His teeth were covered in braces, which I saw as he cried out loud. The other boys were jocks. They wore the school jackets. They kicked the boy in the stomach. They laughed as they beat him blue. Blood came out of his mouth. When he let go of the bag, they grabbed it; one punched him in the face one last time, then walked away.

I didn't want to watch. I didn't want to look. But they called. And I didn't want to be confronted with them at all. They would make my head spin, and then come to me in the night, which made me break out in a sweat and whine. He was lying on the floor crying. I walked over like I didn't want to do this, but I did. He held his head as I walked up. I kneeled down next to him and touched his shoulder. He jerked back.

"Hey . . . Hey it's okay." I said.

I helped him sit up. He wiped his tears away with his sleeve. He looked at me through his broken glasses as though ashamed. "Who are you?" Asked the boy.

"Just someone who was passing by. I saw those boys take your bag." I said.

"That wasn't my bag." He said looking down at all of his belongings, which were scattered all over the place.

"Who's was it?"

"I found it against the wall right there. So I opened it up. I found some videotapes and drugs in there. I was going to take them to the principles office when those two football players came to me. They asked me where I was going. When I told them where, they wanted the bag. I asked if they knew what was in it. That's when they beat me up and took the bag. I was only doing the *right* thing."

"Well there's nothing wrong with trying to do good in the world. It's a good thing you're all right. Just get home and don't mention this to any," I felt pain in my head, "one. If you can keep a secret, I can keep a secret."

"But"-

"*But. But.* Trust me, it'll save you the embarrassment of being that one kid who got beat up and it'll save you from being branded a snitch. Just keep your mouth shut and I promise that bad people in this world get the ugly end of the stick."

"Like what?"

"Well, you could end up rich and they can end up in jail. Whatever scholarship they think they're getting, they'll lose. Did you need a ride home?"

"Yes sir."

As I drove him home, he pointed out the boys who beat him up. They were hanging out in a hamburger joint. They laughed and carried on like nothing. It made me very angry to see them as if they were on top of the world. I swerved the car and the boy grabbed the wheel. I held my head.

"Mister! Mister, are you okay? Oh please stop. You're scaring me." He cried.

I forced the voices away. But you know those voices, when they want something done, they want it done now. I looked in the back seat where slight visions of them were forming. I just nodded my head at them to let them know I was going to do, as they wanted. I took hold of the wheel and continued on slowly.

"I'm sorry kid. I have quite a headache."

"Sir, do you also do good deeds?"

I looked back at the shadows and they were going away. I smiled as I looked back at the boy. "Why, yes I do." I was proud.

"What kind of deeds?"

"Well, you see, I rid the world of the scum that hurt others."

"Do you put them in jail. Are you like a policeman or something?"

"Far from it. But there is a type of jail I put mean people in, so they won't hurt anyone else." A death jail. "So how far up is your house?"

"Just up the street at the corner. Are you sure you're okay?"

"I'm good."

I let him out at the house with the plants growing every which way in his front yard. He thanked me for taking him home. I had to be somewhere. I drove back down the street I came from. I parked at the hamburger shop. As I went inside, the two looked at me. They had red eyes as if they had been swimming pool of chlorine. I sat down with a cup of coffee in my hands. I muttered to myself as they spoke softly in my head. I would like for one time to be mine and mine alone. I didn't need their help anymore raising the knife over my head and coming down in a rhythmatic sacrifice. I sacrificed all the people in the world to satisfy them.

I went outside to smoke a cigarette and it just so happened that they walked up to talk to me. I pretended not to see them. I looked out into the world, as any man would see when he held the secret to life in his grasp.

"Could we bum a smoke?" Asked one boy.

I said nothing. I pulled out my cigarettes. They took two out of the pack. As they lit their smokes. I stared at them. Who did they think they were? One boy had a military hair cut which he greased up with moose. The other boy had dark hair that was brushed back into a little bulb on the top of his head.

"Damn, that's one cherry!" Said the dark haired boy.

I looked at my car then back at the two who stared in awe at my vehicle. I smiled for the simplicity that hallowed over us. This couldn't have gotten any better or more perfect than it had at that moment to seize the opportunity of their lives. I pointed to my car with a cigarette between my index and middle fingers. "You like that?"

The boys nodded their heads like little children.

"That's my baby." I said.

"Really? It's bad ass!"

"Wanna cruise in it?" I asked knowing the fate of their answer whether they wanted to or not.

"Fuck yeah."

I was myself all over again. My smile could not fade at all that day. They got in my car. They smiled as I turned on the ol' Chevy to hear the engine reeve and purr in all its hard work of glory. I sped out peeling away at the tires. How they whistled and yelled about wanting a car as fast and as *cool* as mine. As I looked in my rearview mirror, I saw the bag. I wondered exactly what they had. And I would know soon enough.

"Do you mind if I smoke a joint?" I asked as I held it in-between my fingers.

They smiled. They wanted some also. And how it got better by the seconds that passed unknowingly. I would make them forget all about the reality of time. They would smoke until they couldn't move and I would be at ease trying to handle two football players at once.

I lit the joint passing it as though I had a good hit of it. Only I didn't smoke any of it. They went through about three joints as we all laughed in the car. I found a good chance to pull into *my* creek. Which was only used on a few occasions. They followed me down the creek where all the water had once run through. There were rocks and dirt over ten feet high and sometimes at certain points, it was fifteen feet high.

I stopped walking near a small stream of water. Above us, on the top of the creek, where the *real* world circulated, were some bushes and trees; so much that no one would be able to see down unless they were willing to get stuck in brush and thorns. I pulled out a joint and lit it once again. I had a bottle of beer in my hand, which I just opened. I felt the pockets in my shirt.

"Awe man, I left my cigarettes in the car."

They looked at me as they laughed. They didn't see *them*, but there was one of my friends, a shadow wrapping his hand-like image around the blonde boys' neck. I tried to push them away. *It was my doing! Not theirs!*

"Could one of you get my pack of smokes from the car." I asked like a true gentleman. The dark haired boy held out his hand as I tossed him the keys to my baby. He smiled as he walked away from sight. The other boy was smiling as he crossed his arms. He sat down on the floor tossing rocks into the creeks stream next to us.

I stood next to him, watching his every move. "Say man, do you know how to fight?" I asked.

"Hell yeah."

"Do you think you could show me some moves? I have no clue how to fight. I've never been in one, if you know what I mean."

"Sure," he said as he stood up wiping the dirt from his pants. He put up his fists as he tried to instruct me. I played along as if I were clueless. I could tell he was stoned because he kept laughing and making fun of everything I did. After a while of my *adjusting* to a fight, I socked him really hard in the face. His smile faded a little.

"Hey man, be cool. I think you've got the hang of it. Just don't hit so hard when we're only playing." As if that would stop me now.

"Oh come on. How am I supposed to know if I'm doing well, when we barely tap each other? Besides, you're a tough guy who likes to beat on small boys, ain't chah? You can take my little punches." I put up my fists. "Come on."

He looked at me in surprise. "Right?" He looked at me up and down.

I took off my shirt. I put out my fists again. "Come on. Let's kept going. We could kill time like this."

"Nah, it's getting kind of late. We got to go."

He turned to walk away. I kicked him in the legs.

"HEY! What the fuck!"

"Oh come on kid. You scared of me? I saw what you did. It wouldn't hurt if it happened to you too." I smiled at the boy. "Just one hit." I told him as I pointed to my chin. He looked at me scared as if taken back.

I assumed his idea would be to knock me out, find his friend, then run off. But I didn't go down so easily. He punched me as hard as he could in my chin, which did set me back a little but not much. I went at him. I grabbed him by the shirt beating him over the head non-stop. He didn't deserve to live. The voices began to call. They swerved all around his body screaming loudly. And he saw them too. I pulled out my butterfly knife and slid it right into his throat. He kicked as he held onto the knife falling back onto the rocks without one single whimper to call. I knew the other boy would return soon. I pulled the dead one behind some bushes near by.

I sat by the water throwing rocks like nothing happened. All was well. The other boy walked up as stoned as Cheech and Chong. He had the cigarettes in his hand, which I grabbed quickly. He looked at me wondering where his friend had run off.

"Where's Eric?" He asked.

"He's taking a piss," I said as I lit a cigarette.

He looked at my face, which had sweat dripping off of it. He noticed I wasn't wearing a shirt. That's when his smile faded. He looked around for his friend. I came closer to him not worried for an instant.

"You know," I puffed on my smoke. "You boys are lucky that there are people like me in this world." I said.

He was barely listening to me. He was trying to see where the other boy was; maybe hoping that he would pop his head out from the top of the creek. Not possible. I stepped closer to him.

"It's people like you boys that make people like me crazy. I can't thank you enough for giving me a reason the find you two."

He put up his hand as if to answer me with it and I *really* hate when people try to brush me off like that. He wasn't hearing me. He was getting hotter to the spot. "Eric!" He called. No reply was in the air. He saw the legs sprawled out as he came closer. "What the fuck?"

Before he could react or do anything at all, I had already pulled out my hatchet, which was perfectly strapped to my boot, and swung it down into his neck. His arm went up to feel it in his body. He fell to the ground squirming. Blood was on my chest and I was prepared for that. I cut down over and over. All together, the voices and I moved and I felt the blood rushing to the tips of my fingers as I rampage on this boy. I was surrounded by the lot of *them* and when his heart was gone, so were they.

That night when I went back to my dorm all alone, I wanted to see what was in the secret bag. I was in a single dorm, which was lucky for me, for the roommate would probably be dead before the semester was over. I was lying on my bed with the TV on, when I looked at the bag.

I opened it up. It had a large bag of weed, a bag of pills, and some cocaine. There were videotapes that weren't labeled. I pulled them out thinking they were probably filming themselves at a game or with their friends. I hit play on the VCR. It was a party. Nothing unexpected. The same two boys were sitting on the couch having a good time with some other football players. It was nothing but drinking and joking, which I forwarded to the end.

On the second tape, it was the same thing. The party was over and everyone was gone. The camera, which *Eric's* friend was probably holding, followed Eric into one of the rooms, then into the bathroom. There was a girl who was lying on the floor. Eric picked her up and threw her on the bed. As the camera closed up on her face, I could see she was so drunk, she couldn't move. She just smiled. Eric took off her clothes. She tried to push him off but he just smacked her across the face and kept on. I was disgusted. Eric's friend took on her body as he climbed off. She cried all the while. The tape shut off.

As I was about to turn it off, the picture showed back up. They filmed the woods. Eric was carrying the girl he had raped. She was tied up with duck tape around her mouth so no one would hear her. Her face was red, covered in tears, and her eyes were bloodshot. She looked completely terrified.

I wanted to throw up. The girl was fourteen, maybe fifteen if there was a chance of that. The one holding the camera smacked her in the head with a pipe. She was out cold. They tossed her in the river. There, she sank to the bottom beneath the water.

How sick those boys were. Now that I think of it, they might think I know about what they did. I was talking about the small boy, but I could have been talking about the girl they raped and killed. Did I do the world a favor or what?

Most say, let the past be in the past. It's hard for me to let go of what hurt. I dwell on the past on many occasions and I find myself talking about things that happened when I was a teenager and so far back to when I was a small boy. I can't run or hide from my past. So I face it. Nobody knows about the things I see or know what I hear. I thought I needed *them* but reality leads me to believe I am crazy. They were and are my only comfort now.

Sunday 7pm

Here, I don't know why, but I sit in my penthouse living alone, sitting in one of the corners of an empty room. Pitch dark. I had every window in this penthouse-tinted solid black. The moon is standing high which I can barely see.

They sleep with me, in my head where it hurts, in my mind where little children chant my name in a tune that only frightens me. The demons hum in my head like the ones you only wish were in a movie and not real. The chickens are clucking with no heads, bleeding, cooing the morning sunrise; flapping their wings going no where.

There is a beautiful silent emptiness about her as she cries black tears. This girl is a dream that I have never seen. Never seen the color of her eyes, only an image of her they flash. She is the blackest of all the shadows that cries in the night. I have to feed her or they feed on me. They only want one thing.

I stepped out of the corner away from my thoughts and into myself. I was going to get out of this place. I wore my trench coat and a round black hat to hide my face as always. Whilst driving down the highway I listened to my death opera. It was going to be forty-five minutes to get to San Francisco.

Arriving there I was swamped out on the streets by beggars and bums. Not many of the rich roamed around this neighborhood unless they were shopping, came in for the Opera, or working in one of the old buildings downtown. Teenagers were skateboarding down the streets and I saw the image of me on one of the boys. Lights were flashing were the bars and strip clubs were. I could hear everything clearly but still they spoke to me out loud.

"That'll be fifteen bucks man. You got Id?" Asked the man at the door.

I pulled out my wallet with hundred dollar bills sticking out. I showed him my ID as I stood looking around. He looked at it for a minute then smiled.

"Hey I know you. You look familiar." He smiled and I knew what he was talking about.

"I don't think so."

"No, no. You're from the commercials, with the sports cars."

"You must be thinking of someone else," I said as I grabbed my ID from his hands. I dropped the money on the counter as I walked through the door. He just looked at me real funny then went on about his business. Maybe next time I should wear some thick nerd glasses to hide my eyes. There has got to be a better way of hiding myself.

I stayed for a short while. After that guy spotted me, I couldn't get comfortable. I drove down to the other side of town to a different strip club. I wasn't noticed at the door so I went into the crowd of perversion as all the others.

I walked up to the bar. "Shiner." I said to the bartender. He slid a beer across the counter and I caught it. I felt like we were rehearsing a scene from a movie. I turned around on my stool to watch the ladies on stage shake their tail feathers and felt hate creep up into my system. They were shoving their tits and ass into men's faces just so he would slip her some money down her panties. They were flaunting what I felt should be kept covered. It makes me sick. I know, *what am I doing here?* It's either kill or be killed.

The eyes on stage stared directly into mine. But I didn't let my face show. I took my beer leaving money on the counter for the bartender. I sat at one of the near by tables in front of the stage. I could feel her eyes following me. What was she staring at?

She was *pretty.* She had long curly hair that dangled down on her breasts. I could see her wine colored nipples through the strands of hair. Her buttocks were nice and firm, which tightly clenched onto the g-sting she was wearing. I flashed a fifty-dollar bill at her.

She danced towards me in her shinny black pumps. She got down on her knees then slid her legs open. She rubbed her chest into my face. The *slut* danced to the pole and lifted herself up. She turned around to jiggle her ass in my face. I sat still . . . motionless . . . Not a single feeling in my veins. I was disgusted.

The lights went off. Every perverted man cheered as the man over the intercom had her exit off and announced the next girl. Disco lights flashed along the ceiling on the stage. Old dirty men were getting hard underneath the tables of putrid filth. They were jerk offs. Losers. I can't understand one man in here that has a wife, then comes in here every lunch break, and slips away every night from the family. Sick men. If they weren't attracted to their wives, why the hell did they marry them? Then again, look but don't touch, seems okay to me. But men don't look and *not touch*.

Out came a skinny buxom black woman with straight long hair. Her lips were shinny like the oil she rubbed onto her body. Her chest was fake. I had no need for her. The voices didn't surround her like they did to the other girl. I went through the crowded room to the back area. The hall was beaded with pink balls. I knocked on one of the doors where the women were changing. They yelled and cursed me not to come in.

I had to disguise myself, which I found to be a joy doing in my day. British were good for this evening. "I'm looking for the girl who was just on stage." It was silent in the room. She cracked the door a little.

"Wha do yah want?" Asked the bitch.

"I was wondering if we could have a little chitchat about you being in one of our British magazines. We can discuss it over a cup of coffee, yes?" I spoke so eloquently with my accent.

"Are you crazy or psycho?"

"What? You don't like taking pictures?" I asked.

"I sure do. How do I know you're really from a magazine?"

"Come out for a walk and I'll give you my card with phone numbers to the office. I can set you up with an interview. It's all up to you if you want to take a chance at good pay and a great job."

"Alright, meet me outside and give me a chance to get ready."

I waited outside. When I stood in the doorway, I didn't quite put my head in view. I didn't want them to see me. Which they didn't. I always made sure I was unseen. When she walked out, she was wearing a black skirt, a T-shirt with the bars' logo on it, and her hair was pulled back in a ponytail.

We walked away from the hellhole. She looked at me as we walked up the street. I was glad that most people had gone home. The night was left in my hands. And I wanted it all.

"Did you tell anyone about me?" I asked trying not to sound secretive. "Because I might want to see some others, you know."

"Actually, I didn't tell anyone. I don't want them to steal you from me. Why don't you take off your hat so I can see you." She reached out but I pulled away. "Are these going to be naked pictures? I don't mind taking nude pictures. I have a nice body."

What the hell was that? What a sick, disgusting woman, who has completely no shame for herself. I felt like smacking her while she spoke. I wanted her to choke on her words as I squeezed the life out of her. Maybe while she's swallowing, ask her if being dirty tastes good.

"So is this magazine in England?"

"Why sure."

"So why come here, into a bar like that?"

"Well, we wanted a few American Faces in our magazine. Some of the British men like American gals. If you have what we want. If you look as good as you say."

We went into the shop. She had a coffee and I a cappuccino. I was staring at her legs. She thought I wanted her and it turned her on to see me staring at her. I was staring at the voices. They were swerving around her. I hated her. I hated everything about her. She continued to jabber on about life *what have you*, and I continued to ignore her. My mind was confused. I couldn't hear one damn thing she was saying.

"When I was fifteen I thought being a stripper would be glamorous. I like to show off my body. It's nice."

Stupid comments . . . Stupid slut.

I ashed my cigarette.

"So are we going to have a private interview or what?" My eyes widened and I was not expecting that. So I just smiled knowing what she meant. She knew I was on the same page with her. We just picked up our things and left. We walked to the nearest hotel. All the while I had an ugly feeling within myself. I didn't want to do this. I didn't want to have sex with her.

As soon as we shut the door, it was all porno. I kissed her as she was held against the wall. I rubbed my body against hers. I ripped off her clothes. She pulled off my hat, which she had been waiting to do all night. Underneath she wasn't wearing any panties. Which didn't drive me to her. Most men would love to tear at her and make love to her. Being who I am, interested in a completely different type of woman, I found it hard to continue on what we had started. I was having a difficult time trying to have intercourse with her.

As she lay on the bed gripping tightly onto my jeans to pull them off, she swayed her hair back and forth and said, "So tell me what you want."

"Well, you're in the perfect position." I smiled. She knew what I wanted, but *didn't*.

She did what she must have done almost every night of her life. All the while I wondered what made these women do these things. I can find it hard to believe that it was in their nature to be so promiscuous. From the beginning of time there have been wenches and hookers, there has always been access to sex with a complete stranger and I can't find any love in it at all.

I looked at her face and tried to imagine she was a respectable woman. And the moment I saw a decent woman before me, I became aroused. She had been trying for thirty minutes until my imagination ran away with me. I wondered about her past and what made her become such a dirty little whore. Was it just the pure pleasure in using people for money? Could she make more money with her mind? Probably not. And when I saw her for the truth, all of my firmness went away.

I had to keep trying. So there she was, in a business suit. I pretended she was a famous artist. She was with me now, because she had met me a year ago and this was the first time we touched skin. And there, she became whole to me again. A real *woman*. She waited for me because she loved me. I was now into her as much as she was to me. Though both of us were probably imagining a million different things. She was probably imagining that I was rich and wanted to take care of her and I in my own thoughts.

The first moment our bodies became one, all hope of my imaginations coming into my head, were lost. It was far from what it looked like. It wasn't good. Everything that I first saw her as was right there as soon as I felt her. All truth that she was used and *whorified* was true. She continued moving to the rhythm but my mind was all over.

When the truth came to my senses, I lost all my dreams, and I saw them standing there. They had been standing there all night but I blocked them out. They got loud and angry with her and me. My head was spinning. I wanted to throw up. But she was going on. She was loud and so were they.

"I want to be rich!" She moaned. "I want to be the number one playboy! *I want all men to want me!*" She yelled.

I grabbed her by the throat. I laid her on the bed. She thought this was all part of the game but it wasn't. I hated her! She must be through with this life she made for herself. She pushed me off of her. I laid on the bed wondering what was on her mind.

"How do I know you're a real producer?" She asked standing by the bed.

"How do you know?" I asked in my regular voice.

"What happened to your accent?" She asked.

I could tell she was shivering. I grabbed her by the leg and yanked her onto the bed. I got on top of her while covering her mouth. I got right in her face. When she looked around my head, I knew she saw them too. They were going up in frenzy swerving through the air. "Look you little bitch, do what I say. Don't make one peep." The whispers got louder. The ones who control my thoughts were screaming in my head. I felt shocks in my brain. The children were chanting in my head. "What are you doing?" I asked. I wanted to know what she was doing with life.

She shook her head. Her eyes couldn't tear away from the voices.

"What are you doing with me you slut!" I smacked her across the face. "You loose brainless bitch!" I cried. I closed my eyes. What was wrong with me? I have never been so angry in my life. I saw Lila! Lila! *LILA!*

As I was thinking to myself how much I hated her, she grabbed the phone from the stand and smacked me in the head. She kicked me off of her. She tried to run. She wanted to escape this escapade of hers. I grabbed her by the leg pulling her back onto the bed. I punched her in the face. I held her down with one hand and held my head with the other hand. Blood was coming out of the back of my head. "Fuck!" I yelled. I wanted to whither away from the pain.

"Fuck you psycho!" She yelled as she smack her knees into my balls as hard as she could. I fell over to the side. She tried to jump off of the bed. I grabbed her by the hair and threw my weight onto her.

"I don't think so bitch!"

I took the sheet from the bed so I could tie her up with it. Legs and feet were at each post. I got off as soon as I knew she was not able to move. In my jacket was my knife, which I pulled out. She started to scream so I stuffed her mouth with a hand towel. The voices were surrounding me. And she saw them. I could see the terror in her eyes.

I put the blade to her chest. I saw so many images of her sins that I did not want to see. I screamed out loud. I stabbed her in the chest over and over. There was nothing I could do to stop them. I could still hear her. There was a slow chanting in my ears as the life was leaving her body.

"You like screwing people!" I cried. "God damn it Lila!" I yelled as I stabbed her in the chest. Once I dropped the knife, it went dead silent. There

was no crying from the girl. The voices were gone. I was all-alone and once
again I was left to bare the pain I had inflected. It was me, all me.

I cried, "What have I done." Not again! All over again was the sight of
horror I had committed. I banged myself on the walls. I cried and cried. What
was wrong with me? I can't control one single thought.

As I pushed myself to catch reality, I just stared at the body on the bed.
I pulled out the knife. She had tears dried on her face. There was blood all
over the bed. I washed off my knife in the sink. I washed my face and hands.
Once I was dressed and able to enter the public eye, I began to clean the whole
room. I wiped the phone, doorknobs, and walls of my very touch. I burned
the towel then flushed it down the toilet using my elbow on the handle.

I locked the door as I walked out. It was six in the morning when all
people were just getting up for work. I headed down the streets with the key
in my hand. As I walked down the street with my head under my hat. As I
tossed the key into a dumpster far away, I wiped it off with my sleeve before
tossing it in the can.

What makes me do these things, they will only know? I know deep down
inside that these voices are trying to control my mind and want me to kill
those who deserve it. I make sure that from all of my intrigues, I am tested
every six months for STD's. So far I have nothing. What makes me so special
from not contracting what these whores have? I use protection with each girl,
but hey you never know.

That last charade was more of them than it was me. I can't understand
what makes my mind go crazy. Sometimes I think it was all Lila's fault for
hurting me the way she did. The little whore. Why do I let her get to me?
Her face is the very whore that I see in every woman. Her beautiful face and
the lies she told are all on them sometimes. Maybe the voices make me see
her. They find what hurts me the most and they use it to help me strike down
on those that they hate the most. So I do what I must.

CHAPTER 4

The alarm going off in the morning is one of the most annoying things. But sometimes, it's really great to be *me*. I will dwell on the past often but today, in the present time, it really is a wonderful life.

"Good morning Mr. Dugan."

"Yeah good morning."

"Good morning Mr. Dugan."

"Yes good morning."

I unlocked my office door and barely stepped inside.

"Mr. Dugan! Mr. Dugan." One of the employees chased me to the door. "Mr. Dugan the manager, Stan Gale said for me to give you these slips to sign for approval."

"Look Frank, just because he's too lazy to come into my office and send you for these petty signatures, doesn't mean I'm going to do anything. Call his ass in here please because he knows he can approve of all these things. That's why I hired him." I smiled.

"Yes Mr. Dugan."

Frank was a good kid. He just got out of high school, maybe eighteen years old. He makes about between five hundred to seven hundred dollars a week. He works on commission detailing cars. I remember when I was younger and couldn't find a good paying job. I thought it would be nice to help him out.

I took off my coat then sat down at my desk. I had my assistant bring me a cup of coffee. It was my own special kind of Bavarian coffee. It tasted perfect for winter mornings such as this one. It was about nine thirty in the morning. I had a routine that I had for myself and it hardly ever changed.

I own a car lot on El Camino, close to Red Wood City. My hobby to escape the childhood beatings, was old-fashioned cars from the earliest I can get my hands on to some models made in the 1970's. I was a car junkie.

I majored in mechanics and business in college. Now I sell old Mustangs, Chevy's, Buick's, Porches, and sometimes, Volkswagens, such as the Beetle, Karmangia, or The Thing. I buy junk cars for cheap, and we fix them up to showroom floor view. Once they are in tiptop condition we slap a damn good profitable price on them. I recreate bodywork, interior; put in new engines, new tires, and rims. I make beautiful cars out of ugly old clunkers. I also make many racecars for drag racing; a lot of the professional racers come here for their cars or engine work.

People love my cars. I have one of the most successful shops in California. I'm not the number one dealer here but I am at the top. Half the movie producers come to me for cars to fit right into the movies. Right now I'm trying to design brand new cars that look like the Classics but they are made out of fiberglass and plastic. They will have all the assets of new cars, the space age curvy body, the plastic dashboards, and all the things you see in your car today.

My lot is called, Dugan's Classics. I had a feeling that my first car would be a success. Not bad for a psychotic.

"Yes, Mr. Dugan."

Now there's Mr. Gale, the main manager of this place. He's worked for me ever since I rubbed my own two pennies together. He's a good man. He is about 55 years old. He can run this place without me, but I choose to be here. He keeps all the salesmen in line. I don't allow any pushers here at all. I've had a few. I've caught them trying to make that sale to people who aren't ready and I've fired them right there and then. I told one of them to get their things and get the hell out of here. I've sometimes offered a free dinner at a nice restaurant to those who were being pushed.

I have floor salesmen and for the more experienced salesmen with degrees, they work over the phone and on the Internet for the racecar drivers' orders and some of the movie producers. They deal with the *higher buyers*, as I call them. And man do they have an itch for my cars.

"Yeah, have a seat."

He sat down.

"Now, you know you can do all this work by yourself. If you think that you need help, I can get you an assistant."

"Well, it's not that, it's just some people don't look all that good on credit. The salesmen come to me to sign all these papers but when I'm not sure, that's when I want to get you to decide on whether you want to take a chance on an unknown applicant."

I came around from behind the desk. I patted him on the shoulders. "That's good. I can always count on you." I made him face me. "You're the person who checks these deals out. I want you to use your best judgment on whether you want to trust a person with bad credit. I want people to be able to afford my cars. I want people to buy my cars."

"Sir, don't you think that since the beginning of the shops opening, we've grown a hundred times with money and sales?"

"Yes we have. As a matter a fact, I have already paid for a lot in San Francisco and I'm planting a small seed in San Jose. The Chinese really love our old cars. Just wait till the new car comes out. It's going to be called, *The Dug.*"

"You've made me rich and probably richer."

"And I've made myself a millionaire. Think of all the money we'll make from these two shops and what will happen with my new car. It'll be perfect. Maybe I'll finally find some one to fall in love with me." I looked at Mr. Gale. "Will you marry me?"

"Get the fuck out of town." He laughed.

We laughed for those few moments where memories of us poor and going downhill passed through our minds. We were in the gutter before. I was still in college at the time and didn't know much of how to get started. But here we are, sitting on a mountain of money.

I took a sip of my coffee then snapped. "Well I've got to get on my rounds." I left the cup and walked out of my office leaving the door open. I like to keep busy. I have to work or I am nothing. I can't just sit back and enjoy the money. I'm a good mechanic and I was a six-year graduate from Stanford University. I was only twenty-three when I was done.

The first place I stopped by was the make ready, where the cars were detailed. I passed by the lot inside where the cars that were going to be cleaned. I went into the back warehouse where everything was being washed right down to the engine.

"How are things?" I asked the one who was in charge of the three men who detailed. His name was Charlie. He was kind of old but he's been doing it ever since I hired him.

"It's going okay. And how are things in the designing department?" He asked.

"Just fine Charlie. Catch you later." I waved at the men as I walked away. I headed back towards the front. I went to the mechanic warehouse. Some of the engines, if they were good enough, were rebuilt, and others were brand new. Most of the cars people brought here to get rid of, thought they were junk.

There were six men working in this department and one of which was in charge. These men didn't have to have a degree but I did test them on parts of the car and how-to-fix quizzes. As long as they did them all correct, they were given a weekly paycheck and good benefits. They were working on an engine of a 57' Chevy when I walked in.

Connected to this building, next door, was another warehouse where the bodywork was done. There was usually a order that's given to me by the end of the week with a list of cars. I am supposed to pick the style of painting whether we want to put flames or race stripes. Sometimes I'll check the cars that are being sold to us.

We put new stereos but they are usually the old fashioned kind. We do install CD players and air conditioners. Which a lot of the rich customers request.

As I stood there looking at the list of cars that are to be painted, in drives an ugly old Chevy. It was a 1954 model. The outside was pretty horrid. Someone tried to paint the body with regular paint on the hood and the trunk. The rest of the car was burgundy. I could hear the engine popping as he drove in.

The receptionist walked up to me as the man stepped out.

"Sir."

I put out my finger as if to say, *no*, or *wait*.

He wasn't much taller than me. He was old, chubby, a workingman or schnook, wearing brown slacks, white button up shirt with short sleeves, and his hair was greased back. He held a cigar in his teeth as he shut the door. He walked up to me as he pulled up the inside of his pants with his thumbs going around the waist.

"Can I help you?" I asked.

He took out his cigar with his index finger and thumb. "Yeah, you can help . . . How much can I get for this car?"

"Well let's take a look." I gave my clipboard to the receptionist. I walked over to the passenger side of the car. I checked all the doors; I turned on the engine and listen to it while I checked out every crack and cranny on it. It was popping. I could tell he hadn't changed the oil in a *very* long time. The transmission didn't sound too good when I took it for a drive. When we returned, I stood behind the vehicle with the sun on my back thinking what to give it. In the trunk it seemed pretty clean.

"I can work with this. Why don't you come to my office and we can talk price." I said while rubbing my chin.

"Sir?"

"Yes Ms. Samot?" I was annoyed with what she wanted, though I did ignore her through a test drive and inspection. She couldn't hold out any longer.

"All the salesmen are missing. Half of them didn't show up to the morning meeting and we're getting quite a bit of customers out there."

"Well see if you can call them all to the front and for the customers waiting for a representative, give them my humblest apology, and pass out a few of those free dinner tickets we have. I'll deal with the men in a minute."

She handed me the clipboard as she walked away. I took the old man to my office. He looked around with his hands in his pockets and a cigar between his teeth. I pulled out the chair waiting for him to sit down.

"Have a seat sir. If you'll excuse me for a moment please, I'll be right back. I'll have my secretary serve you some coffee or something." I said as I walked out. My secretary was sitting behind her desk putting some paperwork away. "Lisa could you please keep an eye on this guy," I whispered. "I don't trust him. Oh and get him some coffee please."

I walked to the front of the building where the receptionist sat behind a tall desk. Most of the salesmen were there waiting. I pulled on my tie as I walked up. Ms. Samot was looking at me in fear. She didn't like to see me in one of my moods. I waved my finger to her and she handed me the telephone that went on speaker.

"Would all of those incompetent floor people please come to the front desk, Mr. Dugan is waiting on your abrupt appearance." I handed her back the phone. "Ms. Samot could you please make sure that if anyone needs help, tell them we'll be with them in about fifteen please, thank you." I turned around which I could see the last of the salesmen slipping in. "Alright, conference room, *now*."

They followed me to the large office, which was just next door to my office. All the salesmen stood around the table as I was at the head waiting for everyone's attention. I looked around with a discrete look in my eyes. Mr. Gale stood by my side.

"Okay, now that we're all here and accounted for, let me just say that I am very disappointed in the half of you. I expect you all here by a certain time. If you cannot find it with in yourself to show up on time then I can see that your job doesn't mean much to you. I can find a million people who would love to take any one of your places, okay. I don't have a problem letting go any one of you. You guys make a lot of money here and I'm not the one losing out. I don't believe that all of you were so busy you couldn't help the clients"

"Well sir some of us were just going over paperwork and"-

"Hey, I don't want excuses, I want you out there *on time* or I'm getting rid of you. It's as simple as that. Now I have a customer in my office." I turned towards the door to my office from inside the conference office. "Just go out there and treat everyone with respect. But get out there now . . . or you will find me to be a very unpleasant person." I walked through my door.

The old man was sitting there sipping on his coffee. I stood there for a moment with my eyes closed. Then I took a breath and sat down behind my desk. I rummaged to find the right papers in one of the drawers. I threw some papers on my desk. I looked at him strangely, watching him enjoy his coffee. He looked like the type to go for a liquidation sale that had free hot dogs and juice on any given occasion, though he didn't ever buy anything.

"Now that I've got everything out of the way, let me introduce myself, my name is Alex Dugan. I own the company. Primarily it's the head of each department that looks over the car. But you caught me just in time."

"Uh-huh."

"Now I need to have these forms read through before anything else and if you agree we can move right along here. We need you to understand that this car will be ours and you must give up rights of the title."

"Sure."

"I believe that my judgment on you car is fair and that whatever I pay you for the car can be explained in full report, if need be. You can however stop by the shop in a couple of months to see what it looks like then. We do also send you a postcard with your car, completely restored in the picture. It's just something we like to do here. I'd say your car is worth eight hundred no more no less."

"How about a thousand."

"Eight hundred."

"One thousand."

"Eight fifty."

"Come on guy, it's only a couple hundred more."

How dare he try to make me feel like what I said means nothing. "How about five hundred, it's only a couple hundred less."

He looked at me with those hound dog eyes, which squinted with the cigar smoke blocking his view. "Eight fifty sounds just fine." He took his cigar and crushed it in my ashtray. He sat back in the chair with his hands twined in each other resting on his fat stomach.

"Alright then sir, just fill out these forms here and I'll be back in a moment." I handed him the forms. I walked out of there not being able to stand the sight of him. I stood by the glass window that gave view of the whole lot. I watched the salesmen helping out the customers that were out there. I shook my head. I needed to get away from some of the stress I had to deal with.

Fifteen minutes later, I went back into my office. He had finished all of the forms. I sat down then took hold of the papers.

"Says here, you're retired."

"For a year now."

"Must be nice. Well I think this is a good deal for you. There's also a buyback deal in here for you stating if you ever wanted it back after fully being restored, we will knock off half of the showroom price."

"That's great." He said as if he didn't care.

"Alright then." I signed all the forms. I put them in a little folder. "Well that's it, we're done here." I said as I walked towards the door. I stuck my head out. "Lisa could you make out a check for eight hundred and fifty dollars to this gentleman here." I passed the folder to her. "And get this information into the computer." She just nodded her head. I walked back into the office trying to get the guy out of my place. "Well my secretary can take care of you now. She'll get you the check."

He stood up then pulled on his pants at the waist again. He shook my hand and I walked him out of my office shutting the door behind him. I sat back in my chair putting up some of my other paperwork. I began to scroll through my Rolodex to find the insurance company that I was going through.

There was a light tap on my door. Mr. Gale popped his head through the doorway. "Hey are we still on for lunch today?" He asked.

"Most likely."

"Hey there's a real cutie out here that Albert's helping out. She might want to get with yah." He smiled.

"Really?" I sprayed my breath and stood up. The two of us walked out of my office into the front. I saw her with Albert. She was wearing this pastel yellow dress and these movie star sunglasses. I liked talking to women who thought the world revolved around them. They loved it when I spoke with them. They knew I had money and didn't have any shame in flirting with me.

I walked up to them and smiled at her. "Mr. Flyne, can you get with Mr. Gale about some of those sales figures please. I can take care of this lady here."

"No problem."

He wasn't mad. He knew that if I take over a sale I give it to them. I'm the one making most of the money what should it matter. They all knew I was single. They could tell that when I spoke about how lonely it was for a rich man it wasn't the joke it seemed to be.

I had a good look at her while I was talking with Mr. Flyne. She had yellow blonde hair, which matched her dress. Her eyes were a light blue color almost turquoise. Her legs were long, slim, with just a tad bit of muscle, close to a runway models leg, which to most men were attractive.

"So what can I do for you today?" I asked as I shook her hand. "I'm Alex Dugan, the owner."

"Hi. My name is Sandy, nice to meet you." She had the squeakiest voice next to a mouse. "I've been searching around for a new car for the passed week but everywhere I have gone it's . . . I don't know, their pushy and trying to up the price once we get down to all the paperwork."

"Well you've come to the right place. We don't jack up the price once you've taken a ride. We jack up the price after you've already financed." I looked at her. She just looked at me funny without smiling. "Ah, that was a joke." She went up in a roar as if it were the funniest joke she had ever heard. And I with my mouth halfway open, let down my eyebrows as if I can't believe she thought it was that funny. She was an airhead I know that.

"Seriously though, we're not pushers and we have great deals. If you want we can search the lot for something you might find of interest. Was there a particular year and make you were interested in?"

"Old." Said she who had a brain the size of a peanut.

"What about color," I asked. She must know that much.

"Ah . . . Light blue and white."

"So you like two tone." She just smiled as if she didn't know what that was. "Well come this way miss, we'll find you something." I put my hand slightly on her back to show her one I thought might be small and easy for her to drive. We walked around until I found the one I was looking for. She spoke the whole way there. We stopped in front of a 1959 Chevy that we had chopped into a miniature vehicle with a good engine. We chopped about three inches off the top and on front and back we chopped off about five inches. "What do you think of this one?"

She walked around it looking astonished. I looked at my watch. It was eleven o'clock. She loved the car. I also showed her a 1965 Karmangia which she fell in love with right away. I told her to wait there while I sent Mr. Flyne to get her a key and give her a test drive. As I walked away she was checking me out. I could always feel things like that. So much for love with the blonde bimbo. I feel that it's hard to find perfection in one woman.

Business was good. These cars were all my pride and joys. The least I would sell a car for was 4,000 dollars and at those prices had to be cash. Which were the Beatles and some other small cars.

I have plenty of money. We sell between four to twelve cars a day. I have money saved in the bank for *just in case* situations. The money we do put into the supplies and the buildings come right back three times as much for everything is not that expensive. And the San Francisco shop is also doing well. And when the one in San Jose goes through nicely, we'll be making more. If my new car makes it through, we can charge them twenty to twenty-five thousand per car. Then I'll be more than stinking rich. It's not the money that attracts me the most; it's the fact that I can do it. It's the fact that a person with my background is making deals with large companies and is invited to special occasions by producers.

It all started before I went to college, I bought a piece of junk old Duster. My uncle and I hopped it up and sold it for a good price. More than what we put into it. With the money I made off of that, I bought two more cars and did the same thing. At the time it was just a hobby. When I started going to college, I opened up a small shop, the kind where no one stops in but people who can't afford cars. When I received my degree in Business and Mechanics, I borrowed money from the bank and opened the one I have now. I paid back the bank as soon as I was getting in good business, which took a year and a half. It's surprising that the lot did so well from the start. After I gave the bank all I had, everything else was profit.

A year ago I put my brother Tony's' name in my will to inherit the place if anything should happen to me. If I get locked up (for reasons unknown for now), I have insurance to cover everything. My brother gets all the glory I once had.

I've grown successful. I own a penthouse on the thirteenth floor of one of the most respected private communities. I still have my first car in perfect condition. I have a 1969 Camero, an old Chevy, and a Toyota pick up. When I was young, my parents didn't get me much of anything, now I have everything I ever wanted. Except for a woman. And a son.

I know I'm wealthy and successful, but I want more than that. I want a good woman, though there might never be one in my grasp. I want to be able to set my eyes on her and know I want to marry her. I want her to feel the same, without them seeing all the money I have.

The women I get are usually gold diggers or sluts and I can't understand why good decent women wouldn't want me. I'm tall, a little over six feet, my eyes are gray and women loved colored eyes, and my hair is brown, my nose isn't perfect, kind of like Tom Cruise with the little nook on the top, but it's not bad. I work out and my muscles are defined, toned, but I'm not huge. Why can't I get a good woman?

Over the phone, my brother sounds like a fiend. "Come on Alex, let's cruz in your car and drink some beer at the club tonight."

"Nah, I'm not in the mood. Besides, clubs aren't my thing."

"Alex . . . Alex come on. You're my bro hang with me man!"

"Fuck it. Alright just shut up already."

"Pick me up in an hour."

Great. I'm going to a club where the slut of all sluts are going to be dancing all around me. I'll be there all night trying to kill them. But he's my brother so I have to go. I remember when we were younger he wanted to go to some teenage club where girls wore practically nothing. I went of course and he left to mess with all of the girls and I sat there on one of the couches while everyone danced around me.

Well what to wear? I'll dress how I always dress. Black T-shirt, black slacks, leather jacket like Al Pacino in Donnie Brasco, and my steal toed boots. Even though my brother and I didn't look the same, we got along like no other brothers did.

I shaved my face as always but I kept the mustache and goat tee. I locked my front door thinking that I was completely safe. Standing by the elevator only lasted seconds. The door slid open. The boy who was in there, smiled at me. He thought I was the funniest tenant they had.

"Going down Mr. Dugan?"

"Of course, where else would I be going?"

I could hear the symphony in the elevator. As the elevator moved down the bellboy was smirking like a stupid ass and I wanted to know if he was on drugs or something.

"So where are we headed tonight?" He asked.

"*We* are headed no where." I laughed.

The door opened and I walked out. He popped out his head. "Have a good evening Mr. Dugan." He waved as I walked away. I walked into the parking lot where the drivers sat waiting to drive around somebody's car. "Hello Mr. Dugan, which car is it tonight?" Asked one of the valet parker's.

"The Camero."

"Oh that car is awesome." He took my keys and then step n' fetch. He drove around in my beautiful black Camero. I tipped him and was on my marry way.

On the freeway I drove like a maniac. I sped all the way there, *because I can.* It took me twenty minutes to get there. As I pulled in the driveway I honked the horn waiting for my only brother. Out he came in stylish black slacks and blue button up shirt. His hair was slicked back and looked darker than usual. It made his hazel eyes stand out much brighter.

"Hey bro, what's up? You ready to roll?" He asked.

I pulled in reverse and sped out peeling at my tires. I could see from the corner of my eyes. He pulled out a tray from under the seat. He rolled a joint perfectly even though I tried to swerve the car to make him mess up. He lit it up. We smoked on the way there. When I was younger, I was paranoid about smoking weed on the road. The roads seem to get longer and the stop signs were there for hours. I figured it was because I would stare at those red signs daydreaming and wouldn't move until I snapped out of it. One time I was waiting for the stop sign to turn green. *A sign turning green.*

At the club, it took forever to find parking. It was crowded. I locked up my car making sure there wasn't any way someone could break in. I had an alarm, the club, and automatic locks. I was a little stoned as we walked up. As soon as we entered the doorway, there were people dancing all over the place, loud rave music, and drinking. Tony barely stepped in and some girl walked up to him wearing tiny little shorts and a talk top.

"Wanna dance?" She asked him.

He looked at me with a smile. "How can I resist?"

There he goes off into the crowd. And there I was all by my lonesome with no one to talk to. I decided to go upstairs to the bar. I sat at a small round table that overlooked the dance floor. There were many college students there. I could hear a bunch of them chatting next to me about *world issues.*

The waitress finally walked up to me. "What'll it be, cutie?" She yelled out over the noise.

"Guinness."

"Sure thing hot stuff." She cleared my table whilst sticking her breast into my face. I backed away for that was not what I wanted.

I took off my jacket. From behind me I heard a voice but it wasn't them. "I just want to kiss you." A whisper in my ear. She sat down in the empty seat next to me. She was pretty but you know how I feel about these sluts. She had long curly black hair, slim body, a tight black dress, and flat chested.

The beer was tossed onto my table. "Four fifty," Said the waitress. I gave her a ten.

"Keep it." I said to her. She walked off a little angry. I took a drink of my beer. I didn't take my eyes off of the girl. She rubbed her hand on my inner thigh. I spit up my beer.

"What's wrong?" She asked me.

"Keep you're fuck'n hands off of me." I told her getting aggravated with her very presence.

She scooted closer to me. She rubbed her chest on my arm. "What's wrong? Is the good looking man still a bit shy." I looked at her as if she were crazy. "Just give me one kiss. I saw you when you came up here. Please kiss me one time and if you don't like it I'll leave."

I closed my eyes trying to show her that she has her moment so hurry up. She kissed me. It was good, very good. I'll give her credit for that. It was wet; there was an exchange of passing tongues. When it was over she smiled at me waiting for me to do it again.

"You have beautiful eyes." Said the Squeezer.

She leaned towards my face. "Sugar, why don't you go and dance with some other sucker." I took a drink of my beer.

She let go of me. She tried to shove me but I didn't budge. "Fuck you!" Then she walked off. What a slut.

After I finished my beer, I looked around to see if there was anything I could do besides wait for my brother. I looked at the bar. I grabbed my jacket and there I sat on the stool for my whole night to revolve around.

"What'll it be lad?" Asked the Australian bartender.

"A shot of whiskey and another one after that . . . Just keep them coming."

"Sure thing mate."

I sat there and did non-stop drinking for an hour. I was really drunk by then. I was used to liquor. I had plenty of bottles at home. On half of my nights I would stand out on the balcony watching the city with liquor or beer in one hand. I would drink until the very end of myself.

I had to use the restroom unbearably. I walked very crooked, I followed the end of the bar where the men's room was. I think . . . I stood in front of the urinal or sink. I leaned on the wall to let it all out. I wanted to moan it felt like I had been holding in that one. I was pretty drunk.

"Damn! Miss thang is fine!"

I looked at the entrance. It sounded like a girl walked into the bathroom. I looked in the mirror when I was done. I always look at myself when I'm drunk. It was just a habit to see how far-gone I was. All I saw were squinting eyes and everything else was as it should be.

I sat at the barstool again. My head got real heavy and I hit the bar. I just couldn't hold up my head anymore. But this is what I wanted. I wanted to pretend like I was having a good night

"Give me . . ."

"Excuse me?" The bartender put his ear towards me. "What's that lad?"

"What?" I looked at the bartender.

"No more for you." He laughed at me.

"Damn boy, you fine."

I turned to my side. There sat a weird looking woman. She looks like she had fake breasts. Her make up was caked on as if a baker was having fun on her face. She spread out her lips, which had shinny red lipstick on it. She acted like . . . like ah . . . Like a woman trying to be too lady like. It was the way she sat, the way she moved her hands when she spoke, like she was grooving to music I couldn't hear. I had no idea what she was saying. I just stared at her.

"So you know what I'm saying? I saw whatchoo been hiding in the bathroom. It's big girl."

I looked at her with my drunken eyes. "What?"

"Boy you look good." She rubbed against me.

I tried to smile but nothing came to my lips. Maybe drool. She kissed my ear then blew into it lightly. I felt disgusted. I had no idea what to do at this point. I couldn't even tell what was going on. She rubbed her crotch against my leg. It didn't feel like no flat flower, it felt like . . . Oh no! I threw up knowing it was what I had.

I fell off of my stool, as he got closer. I looked up at him. I could see its masculine legs and tell where everything fake was.

"Damn boy, what's yo problem?" Another drag queen popped his head next to him.

"Girlfriend, he is tripping."

"Uh-huh girl, you know it."

The man helped me up. I stood there staring. "You're a . . ." I pointed at him slurring my words. "You're a dude."

"She opened her mouth. "Well thank you miss thang. I didn't know that. And what? You know you want some of this."

"Fuck'n faggot!" I slurred. Then he slapped me. I didn't do anything wrong. I fell to the ground again. I watch the two snip snap off. I felt someone's arms around my chest helping me up. I was then set on the stool again. I turned around to see who it was. I smiled. There was my long lost bro. I thought he was gone.

"Tony!" I yelled with joy.

"Hey Alex, looks like you drank a shit load."

"Where have you been."

He looked at me weird. "Ah bartender, how much did he drink?" The bartender pulled out the empty bottle I was drinking from. "Oh fuck Alex, you're wasted. I got a couple of lines of coke. The shit was smooth. I'm feeling real good right now." He sat down next to me and turned towards the bartender. "Can I get a blackjack." Tony gulped it down.

I put my arm around Tony's' shoulder and came closer to his ear. I pointed my finger towards the end of the bar. While I spoke I stared at the wall behind the counter.

"Did you see that guy?"

"Where bro?"

"Right there, I swear to god." I shook my head while I spoke. "Aye get this, he tried to hit on me."

"No way!"

"Yeah!" I moved back because I didn't think he believed me. "I'm serious dude."

"That's fuck'n sick bro. Oh . . . I see them. The one dressed like a girl? Nasty." He turned back and looked at me. "Well bro, I'm gonna dance cause that coke gave me a rush. Meet me out there fuckhead." He walked off.

"Yeah, dancing sounds fun." I pointed to the bartender. "Last drink of the night. I'll take a shot of Jack Daniels."

He poured it; I gulped it.

I paid the bill. I made sure I gave him a good tip being that I sat there drinking for a while. When I turned around there was a girl standing next to me. A *real* girl. She was kind of cute. She smiled at me shyly. We went downstairs together. I tripped on the last step. She helped me up. We entered the crowd of music. I felt my body moving on it's own, like I couldn't stop my drunken dancing. Soon it felt like I had been dancing for hours. I fell.

Someone picked me up. I saw bright lights. I thought it was the cops but it was my brother. It was always my brother who picked me up off of the ground. The disco ball was reflecting in my eyes.

"Come on Alex, we gotta go home." He pushed me to the exit. We walked out of the club; everything went silent as if I went completely deaf.

"Go home? But we gotta groove." I slurred. "You know what I mean?" I sang and did a little dance.

"Alex I'm gonna have to drive your car. You're too drunk."

Tony practically carried me to the car. We heard voices behind us.

"Oh there's that bitch right over there." It sounded like the faggot from earlier. He walked up to Tony and me.

"Get out of here you queer. Leave my brother alone." Tony gave them dirty looks as he was trying to get me to the car. "My brother's not into dudes."

"Oh, you think you're too good now huh. Well let your *brother* decide for himself. Is he such a bitch you need to talk for him."

"I don't even have time for this shit. You two want to take advantage of a guy who can't even walk right now is pretty pathetic. Now get the fuck out of here before I make you my bitch!"

"Fuck you too! You just wish you could have some of this!"

Tony dropped me on the ground. He pushed the faggot and I could hear them yelling at each other. Tony started beating the crap out of him. I found the strength to get up. The other guy smacked me across the face. I just threw my drunken body at him, which sent him to the ground. Tony was kicking the other guy in the back and head telling him he was nothing but a dirty faggot. I kneed the other guy in the balls. He tried to kick me off but I couldn't even hold myself up. I smacked my head into his. I felt someone touch my shoulder. I flung around with my hand in the air. Tony backed up then helped me to my feet.

"Get the fuck up little brother. We got to get out of here."

I lost all sight of everything. I felt as though I wasn't even touching the ground with my feet. Maybe I shouldn't have drank so much that night.

I woke up screaming.

The light was in my eyes. Tony ran in. He looked at me and said, "What's wrong? I heard you screaming!"

I ran to the bathroom and threw up everything that evaded my body the night before. I was on the floor like a dog licking the bowl.

"I cooked some breakfast," yelled Tony. What a dick. It just made everything worse. I don't ever want to remember how sick I felt that morning. The world was spinning in my head and in my stomach. I just wanted to die so I could escape the pain. After a half an hour over the toilet, I came into the dining room where Tony sat at the marble table. Tony had out a small cup of pepto and a coffee waiting for me.

"Man, I envy you."

"Me? What the fuck for? Look at me, I'm sick as shit!" I said.

"Look at this place. You've got it all. Everything in your hands is gold."

"It means nothing if you have no one to share it with." I looked at him with my eyes squinting. "What are you doing here?"

"What? Oh, well I couldn't go home because you were too drunk to drive. But later my wife is going to pick me up. You want to come over later?"

"Tell everyone to come over here. The kids can go swimming at the pool downstairs on the first floor. We can sit in the hot tub or the sauna."

"I don't know, my kids might not want to leave this rich life."

"You know this is all yours too."

CHAPTER 5

I dream of the past often. What I remember were shattered memories and sometimes the funniest things that happened to me. We sometimes pretend in life that there are open doors and opportunities for us. But not for me. The doors I go through are not abstract in the sense that these things *can* and *will* happen. I make things happen. All things must be concrete for me.

They tried to help me before. It seemed to be a control problem for most parents it was different with mine. They didn't care what I did or became as long as it didn't interfere with their plans. Old stepfather Patrick made sure I wasn't in the way of things. What was difficult for everyone, was where and who to send me with. How had I burnt the bridge with my uncle can be described as stupidity from someone who didn't recollect the pain he once went through. I wanted to get away from Patrick. I hated Patrick. He was not my father and didn't care to be. He did however find it amusing to use me as his personal punching bag. I don't want go on remembering what they did to us forever.

"Alex I know it's difficult with your mother and father," He looked at me with the words *father*. Was it an understanding from everyone that this monster, this beast was my inheriting father? I think not. And I cringed at the word *father*. "I know you want to stay here, but yah just can't. I won't allow it. My hands are tied you see. And you haven't proven to me that you have changed. Frankly, you're not my responsibility."

Why did he have to bring this up at our most intimate moment? Where I pretended to be the best-behaved child in the world and he pretended to be a well thought out uncle. I was sitting in my favorite Mexican restaurant eating a monster taco salad that no one else in this world made so good.

"Can we talk about something else for now?" I asked trying to avoid the moment of clarity he was having.

"No, I just can't. I knew that with this visit you would want to stay with me. But this was just a visit. I have my own life now. I don't ever plan to have any more kids nor do I feel like making any more mistakes with you."

"Look, I just want to finish eating. Please, let's just let it go for a little while."

"Sure. But I'm telling yah, I have no interest in changing my mind."

I *was* happy stepping off of that plane for a summer visit. I was stunned. In the whole world, out of all the places I had heard was so cool, this was it. This was where I wanted to plant my seed and make it grow. My brother was here, why can't I be here?

Uncle Mike was a hard person to deal with. If I can just show him that I won't be in the way, maybe I'll be home free. Away from the beatings, the teasing, and Patrick. That's all I wanted to do; *get away from Patrick*. He was a complete asshole. My mother loved him though. There must be something about him that she has seen in him for all these years that makes her want to stay. My wife wouldn't ever lay a hand on my child. For he is my son and I must be his protector. She protects no one. She didn't care. She called me, "her little shit."

As the visit ended, I cried on the plane back to Texas. These old people who sat near me, thought I was crying because I would miss my family. I was crying because I had to go back to them. I was already seventeen and already committed the ultimate crime. I stayed in most of the time. It was strange when you see the old folks going out to party and the kid stayed inside, locked away from the world. And as opposites happened in my home, you might think I was the one waiting late at night hoping they would get home okay after I specifically told them to be home by a certain time.

The reality was, I hoped they would crash and burn. The reality was, I hoped they got drunk and drugged and killed each other in a most psychotic form of pain. The reality was, I didn't care what happened to them as much as they didn't care about me.

On a Saturday I sat there staring at the tube letting the fan blow in my face. The summer here was like sitting *on* the sun after it had been covered with water. I thought often about my loneliness. I did let it get to me.

"Where are you going?" I asked my mom and Patrick.

They were dressed up. My mom had on kaki shorts with a nice blouse. Patrick was wearing his *clean* pants and cowboy hat. The two smelled of cologne. As much as I hated him, it was nice not to smell the grease and sweat he smelled of everyday. Like chili beans and armpits. He didn't care if he smelled up the kitchen with his sweaty fungous feet while we ate dinner.

"We're going to Jesse's, you want to come?" Asked my mother. But no pity for me. Not only that, but Patrick gave her this look of, "*how dare you invite the boy.*"

"Nah, that's cool. I'll just stay here and lick my own ass."

"Well have fun." Smiled Patrick. They shut the door behind them and I was all-alone. Not that I felt like they were company when they were around. It was as if I were never around to them. I would rather not be around them ever again in my life. There are ways to pretend that I am not alone.

I don't know how to feel about them not caring about me. I can't feel anything. I think I am crazy, for nothing in this world surprises me in the least bit. No friends at this point to care about. No Alex for friends to care about. But that's my life and some others have the same existence of being alone. This is my eleventh week home since I came back from visitation with Mike.

I dialed the number of my dealer. I had to get something in my hands of loneliness. He wasn't my friend nor would he ever be. He was a west side gangster. I didn't know what gang he was in, some kind of Vato Loco gang. It didn't matter to me. I wasn't in a gang nor ever would be. He knew I was different but he thought I was cool. He offered one time in school to sell me some weed and we were almost caught smoking out. He said if I ever needed anything to give him a call. So here I am.

When he received my page, I got the call. I dodged for the phone, "Hey!" I yelled out of breath.

"What can I get for yah, freaky?"

He always called me freaky. "Quarter sack and three hits of acid."

"Well I'm a bit busy right now but I can swing by in an hour so have your shit ready. See you in a bit."

"I'll be here."

Chewy Garcia got me what I needed most of the time. I can't explain my enjoyment for drugs. I just do. When you're as lonely as I am, drugs and alcohol make you feel like you aren't alone and you are laughing and having a good time without anyone in the world.

My plans for this evening would just be, *get high*. The TV would be funnier than ever, the movie would be scarier and make me fear turning off the light and another would make me tear and want to fall in love again. When reality hit, I would never want to be in love. I will make it a point not to fall in love.

The three taps on the door made my heart pump and I ran to open it. There he was. Not as tall as me, tan, his hair slicked back, Dikie slacks, and a white t-shirt. There was some other guy with him. He looked the same, appearance wise, but he was thinner and a lot taller. He looked a little Lurch.

"How's it gong?" I asked.

"Pretty good." He looked at his friend and tapped him on the chest real quick. "This is my homie Ed. Ed this is Freaky, he calls me from time to time to get his shit."

"Sup," said the newcomer.

"Hey." I looked around. "Well, let's go into my room here."

The three of us went into my room. Ed sat on my one-seated couch and Chewy and I sat on my futon couch. Chewy pulled out a large bag of weed from under his jacket, which he held in his arms. It was laced with red hairs. I wanted it more than anything else in this world at that very moment.

He made a separate bag, which he weighed out a little extra. "Is that good for you?" He asked.

"You know it is." I took the bag and gave him the money. He pulled out his wallet to put the money away. Then he took out a little piece of foil.

"What kind?" I asked.

"Blue moon dipped twice. My boy and I tried it the other day."

I gave him fifteen dollars.

"You want to smoke a J before you go?"

"Yeah."

I rolled a beefy joint for them to get really high. I always liked to smoke with Chewy before he left my house. It was my one moment of *real* company I had. I took a hit then passed it to Chewy. After that I couldn't feel anything. I knew I wouldn't be stoned as much as we just smoked. This was the kind that liked to creep up on you when you didn't expect it. And it would be in an awkward moment when you were out doing something that took a lot of thought in the state of mind you would be in.

"Well call me again when you need your shit. We gotta split for now." I gave them both the gangster handshake. They said their goodbyes and I was alone once again. But it bothered me no more. I was going to have company with my drugs.

I locked the door and went back to my room. It didn't smell like weed to me, but I'm sure it did. I opened the doors and windows to let out the smell. I turned on the fan then sprayed some air freshener. After hours of sitting around, I finally decided that I should get out of there and go to the punk club. I hadn't been there since I was jumped but now was as good a time as any.

I took one of the hits of acid. I tripped out for a while. I dressed in ripped jeans, black combat boots, and a black t-shirt. I barrowed some cologne from Patrick. It was seven forty-five at night when I decided to prowl out into the world.

I hopped in my Camero, which was barely running at the time. I cruised over to jack in the box. I had the munchies. On my way to the club I stuck my switchblade in my pocket. I parked across the street from the club. The entrance was memorable to me. That was where I seemed to hang out with my friends.

"Who's playing tonight?" I asked.

"Ah . . . Chaos log and the Band-Aids."

"The Band-Aids? What kind of band?"

"Alternative. Chaoslog is a little punky. It should be a slow night. I heard there was a punk tour over at another club."

I gave him five dollars then walked through the gate. There was hardly anyone here. The only people here were some kids drinking by their cars. There were probably fifteen people here. Some of them were friends of the band I suppose. I decided on playing pool. I put in the quarters then began the lonely game.

The band was done setting up. The kids outside came in and stood by the stage.

"Okay everyone, get the fuck up here!" Called out the singer.

I walked up with the rest of the crowd. When they began to play, I thought they were okay. Not too much my type but it was okay. As I stood there enjoying my acid, I saw something out of the corner of my eye. I was the same fat guy that was with Steve at the skate park. He was one of the guys who jumped me. I may have been too fucked up to see straight but I have not forgotten one single face from that very day. I even remember what each of the sponsors looked like. But his face remained etched in my brain.

Something was happening to me. I can remember only one time before this one. It was the night I took care of that red head. This would be my fourth pain. I couldn't understand what was happening to me yet. It was just the beginning. There was weeping in my head. The music was muffled and all I could hear was a moaning, crying, and screaming; three different voices crying out. There were shadows floating around me. They stood in the background like the shadows we give off when light reflects off of us. They were yelling at me. My heart was pounding. I was afraid. I knew it wasn't the drugs that were doing this to me.

He was jumping in the mash pit. He was big, tall, fat, wearing dorky glasses. He had his head shaved with only long bangs over his face. He was of massive size. He was laughing, having a good time. He gave his crotch a quick squeeze as if he were irritated. He walked away to the bathroom. I followed him. It was quiet in there. I stood in front of the urinal. The guy next to me flushed and walked out.

There he was, all alone looking at himself in the mirror. It was big fat John. He pushed up his glasses then went into one of the stalls. As soon as he locked the door, I snuck over to the front door and locked it. I turned off the lights. We were alone. My perfect chance.

"Hey! What the fuck? Who's fucking around?" He yelled out from the stall. "I know that's you Joe. Cut your shit out." He realized it was too quiet for an ignorant friend to be playing a trick. "Joe . . . Joe?" He was sitting on the toilet now scared.

I turned on my lighter. I had my switchblade against his neck. I was slightly behind him off the side. My ideas for all this was not my own. I just went with it all.

"Hello mate, remember me. Alex." I whispered in his ear.

I was not as tall as him but I was close. He was big but my anger was bigger.

"Alex," they called again.

He was about to get up but I pushed down the blade breaking the skin. He knew this was not a game. "Now, if you get up, I will slice your throat. Do as I say and everything won't be alright." At least I'm honest. I got ready. "Get up slowly." He stood up and so did I. "Now, walk out so we can turn on the light." We tip toed to the switch. He turned it on. "Do you see yourself in the mirror?" He nodded his head. "Good. Now," I said calmly. "I'm going to let you go. I want you to turn around and *try* to kick my ass."

I backed away. I took the blade away from the bastards' throat. He turned around. I had my hands out ready for the kill. He yelled as he went at me, which reminded me of the fat guy from "Better off Dead," at the end where the fat guy screamed and was dumped into the snow. I moved at the last minute. I grabbed him by the shirt then banged his head against the wall. I rammed my knee into his stomach as hard as I could.

My uncle always said, "Once you get hold of them, don't ever stop hitting them."

He fell over. I kicked him in the face breaking his nose. I kept kicking him over and over to the point where my leg *should've* gone limp. Blood splat out of his mouth and nose. I wouldn't stop.

"You want to kick my ass now! You ain't shit without your friends, are you?" I was furious and ready to cry. I was so mad. I knew it was an insult. He couldn't even hurt me without anyone else helping.

I grabbed him by the shirt and punched him in the face as hard as I could. It must have hurt my hand because it was so red and swollen. I felt him grab my leg then yanked me down. I still had my knife. I didn't have time to think. He crushed me with his weight, but I held the knife in front of my chest.

Oh god! It was worse than the first time! *Dead silence.* They left me all alone. I crawled out from under him. He held the knife as he looked at me. I flipped him over ripping the knife out of his clutch. All I could see was blood. He never cried out. I jabbed the blade into his neck and it was over.

It was worth doing. But now I had feelings again. A conscience. I used all the strength I had to pull him into one of the stalls. I set him on the seat then locked the door. I crawled out from the bottom, which smelled like pea on the floor. I tripped all over myself and I felt like a wreck. I wiped the blood off the floor. I cleaned the knife free of all prints. I put the blade in my pants then walked out.

"Man, what the hell? I had to fuck'n piss." There was a boy by the door. I kept my head down so he wouldn't see my face.

It felt good. I knew they wouldn't trace it to me. It would be a while before they realized he was there and I would be long gone. No one can remember who was in the bathroom with him.

I didn't feel like I had a problem with drugs. Others believe drugs are a problem. My brother does them. I take them. I know why I do them. I have fun getting high. I can tell you the main reasons why I do drugs . . . I can't hear them when I'm high. There are no children chanting my name. But they like to invade my dreams and turn them into nightmares. I feel like I'm in hell. My reality doesn't exist.

No dream women exist. It's all just a game of who can impress whom until the truth comes out of how their whores and cheating lying bitches. They turn on you like dogs.

"Alex, we're leaving. We'll be back late. If you go out, don't forget to lock the door." Said my mother. I was going to be alone. Waiting up for the two.

"And stay the fuck out of my room, you little shit." Yelled my stepfather.

Like I want to be in their smelly room. They shut the door gone in a flash. What to do? I decided on downtown exploration. I ran into some drug dealers and bought some acid. I thought it would be a good idea like all of my same ideas, to get messed up.

I dropped the acid into my mouth. I had left my car at home. I didn't like having my car downtown.

As soon as I stepped onto the bus, it hit me like a ton of bricks. I was far beyond okay. I had triple visions. The bus almost knocked me over when it drove on. I didn't even think I would remember where to get off. But there was this restaurant, which was my landmark to safety. So I pulled the plug. The bus stopped and I was back out on the streets. There was honking and yelling but from which way, I couldn't tell.

As soon as I found my house, I fell on the front steps. As I lay on the ground, I searched for my keys. They were at the bottom of my pocket. I had to bend myself backwards just to get them out.

"Ah-ha!" I yelled out when I had them in my grasp. I pulled them out with the tips of my fingers. I found the strength to get up and unlock the door. It was quiet inside. Very dark. An elephant rumbled passed me the size of a dog. I jumped back.

"What the fuck are you doing in my house?" I said as if it were normal.

I grabbed a poker from the fireplace. I held it up ready for the elephant to try to attack me. Instead it just ate my mother's chocolate cookies. I walked up to it. I pointed my poker at it. I jabbed it a couple of times.

"Hey! Stop eating my mother's cookies!"

But it just kept eating. I tapped it again. It got mad. It turned to me then blew its little trunk at me. It was after me now. I backed up then ran into my room. I locked the door. I looked around the room once I turned on the lights. My posters were staring at me. I knew now it was the drugs. But I couldn't stop. I was afraid. Everything looked so real.

There were posters all round my room. Most of them were monsters, mummies, and skeletons. I lay back on my bed. I watched the door with my poker, ready for action. I saw something that made me want to scream. The monsters on the posters were climbing out of their pictures. They were reaching for me. I moved into the corner of my bed.

"No!" I cried.

I grabbed the poker and tried to swing it back and forth at them. I jumped around my room like a monkey trying to dodge every move they made against my own. I jumped off the bed and ran into the bathroom. The statue of the dog was barking at me. I ran back into my room.

"Leave me alone damn you!"

But their hands reached out for me. I heard a bang on the door. I knew exactly what it was.

"Go away elephant! You can't eat my mother's cookies!" I yelled as I tried to escape from the zombies. But the banging continued. "Somebody help me! The creatures are trying to eat my brains!"

The bang broke apart the door. I swung the poker at the strange looking creature. The elephant had changed form.

"Alex what in hell has got into yah?"

The elephant sounded like my stepfather.

"Oh no! You ate my mom's asshole husband!" I swung the poker at it. "Get back! Get back you bitch of the devil! You must leave before I kill you! Eat the zombies and run away!" I screamed like a maniac.

"Alright boy, that's enough nonsense." Said the elephant.

"No! No! Patrick, you have got to cut through! I'll set your dumb ass free." I said. Then I tried to stab him.

The elephant rammed me onto the bed and held me down. "You had better sober up off of whatever you took boy!" He looked at me funny. "What in hell did you take?"

"It's not the drugs that are effecting me. The creatures are coming to life." I looked around and my eyes were almost black from my pupils dilating. "It's okay that you ate him. I hated him anyway."

"Alright boy. I think it's time you shut your fuck'n mouth." Said the elephant. He started hitting me really hard in the face until I completely knocked out. All I saw was blackness. The last image seen was Patrick.

I woke up in a strange bed with white sheets. I looked around the room.

"So what's up with the boy?" Asked Patrick.

"Well it might be heroin, but I don't find any signs on his arms. It just might be acid. I don't know if this has been a problem before with him. But whether he took acid today or a while back, it stays in the system for life. You say your son thought you were swallowed by an elephant." Asked the doctor.

"Yep. He kept telling me to get out of the *elephants* stomach." Said Patrick.

"Was there any prescription drugs he could have gotten into?"

"All my pills for my ulcers have been locked away, besides it couldn't be that."

My mother stepped closer. "Well we had just bought this new statue that we put by the refrigerator. That might be what he saw."

"Well I won't know until he comes to." The doctor turned around. He stuck a needle in my arm and gave me a shot that just put me to sleep. "Best I can do is stick him in drug rehab or a mental institute which is free for people of your sort."

And then my eyes close.

"Okay boys, let's talk about what we can do to trample our problems. What can we do to help each other? Is there any ideas?" Asked the lady.

"Well I think maybe you guys can ask yourselves why we do drugs, then maybe we could solve the problem." Said Tommy the taker. He took anything he could get his hands on. Even his mother's menstrual pills.

"That's a good idea Tommy." The lady looked around the room. "That sounds just about right. Why don't we start with Adam."

Adam looked up from his sneaker. "Well what do you expect me to say? My parents put me here. I didn't." He was already mad that all eyes were on him.

"Okay, let's move on. Thomas why don't you give everyone an example of what we're trying to do here. What makes you do drugs?"

"Well miss, I couldn't tell yah. I mean, why does there *have* to be a reason? It's like there are voices that tell me to do drugs and I can't stop them."

As soon as he said that, I zoomed in. I knew what he was feeling about the voices. I knew there had to be some sort of connection somewhere along the lines. I was hoping I wasn't the only one. My eyes set on the other boy.

"They want me to take drugs . . ." He was quiet for a moment then hit the guy sitting next to him and the two began to laugh together.

The councilor was mad. She hated dealing with punk kids like us. But it was a living. Maybe she was a volunteer. She looked at all of the boys. She made eye contact with me. I looked away. I wasn't much of a talker.

"Please Alex . . . can you shed some light on the subject? Do you know why you take drugs?"

I gave her a cold look that must have made her have nightmares for weeks after that. She had this scared look on her face like she grew sick from the sight of me. But then I smiled most unpleasant. It only made her feel worse.

"Well my parents put me here because the acid I was on gave them an excuse to get rid of me. They don't give a fuck about me. I'm only here because this was free and an easy way to get me away from them. But I'll tell you why I do drugs, because I can't hear them. I can't feel the shock of pain in my head."

"Okay Alex, I've had enough of these games from you boys. I'm trying to help you all and you just seem to like mocking me." She turned away.

I looked at her with crazy eyes. "I'm serious lady. They seem to want me to kill. And I have. She was nobody to me. She wanted to fuck around so I put her out. Can't you stop this? Can't you stop the screams? All I want is a normal life. And I can't see straight. Why can't you stop the voices in my head!"

Everyone freaked out. The next thing I knew, I was being rushed to the Dallas mental institute. I convinced them it was just to scare the councilor and get her off of my back. How about you, do you believe me?

CHAPTER 6

In all my experience with life I understand one thing, I am not alone in my own head. I watch the world grow around me and I hate what I see. I am disgusted with the life that people chose to lead. What happened to faithful loving marriages? It always comes back to relationships. The relationships we have made with every type of environment such as family, work, friends, and strangers.

My family shit on me all my life. There goes that relationship. My friends beat me up. There goes that one. My girl cheated on me. There goes that life. The people I work with suck up to me, for I am their golden paycheck. The strangers disgust me. I cannot seem to find someone in this world who feels as though I do. It was just an unlucky life for me, I suppose.

I know that many people say they wish they were as rich as me, and then they can do anything. It is true. I can do anything. The only way I find comfort is to rid of those who I can't stand at all.

One other comfort I find in this life are my nephews. Their innocence in this world is precious to me. I would do anything in my power to care for my brother's kids. I've started a college fund for each of them. He wouldn't let them go, not even for a million dollars. I would never try to steal them from him. Even though Tony and I fought when we were children, it didn't matter. That is how most normal brothers and sisters are to each other.

I just hope that they find happiness in what I cannot.

Society seems to let these things happen. People who have leading roles sometimes have no business up there making decisions for us. It's been going on for years. I wish I were born in another time.

No one has any morals. I see mothers who allow their girls to do drugs and sleep around and some do it with their kids. It's been *in style* for women to look as though they are starving to death. I mean these runway models may look good to some guys and to all girls but reality needs to look them in the face. Some of them have ugly faces, but because they have stick figure bodies and a flat chest it's *supposed* to be good looking. I like the type of women who have shape. I'm sorry but eight-year-old boys are not attractive to me.

The men these days become gayer. I guess it turns on the world that all the men look gay. I would never be caught dead wearing a tight see-through button up and slick my hair back into a mound of shit.

I can't see myself with these people. I find the most interesting people to be people with conviction in life. Those who want to change the world and not care if anyone else is with them. That's what I'm doing; mopping up all of the scum from the face of this earth so we can start all over.

I can rid of all the scum of society, and then it will be a new beginning. If I could choose a time period to be born in, it would be between the nineteenth century and the beginning of the twentieth. I would be able to see more people who believed in the word love. Of course there would be whores. There have always been whores since the beginning of time. I can't change that about the world. But I can empty out their existence around my presence. Jack the Ripper couldn't have said it any better.

In my dreams I can fell both hot and cold which causes me to shiver. I wake up sweating or I wake up freezing. My heart beats a million miles a minute. I'm confused for a while and don't know if anything is real. It's always in the same episode when I awake in such horror. To see the faces of those who stick in your head after you've rid of theirs.

It was always the same girl that I can never rid out of my head. This woman is a demon. Her beauty . . . Her significance. I'm always running away from her. She is not a real beauty that I had always thought her to be. I fear the Demon is my own. My Lila. My heart was all hers when she was mine. That was my mistake. I let her take everything from me, every last feeling I had, that was real, was given to her and she shut it out. Because she was a whore just like the rest of them. And I can't remember the last time I dreamt of a woman and it not turning into her face.

I closed my eyes and I am in pure rest. It comes on slow through the night. The flashes of death. The quick screams of their last breath.

I started running on the hottest pavement while my feet are melting. I ran from the screams of women I have murdered. They are crying always in my head. I can't breathe. I choke on my own sweat.

Out of the tunnel. Everything is red; the sky, the pavement, the hills far off, so far I'll never be able to touch them. I stopped in the middle of nowhere. Behind me in a far distance I could hear all of the girls crying in a sexual moan of pain and others are crying as if I broke their heart. The noise got louder and louder, until there is a strange pattern like a fan blowing loudly next to my ears making that swaying whacking noise.

My ears started to bleed. I try to breathe in and out but nothing. She knew that this would drive me insane. And I believe I woke up screaming my head off. As soon as I sat up into reality I started to panic and had an asthma attack.

"Lay still Mr. Dugan." I try to lay back but my body is going into convulsions. Every vein in my forehead down to my arms were pumping so hard they bubble up as I strain to get out.

"Get the anesthetic! He's going out of control!"

"Is he psychotic?" Asked another doctor.

"Let's just get the respirator on him and put him out!"

All these doctors and nurses are trying to calm me down as I had my fit of rage. I sat on a bed with wheels as they glide me through the hospital. My vision was blurry and I couldn't see anything but people behind counters in white uniforms. The people pushing my bed were looking at their watches and shouting at each other. My ears were *really* starting to bleed. I started to scream over the voices that are so loudly shouting at me. My mouth hung wide open as we reached a room filled with many different surgical tools. They want to play with me I thought.

As they tried to hurry and stop the bleeding, another doctor hooked up a respirator to my mouth, while a nurse just shot me full of something in my arm. It went straight to my head, for my body went limp within a minute. I laid back in my bed and looked at the characters of life that worked to save a crazy from having a heart attack or something. Now my life is over but I could hardly care. Had my dreams really messed up everything for me? They just showed the crazy side of me.

I looked at the nurse who was checking my pulse. The doctors were talking in a low tone to each other next to me. I knew it was about me, but I wasn't all here you see.

The room was lit up with bright lights and the walls were purely white. It was too bright for me and my eyes began to squint as the drug was taking a large effect on me. I fought it. I wanted to know what was going on with me. But it was too late. My eyes closed and all thoughts are gone.

In the middle of everything, this whole ordeal, which I can't plainly get myself out of, I woke right up still dazed from this drug. There was a nurse checking over me. She had a clipboard in her hands. She never looked at my face. Her hair was done up behind her white half cap. It was a dark red. I looked at her face.

"Lila?"

"Don't try to speak sir, you'll only make things worse for yourself." Said the nurse.

"What do you mean?"

She looked at her watch. The nurse put down her clipboard then began to wrap my wrists and feet in straps.

"Why are you doing this to me?" I asked. "I'm not crazy."

"Who's Lila?" She asked with a drill buzzing in her hands.

"What?" I backed away. "No, what are you doing!" I screamed. "I'm not crazy!" I cried. "I'm not crazy."

"Sit still, this will only take a moment."

From a distance I saw two other doctors coming up to me. They smacked their gloves on their hands as they smiled at me. They began to drill on my head and I screamed.

"What's the matter Mr. Dugan? You shouldn't feel a thing." Laughed the doctor.

I looked around the room. I knew what I saw was not my imagination. There was a man walking around with no skin on his body. He stumbled around like a fucking zombie. What the hell was going on? Okay, calm down, anything this crazy has got to be a dream. But when that doctor with the cigarette hanging from the end of his lip started drilling, I felt everything. I must be feeling every inflection of pain I put onto others. I screamed so loud I thought I was going to collapse a lung. I know what this is; I'm in the mental hospital already.

"Fuck!"

The doctor laughed then handed the nurse the drill. His hands reached down when they came back up he held in his hands, part of my brain. The smoke was rising from his cigarette and he smiled, "Ah," as he pointed to the brains in his hands.

"This is where you hold all of your memory which I am plainly taking out right now." He held it over my face so I could see every crevice of the organ. "You see," he pointed, "this is where you hold all of your memory here." He took the cigarette out of his mouth then pointed again. "This is where all the memories of Lila are, which you can see take up are large portion of your memory. Oh," smirked the old man, "this is where you memorized your childhood beatings, yes. Yes . . . And ah, here we have the memories of screaming women which you killed." He tossed the brains in clear glass bowl.

"All of which is making you insane right now. You are no longer crazy." He patted his chest. The nurse handed the doctor a clipboard and a pen. "Oh thank you Lila."

"You're welcome Doctor." She smiled at him then me.

He signed the papers. He leaned closer to my face. "I guess we've all had a piece of her ass, wouldn't you say so, Mr. Dugan." He laughed. "And a good piece of ass that is." He looked at her body then winked at me. "Well, now you have no memory, which means you can't function with the rest of society but that's alright, you can stay right here with us." He turned around and grabbed Lila by the waist. They started to make out right in front of me. Then they started to take off each other's clothes.

The skinless man headed towards me with a scalpel. He smiled at me then laughed as he began to cut into my chest.

My echoing screams stayed embedded in my head for the whole day.

"Doc, you gotta do something about these dreams I'm having. Is there anything you can give me for dreamless sleep? It's really messing with my head."

"Do you want to schedule a session so we can talk about these dreams you're having. Maybe there is some related problems we can talk about that might help these dream occurrences to go away."

"I'd rather not. Now do you got anything to cure this shit?"

He looked at me strangely outside of his glasses that were hanging off of his nose. "I think it's best if you just try to cope with your sleep with therapy, now I'll be happy to schedule you in and if I see that you need something for sleep, I might be able to get you something."

I walked out.

In sight of each other for the first time. Underneath my sunglasses are my eyes fixated on her. She glanced at me. Her body swayed from side to side as she strode down the street passed the restaurant I was sitting at outside. Through the tinted glasses it mattered not to justify her.

I can picture her laying there next to me with those red lips smiling at me. I had flashes of her moaning as I sat here with my Chinese connections. We were eating lunch. In front of me were some figures they had come up with on the percentage rates of my cars sold in the southern area. They wanted me to manufacture with them.

I couldn't pay any attention to them. I had my eyes set on her. Her long brown hair swayed with her. Her big brown eyes caught me for a moment then she was still in motion of her destination. Her lips were red like cherries, bright and nicely shaped and no smile was attached to it. She was wearing a tight red dress that was not lengthy at all. Her legs were shapely wear shape was needed. She was on a runway and there was no show. I didn't even smile at her.

I paid heed to the gentlemen at the table who wanted my attention and my signature. I made another appointment with them. After I saw her, from that first instant, I knew it was death. Can you imagine? It used to be, "From the moment I saw you, and I knew I was in love." Ha! *Love.* What does that mean? I don't even think it's in the new *Webster's Dictionary.* A hypothetical term now.

I got up leaving money on the table for the waitress. I followed within her footsteps. I imagined she was next to me and I was not alone. She walked down to the shopping center and into a very expensive clothing store. I watched her from outside of the window. I pretended to stare at a dummy by the window.

"I'm sorry miss but this dress is not refundable. It was on sale." Said the woman behind the counter.

"Look miss, I'm not trying to cause a scene but it was a gift and I don't think a dress of this kind looks good on me." Said my lady in red.

"I don't care what you think of how it looks. This is not refundable and now I'm gonna have to ask you to leave."

"Get out your god damn manager now."

The retail clerk turned and walked away. The woman in red saw me outside by the window. She smiled at me but I pretended I never saw her. I looked away at the people who walked by me. She turned around again when a gentleman stood behind the counter. As soon as he looked at her face, his stern expression changed into a polite pleasant look.

"You wanted to speak with me?" His voice trembling a little.

She turned around. As soon as she saw it was a man, it was putty in her hands. She leaned in to show the cleavage down her dress. The other clerk was staring from afar with another girl telling her that the red dress woman had a lot of nerve. They watched how he fell into her web.

"I have a slight problem with the dress. This color is not me. Now I know this isn't refundable, but could you work out something for me?" She asked in her sexiest voice. Then she wrapped her fingers around his tie. He began to sweat.

He smiled. "Miss I'm sorry but"-

"Shh." She put her finger to his lips. Then pulled his tie a little harder. "Pretty please. I'll make it worth your while."

"And how so?" He asked. She winked at him then nudged her head. He looked back at the two girls who curiously watched them. "Um I see. Well," he whispered, "If you leave the dress here and the receipt, I can meet you at the coffee shop down at the corner."

"Hmmm."

"We can work out something as long as you can walk out of here upset for them."

She looked at him with her head down and her eyebrows pitched at him like a vulture. She secretly winked at him. "So this is your god damn policy? You can keep this piece of shit dress. I don't need it." She tossed the dress on the counter and it just so happened that the receipt landed well with the dress.

He stared at her as she walked out of the store. Soon after, the clerk came up from behind him and looked at the dress. "So you denied the refund? I didn't think you would do it with the look on your face when you saw her. I'm glad, she had a lot of nerve coming in here like that." She spoke as she looked at the dress. The receipt fell on the floor and he hurried to pick it up.

"Mark that dress down by five percent and put it out on the racks please." He said as he walked away. "I'll be leaving to lunch in about ten."

I followed the girl up the street. She walked into a coffee shop at the corner and sat down with a steaming plastic cup. I stood by the window but not in her view. Ten minutes later, the manager of the clothing store came rushing up the street. He looked anxious. He smiled as he saw her sitting there. He sat down with her. They spoke for a short while. They smiled at each other. I followed them to a hotel right outside of downtown.

Now this is what gets to me. This is what bothers me. What was I doing following these perverts to a hotel? I was real curious. It's better than watching a movie, it's the real thing.

An hour later the manager rushed out tucking his shirt into his pants. He sped out of there very quickly. She came out ten minutes later with a smile on her face. She was proud of the slut she was. Little did she know I was watching her very disgusted with every orphism in her body. She was a disease that spread to other girls like the plague.

I did follow her home. She lived in Santa Clara County. She never noticed me following her. My car trailed onto hers through the suburban neighborhood. She parked in front of a duplex. I continued straight on as if I were just passing by. I never stopped until I was home.

Later that night I came back to the spot I so wanted to stop at. She wasn't home though. I parked down the street at the corner and walked to her house. When I was a teenager running the streets of California before I was *shooed* away, my friends taught me how to break into houses. I have found myself wondering the gadget stores to find better-advanced tools to help me break in to other peoples' homes. It was for drugs when I did it as a pre-teen. Hopefully, she doesn't have an alarm.

When I got the door open, I shut the door quickly so no one would see me lingering. It was a decent one bedroom duplex. It smelled like flowers in her house. Pictures of her hung all around the bedroom. She was completely in love with herself. She posed as if she were a model.

After snooping around her room, I took one of the pictures off of the wall. I sprayed the back of it with her perfume. I left for her a pretty white rose on her pillow. Out the door I came through and locked it on the way out as if I lived there.

I hung her picture on my bathroom mirror. Every time I looked at her, I pictured her saying to me, "Come on, I'll do anything for you." I could hear her voice, her smell, her sluty smile. The more I stared at her the more I hated her. As I ate dinner, I pictured her sitting across the table from me. There were two candles lit and two plates of stir fried shrimp.

She smiled at me while she sipped on her wine. She was wearing red lipstick. She crossed her legs so that I could see her thigh highs underneath.

I ate my dinner quietly staring at the empty seat across from me. Afterwards, I smoked a cigarette. I gulped down the rest of my wine. I took her plate and tossed it into the trash. I left the rest of the mess for the maid. And that's when I decided.

. . . and for hours I sat in the reflection of her window. Time moves on and I care not.

It was about eleven forty at night when she came home. That's when I got out of my car. I was one with the night in my black jeans, black shirt, boots, and a black cap to hide my face. I had new leather gloves.

I climbed through the darkness watching the dark men follow me from the lights that reflected down on me. I hid behind the trees watching her pull down her red thigh highs that looked so good. She slid down these purple panties and then . . . the wind blew in lifting up her dress. I was not thrilled to see her body. She let down her long hair brushing it against her ass. She let down her dress; letting whoever was out in the night, see her body. I threw up on the side of her house.

She left the room. Where the bathroom was in the hallway, a light came on. I waited until I saw steam coming out of the room. I was on my way. I crept to the window. I pulled out my magic keys. As soon as I opened the door, I could hear the shower going. I checked around the house to see if anyone was there. It was clear. I turned the blinds so no one could see in. Into the bathroom I went locking the door behind me. She couldn't see me through the shower curtain.

I came close to the curtain to look in. She was facing the showerhead. I watched the drips of water rolls down her curved hips. I stepped in the tub almost slipping as I put my feet onto the porcelain tub. She was about to turn around but I put my arm around her waist grabbed her right arm as hard as I could. I held her arms down. She let out a cry.

"Don't think of moving! I swear I'll gut you like a fish." I grunted.

I turned her body around so she could face me. I grabbed both arms with one hand holding them behind her back. We were face to face. As soon as she saw me, her face wasn't as frightened. She moved close and kissed my stiff lips. She slid her tongue around my lips as I stared down at her with anger. I looked down at her wet body. Her nipples had hot water running across them.

I took my right arm and grabbed her by the jaw. "Don't play your games with me you little slut. I know what you do in your spare time."

She looked at me strangely. "What do you want from me?"

"Your death."

She took in her last breath. I covered her mouth with my hand. I pulled her out of the tub. Her face was terrified. I pictured her with a room full of men as they pass her around to use. And she smiles with every touch. I know that she didn't regret anything she did in this life; I was the only regret of hers. It's just so sad for her that it ends this way. A picture of her fell off of the wall and onto her chest. I picked it up, looked it over, and then smiled at her.

"Cute picture. What the fuck do you think you are, the fuck'n queen of beauty? Trust me though, you're not all that great when people can see right through you." I tossed the picture on the floor. I took off my shirt. Can you believe that she thought I was going to rape her? I think when I tossed my shirt in the corner and she spread her legs willingly, that was a subtle hint.

It started quickly as she tried to lift her eyebrows for me in a continuous matter. They called all at once. The shadows began to fling around her body. She saw them. Her legs closed and she began to shake the bed trying to escape. The whispers began to echo loudly in my ears. I closed my eyes for a moment; my vision was beginning to get blurry. There were loud cries and screams of women in my head.

"Do it!" Cried the voices. "She likes to sleep with strangers."

The voices wouldn't stop crying. I heard her whimpers as if the cloth wasn't in her mouth. They flashed all the men she cheated with for money.

"*Now.*" Hummed the Demon voice that was calling out.

She closed her eyes as she tried to rip free. I sliced from top to bottom and as I did I heard the voices of many women crying in a heart broken melody. I felt the strain release from my veins and my body was relaxed with the first cut. Her eyes were wide as melons and her eyes were streaming tears.

Blood poured out like a stream of water rushing out of a creek. I smiled at her as she bled to death.

"What a terrible web we weave." I said as I held the jungle knife in my hands and waved it around like a wand of power over her. Her eyes followed the knife like I was using hypnosis. "You see its people, no smash that, *women* like you who make people like me go crazy. You're a *fuck'n* whore and I have to rid of you. No one will miss you because all you do is cause heartache and pain. Goodnight sweet child of the devil."

I brought the blade over her chest and slammed it into her until I heard that grunt. The grunt that lets me know it was all over. I felt her pulse and it slowly faded into nothing. I was in utter satisfaction. The shadows that stood in the background of the room turned around and disappeared into nothing.

The phone rang louder than any phone I had ever heard. My heart began to race into reality. I was glad the gloves saved me from cleaning the places I had touched. I cleaned my knife. After cleaning my face and arms I put my shirt back on.

Before leaving, I stared at the body on the bed. She lay on her back staring at the ceiling, face to the side with splats of blood on her face. She had streams of tears on her face. I kissed her on the cheek.

I left the house checking to see if anyone was around. It was empty. Not a soul out on the streets. I kept up against the walls so no one would see me. I made sure that no one was peeping out their windows. The only lights were from few TVs and front porches. I ran across the street, jumped into my car, and drove out with no lights until I reached a main street.

By the next weekend I was sitting out on my balcony eating breakfast on a beautiful morning. The birds were chirping and flying through the air trying to shit on my head. The wind was lightly blowing in the air. And the sounds of the world were at my disposal.

Knock. Knock.

I sat there in my silk boxers and rob not wanting to be disturbed. I opened the door. "Here's your paper sir." Said the maid as she handed it to me.

"Thank you, I'll be sure to put a tip in your pay check," I said as I grabbed the newspaper from her then shut the door. I smiled at the thought of my good days I can achieve if I try.

The day was so perfect. The weather was well. I sat back down and drank down my sunny delight. I opened the paper and read the headline. "Forty niner picks a fight with the wrong person." Is it just me, or was the rest of the world as violent as I was.

On the side of that story was a blurry picture of the light brown haired woman. The one in red. The headline said, "Beauty was killed by the Beast." I read the whole article through. She *was* a model. Not a big model. She did adds for department stores and such. One of her lovers killed her by slicing and dicing. Suspects were her x-lovers, whom she cheated on, Roger Morgan and Thomas Wrigle. No one was scene going in or going out.

Monday morning is always a favorite day for me. For most people out in the world they hated the first working day of the week. They wanted to recover from their weekend fun yet that's what Sunday is for. People who don't like to wake up in the mornings are usually people who have shity jobs and are unhappy about the way their life is going. But in my life, I had say so. I was the owner. It repeated in my head and I smiled as it did. *I own my own company.*

The first thing in the morning after the regular presentable look was breakfast. I went to Denny's to enjoy a light breakfast. As I sat down the waitress already came to me, asking what I wanted. Eggs, ham, and hash browns were always good to fill up on. She brought me a coffee and I smoked a cigarette.

Some things I look at twice. They come by slowly so I can see all of its difference in this world. Why these things are drawn to me is not a question I can completely answer. But there she was. She walked passed my table, her hips moving side to side. She had nice legs. As I looked over her face I noticed she was anxious.

She sat down alone. Soon after a man came and sat across from her. They weren't far from my table. He took her hands in his then kissed her passionately on the lips. She smiled as she pulled away.

"So he doesn't suspect anything right?" Asked the man.

Her voice was low as she looked around. "No, I don't think he knows."

Her eyes looked up full of fright. A man came rushing in right at her table. I looked back to watch them. I didn't care if I were nosey. What were they going to do, turn around and tell me to mind my own business?

"What the hell is this?" Asked the stranger.

"Honey, this is"-

"Ah no, don't give me that shit. I've had my eye on you for a while. What the fuck did we get married for if you were going to go behind my back and sleep around?"

"You don't understand. I don't mean to hurt you . . ."

CHAPTER 7

I've tried to ignore the many women in todays' world to rid my self of all human era. What happened in the twentieth century? Here we are in the 1800's discovering technology and at the same time we were still very respectful. I mean, to show a woman's' ankles was considered disrespectful. I think our ancestors would be ashamed to see todays' society.

Do I kill every woman that I see as a whore?

Unfortunately no. I do not kill all women. Of all the demons that I see, there is but one that controls them all. He is the leader. He represents all horrific images I dare not explain that I see. He chooses whom dies. I know I may have my hate that I hold onto each day but he decides their fate.

Yes, my first time, I chose the girl. I chose many. But if they weren't there, if *he* wasn't there to scream in my ears, then I would never have killed a soul. He knows what hurts me. He knows what secret pain I have hidden deep within me.

It's *her.* Lila. She is on their faces. I hear her voice. I see her on top of Nick! I try very hard not to suffer her beauty. I try very hard not to force my hate for her onto others. She's lucky it's not like Anthonys' situation. That bitch doesn't care about my nephews! I hate women! What's happening to me?!!!

Calm down, stay cool. I have a life. I am a *God!*

This weekend is my company Christmas party. I throw the best parties known amongst company parties. You see, I'm rich, single, I can do whatever I want. So what I like to do, is I rent an entire penthouse suite on the top floor at one of the best hotels in San Francisco. It over looks the ocean. We get catered the best food. I provide as much alcohol and beer as they want, they can bring three friends max.

I don't really plan the parties anymore because they already know the routine of how I like them. And my employees can get pretty crazy. I love my team. I don't treat any person different by department one guy makes chump change while the other guy makes bank. I really don't care who they are as long as they're polite and they respect me.

This year, like every year, they urged me to bring a date and so many of them wanted to hook me up with a friend or a family member. I laughed every time someone tried to set me up. They would always ask why I wasn't receptive about it. Then there had been the long illusion of, *am I gay?* Of course not. Just because I can not trust women to be true to me doesn't mean I'll turn to a man. Just the thought of it makes me want to slap people for thinking that about me.

I was going alone. I invited my brother and his wife. They always showed up to my parties. This is where people got to know the average Joe, Alex. And it seemed like people loved when I was a social person.

I still have rules and class to my parties though. This is a formal occasion, I do expect people to wear suites and dresses. There wasn't going to be any teenage bullshit of running in and out of the rooms nor all over the hotel being loud and obnoxious in any way shape or form. I draw the line at public embarrassment.

I wore my best black suit. I had white gold cufflinks with three diamonds on each. I had a tie pin that matched the cuff links. I was smelling great and ready to go. I took my Camero. I could have any fancy sports car easy. But this was my sports car. I had a great sound system, the back tires were thick, wide, and lifted, and I've also dropped a nice race car engine in here. You can hear her a mile away.

The party doesn't start in the penthouse. It starts in one of the large banquet halls. As I drove up to the valet Parker, I saw many familiar cars. I looked around at the entrance where many people were gathering inside to their own parties or rooms. As I looked out the window, a young man tapped on my window.

"Sir?" He asked through the glass wall between us.

I put the car in park and got out. He looked at me and then in my car which was blasting Rammstein. I looked back as I grabbed my jacket and then turned down the radio. I handed him the keys.

"Now, if anything is amiss, I'm coming for you." I smiled.

He laughed turning his head away a little as he grabbed the keys. My hands were stiff as a board. I didn't let go of the keys. He let go and looked back at me.

I slowly shook my head left to right. "I'm not playing." I smiled at him, my eyes reflected red for a moment and then I dropped the keys in his hand. "Thank you." I said politely as I walked away.

I walked through the door staring at the huge water fountain in the center of the front room. I walked down the long hallway where people were walking to and fro. I looked down at my feet staring at the beautiful marble tile that seemed to be in almost every room.

"Alex!" I heard above the loud voices.

I looked up. It was one of my salesman Jack Hamilton. He's an internet salesman. I smiled as he walked up trying to get through the crowd. I shook his hand as he approached. We walked towards the main desk together.

"So, everyone's inside the banquet hall down that left hallway there." He pointed.

"And the room?" I asked.

"Stans got the key."

"Maybe I'll go up and take a look." I said.

The two of us went up to the room to look around. There were three bedrooms. There was a huge living area that was carpeted with the finest quality. There were three steps surrounding the entire living area. Outside there was a huge balcony bigger than the size of one of the rooms. And of course, I couldn't do without a large hot tub to the right of the balcony.

I turned around and looked back at Stan who stood by the doorway smiling at me.

"Wooh!" I laughed. "We're gonna get fucked up tonight, let me tell you!" Stan smiled at me. Jack put out his hand for me to smack it, *and I did.*

"Fuck yeah bossman!" Shouted Jack.

We went down the to banquet hall where it looked as though it had double in people. There was a long fancy table in the front near a podium for me, my family, my managers, and their invites.

There was going to be music and dancing. I actually loved having these company get togethers. But outside those walls would I let no one penetrate my life. I walked around greeting many people. Many employees wanted me to meet their families. Everyone was eager to show me off. There were a lot of single pretty ladies there.

One of my top sales person, was Annie Lubbock. She was great with words and took care of a lot loose ends for Mr. Gale. She was management over the floor salesman. She pulled me by the arm towards the long table.

"Let's go ahead and make our announcements and then we can start the dinner." She said.

I followed her to the front cause lord knows I starved myself all day for this. I was about to eat lobster, crab, and shrimp. I wanted to eat like a pig, dance it off, and get wasted. Most of the time, people saw me a little unfriendly, uptight, serious. And that really just isn't who I am. But why expose myself to any person.

"Alright everyone let's please find a table with our friends and families. Stan get up here, you're the last one." She said over the mic. She wasn't fat, but a little heavy, so sometimes I could hear the fat in her cheeks as she spoke and that was very annoying.

"Thank you all for coming this evening. The owner Mr. Alex Dugan thanks you for being here to enjoy the holidays with everyone here from Dugans' Classics. We have a wonderful evening planned for all of you tonight." She saw that mostly everyone was seated at their tables. Anthony and Jennifer slipped in besides me on my right. "Now, let's welcome our manager Stan Gale who will be passing out the awards this evening." She clapped so everyone clapped.

Anthony tapped me on the shoulder and nudged his head at me.

"What's going on?" He whispered.

"Oh, top salesmen and stuff." I whispered.

"Thank you for that lovely welcoming." Smiled Stan as he stood behind the podium. "First off I'd like to thank Alex, Mr. Dugan for inviting us to this fancy hotel for good food and company. E very year he puts a lot of money into these events." I nodded my head as he looked over at me. "Without this guy here, we'd all be out of a paycheck." He laughed. A few chuckled out in the crowd. "So, let's get started on the awards!"

He looked down at his cards. "First we'd like to present an award to the fastest climb in sales in a short period of time to . . . Michael Walters!" He called.

Michael jumped up. He laughed as everyone at his table were making comments to him. Everyone clapped as he walked up to the podium.

Stan handed him a plaque and shook his hand. "So here you are, from all of us at Dugans' Classics." Michael smiled as he shook Mr. Gales hand. "*And,* we have here," Stan pulled out an envelope. "A check made out to you for one thousand dollars!" Michael's eyes lit up. He looked back at me.

"Thank you Mr. Dugan!" He smiled.

I smiled back at him nodding my head.

We passed out five awards to different categories. The employees loved getting awards and money. Anything for free.

"So last but not least, we still have one more award we'd like to give." Said Stan as he looked over at me.

I looked around like I didn't know what was going cause . . . I didn't know what was going on.

"Mr. Dugan, we, the staff, would like to present you with this award for being a great boss and an inspiration to us all." The four managers stood by the podium holding up a fancy plaque. "Thank you for everything."

I stood up and smiled. Everyone clapped as I approached the managers. They handed me the plaque. I held it in my hands looking down at it, then back down at the crowd of people. There were lights pointed on me, in my eyes. I squinted. For a moment it was so bright, I felt like I was being watched . . . *by them.*

"You know, I didn't expect this . . . there are moments in life when you think all your hard work is never going to pay off. Or no one appreciates everything you've done. I mean, this," I shook the plaque a little in my hand. "This is what it's all worth." I looked around at all the smiling faces. "I know that financially I'm doing great. But when you bust your back for years thinking no one will ever care . . . you prove me wrong." It was quiet. "Thank you, to all of my employees, this means a lot to me."

Everyone clapped. I felt silly as I walked away. Stan patted me on the back.

"Okay everyone, let's eat. Um, we'll have dancing until eleven and then if you want to stay for the after party it's upstairs on the top floor. Don't forget that we're also having a raffle so if you have your tickets please put them in the bin. We'll be passing out prizes after we eat. Enjoy everyone. And I better see everyone's' asses at work on Monday."

People were laughing and cracking jokes about coming into work drunk on Monday or that they were all going to call in.

We ate like pigs, passed out prizes, and after that, when the drinks and dancing began, we lost ourselves in the commotion of mingling. There were twenty-five prizes ranging from gift cards to a trip for two on a Hawaiian cruise. One of the mechanics won the cruise and one of the receptionists won two plane tickets to New York. Yes, I spent a lot of money on everything but it's Christmas, what can I say.

I started drinking once the music started up. They mixed it up playing some classic dance songs from the 70's and 80's but everyone got wild when they were playing todays' music. Which I can understand, todays' music is a little risqué.

I got down with everyone. They were playing, "play that funky music white boy." Of course *this* white boy was about to get crazy. My brother and Jennifer were laughing as I loosened my tie and slid my legs to the sides from left to right. I call it the *Axel Rose dance.*

We did *the kid n' play*, we did *the robot, the wop, the hippity hoppity!* I was laughing and sweating. All the guys were in their nice clothes, sleeves rolled up, and the sent of beer breath surrounded us all. We were laughing in each others faces. A few of the guys tried to get a little serious with me. Shop talk.

Stan and Anthony were going to go to the top to make sure everything was set. One room was for me, the rest I really didn't care. It was first come, *first come. Ha! Ha!* That's when Ronnie Flask, came up to me.

Ronnie Flask was one of the Floor salesman. He won an award for third top salesman. His cousin that he brought won a DVD player in the raffle. I could tell he was buzzed out. His eyes looked a little off and glassy. He kind of pushed himself to get to me. I walked towards him and put my arm on his shoulder.

"What's the word pal?" I asked him.

"I'm just about gone Alex." He looked up at me. "Hey, I'm glad that I work for you sir. You're an honest guy and treat people fair."

"Well I'm glad. Let's get back for now. Are you coming up later?" I asked him.

"Oh maybe for an hour or so."

"Alright, well don't forget we have a hot tub up there."

"No shit?"

"No shit." I said. He looked at me and laughed.

I danced with the whole group of people. There were sixty of us on the dance floor. My brother and I were hanging on each other falling over as we danced. I saw some of the guys from the detail shop doing break dance moves with the mechanics. I saw my respectful little receptionists, getting down with their husbands.

I stepped back a little. There were some people still seated at their tables talking or eating. There was one little tan skinned lady sitting by herself staring at all of us dancing. I looked over at her and smiled. She smiled at me shyly and tried to hide her face.

Jennifer and Anthony walked passed me. "Time to go up bro or what?"

"Yeah, it's about that time. I'll let Annie know we're going up now." My brother went up while I let Annie know I wanted everything pretty much cleared up.

As I was about to leave the banquet hall, I saw that girl putting on her little sweater. I slowed down as she stood up. She was small, maybe 5'1, really petite. She had a small face with long straight black hair, thin long sexy lips, and large dark brown eyes. She had bangs that were long flowing down and off the side of her face.

I smiled at her. "Are you here with someone?" I asked her.

She smiled and looked around. "That's my cousin Rick, over there." She pointed to one of the guys from the body shop. Rick Gonzales. I know him. I say hi to him whenever I see him.

"Are you guys staying for the after party?" I asked her.

"Um," she looked back. "I don't know. I don't really know anyone here so I don't know. We'll probably just go home."

I smiled at her. "Well, if I were you, I'd go."

"Oh yeah, and why, who are you?" She asked me.

I smiled at her. The nerve. I laughed. "My names' Alex." I put out my hand.

She covered her mouth. "Oh, you're the owner." She hid her face.

"Does this mean we can't be friends?" I asked her.

She laughed as she pulled her hand away from her face. She kind of shook her head a little. "I'm sorry. Now I feel stupid."

"Why? Don't be."

"Well, I didn't mean to say, who are you, like that."

"Hey, I'm not special." She looked up at me with her cute round eyes. "Now just for that, I'm going to have to fire Rick." I gave her this serious look. Her eyes dropped from excitement in fear for her cousin. "I'm kidding. No seriously, come up when you get squared away, and hopefully I'll see you up there."

"Okay, it was nice meeting you."

When I got upstairs the party was already happening. There were people standing around in groups talking around the room, there was loud music, and people out in the patio. I smiled as I walked in. This guy named Jerry from paint and body came stumbling over to me draping his arm over my shoulder.

"What's the word boss?" He asked. "Let's get fucked up."

"You know it." I smiled. "Where's the liquor? *point me to of danger Azeem, I am ready!*" I said in a British accent.

I was pushed into the crowd of people towards the bar. The bartender looked at me and smiled.

"What'll it be sir?" He asked.

"I'll take some Jack Daniels." I said.

As he handed me my drink I smiled from ear to ear like a crazy man and swallowed it down. I felt someone tap me on the back. I turned around and saw Jennifer smiling at me with glassy eyes. I smiled back.

"Hey girl, where's Tony?" I yelled.

"He's out in the tub." She held her drink in the air with it kind of sliding down her palm.

"You okay girl?" I asked her.

She hiccuped and laughed. I grabbed the bottle before I went out and then helped Jennifer to the patio.

Outside everyone was being loud and joking around. There were six people in the hot tub including my brother. I looked at him and laughed. He nudged his head at me as he pointed out the girls next to him in their little bikinis. I laughed.

"Come on Alex, get in."

"Calm down. Let me mingle a while before I just hop in the tub."

Jennifer took off her towel around her waist and got in the water with a glass of Champaign. I stepped back to over look the view of the ocean. Jack was there with Ed my team lead in the mechanics department. They looked like they were just having a serious chat and not the average drunk obnoxious talk that comes with most parties.

I walked over to the two.

"Hey Alex, what's going on?"

"Nothing much. Getting myself nice and drunk."

"Perfect, now we can rob you and rape you." Said Jack.

"Careful now, you may just get what you wish for." I pointed at him with my rocks glass in my hand.

"You sick bastard." Laughed Ed.

"Only around you gentlemen." I laughed.

Ed started going into a debate about politics that he and Jack must have already been talking about. I looked through the opened sliding door at the crowd of people drinking in the living area. I took a drink of my liquor.

There were a few loud cheers as Rick, his friends, and his cousin came into room. Everyone greeted them with things like, "come on let's get fucked up," "Where yah been," and "there's a hot tub out back."

I saw her long lips from across the room. I saw her innocent smile. I saw her.

I drank down the last in my glass and set it down on one of the glass tables. I walked passed all the people towards her. Rick stopped in front of me.

"Hey boss man? You fucked up yet?" Asked Rick.

"Just about. So who's this over here?" I asked.

Rick looked back at his cousin and smiled. She looked down as she smiled at me. He tapped her on the shoulder.

"This my cousin Lexy. Lexy this my boss Alex Dugan."

She reached out her hand and I leaned down and kissed it. I didn't see Lilas' face. Nor any demons standing next to her confessing her sins. I pulled her hand so she could come with me out onto the balcony but as I did, I was very immobile. She had to help me up or at least kind of let me put her weight on her.

We sat down on a bench just along the edge of the view. I dropped myself on the bench as if I had no more strength in me. She just sat a way from me a little staring at me.

"So what's up? Who are you?" I asked with my eyes drooping down.

She laughed. "I told you, I'm Rick's' cousin."

"Yeah, I heard that part. But I mean whooo," I held up my hand like the godfather. "Whooo are you really? What do you do? Who is sexy Lexy?" I slurred. She laughed hysterically.

We talked for about forty minutes. Well at least I tried. I was pretty gone already. But I tried to pay attention. She told me about where she worked and that she lived with a roommate. Yadda, yadda!

"Say!" I snapped as my eyes closed on her. She looked at me like I were crazy because I looked as though I were passing out in the middle of what I was trying to say. "Would you like to get in the hot tub with me?"

I hooked her up with a bathing suit. Aside from all the many free gifts people earned tonight, they also had their pick of swimming gear to get into the hot tub. She picked out a plain black bathing suit. No g-string. No bikini. No low cut . . . I liked that.

Everyone in the tub was involved in a serious conversation about relationships and problems they've gone through and what solutions they have for the future to insure better relationships. This was not something I wanted to be in the middle of. But I'm in the water, I can't change my mind now.

My brother put his arm around my shoulder. I could smell the beer on his breath as he spoke. When I looked over at his arm, I could see the water dripping off his armpit hair.

"Eew dude, get your nasty, armpit hair off me bro!"

He looked down at his dripping arm pit and laughed. "Shut the fuck Alex, you like it you faggot."

"Ohh!"

"He called the boss a faggot!"

Everyone was laughing and carrying on while Lexy sat quietly next to me in the water. I leaned on her almost passing out. Everyone noticed me with her. Everyone was going to make their comments about it later at work. *Alex was with a girl! Alex hooked up with someone.*

But as drunk as I was I didn't care. By three in the morning mostly everyone had gone except for those few stragglers who like to stay until they pass out themselves. I found myself laying in bed with Lexy. We didn't do a thing. I passed out on the bed and she fell asleep next to me.

That was one of the only times I lay next to a woman who didn't try to sleep with me. That was one of the few times I didn't have to kill them.

Nothing ever became of Lexy and I. I met her that one time and that was it. I never asked about her again. Rick mentioned on occasion she said hi every so often, but that was it.

Thank god for that otherwise, who knows what I might have done to her.

CHAPTER 8

The world turns no matter who's in it. Each and every one of us has our own lives and our own worlds. The world I live in people couldn't handle nor understand. It's unfortunate that even in your very last moments, when you think there is at least one person who loves you enough to suffer with you till the end, there's no one. Absolutely no one. And your lucky if people mention your name once you've already gone and past away.

Lila and I had that love. Lila told me that I was her soul mate.

In dreams we all do live. In dreams I do live. I dream of her when I close my eyes. And I can remember so many special moments.

"Alex, where are you taking me?" Asked Lila.

I had her eyes folded blind as I walked her down the path of shrubs and bushes. She smiled as I held her hand.

"Don't worry little lady. I'm gon fix you up real good." I said.

She laughed. I stopped by a large tree all by itself surrounded by grass. I pulled the blindfold off and she looked around. There was a blanket laid out with a basket of food. She looked at me then reached over and squeezed me.

"This is so sweet. Why did you do this?" Shed asked as she sat down.

I helped her then sat down next to her. I pulled the basket close so we could start eating. I pulled out the food as she watched me.

"Oh Alex, cheeseburgers and fries, you're such a chef." She kissed me on the cheek as she took her food.

We laughed and ate together. After we ate, she lit a joint and we just lay on the blanket together staring at the sky. It was baby blue with different sized white clouds floating across the sky. When I was a kid watching the clouds, I used to say, the clouds aren't moving, it's the earth rotating.

She looked over at me as I stared at the sky. She wouldn't turn her head away so I looked at her. I smiled at her gorgeous face.

"You're so beautiful." I said as I touched her face.

"Why are you so good to me?" She asked as she stared in my eyes.

"Because I love you. I love you more than anything."

She leaned over my face and touched my cheek with her hand. "I love you too." She lowered her head and we kissed.

And when we kissed it was like magic. It was like fireworks were going off in my mind. It was like I felt weak in the heart and the chest and I couldn't breathe. It felt like with each rub of are lips together made me want to shiver. Why did she have this affect on me?

As she pulled back I looked at her pretty face. I could see the sky just behind her. I pulled her on top of me and squeezed her.

"I love you Lila. Some day . . ." I looked in her eyes. "Someday I'm going to marry you. And I'll spend the rest of my life making you happy."

"But you already do."

It's moments like these where artists like *Boyz to Men* or more of todays era, *Chris Brown,* that make you feel like you are so in love. When you feel everything it is that they are talking about in the song, whether it's just lyrics or an actual event in their life. *I miss you. I need you. I love you. There's no one but you. I only think of you. I only dream of you.* And so on.

In the plight of being a Skater Punk, there's no romantic songs you can play that will make you feel like you're in the mood to fall in love. If there was anything mentioned about love with Punk Rock it was always things like, *Punk girl, she's so cool, she's so crazy, I saw a girl in combat boots, bla, bla.* Also the fact that if there was anything said about love, it was always shouting into the microphone. Of course they were good songs but it's not what I hear in the back of my head when I stare into the eyes of her.

We had many moments like that. I didn't have a car or much money, but what I could muster up for her I would do it in a heartbeat. She promised we'd be together forever. She promised she'd never hurt me.

I had just finished up my day at work. I wanted to swing by the grocery store to get some food. After I did my shopping, I pushed my cart out to my car and began to load everything in. There were cars trying to find parking and people walking in and out of the store with carts.

I was in my own life. Everything was silent. In the back of my head I heard her cries. Her moaning. Her pain within. I heard them talking, whispering to each other in the back of my head. What were they talking about?

I looked around and saw a man about forty years old, Caucasian, at least 6'3, with a dirty blonde goat tee and a dirty cap over his greasy head. In an instant, I saw Patrick. In an instant it was a stranger. But he so resembled the man I loathed for so long.

I continued loading my things as he walked by with three kids and a chunky blonde wife pushing the cart.

"But daddy I don't want to stay home tomorrow." Said one of the little girls.

"Now, hold on, you're sick. You cain't go tah school. No more about it yah hear." He replied.

Patrick. Patrick I saw. I finished loading and pushed my cart back as he and his family began to load into an over beat up Volkswagon Bus. I stared at him a little as I walked back to my car.

The Demons were there. They surrounded the car. But *he, he* stood right next to that man without him even knowing. The demon reached over and touched the man. *He* looked at me and I saw everything. I saw what people won't want to know or hear.

That sweet little girl was losing her innocence. Her blood father, her daddy, her protector, was not protecting her. He was her predator. He was going to steal her innocence. He had been working his way until he was ready for this day.

I saw it. I saw all that he had ever done to her. I saw what he did to his own daughter. I saw what he tried to do with his cousins but they refused. I saw him trying to get what he could off the children who didn't know what he was doing. *The sin!* A disgusting fowl being just as bad as my dead whores.

It was hurting me to see these images. It was hurting my head. I heard clucking, women crying, demons whispering, blood, body parts! HELP ME!!!

I screamed from the fear. Instantly, it all disappeared. I was alone in thoughts. There were not more images forced into my memory. I looked over at his van. He kissed his wife before he backed out. His wife had no clue. As he turned the car back I caught a glimpse of the inside. She was in there, the little girl, staring at the floor not playing with the other kids.

I'm coming for you.

How many of us see ugly things in this world and don't do a thing about it? How many of us have walked by a parent mentally breaking down their kid or abusing them in public and thought, *my god, you're abusing that child.* How many of us stop them? How many of us try to protect the child in harm? How many of us *want* to say something about it or do something, but never do?

Years of my life I walked passed things I didn't want to know this world was doing. I wanted to tell all those psycho mothers they're ruining everything about that child. I imagine taking those abusive parents of mine and choking them until their eyes popped out of their heads. I wished someone like me came across young Alex Dugan as a child, seeing my stepfather beating me, and then they stopped him. But no one ever did stop my parents from beating me. No one ever did tell my stepfather that beating on me and locking me in the shed was going to ruin me.

Ruined. Ruined is far from what I am now. Ruined is far from what I've become. And ruined is what will become of him.

No one stopped them! No one saved me from all the abuse! NO ONE!!! I'll fuck'n kill you Patrick! You fuck'n redneck son of a bitch!

As soon as I walked into the bar, I heard the sound of pool cues hitting the solid balls on the tables, there was classic rock playing on the juke box, and the room was filled with hill Billy's drinking beer and smoking cigarettes. I swung the door open and walked over to the bar.

"I'll take a bud." I said to the bartender.

He cracked open a beer for me and set it in front of my hands. I looked around at all the regulars hanging out. I didn't know anyone there. I turned to my left where the replicate of Patrick was drinking and smoking with his friends. He was wearing a dirty mechanics uniform with grease stains all over it. His shirt had his name sewn on it. John, John Mcree. Ha !

I stayed for a while, trying to just be alone and watch the environment. I sat close to his group of friends. I could hear pretty much everything they were saying.

"Oh man, this girl is so cute. And I can tell her what to do. She listens to me." He laughed before he took a chug of his beer.

"That's all them sluts is like. You make her yours and she'll treat you good." Said one of his *inbred* friends.

"How long you been see'n this gal?" Asked another.

"Oh for a few months now." Said John.

"And the misses doesn't suspect you're out with another woman?" Asked another.

"Oh no. We hang out when she's gone. She has shop'n to do and my lady don't live too far."

"She good in bed?"

"Well, I'm about to find out. We got plans for tomorrow."

"Oh man, yous' lucky. If you can, have her swing by the shop so's we can look at er. Or maybe just bring in a picture."

"You try'n to steal my girl?"

"No. But you claim'n she's cute and petite like one'a them Asian gals."

"That she is. Well, I guess I may be able to." But I knew what he was talking about. Maybe the son of bitch can muster up a picture of one of his wife's friends or family members.

By one in the morning, he was done in. The bar had mostly cleared. His friends and him walked out to their cars laughing and carrying on. I walked out before them. I sat in my car waiting. Biding my time. They were making last minute cracks on each other until all the guys were in their cars and on their way home.

I stayed close behind. He pulled into a lonely gas station but went to the back to use the restroom.

My demon was with him. My demon was anxious. I love moments like these where I am given full open range to feed on the sinners. To hate them with such rage. To pay them back for all the pain they put onto others.

As soon as John walked out the back door, I clocked him over the head with a bat. No one saw. No one was around. The highway was just below with barely a few cars on the road. The gas station clerk was in his booth, locked away, at the front of the building. There were no other convenient stores or shops around unless you drove down four or five blocks.

My car was five feet from the back door. I propped him in the front seat and we were on our way. I had on my black leather gloves. I pushed in a CD. It was classical. My favorite was piano, violin, and opera. It was my theme music. I loved to create the art of death to sounds of sweet sad violin playing in the back of my mind. It's art. It's beautiful.

After three hours of driving into the night, I could hear him waking up. He was moaning probably because his head hurt. He was smacking his lips like he could still taste the beer in his mouth and he was thirsty. He started to move his head a little until he opened his eyes. Once he snapped into reality, his eyes got wide and he looked at me.

I looked over at him, smiled, and tipped my head at him. I looked back at the road like everything was calm and orderly.

"I bet you're wondering who I am?"

He looked at me in anger. Then he looked at his hands.

"Don't try it. You won't get the rope off your hands and feet, nor the gag in your mouth. *Yes*," I said. "This is really happening."

He looked around the car for a way to escape. He looked out the window.

"Too bad, buddy. Everything's locked. You're SOL this time buddy." I laughed at him then turned up my music.

He just looked at me with wide eyes in fear. He was taller than me. He looked like a long stick of a man. I could tell when he felt a little more alert he was going to try and fight his way free.

I pulled the car to his last destination. I turned off the car but left my door open for light. I came around the other side to open the door and get him out. As soon as I opened the door he tried to kick me with his long legs. But I swing my bat into his knee caps. He yelped spitting saliva out the side of his gag. This was real.

I grabbed him by his arms and dragged him out the car throwing him on the dirt. When he hit the ground I heard him grunt as his chest hit the floor. A blast of dirt blew into his face from his harsh exhale. I flipped him over. He looked so afraid. He tried to crawl backwards away from me. I kicked him in the hip.

"Stop trying to escape. You're going no where."

The demons laughed.

I ripped off the electric tape from his mouth with the gag flying out onto the floor covered in blood and saliva.

"What the fuck man?! Who the fuck are you? What the fuck are you doing?" He yelled at me as I tried to back up.

My eyes were wide and I carried a smile as I came closer to him.

"Who the fuck am I?" Stopped walking and held out my arms. "Who the fuck am I." I laughed. "Let me tell you who the fuck I am."

I stood still as he stared at me in fear. The Demons revealed themselves to him. He saw them next to me. He saw them surrounding us. He saw their eyes, shadows; images of men standing in the background of a hot dark Arizona night.

I looked down at him. When he saw them I think he wet his pants.

"How long have you been molesting your own child?" I asked him.

He tried not to make eye contact when I said that. He looked away in shame. "I don't what you're talking about! I don't know who you are? But if I get out of this, you're a dead man!"

"I think not." I said. And I swung my bat at his elbow because he tried to block his face with his arms up. He yelped in pain and began to whimper.

"What do you want from me? Why are you doing this?" He screamed in pain.

"So is she the tiny petite lady you've been bragging about at the bar?"

His eyes squinted and he looked closer at my face. "You're the guy from the bar."

"No sir, I'm the demon who takes revenge for the innocent." And with those words I swung down my bat over his head. He knocked out for a moment. I dropped down on the ground next to him and touched his head.

"Oh no Johnny boy. Don't go to sleep. We still have much to talk about." I rubbed his head.

He shook a little as he was waking up again. He looked up at me.

"Please don't do this to me. I didn't do anything." He cried.

I huffed at him. "Please Johnny boy. Go out like a man. Man up and confess to them now." I held up my hands to them.

The demon came out from behind all his disciples. He stood behind John as the man whimpered on the ground in fear. I snapped my finger at him.

"Hey! Don't be afraid of them. It's me who you should fear."

"What the fuck is going on!" He yelled.

"No one can hear you. So what have you done to her? Why to your own child? Have you put your disgusting being onto the child?"

He didn't want to look at me. I walked over to him and crouched down. "You can't lie to me. These shadows in the background already know what you have done. Now you can be a man and confess or you can die a coward."

"I didn't do nuthan!" He yelled staring at the ground. He couldn't even look at me.

"Ent! Wrong answer!" I swung my bat over his shin. He yelped out.

"Oh fuck! Son of bitch!" He cried. "Alright!" He screamed. "Alright I confess!" He touched his leg. "Fuck!"

"Do you take full responsibility for what you did to her?"

"Please mister. I'll do anything."

"*Do you take full responsibility for what you did to her?!*"

"Yes!" He cried.

I got down on my knees next to him. I began to cry. "Do you know what you did to her? Do you know you ruined her? Do you know you killed the innocent child within her? Do you?! Do you fuck'n know what it feels like to be hurt by people you love?!"

John could barely hold himself upright. He was crying with me as if we were finally confessing all our pain to each other in group and we were crying the life out of us.

I barely had a voice. "You destroyed her!" I stood up pacing. "So what did you do? Did you touch her? Did you make her touch your nasty disgusting body? Did you put your fuck'n dick in this child you fuck'n sick bastard?!"

"No! No! I didn't fuck her!" He cried.

I leaned over in his face. "But you did molest her. You did make her touch you while you put yourself onto her!"

"Yes!" He cried.

I stood up straight. "John Mcree, do you accept and admit to all these sins you are confessing to right now?"

He cried. "Yes."

"Do you regret what you did?"

"Yes." He could barely say.

"Do you accept your fate for the sins you have committed?"

He was trembling. Shaking. He looked up at me as I stood over him. The red sky was just behind me with miles of empty land surrounding us. He looked around at the demons surrounding us.

"Yes." He said.

I swung down. I swung down as hard as I could. I could hear the crack in his skull. I beat everything. I could hear him trying to fight death. His last breaths. His last words.

"She was a child." I whispered in his ear as he could barely move.

"I'm sorry." He whispered as he fought for a few last breaths of air. "I'm sorry Katelynn. I'm sorry baby." He was breathing in the dirt now. "Daddy's sorry." He said.

I stood up. He couldn't move but his eyes looked up at me. He watched the bat swing from the red sky over his head and crush his sight to blackness.

I dropped the bat next to him crying. I sat next to him holding his head in my lap as it hung limp from his body. I pet his head like he was a cat.

"It's okay John Mcree, you're saved now. You confessed. She is safe now." I rocked back and forth covered in blood as the demons began to walk away into the night disappearing into nothing. I turned his face towards me. "You better hope she doesn't turn out to be a whore. You better hope you didn't kill her twice. If I have to come back for her because of you . . ." I rocked back and forth. "Well, let's not think that far ahead. But I shall remember the name Katelynn Mcree for I can never hurt her if I tried to save her."

I was still crying. I tried to calm down. "You fuck'n bastard," I whispered. "You fuck'n dirty son of bitch. You touched her!" I cried. "You hurt her."

I stood up thinking it was over. But it wasn't over. I looked down at his body and I saw Patrick. I couldn't help it. I took the bat and just beat on his dead body.

"Patrick!" I screamed. "I fuck'n hate you!!!"

CHAPTER 9

It feels good knowing you can smile about the things you have done in your life. Friends can last a long time or they can last a short time. You never know when it'll happen; you just know it *will* happen. You won't forget the past no matter how hard you try. It was perfect for me to just take action years from now.

I remember my best friend with the greatest smiles and the funniest jokes. He had all the girls. He didn't care if they were passed amongst his friends. But when it came to me, he was taken back. How could any girl possibly want me before him? How could a girl as beautiful as the sun, want someone like me.

I can't understand why I won't get this out of my head. I reminisce on all of my unhappy days. The only days that were good was when I was skating with my friends in California. Even if I did stay, they wouldn't have lasted forever. I can't judge correctly. I can't see through everyone. I can only see the bad things they have done in their life. I try to move forward and not think of them, but they're always there, in my dreams, in my thoughts as I am alone. It's like a plague that has no cure. The only way to go forward is to move backwards. I have to fix the wrongs to what feels right.

I've packed the simplest things I need for this trip. I am sleepy and my flight leaves at seven in the morning. I have to be there ahead of time. I took a few glances at what I had in my possessions. My penthouse. Yesterday, I let Stan at the shop, know, I was leaving town for a short while. My destination was Florida to them. But for me, it was different. It might be one week or two. I was going to face my past.

I enjoyed my trips around the world. The plane rides were relaxing. I sometimes flew in first class. But this time I didn't. I didn't want to make this trip a big deal to anybody. I kept thinking to myself, it would be over soon. I wouldn't be a failure or a loser that I used to be.

I handed them my ticket then boarded the plane. I put on my seatbelt as I listened to the aircraft warming the engine; the air conditioner was in a loud winding roar and sounded electrical. All the bright lights were on overhead, which made my eyes squint.

"Good morning ladies and gentlemen. I'm your flight attendant Susie Banks and this is our other attendant Christine Mills who will be helping me serve all of your drinks whatever you may need. First we would like to point out on this flight . . ."

I hated listening to their high-pitched airhead voices over the intercom. It was always the same seatbelt instructions as if we had never buckled a belt before. The breathing problem instructions that are there incase of emergency as if during a crash, it'll be the first thing on our minds.

"As you can see, the seatbelt light is on so remain seated until the light is off and you can walk about the cabin. Thank you for choosing Delta Flight first. We hope that you enjoy your flight and come see us again."

I could hear the jets turning and the air was blowing hard. Everyone was talking quietly as if we were in church, to their family and friends. I turned to my side to fall asleep as I always have on the plane rides. At my window seat I look down at the city getting smaller and smaller. Soon the clouds began to cover the city and I can see the high skies magnificence.

I leaned back in my seat thinking it would be a very long day. I could feel it. I opened up a good book that a friend of mine from before high school, gave to me. She and I were friends for a short while. She thought I was cool for but when I was beat up, she didn't want to talk to me too often.

"What would you like to drink?" Asked the stewardess.

I could barely put the words to my mouth. "What kind of alcohol do you carry?"

"We carry beer, Martinis, some liquor. I'm not too sure but I can check." She sounded exactly like the airheads I was speaking of; the way she put her finger to her chin and looked up at the ceiling for an answer."

"I'll just take a Heineken thank you."

She wrote down what I wanted and then asked the person in the seat behind me. I sat back. I shouldn't drink beer right now. Not that it's a big deal but I smoked out before I came out here and I'm still pretty stoned. I feel like getting a beer buzz now. It'll get rid of my cotton mouth and refresh my throat. I could feel myself falling asleep, but I shouldn't do that either because that would be a waste of bud. I could sure go for a cigarette.

"Here you are sir, one Heineken." She smiled.

I pulled out my wallet and gave her five dollars. She handed me my change but I waved my hand for her to keep it. It was only a few bucks.

"Oh I'm sorry sir, we're not allowed to accept any tips." She said.

"Well let's just say it's just cause I think you're a polite lady." I took a sip of the beer and felt my throat sooth. I noticed a few people staring at me as if I were a strange person. I didn't care. Who were they? I wasn't here for amusement.

I gulped half of the can. I almost spit out the beer when some guy popped his head over the empty seat.

"What the fuck?" I yelled.

"Hey mate. How's it going?" He had an Australian accent. "The name's John McKracken, please tah meet yah." He spoke really fast and I couldn't understand one word he was saying.

"Yes ah"-

"Aht! Ah, you're Alex Dugan aren't you?"

"How do"-

"You sell old cars. I've seen your add. A friend of mine bought one of your cars." He swung around and placed himself into the empty seat next to me. I looked at him as if he should've asked permission.

I drank the other half of my beer. The stewardess came around again. "Would you like anything else sir?"

"Sure, I'll take a bud light beer, sweetie." I laughed at the way he said beer, *bear*.

"I'll take another Heineken."

"Sure thing," she smiled.

"So tell me who the hell you are." I demanded.

"Well I'm a photographer. I took a couple of pictures of that car. It was a beaut mate. Runs great. Yeah, me friend took me for a spin in it for the whole day. Everything's perfect. He's had no problems. They make me think back to the good old days where the women were 'appy and the men were 'ard work'n"

I turned towards him. How this man read my mind. I knew we might get along just fine. "So what is it I can do for you Mr. McKracken? Did you want to take pictures of my cars or something?" I smiled to the side because I was kind of joking.

"No my good man, I want to buy one." He laughed like he was overwhelmed.

The stewardess put the beers on our trays. "Would you like anything else?"

John looked up at her. "Such a sweet lady. No miss, this is good for now."

He was such a brown noser. I drank my beer as if I were downing liquor. It tasted good after all the weed I was smoking at my house. I didn't care if I got drunk on the plane. I wasn't going to handle any equipment nor was I going to drive when this ride was over.

"So where are you headed?" I asked Mr. McKracken.

"Oh I'm out for a job in Tennessee. There are some great landscapes out there. It's one of me favorite jobs, pictures of the different cities and states. I'm working on getting a better recognition than my short work."

"I've traveled"-

"A great deal. Why you've been all over Europe!"

I finished my beer. The stewardess knew that we were drinking heavily on the plane so she continued to bring us beer. I was drinking one after another. I can drink like a fish when I want.

"How do you know so much about me?" I asked him.

"Why, you're a star. You've got one of the best car companies in California. You get recognition from all those movie producers who use your cars in movies and especially when they drive theirs around. You have articles in the magazines and pictures. People talk about your cars mate. You've got a good name for yourself."

"So tell me about yourself and your job."

"Well I'm from Australia. I'm not married. I've been a photographer since high school. Let's see . . . I don't think there's much tah say but I travel a lot. I work for several different companies. I don't have me a girl."

After seven beers I felt a little buzzed. I could tell he was too. I lost track of the conversation and sometimes I would get back on track being in the state of mind I was. He was a very interesting person to talk to. We spoke at length on how I started the company I have. When we spoke about people and marriages, I could see we were somewhat on the same page. He wasn't at the point where I was hating everything about women to the point of killing. He was probably in the middle level and would be there for the rest of his life. Some of the models he had taken shots of, flirted with him. We had a connection somehow though; he took shots of the girl I killed, in remembrance of Beauty and the Beast.

"Well Ladies and Gentlemen we have just arrived here in Texas. We will be landing in El Paso in thirty minutes right on Schedule. Thank you for choosing Delta. We hope to see you with us again and enjoy the rest of your flight." The Captains voice was deep with no bit of energy at all.

It took me a while to realize whom it was being that I could hardly pay attention. It was the pilot. I tried to play like I knew who it was after I made that curious face.

"Well looks like we land soon mate." He got up and buckled himself into the seat behind me. I could hear him slurring back there to the people next to him.

I could feel the turbulence from he plane moving lower. I was giggling a little, low enough for no one to hear me. I looked out the window to see the schematics of a city. The ants were driving down the highway. Texas looked different from the last time I was here. El Paso was completely different though. My secret trip was on the way.

The plane landed within minutes. When the plane stopped, everyone got out of their seats and started grabbing their bags from the overhead compartments and started towards the exit.

"Aye mate, ere's my number, just ask for John McKracken. I'll be out of town for two weeks. If you could leave me a number so I could get hold of you. I'd really like to get my hands on one of them cars."

"Sure thing." I shook his hand. "Nice meeting you. I'll definitely give you a call when I return to California."

The stewardess passed by me. I grabbed her arm gently. She turned around and smiled. She had this look on her face as though I was about to hit on her and it would please her.

"May I help you?" She asked trying to wind her fingers within her hair even though she was having trouble and at the same time her chest grew closer to my face.

"Ah yeah, I need a cigarette. Where can I smoke cause I can't smoke on the plane and we're not allowed to smoke in airports anymore."

"We'll be here for an hour, so let me see." She put her finger to her lip. "I'm going on my break now, I can show you where there's a bar we *are* allowed to smoke at."

"That would be great."

I followed her out into the airport. It was crowded with so many people. I had to make sure I didn't get lost with me being buzzed. We made it to the bar just fine. I rushed to the restroom near by. I hated using the ones on the planes. It was too small. I sat down at the bar and she was there.

"So what's your name?" I asked as I looked around the bar. I took a drag of my cigarette.

"Belinda . . . Harting," she said with her hand out. "And you are?" She asked trying to catch my eye.

I took another drag of my cigarette. "Alex but that's all I'll say. I'm not here to catch a date with you miss, no offence. I just needed a cigarette."

She looked down in disappoint. It didn't matter to me. Sometimes I was just careless and didn't care of other peoples' feelings.

"You head' out to Dallas or are you connecting with another flight there?" I asked her.

"Well I'm heading home to Kentucky, that's where we're going after Dallas." She took out a pack of Doral's, which to me were cheap and tasted really bad. She looked around with a different perspective of things with me. She was angry about what I had said. It was the way her blue eyes glistened with anger when she crossed glances with me that gave it away. She wasn't attractive. Her hair was frizzy as if she didn't take care of it. Her lips were cracked with metallic pink lipstick emphasizing the crust of her lips.

I took another drag of my cigarette. "Well you're a nice lady for showing me which bar to go to. It was nice talking to you but I have to take another leak and be on my way back to the plane."

I got back on the plane after I went to the restroom. The minutes passed and I was back relaxed in my seat. We went through the routine again while I closed my eyes burying my ears in a pair of earphones.

After another half hour we were in Dallas. As soon as the plane landed everyone rushed to get off the plane, me especially. As we walked out of the ramp and into the airport, there were families waiting for their loved ones. No one loved me except for the cab that was waiting outside for work. I could have had a limo easily, which I was going to do, but I didn't want my name on anything here.

"So where to mister?"

"Upper side." And he drove off.

I moved my parents to a nice area where the crime rate wasn't so bad. They used to live in the Ghetto over on the southwest side of town. There were nice areas on the Southside but my parents were in the midst of drug dealers and gangsters. Once I hit it rich I helped Tony get a place of his own and I put down on a house for my parents.

They didn't know I was coming. I had my own room in the attic, which was locked, me having the only key. The driver helped me carry my bags to the door. I paid and he was gone, not knowing who I was or where I was from. I opened the door grabbing my bags and running upstairs almost falling because I was still out of it. I took a hot shower to wake me up. I had my own restroom built up there.

I walked out clean and I would on other times in my life. I brushed my hair and was dressed real nice. I wanted to take both those bastards out to dinner. Downstairs I could hear my mother cooking. I popped my head from the side of the entrance of the door. "Hey ma."

She screamed with the sudden danger of me then kicked me right in the balls. Oh the pain. I could feel numbness through my whole body. My nuts curled up within themselves knowing they wouldn't be able to produce for the next ten years. My eyes fluttered and I fell over.

"Hi mom," was the whispering voice of what was left of my strength.

"Oh Alex!" She cried. "My poor boy. You scared the shit out of me. What the hell did you expect not call'n or nuthan."

My stepfather ran in with a beer in his hand, a picture I knew all too well. "Cassy, what's wrong."

"Honey our boy's home." She helped me up.

"Just for a couple of weeks." I whispered in a raspy voice still holding onto what precious jewels I inherited from my father. "I have a business to run. Right now get dressed so we can go out to dinner."

"But I already started on the Spam stew."

"Ma, whatcha got done?"

"Just the water boiling."

"Get the hell upstairs and put something on for I smack yah." I said.

Patrick stepped forward. "If your mama didn'ta tell me yous here, I'd kill yah from the surprise."

"Go on."

They looked at each other, smiled, and then went upstairs. I began to clean up what she started in the kitchen. Then as time pressed on, I would clean up a few other things in my life. Over the boiling water I began to daydream. I saw the faces of the kids that made me look stupid. I know my only reason for being here was purely something the voices and I concocted.

The water began to over boil as my mind came to.

It's been two days since I've been here in Texas. I still don't have as much fun as ever. Things seem to never change in life. They only change when you don't want them to and what you want changed is always repeated. My mother is still working at a diner. She hardly smiles but she seems glad to see me. She's getting on in age but she's still the same inside. Patrick is unhappy as always. He seems like he stays with my mother because they've made their lives together. I'm positive that he's cheated on her a few times and she to him. All I can do is pretend that I wanted to see them.

I took my moms jeep. I decided to go look around the old neighborhood where troubles come in many forms of pain. I haven't seen these faces in over ten years. I wanted to be forgotten amongst the others who enjoyed making my life miserable. Of course, they won't recognize me. I have grown tall and built.

I drove down the highway till I reached Downtown towards the strip. I slipped in some music that reminded me of my past. They were songs I could never forget. Songs that create a picture in my mind of all the memories tied into that one song, to that one specific moment in time. On a sheet I made out specific names that I hadn't just picked out of a hat. It was done in order starting with Steve, whom jumped me, Nick who put his filthy member into my girl, and last but not least *Lila*. The names repeated in my head over again through the wind, through the whispers which came to me often, through the roar of any noise that came in my very presence.

I saw it like a dream I wish I could be. The club was still there standing on all fours. I had concluded that it was torn down as many times as it had closed. It seemed to never stay in business. New children were there, new to the scene, new to me. They had little knowledge that they were just inbreeds of the punk culture that fascinated those who had shitty lives. They had one invitation to their own beatings.

I parked my mothers' jeep in the back alley across the street locking the door as I was prepared for what I might encounter again in this life or the next. I stood there thinking of what they did to me as I smoked a cigarette. I headed to the entrance holding my head high afraid of nothing anymore as I did being a teenager. In the dark alley, I passed by the kids that were smoking and drinking as a ritual that was done with every group of teens who were not of age. At the entrance was the owner.

"What kind of music tonight?" I asked.

"Punk rock and some hardcore."

I could hear the band playing inside. I slapped the ten dollars on the register as I walked through as if I were not to be told anything. I ordered a Heineken which I loved and sat there staring at the young ones who thought they were the first ones to ever discover the *scene*. I liked watching the bands play so I stood with the rest of my fellow freaks. Next to me were two punk rockers that seemed like they would know what I needed.

I turned to my side and yelled in one of the boys' ears. "Do you know a guy named Steve, he's real fuck'n fat?"

His face was questioned. "I don't think so but there are a few fat guys around here that we don't know. You might want to check with them. You know how fat people flock together." He laughed.

"Yeah."

I had to use the restroom but I remembered what it was like in there, disgusting, smelling like piss and ass, the walls were covered with bands that people drew on there, and the porcelain toilets and urinals were half broken leaking pea and shit and sewer water. I walked in. I stood there staring at the whole room. Flashes of death. Flashes of John and me fighting. Flashes of me dragging his body into the stall. The memories come back. I had decided I would go outside in the corner of one of the drinking spots.

My ears ringed with the noise of what was going on in the club. Right to the side passed a crowd of guys drinking in an empty corner. There I relieved myself on the wall of the building that I hated. Not but five feet from me was a guy who just walked up after me, to piss. Here I was, in plain jeans, a blank shirt, and combat boots, roaming the club for someone who just walked up next to me to take a whiz. I zipped up my pants then faced him with a smile.

"Steve?" I asked.

"What?" He was leaning on the wall a little as he let out.

"How's it going?" I asked as I crossed my arms then leaned my shoulder against the wall.

"What are you? Fag?" He asked trying to move away a little.

I moved towards him with an insane look in my face, eyes wide without blinking and a smile that could make you cringe. It wasn't the voices this time; it was my anger. They knew to stay away at this point in time. Madness and hatred both coming into my veins in a sudden rush of adrenaline.

"Oh, you don't remember me? It's typical though." I came face to face with him so that the streetlight shined in my face. Only this time I wasn't looking up at his fat gigantor face, I was looking down. "Over twelve years ago, you got several punk rockers to jump me."

He looked deep into his thoughts to find one of the people he jumped coming back to him. He looked a little frightened but not remembering me, he couldn't find an answer. I wanted him to fear me.

"I was going out with that redhead Lila and you guys jumped me at a skate park. I guess if you needed all those people, you must be pretty weak."

His hair hung in his face a little and his fat mouth was always in this pit bull frown, for obese people could not have the muscle capacity in their face to look any other way. He remembered. He looked into my eyes. He nudged his head at me then said, "Oh yeah, what's up." He took a swig of his beer then walked towards his friends who were drinking by an old broken up van.

I followed right behind him. His friends were wrapped in conversation as we walked up. I stood right behind him with my arms crossed as he tried to ignore me. I kept that expression of a psycho on my face as I looked down at him. He was trying to hear his friend's conversation, but I am to interrupt.

"What's the matter Steve? Are you afraid of me now? What is it? I want to know what the fuck is going through your head right now." I said in a normal tone of voice but not over the voices of his friends. But they heard me. That's when everyone stopped talking and looked at us.

With his right arm he tried to push me back to get me away from him. "Man get away, I ain't got time for this shit."

Everyone's attention was on us. His arms didn't even move an inch of my body; I remained smiling waiting for the right moment.

"Steve is there a problem with this guy? What the fuck's his problem?" Asked one of the tall beer drinkers. He was my height but very skinny.

"He's just pissed off cause I kicked his ass back in Nam." Laughed Steve. He looked back at me again. "Go away, I ain't got time for kid shit."

"What's that matter Steve, afraid you can't kick my ass?" I asked him.

His friends looked at him waiting for a response. It was rumored that he could kick anyone's ass when I was younger and being that he still hung around, I'm sure he still did it even though he was old. He turned around to face me.

"Just cause I kicked your ass ten years ago doesn't make you look good trying to front me now. Get over it." He said smiling, trying to impress the others. They waited.

"I think your just scared and trying to get out of this situation."

His friends looked at him as if to say, *shut this guy up already and kick his ass.* There was nothing left to say. He moved towards me then swung his bottle towards my head but I blocked it with my forearm. With my right arm I swung right into his gut and gave him a blow that scared him. No longer was I this skinny little boy who was thrown around like a rag doll. He was flung back a little. Then with his fists out he rammed me with all his might knocking me down onto the broken up street that had been smashed and torn up from decades ago.

He tried to squish me with his weight. He began giving me these blows to the head that I couldn't even feel. It was as if I were on angel dust and shoved his blubbering body off of mine with the strength of ten men. He was on the floor next to me. I rose up feeling like I had just drunk down twenty gallons of Rockstar. I jabbed my knee into his back in such a way where he would feel numb. I held his body down with one knee resting on his stomach, which felt like a waterbed and my left arm holding his throat with my thumb holding a pressure point. With my right arm I began to strike blows that made his face gush blood. And with the first strike there was a loud crack that everyone must have heard for there were background noises of "Woh," and, "oh shit!"

He couldn't move nor could he believe this was happening to him. My arm was dripping blood from he bottle that he broke against it. With my hand rising from his face I could see he was falling deeper out of reality.

"Would you like one blow to the gut to make you remember this," I said as I shoved my fist into his stomach, under the ribs so that he would feel it down his back and lost his breath for a minute or two.

"Woh! Woh! You're gonna fuck'n kill him!" Yelled a guy who was standing near enough to see all my damage to his friend. I felt the hands of several people pull me off of him. That's when I felt all reality come into place. I could breathe again. There was blood on my face from his weak punches and there was blood gushing from my arm.

"What the hell is the matter with you?" Asked one of his friends.

As I came to, I looked around myself to find a larger crowd of people watching from near and far. I'm sure that the people who were trying to care for me, wanted to do that to him for a very long time. Some guys pulled me across the street. They rushed with napkins and rags to wipe away the blood and stop the blood from my arm. I thanked them politely. One of them brought me a beer. I was happy and the adrenaline was gone for me.

When things were calm and I was relaxed with my beer, about ten other people came to hang out with me. They introduced themselves. I was popular, which mattered to me no longer like it did when I was young.

"So what's your beef with Steve?" Asked one guy.

"He jumped me a very long time ago, probably while you were in grade school. Anyways, I got him back." I looked across the street where they pulled Steve into the back of the van to wake him up. "Gee, I hope I didn't kill him."

"I don't." Said another guy.

I told them I wanted to get high. And they did. They sure did. We sat in that parking lot for over an hour of straight smoking. They followed me into the club because if Steve came back at me with his friends, they wanted to back me up. It was all high time we stood up to people like him.

Sometimes you think that getting back at people will make you stronger or bring you back to your old self again. But it still plagues you from your past and it can never be erased. I will hope that people I used to be friends with saw that, and saw that they dumped a friend who ended up rich and kicking ass all across the world.

"Where are you going today, Alex?" Asked my mother as she set the table for breakfast.

Patrick sat there waiting to leave for work and was complaining about everything that crossed his path. We hardly paid any attention to him. I made it known that I didn't give two shits about him. He still tried to be nice. He started to change the tone of his voice when I got rich like, "I helped you get there, son. I pushed you to your dream, right *son?*" Of course he was nothing but dirt to me.

"I think I'll go shopping, you know, take a look at the town now."

Patrick got up. "Son, I need to speak with you outside. Walk me to my car." He said as he was heading out the door. Ever since I hit the big time, I became his son. Before I was the *bitches kid.* He has the audacity to call me his son after he said I was just something a whore accidentally had.

As we walked out to the rusty old truck, I squinted my eyes at the sun that shined right over us rising from the East. He touched my shoulder as I thought of knocking him out then running him over with his own car.

"How's your brother Tony? Is he okay?" Of course the run away son was not his. Tony was not rich and he didn't care about Patrick or my mother. He *would* take his bare hands and kill them both if he had no family in his life. "Tony never calls." He said. And I thought to myself, of course he doesn't call, you two *fuck'n* abused us to the point of death. "Anyway, I never recall us getting together for a couple of bruskies. I have the day off tomorrow and thought we could take a drink together at the bar. My friends at the bar don't believe you're my son." That's because I'm not.

"Well it sounds good *dad*, but I think I'd feel more comfortable here at home. If you don't mind." I looked at him strangely. "I have a date for tonight and I might be here at around ten."

"*A Date?* Have you finally decided to get you a woman? Some times, I thought yous gay."

"Great." I opened the door to his truck. "See you tonight."

It's about that time to go and find the gang of my past. I took the old bitches' jeep downtown. That's where they hung around many of times. Anywhere Steve hangs out, Nick would be there. I'm not going to do anything once I find him, but I will see where he is and what he's up to.

I parked in hotel parking. I walked down Commerce Street to where the Hollywood Rock and Roll used to be. Nothing but broken down buildings and bus stops. There was nobody around that I knew so I headed towards the mall. They like to hang by the park downtown, but there was nobody there. Walking downtown finding nothing, was a big disappointment. I walked up and down the street until I was hungry. At a restaurant I sat outside eating my lunch.

I stared at the people who passed by me, businessmen, kids, the employees from fast food and museums. When I turned my head back, I noticed a guy with black hair walking with a short male with a Rockabilly hair cut. It was Nick. He was different. He had a normal haircut and was dressed in your average everyday clothing. The only thing that was the same was his face. He looked at me while he walked passed me. He didn't recognize me.

It saddens me that this moment comes and he can't remember me. Yet I can envision every moment we hung out together; good times and bad. We used to hang out at shows. I can remember where he lived as a teenager. I had a little incentive though. I need to show them in four different directions in the their heads that I am *Alex Dugan* and no one will fuck with me again. I don't have time to go about every way for them to understand. I will show them one way who the hell I am. The lights will go out and they will remember and it will be too late.

As he passed by my table, I caught onto each of his pathetic steps. He walked down a few blocks. He stopped at a bus stop with all of the other dirties. A Dirty: Any person who lives life off of other people and cares for nothing but getting wasted at any given moment

I stood near him. I listened to his conversation. I think he said he was taking the number 58 bus. I left as soon as I was sure of which bus he was taking. I got in my car to follow. When the bus came along, I followed right behind it and stopped at every stop it made.

It had been an hour and still there showed no signs of Nick. I thought I might have missed him. Maybe I had the bus number wrong, but I heard him loud and clear. He couldn't have gotten off without me seeing him. I had been eyeing every person that got on and off of that bus.

I tried to think of where else he could be. I tried not to think of anything else but he was the one who got Steve on me. When school started we were close friends. At first I didn't like him. Steve said he was one of his best friends, so naturally I wanted to be friends with all of them. I thought he might have been cool being that the first night I spoke with him he beat someone up right in front of me. Tough people were always good to hang around with.

No sooner he claimed we were the best of all his friends, that I found him rocking the mattress with my lovely Lila. I wanted, with all the praying in the world, to beat him up in front of everyone. But I was weak, small, and had no clue on how to fight. When I was jumped I lost all hope that my life would ever move forward. I had nothing left. I lost it all that week.

Every time I ran into Nick at school or anywhere he was with his friends, he pushed me or called me names. I said nothing. I was too frightened of everyone. I let it go on. I would imagine that when he teased me in front of everyone, I would lunge at him with my fork and stab him in the neck over and over. The two of us covered in blood. That's how I got through it all. When he spoke, I believed something else was going on.

The bus drove off with a cloud of black smog trailing behind it. Nick walked down the first block by himself. His friend went the opposite direction. I followed him slowly. He made a right and went down two more blocks. He walked into an apartment complex which was cheap and ugly. I remembered the apartment he walked into. I couldn't see the number, but I did remember the very one he pulled his keys out for and opened.

On my way back home, I bought a twenty-four pack of Budweiser. Walking into the house was always hard for me. It was always a scene I had feared as a child; afraid to walk through the door for another beating. Patrick was watching TV in the living room and my mother was in her room.

"What's going on? You still in the mood to drink?" I asked as I walked in the door.

He stretched throwing the remote control to the side of the couch. "Not much son. You ready to drink?" There he goes with that word *son* again.

"Sure."

The two of us went into the backyard and sat in the patio listening to his hillbilly music. I opened a beer and gulped down at my normal pace. By the time I had finished two, my stepfather had finished four. He was always quite the drinker. And when he reaches the point of sixteen and me at thirteen, I was pretty drunk. I thought he wouldn't mind smoking some weed with me. I pulled a joint out of my cigarette pack.

"Here *dad*, take a hit." I said passing him the joint.

He looked at me funny and I wondered if it was either the fact that I passed him a joint or the way I said *dad*. He grabbed the joint with a serious look on his face. "Well it's better to be smoking with your kin than out on the streets with some trouble makers." He laughed. I could tell the old bastard was getting pretty drunk.

A few hours of nothing and he finally went to bed. He tried to talk high and mighty with me about him being *learnded* but I wanted to laugh. I stayed up late going over some figures for work. I went to bed at 4:30 in the morning and woke up and 5:00 in the evening the next day.

I quickly washed up and ate dinner with the folks. It was around nine that I took off in my mother's jeep again. I went back to the club. I couldn't let go. I had a dream that made me understand my reason was to hurt them, humiliate them, and end them.

I sat in the car smoking cigarettes and watching everyone that was there. I had a hatchet under my seat. There he was. He walked out with a busted face and a broken nose. *Yeah I see you. I see how you feel embarrassed with no more pride.* I still felt the pain. I feel like shit because of everything they did to me.

I watched him get into a shitbox car. I followed perfectly behind him. His home was worse than Nick's. I wondered if they were even friends anymore. He lived in the ghetto on the west side of town. I parked on the side of the complex then got out. He parked inside then proceeded on foot.

I could tell he was drunk by the way he was crookedly walking. He went straight to the dumpster to toss some beer in there. Behind the large can he peed on the bushes that were along the wooden fence. I got behind him with the hatchet at his neck.

"Shhh!"

I could feel his body trembling, shaking with fear.

"What a predicament . . . You had no reason to get me jumped you fat worthless piece of shit."

"Hey I kicked your ass you kicked my ass, let's just let bygones be bygones."

I chuckled for a moment and in an instant I stopped. "Let's not and say we did."

It was pitch black. I could hear the crickets calling out in a beautiful tune. The voices were whispering in the wind. "Do it . . . kill him . . ." The shadows came from the dark. They began to choke him but their grasps were my own. I slashed down the hatched and sliced into his groin.

"Fuck you!" He cried. "Fuck you!"

He fell to the floor holding himself crying. I swung down over and over cutting into his stomach. I smacked his body with that mallet as hard as I could. Every time I lifted the blade, blood shot out onto the can. Oh god! The blood, so much blood. It was all over my hands and face. He turned over and I smacked into his backbone. It was over. The voices, the screams, and then I couldn't feel bitter anymore. He was dead and I gained some confidence.

I buried the hatchet in my jacket taking deep breaths with my hands on my waist. I could feel myself shaking. I grabbed his body shoving the whale under the bushes. I ran out of the parking lot as a car pulled up next to me. I put down my head so they wouldn't see the blood.

"Do you know where apartment 115J is?" He asked as he rolled down the window a bit.

"No, sorry." And I kept on walking. I ran to the car wiping my face down. I used my shirt to clean myself off. Oh god of which you are not, please take the voices out of my head!

I made sure I was cleaned inside and out before I stepped into the house of the hillbillies after my affairs with Steve, the fat drunk'n loser. For the past few days I've done nothing but lounge around the house. I help my mother with the groceries and moving furniture where she wanted it changed.

But tonight . . . Tonight I must prowl and seek the boy who started it all. First comes the words I so long to say to him. Then it ends; everything from the pain and the sorrow to the embarrassing moments to which he so precluded. His words haunted me for years. He screwed up every bit of self-esteem I had left. It made me cry as a boy. He stole the one person I felt was my one and only. He jumped me to get to her. For the man that I had become, I find it hard for tears to welt into my eyes for any reason. I feel ice in these veins now.

That's when I began to dream of Lila again. She was like a beautiful dream and an endless reality. She was such a sad girl and I feel sorry for her now with what I now plan to do to her body. Her mind was wondering aimlessly for no reason at all into a dream that was never there, a dream too fake to even believe was imagined. Before I say goodnight, I must leave a bloody kiss for her to remember me by; the kid that lied; the boy who died in front of her while she was fornicating.

There's something inside of me that just wants to murder the world with my bare hands. The spirit that lies inside each and every one of us can die in an instant and I died as a boy. I lost it all and am left with a head full of anguish. I wanted to cry. But it won't come out. There is no sobbing or whining or a single tear can come out of this heart. My life is only happy with the souls of the murdered. I want to talk to anyone and tell them to hold me for I have no one who will. I want them to pretend that they hear me in a crowded room and lie to me that I was significant. Tell me I'm the only one that matters to them.

I have no companion. I expose myself through the words on paper so that *people* can listen to everything I have long to say. My life is just words. I am nothing but a story. I should not let this story be told of how a boy loved a girl and the girl murdered his heart and then he went back to murder her. But I need to remember why it came to be so tragic. Why can't I love and why have I no feelings on the inside? Reality is for the weak. And I believe I lost that a long time ago.

So sad it is to hear that we all have problems to deal with. Sometimes people feel like holding all the anger inside because they're too ashamed to tell anyone. And when a person takes a chance to show someone the *real* them, that person turns their back on them as if they were strange. I'm pathetic because I have nothing.

For those people who fucked over the innocent so bluntly without even a sense of remorse . . . I'm coming for them. Satan is coming for every one of them. He sends his demons to those who have the courage to do what you want and lets them torment your rage.

Tonight I use fire. It's always been a painful way to die. Something all of us do not want to perish like in the end.

My mother is getting ready for bed and Patrick is plopped on the couch watching old movies and drinking alcohol another scene of the everyday life in his home. Especially on those nights where I came back from a party and he was there, waiting for me.

"What are you doing in the garage son?" He called.

Quickly now. I have to get out. "Yeah dad?" I ran into the house. "What?"

"Oh, I just gotta get some stuff. I'm going to take off soon. I'll be home late. Just wanna let you know so you won't lock the chain."

"Alex, where is it that you go all the time? I mean, I really don't give a shit, but you've been awfully busy for someone who hasn't been here in a long, long time. What's going on boy?"

I hated when he called me boy, it was just as bad as calling my mother, woman. He used it often. "Boy," is a term used with the lower class who don't have enough respect for those to call them by their first name. "I just hang out at clubs. I have to do something. I can't get stuck in the house or I'll go insane." As if I weren't already. "Well gotta go."

I locked up the garage taking a large container in my arms. I put everything in my mother's jeep. She didn't mind that I used her car all the time, being that she hadn't seen me in years. It was ten o'clock as I reversed the car out of the driveway. In fifteen minutes, I was there, at the apartments a' La Cheap. I wanted to make sure he was not home. When I parked to the side of the complex, I pulled out the special list of names and crossed off Steve's name.

I was in a hurry. No lights were on in his apartment. I guessed he wasn't home as I had hoped. I held the blueprint in my head for the whole night. I wore black as usual. In my left arm I held the can of gasoline. I splashed it along the walls of his apartment. Back at my car, I tossed the can in the back then sat down. I slid on my leather gloves. In my hand I held a Zippo I had special made. Engraved on the shinny piece of metal was, "Nick." I wiped it down making sure I left no prints. I pulled out a note, which said, "For you Nick." Then I put on some lipstick and kissed the note.

I wanted to pat myself in the back when it was all over. He used to smoke cigarettes all the time and I doubt he ever stopped. This idea had nothing to do with anything I had every performed. My deaths were usually sought out with a blade of some sort; knives, axes, or hatchets. My rage was going to burn down the whole world, which he started for himself.

I broke into his apartment. I was nervous like I hadn't been in so long. I had to check all rooms to make sure there was no one there and I wasn't walking into a trap. It was clear as crystal. I pulled back the stove and ripped out the gas line. Right away I could smell the gas.

The front door opened. Oh no! He's back! I stood up against the wall of the kitchen. The person walked passed me into the bedroom. But it was not Nicolas. I grabbed the hatchet from my back pocket. I crept to the room where they were undressing. What a moment of clarity, watching the clothing fall from skin that looked as soft and rosy.

I was about to swing into her skull when I realized that her cracked cranium would give away a few ideas about their death. I pulled back shoving the hatchet back into my back belt.

She turned around just after she took off her shirt. She jumped at the sight of me screaming. I smiled and nudged my eyebrows as I stared at her chest. *Quickly now, Alex, we don't have time. Shut her the fuck up!*

As she tried to punch me I blocked her arm twisting my arm into hers. I pulled her close to me covering her mouth with my right hand. We fell onto the bed. I punched her in the face real hard. I could tell that one punch almost put her out. Her eyes rolled back a little. I grabbed her by the throat and squeezed as hard as I could. She was trying to scream and breathe but nothing was coming out. The shadows filled the room lighting up the darkness with their red eyes.

My eyes were wide as they stared down at her crushing her breath. Squeezing her life. Go now! Go to sleep Nick's true love. He took my love so why can't I take his. *Mother fucker! Die bitch die!* I wanted to scream. I wanted to yell. I wanted Satan to come unto me and do onto them.

Her arms became weak. She looked sad in the eyes. Tears came flooding down. I kissed her cheeks.

I whispered in her ear. "It's okay honey. Go to sleep. It's okay. You're free now." I breathed in her ear. I was panting as I lay over her next to her face. No life. No love.

I lay there for just a minute trying to calm myself from the mere emotion I was going through. When you murder someone as romantic as I, this touches your soul. It's not as easy as it looks. These faces, these people will haunt you dreams forever. In the significance of my pain, I inflect on those who deserve it.

She was pretty. She had real short bangs and jet black hair like Betty Page. She had red lipstick on. She was one of those wanna-be rockabillies. Please, you have no idea little girl.

I picked her up and tossed her in the closet. I couldn't stand the way her eyes seem to follow me wherever I was so I threw a shirt over her head. The closet was closed with not even a hint she was there. Back to what I was doing.

The fumes were taking over the house. I got out of there within a flash. On the coffee table I left the note, the Zippo, and a black colored clove called X-tra, which used to be his favorite.

I walked back to my car to wait. I was afraid I might have to wait all night long which I was prepared to do. It happened that he arrived an hour later. Just for my own amusement, I laughed out loud all by myself. I was pleased to see him.

The time I waited in my car I spoke with them. They were telling me stories about their world and were proud of my evil deeds. These demons were persuasive to the point of massacre. They said I would join them for eternal life. They began to make my head pound the longer we waited and when I saw Nick with a roar of laughter, they left me alone for a moment. The shadows no longer sat with me in my car.

As Nick walked into the house, I sat near the window to watch. I opened the curtain, well enough for me to see inside but not enough for me to be seen. I became nervous. The voices were racing in the house and I was the only one who could see them. He read the note and smiled. He tossed his feet on the table. As he relaxed himself, I noticed his facial expression. He could smell the trap. I watched him disappear into the kitchen then walking out with a bag of garbage. I was biting my nails.

He put the trash outside of his front door. I remembered then, I was still wearing lipstick. It was now going to act as my new disguise. When he shut the door, I moved back a little. He returned to his place at the couch eating a bag of chips that were sitting on the table. He read the name on the Zippo. He put the clove cigarette to his lips. I walked out of the parking lot as if it were just an ordinary day.

BOOM!

The whole apartment and the one above went up in flames. I felt a vibrant blast swing me back against the pavement. I wanted to get out before anyone saw me. I was in my car and hurried out without looking suspicious.

I crossed off Nicks name.

I was on my way to freedom. Not in a sense of getting caught by the police but a sense of feeling like I could cry once again someday. And I was hopeful that I could start all over. Maybe run into a wonderful woman who was dreadfully wholesome. I had to find myself an alibi for the night so I drove down 5th street again. It was packed full of different crowds of people in different kinds of bars.

I stopped at a new bar that was loud as I rolled down the window of the car. It was the kind of music I was turned onto now. It might as well end dreadfully well. I parked my car. My hatchet was put under the car so no one who find it. As soon as I walked in the club I was lost in the crowd. It was full of Gothic kids and freaks.

Near the restroom was a table full of t-shirts and CDs for sale. I grabbed a long sleeved shirt. I changed my clothes in the restroom that reminded me of another dirty club that I would dare not walk into again. In the restroom were some guys making out. I wanted to choke them both, the faggots.

"Hey, do you mind?" I asked.

The two Marilyn Manson painted faces looked at me with frowns then walked out. I was relieved they were out of my sight. I washed the blood from my face that I hid under a hat. I threw the bloody shirt into the trash that I wore underneath my jacket. It wasn't that bloody. Just a little came from her mouth when I choked her. There was some blood on my chest that seeped through the shirt. I cleaned up my chest. After I put on the new shirt a boy walked in. He had the white make up on his face just as the others did. Trying to look dead as vampires. I wanted to laugh. He did his business in front of the urinal then stood next to me at the sink. I looked at him up and down. How convenient these guys were to be in my very presence. I shook off my hands then faced him.

"What's going on little buddy? What are you up to?" I asked him.

He looked at me as if I were crazy. "Are you talking to me?" He asked very girly.

"Yeah you."

"Do I know you?" He asked me.

"No, but if you like, we can go hang out by the stage and watch the band together." I was trying my best not to crack up.

He looked at me up and down. I saw the smile form across his face from ear to ear. I know I'm good looking. It was easy to just manipulate this guy to say he's been with me all night if anything should ever happen.

"Well, maybe you can hook me up with a drink since I'm not of age." He put his hand on his hip.

I smiled to the side. Then I nodded my head. "Yes, yes. I can get you a drink."

"Well good, then I'll see you out there in a bit."

I nodded my head.

He walked out. He was four inches shorter than me and he was skinny. He looked like the type to fall in love all gay with some dude and get all emotionally attached once you let him into your life.

I was fit as a fiddle when I walked out. I wore my jacket even though I was warm. I stood with the crowd and relaxed a little. The singer of the band on stage was wearing all black clothing as if out of an Ann Rice movie. The music was loud and I was emerged into the music at once. There was a mash pit behind me and to the sides were people dancing. I pushed and shoved with the pit of people. I knocked over a few of guys. When I stood with the crowd, I looked around at all of the people who were enjoying the music.

I noticed this one guy who was a little rougher than others. He stood near me and I heard his name over the music through the whispers of the shadows that suddenly flowed around them. I did not want this moment to appear right then and there. But I would be in worse pain if I didn't.

He was a face of one of the punk rockers that beat me up. His name was Danny and he hung around Steve often. I would believe that he would have changed but he looked the same. The music was louder and I grabbed my head in a way where no one would notice as if I were jamming with the music. Everything went suddenly silent. It was dark. I pulled out a small switchblade from my pocket. It was so crowded I believed no one would notice. I opened the blade right on him. As I shoved it under my sleeve I felt the blade slice open my skin.

As I had stabbed him, I pushed him forward like I was in the pit with everyone else. I jumped to the other side. I made way through the crowd into the bathroom. I wiped the blade clean then hid it behind a toilet. I wiped the blood away from my arm and tried to cover the cut with paper towels. Mental note, *do not skip your STD's test in 6 months!*

Back into the crowd, the music was ending and people weren't apt to pushing anymore. When the area cleared, I saw Danny holding his back lying on the floor with some blood coming out of his shirt. I stood there with everyone and we stared at him in surprise.

I was near the bar then tapped on the shoulder. "Hey," said the freak who I was to hang with all night. "How about that drink?" To occupy myself, I thought it a good idea to stick with the boy who must have been eighteen or nineteen.

I smiled at him. "What do you want to drink."

"Something like, Cherry pucker." He smiled. I turned to the bartender. He looked over at the crowd of people. "Oh my what happened to that guy?"

"I don't know," I said as I turned around with a drink in my hands. I gave it to him. "So what's your name?"

"Andy."

"I'm Tom, nice to meet you. If you want I can take you home."

"Really?"

"Are you here with anyone?"

"Not really. I just met up with some friends."

The band got off the stage and everyone was wondering what was going on. The police were in there in no time. It was three in one night that I had never done before. They rushed in saying that no one was to leave without being frisked. I wanted to be cool. The club was closing down because of this horrendous killing. Everyone had to near the door and empty their pockets and get checked with a hand held metal detector.

Andy stood near me trying to down his drink as fast as he could. He put the glass on a stool as we neared the door. We stood side by side as it was our turn.

"You two here together?" Asked the officer who looked at us two.

Andy looked up at me hoping for a yes. He wanted me to be his new boyfriend. I was looking for an alibi. I looked at the police officer and grabbed onto Andy's hand. "Why yes we are." The cop wanted to laugh. There was nothing but freaks here and it was hard to pin point a murder with a room full of want to be vampires.

They checked us both and we walked out together hand in hand. I let go of him as he neared my car. As I lifted my hand to unlock the door a drop of blood smacked onto the car door. I looked at him funny to see if he had noticed but there was nothing but a face of boy who was purely in love.

I dropped him off and ended the night not with a kiss, but a pure thank you for the company and sent him floating home with a promise that I would call the number he left me very soon, maybe even when I got home. It was a load of crap I spilt onto the boy.

CHAPTER 10

I patched up the slice I had made in my arm with a needle and thread. It wasn't deep at all but I didn't want a large mark on my arm. It was a good beginning of the day. I woke up to the sent of bacon on the stove. My mother made eggs, bacon, and waffles. I stayed with her for a while. I didn't want to go out that night so I just slept for hours up in my room.

In the middle of the night I started drinking some of my stepfathers liquor. I made it through the bottle until it was three fourths gone. It was two in the morning when I stopped drinking. In my room were some posters but not many. My experiences with posters made me not want them anymore. On my dresser was a mirror. I had forgotten all about it until that very moment when I was really drunk.

I walked up to the mirror to look at myself. My eyes were red, my complexion was pale, and my muscles looked more defined since I last looked through that very mirror when we first bought the place. There she was lying on my bed wearing a red teddy and high heels with her hair down and smiling at me. I swung around in fright but there was nothing but an empty bed.

I slid the drawer out of the way with it blocking the door. There behind the dresser was a small safe. I remembered the combination as if I wrote it down that very day. As soon as I opened it up, I knew what was there. No money, no bonds, nothing of savoir, but I knew I wouldn't be looking for this until I was ready to burn them. I pulled the box out of the safe and sat on my bed.

The pictures looked the same as when they were first taken. Lila was in every picture here. As a boy I may have had a cheap camera, but I took many pictures of her. And though they were cheap, she embraced every picture with her beautiful face. She smiled in every one of them. There were some of her and I when I was a skinny little boy. It mattered to me that these were still in my life and I couldn't let them go.

Three am. No one was awake at this moment watching me standing in front of her house. No one could see that I almost cried for a moment but there was nothing. Still a man like me could not cry. I was glad I did not cry because she was not worth the tears I did shed when she tore out my heart.

I crept up the porch remembering times we had sat at this very porch and kissed the night away. On the side of the house was her bedroom window, which I stood next to for some while. She was lying in bed sleeping. Still beautiful she lay. She looked more extravagant than before it was almost breath taking. I asked myself if I should crawl through her bedroom window and say goodbye before I say hello. I kneeled down and pasted my face to the window of her room to watch her breathe.

She never made a sound while she slept. Her red hair was lying across the pillow looking soft as if it were silk. I wanted to stroke my hands through her hair. The room was dim, but I could still see in the darkness. The house lights were all off so no one could see me. The window was locked but I had my own key.

I cut through the glass and unlocked the window. It sort of squeaked when it was lifted. I ducked low so she wouldn't see me if she were to awake. She was still in her dreams right now. I lifted myself up and crawled through the window.

I was hot because of the gloves I wore and I was still very drunk. I am always a careful man. Staring at her as I came through was like the moon shined on her perfectly and she glowed. The rest of the room, where I stood was completely black. If she opened her eyes, she still wouldn't see me.

Her lips looked soft. Her neck was showing in a sexy curve from her face. I crawled to the bed and sat down next to her. I stared at her without blinking. I could kill her now and not have to think about her again. I took off one glove on my right hand and touched her face lightly. It was very erotic for me. I leaned over to kiss her lips.

I rested my head next to her on the pillow and closed my eyes. I don't know what was going through my head but I fell asleep. I can't remember how long I was out but someone turned on a light and began to yell at me. I couldn't hear them though. I could see him scolding but I was deaf. He held a bat in his hands and swung it at my head. I felt a smack chop off a piece of my skull.

I shook with fear and then woke up. I looked up as she still lay there sleeping. It was no longer dark in her room nor could I hide in the shadows. It was maybe six in the morning. The minute changed on the clock and I heard the alarm go off in the room next to hers. I jumped up and crawled through the window. I made sure I had my gloves on as I shut the window. I stood there to listen.

Footsteps began towards her door. There was a loud knock on her door. I shut the window and ducked down as she got up. I walked up the street to my car. It was cold and the gloves served a good purpose.

I was tired from the night of roaming around into her house. But I took a ride to her house again. I pulled my jeep up to her house and knocked at the front door. Her father answered and I remembered him well from my dream.

"Can I help you?" He asked in a very intimidating voice.

"Is Lila home?"

"Um, well, she's in the shower now. She should be out in about five minutes if you want to wait or something." He put up his hand.

"Okay. I'll wait by my car."

"Alright, I'll let her know. What's your name so I can tell her?"

"It's a surprise. I hadn't seen her since high school."

"Okay son."

I walked to my car. I pulled out a cigarette and lit it. I waited fifteen minutes. The front door opened. Out she came wearing short kaki shorts and a tank top. Her face was naturally pretty. Her red hair was blowing in the wind. She walked up to me with curious eyes.

"Can I help you?" She asked me.

I blew smoke out of my nose. I looked at her. "You haven't changed much. It's been a very long time since I saw you last."

"Do I know you?"

Well yeah you dumb bitch! But I had to hold back. "Take a good look."

She looked at me. But there was no recognition in her expression but there was a bit of attractiveness in the way she tried to figure out who I was, if she was even doing that. "No I don't remember but I would like to."

"Do you remember a little pipsqueak named Alex?"

I looked down and she looked at my face again. "Oh my god. Alex?" She put her arms out. "I can't believe it's you!" She let go and backed up. "You look so good. So tall."

"So how have you been?"

"I'm great and yourself?"

"Oh I live in California now. I got my own car lot. I've been doing pretty good these past years."

"You sure have."

"So where do you work."

She looked down. "Well, I work in the children's department at the University hospital. I'm an assistant nurse there. Its pretty good work. How long are you going to be in town?"

"Not much longer. I'll be leaving in a couple of days. So are you married?"

"No. But I have been dating a few people here and there. I'd rather not go into that though. Enough about me, how about you? Where are you staying? Who are you dating?" She smiled then nudged me in the shoulder. I didn't want her to be touching me. It was strange talking to her after so many years of having nightmares of her. I didn't want to let myself believe this was just another dream. I wanted to wrap my hands around her little throat and squeeze the life out of her.

I smiled then said, "Well actually, I'm staying with my folks." My smile faded just a little as I looked into her eyes. I felt a pain in my neck. "I just wanted to see how you were doing?" I let out a heavily held breath of air. I imagined I touched her cheek then kissed her forehead. Everything went quiet now that I couldn't stare at her. I felt her arms wrap around me tightly. She held onto me like she really missed me. It felt good having her body pressed up against mine. I let go of my anger and put my arms around her as I closed my eyes. I felt warmth again. The last time I had felt this happy was when she was with me. I had no idea what to say to her. "If you're not busy later, maybe I could have the pleasure of taking you to dinner," I asked in a low voice.

"I'd like to but"—I knew it. "I had plans for this evening." I put my head down a little. "But I can cancel no problem cause I know you're leaving."

I looked up and smiled. "Great." I felt a little shy but I had to keep my cool. I didn't want her to think I was after her. I wanted her to be after me. "Well I have something's to do but I can be here about eight thirty if that's okay?"

"Okay. I'll see you tonight." She headed back up to her house.

I drove away as she stood on the porch staring at me. I was going to look very good tonight. I went to some nice shops on the northern area. It wasn't very crowded which pleased me that I was waited on hand and foot. There wasn't much of what I liked. I was a simple person and simple wasn't *in* anymore. I picked a black suit with the blazer and slacks of very good material. Under the coat I wore a short sleeve turtleneck, but not the kind that folded over like a turtles' neck.

It didn't take me long to get ready because I was very excited. She was going to see what a success I turned out to be and she missed out on it all. I wonder if she would get really dressed up to impress me, or if she would toss on whatever knowing it was just meeting up with an old friend.

It was dark as I pulled up to her house. I walked up to the door very nervous which I hardly ever am. I stood there thinking about all the things that brought me to this very moment. I imagined choking her so hard she-

Her door opened and her father looked up at me. I snapped awake. "Oh, what are you doing here?" He asked me in a mean tone. "If you're here for Lila, she's inside. Knock or something." He turned around. "Nah." He yelled out loud, "Lila! Some guy is here to see you." He walked to the car in the driveway and took off. I stood there thinking, I didn't even get to speak.

The door squeaked a little. She was very stunning when I set my eyes on her. She wore a long red velvet skirt with a slit on the left leg and a red velvet tube top with a black velvet jacket over it. She hair was done up so I could set my eyes on her neck.

"You look nice," I said while trying to hide my hard on.

"Thank you." She looked at me with drooling eyes. "You looked good yourself."

"Well, yah ready?"

She locked up the house. I escorted her to the car unlocking the door for her. The conversation in the car was slow and we didn't have much to say to each other. I still imagined it was all too fake to be real. I took her to a fancy restaurant. It felt good having her waist in my hand. We walked inside where an older man stood with his hair slicked and parted right down the center. He was standing behind a podium with a fake smile.

"Table reserved for Thompson." I said.

The little French faggot responded, "Ah, oui monsuer, we have your table ready." He showed us to the table, and then pulled out the seat for Lila. I thanked him and he was back to the front.

"So Alex, this is different, but I guess you're doing quite well." She leaned on her hand resting her elbow on the table with a flirtatious look. She tried to catch my eye. I blew smoke into her face from my cigarette. She knew then, I was not in the mood to make eye contact. I raised my eyebrow as she sat back in her chair.

I pulled out the menu to look it over casually trying to change the odd moment. "So what looks good," I asked.

The waiter came to our table with his hands behind his back. He looked just as the host did with the button up and bow tie. "What would you like to drink?"

"I'll have a Shiner bock." She replied.

"I'll take a vodka on the rocks." I smiled while staring at Lila.

He left us alone again.

"So, you live with your parents?" I looked at her and wanted to laugh at the thought of her still being at home.

"Yeah, I do. I know I should be out on my own but it's so much easier living off of them. I'm still in school. I want to become a registered nurse. For a long time I was going out with my friends and having a good time."

"Well that's good." I put out my cigarette. "At least you're trying to make something of your life."

"Do you go to school?" She asked.

"I received my masters degree in Business and a Bachelor's in mechanics. During the time I was in school, I was trying to get together my car lot. I sell old cars but I restore them to its unique self again."

"Wow, that must be exciting to own your own place. How much income does it bring in?"

"Well I'm not supposed to let anyone know but it brings in a great deal. I'll tell you this much, if I didn't want to work anymore, I'd be well taken care of. I go in because I like to see my product get out there. I actually have two shops in California and another one is being built now." The drinks were laid in front of us. She smiled at me and she put the glass to her lips.

We ordered the best on the menu. We ate empty plates that cost more than what you expected to eat. We could have had a buffet for far less. Every time Lila leaned over to take a bite, she would look up at me to see if I were watching her. She tried to keep eye contact. I sat there with my leg crossed over the other leaning back in my chair with a serious look on my face.

I remembered when I touched those lips they were soft. I was young then and old now. What I thought was sexy is not near what I think is now. But they still looked good. She still turned me on.

We finished our meal. I pulled out another cigarette. With it in my mouth, I snapped open my Zippo and lit it with a click as I closed it. The waiter came by again.

"Can I get you anything else at all?"

"Yeah, I'll take another vodka on the rocks." That would be my third. I downed them like they were shots. I wasn't comfortable with her at moments; afraid she was still going to rip out my heart for the second time. After two more drinks I was feeling pretty good.

"So what made you come down here when you have so much going on, on the west coast?"

"Well I wanted to visit with my folks and get away from California for a short while. I even had a man sit down next to me on the plane and tell me he wanted to buy one of my cars. We had some beer on the plane and ended up a little drunk." I laughed a little at the thought of the stranger.

"Oh really. And you made it off of the plane okay?"

"I seem to have. I can be drunk and go through the process of life with no problem." Another glass was set in front of me. "Awe my drink," I smiled. He laid the check in the book down. I could tell she wanted to know how much it was. She wanted to flip it over and peek. I gulped down the whole glass. "So how are things down here in Texas?" I asked her with a southern accent.

She laughed a little. "You know Alex, I look at you now and think back to what you used to be like." She nodded her head leaning back in her chair with her legs crossed and her hands placed perfectly on her nee. "I am really proud of you. You've done an excellent job with yourself. I mean, look at yourself, you are absolutely sophisticated and well mannered. I couldn't recognize the boy who lies beneath you."

I turned to my side with this face that tried to smile but it came out all wrong. "Well you're doing good too. A nurse plays a big role in our lives. If it makes you happy then that's all that matters. I didn't just end up rich on a whim, I worked my ass off and went through tough times." I pulled out my pocket book, which slightly resembled a checkbook. I tossed some money in the book with the bill then looked up at her. "Are you ready to go?"

"Sure."

I didn't want the night to end. When we got to the car I asked her if she wanted to go dancing. I felt a little buzzed. We arrived at The Dawn; a club I had heard was doing real well. The first place we went was the bar where I had a shot of liquor.

"You better slow down Alex or I might have to drive you home," she laughed. She drank another beer.

I smiled at her with my soggy mouth and my eyes a little lazy. "That's okay. Bartender, pour me a shot of whiskey and I'm done." I drank it down once he handed it to me. I grabbed Lila by the hand so we could go dance.

The night finished for me. I was ready to go. We danced for hours. I was drunk and happy. She was having a good time. She looked good dancing. We crookedly walked to my car.

"Are you okay to drive?" She asked as we reached the jeep.

She leaned up against the car on the passenger side. I pulled out my keys but they slipped out of my hands onto the ground. I leaned over to pick them up. I noticed her legs between the slit in her skirt as I was rising up. Then her hips, waist, breast, and then her face surrounded by that red hair. My smiled faded. I moved forward to kiss her. She liked it because she held tightly onto me not wanting to stop. We got in the car, which was completely silent as we headed back to her parents house.

I wanted to stay far from her. That kiss was not good on my part but it wasn't going to ruin plans I had for this evening. Once we pulled up to her house, I walked her to the front door. I had this vision that I leaned over to kiss her, then grabbed her by the neck and choked the life out of her. Instead she grabbed my hands and touched her face with them. She leaned over then kissed me on the cheek.

"Thank you for a wonderful evening Alex." She let go of my hands so she could unlock her door. "I'm so glad that you found something special in your life and you're a success. Take care alright."

"Will do." I said smiling at her as she shut the door. I felt bad, that fuck'n bitch. I didn't have a chance to choke her. I'll just come back and finish the job. Her face would be branded in my memory if I didn't rid of her. I must come back tonight to finish what I came to do.

I touched the door. I just turned around and walked away. I had some things I was sorting out in my head at that very moment as I turned on the car. I switched on the headlights so I could drive away. I put the car in drive when I saw Lila standing in front of my car. I rolled down the window to see what was the matter.

"What's wrong?" I asked as I looked out at her. I saw tears streaming down her cheeks. I turned off the jeep then got out. Her head was down with her hair in her face. I almost ran up to her. "What's wrong?"

"I just wanted to let you know that I didn't forget how we parted. I am so sorry for what I did to you." She looked up at me with the saddest look in her eyes. "I know it must have hurt and I hope it didn't shatter anything in your life." She pointed to herself. "And I couldn't let you leave here without me telling you how truely very sorry I am." She turned to walk away from me. In a very low crying tone she said, "Sorry again Alex."

I grabbed her by the arm turning her around. I held her face in my hands. "I remember Lila. I remember. And yes it did bother me a great deal, so much that you'll never know what I went through. You were the only girl I ever loved and it hurt me."

"I *am* so sor"-

"Thank you." I said before she could say another word wiping the tears away from her cheeks. She was still so beautiful. We were no longer kids.

And I felt that one part of me fill that I thought needed death. She held my hand close to her chest. I walked her back to the front door. She opened the door holding my hand still as she was going inside.

"What about your parents?" I asked.

"I have my own life. And they have locks on them."

It was dark in the room. She sat on the bed. I sat with her. I felt my heart pumping, I haven't been this nervous since I was last with her. I couldn't even remember what it was like being with her. I kissed her as she lay back on the bed. It was an intimate moment for the both of us. Slowly and softly, I slipped the top of her shirt down sucking on her breasts. She wrapped her arms around me as I kissed her body lower and lower. My hands slid up through the slit of her skirt. Her body was soft as silk as I imagined it was as a kid. I held her tightly in my arms as we moved and moaned.

In the midst of all the love making she whispers, "You sure did grow since you were away."

I made a small laugh and thought the same about the curves in her body. "Don't worry, I won't hurt you." I said moaning with her. It was a passion I hadn't felt in all my life. With all the women I had been with and who wanted me never did once make me shiver as I did with her. I hardly made any noise with any of the sluts who messed with me. But with her, it was different. I couldn't stop moaning and she was getting louder. I was afraid her father was going to come knocking but I couldn't stop. I wanted her and it was an uncontrollable passion that was held inside of me.

When it was over, she leaned on her side with my arm draped over her. It wasn't as dark as it was when we walked in. I could see her face. She touched my cheek. I grazed my hands along her naked body.

"I thought about you." She said quietly.

"I thought of you too."

"Could you ever forgive me?" She asked.

"I've tried to. I think I can now. I really needed you to say what you did out there. I've waited for it."

"Do you think I could ever see you again?"

"I don't know."

"It's okay if you don't. I won't ever forget you." She leaned over and we kissed for a while until she fell asleep in my arms. In the morning I was gone. I didn't even harm a hair on her head. I think that she made peace with me. I might be able to forgive her. I said my final good byes to her that night. It was my one night of passion.

CHAPTER 11

One can only assume that life with regret is what makes mistakes possible. I regret not choking the whore of pain in the palm of my hands. I will for the rest of my life. She deserved what she was going to get and I let her slip right out of my very grasp because I forgave her. She made me *feel* something for her. I still love that girl but not like before. Still no one can touch my heart and she can never hurt me again. Maybe that's what I needed. Has this life that I had made of plucking out those who loved to torment people been wrong all this time? Maybe deep down I could have spared every one of the lives I had taken just be a simple pleading. A drawn out beautiful apology. It seemed like my whole world might turn upside down.

I would not change. I will not change. Those people live all of their lives hurting others. I had to stop it. I will forgive her and only her. She is my muse that helps me seek out those who needed to be justified. If I still have dreams of her I will know that I was wrong. It's all in how I will react later.

"Mom, are you going to take me to the airport or is Patrick?" I asked her.

She was standing over a hot stove with a spatula in her hand. I wonder if she was cooking for me. "Well your father and I thought about taking you out to dinner before you go, if that's okay."

"Sure thing." Heck if I cared. I went upstairs to my room. I had to get all of my belongings together. The music was low on the stereo, which was opera. If Patrick heard the music, he would surely make fun of me and call me a queer. It didn't matter to me what he thought.

Over in my head was the voice of the girl I made love to a few nights ago. She was so beautiful the way she moaned loudly when I made love to her. I wanted to go back and take her home so we could make love all day and all night. But she's not what I thought I wanted or hated for so long. Steve, Nick, and Danny were all part of some plot to ruin my life. I take back now what was rightfully mine, my life. And there are no gaps in my heart. I feel

somewhat like, *The Grinch Who Stole Christmas*. My heart is growing in size
and I felt really good. I was ready to let go.

In that moment of clarity, I knew what I had to do. I took all the pictures
I had of Lila and a few I had saved of the two faced friends in my life, then
dumped them into the sink where I burned every last one of their faces, one
by one, out of my memory with a single match. I smiled at each picture with
a relief that it was over.

I opened the top of my dresser where there were more pictures, but
family pictures I had cared not to take them with me. My memories of this
childhood would remain where it was most remembered, here in the presence
of the ones who hurt me more than anyone else in my life. Yet I didn't find
any reason to do otherwise.

I have mentioned the pain of my parents. And there I lay back on my
bed wondering why I was in their house and had not done what Tony had
done; ignore them, never speaking to them again.

"Tony, Alex, you two get the fuck in here now!" Patrick yelled from the
living room sitting in *his* couch chair right in front of the TV. He had a beer
in his right hand and a cigarette in his left.

My brother and I ran in with smiles. Smack! An unexpected surprise,
which I should have known better. He hit both of us on the bottoms. We
began to cry. It was very fearful to come face to face with the gentleman we
believed murdered our dad and stole our sweet mother. Of course father had
died during the Vietnam War.

"God damn it boys, you listen when I call you! You hear me? You get
your asses in here pronto when I call yah! Now sit down here boys." He
drank down his beer to the very last drop. "I swear I don't know why I got
with that whore if'n she had kids." He said to himself. He tossed the beer
can at Tony's head. "Go throw that away boy, and tell your mammy to get
me another one. You hear?"

"Yes sir." Said Tony. He took the can to our mother. He didn't know
much being that he was only seven and I was four. We did what we were
told but the two of us had a hard time calling him dad. He didn't care; he
liked it that way.

Patrick kicked me on the arm and I started to cry a little. "Shut the hell
up boy and rub my feet." He looked at the child who hardly spoke much and
was crying with his mouth wide open and tears coming out but no sound.
"God damn it." He said to himself. "Shut the hell up, you don't have to rub
my feet."

Tony ran in with a beer in his hand. He sat down next to me on the floor and he put his arm around me for protection. We sat close to each other hoping that we would disappear. I wasn't old enough to understand what was going on; someday Tony would make a promise to rescue me from them.

"Alex, run and get my slippers." I ran to his room while Tony buried his head into his knees. I ran back handing him the slippers, when Tony looked up and put his arm around me.

He took a drag of his cigarette while looking at the TV. He stuck his foot in to the crevasse of the slipper. "Shit!" He grunted as the cigarette fell out of his mouth. He picked up the cigarette from the floor then looked inside the slipper. "What the fuck?" He then pointed his cigarette at me yelling, "Alex, what the fuck is this shit? GI Joe figures in my slipper. How many goddamn times have I told you to keep away from Patrick's things? I know it was you, Tony don't play that shit no more, I broke em of that. Whoop round boy, so's I can punish you."

My mouth opened wide again with no sound at all and the tears already streaming. I was afraid of this man, more than any man in the world. All he did was ridicule and inflect pain on us. I didn't know if he were my dad nor where he came from, all I knew at that point was that he was the one who made me cry all the time. When I turned around, he smacked me several times with the bottom of the slipper on my legs and ass. I jumped because the last one was the sorest.

"And just for jumping," he laughed, "I'm gonna have to do it again." He smacked me once more. "Now scat! I'm in the middle of M.A.S.H. you too Tony."

I ran to the kitchen for my mother. I held onto her leg. "Mommy," I cried.

"Oh get off me, can't you see I'm trying to cook, you little nuisance."

I ran to my room to cry. I sat in the corner all by myself. They didn't show any affection to us and it was hard for a child as young as I to get through life without it. Tony walked into the room to sit in the corner with me. He put his arm around me again with me burying my face into his chest crying like the baby I still was. He didn't mind at all. He was the only one who loved me.

Because of him I made it through life. We had a bond like no other brothers out there. Even when we were teenagers, he didn't pick on me like most siblings do. He always made sure I had enough lunch money and everything together when I was in school. Patrick stopped hitting Tony around fourteen. He wasn't ever hit by Patrick again. Nor did Tony ever step foot back in their home again. I remember Tony's last one.

"Get in here boy!" Yelled my stepfather from his room.

The two of us looked at each other frightfully. We didn't know which one he was calling. We both came closer to see who it was he wanted to beat this time.

"Tony! When I fuck'n call you, you get your ass in here!" He yelled.

Tony ran to my Patrick's room. I followed but stayed behind the door watching through the opening. Tony stood there very afraid of Patrick and worried about what he would say.

"God damn it Tony! Boy, I have tried to teach you to be obedient and what do you do? You disobey your teachers. You didn't tell me and your mammy that yous got a week of detention."

"I know." Tony lowered his head.

"Oh, you tried to hide it from us." Patrick smiled. He enjoyed hurting us.

"Go on now," said my mom. "You tell him what yah up to at school."

"It was because I talked back to the teacher for making fun of my homework."

"She just called right now say'n she thinks you might have a bit of a temper problem. She wants you to see the guidance councilor at school. She also wants me and your mammy to go down there to speak with her. I didn't raise no idiot for a kid. You didn't tell me like you should've when yahs came home." He took the belt off of his pants. "Turn around boy." Tony closed his eyes. My stepfather took the end where the belt buckle was and smacked Tony on the back with it. Tony screamed so loud, I couldn't believe that was him. Patrick whacked him again on the back.

"Mom make him stop!" Cried Tony holding onto his back. "Please make him stop!" She stood there with her arms crossed in satisfaction. "What kind of a mother are you?" He cried as Patrick continued to punish him.

"Don't you talk to your mammy like that." Growled Patrick and he swatted him again.

An incredible moment for my brother. He flung around as the belt came down and punched old Patrick right in the face, which sent him flying back against the wall. "Stop it!" He cried. "Stop beating us you son of a bitch!" Yelled Tony. And right in the present moment as I lay in my bed upstairs from the attic of their house, I began to cry hearing those crying pains from my own brother in pure torture. I closed my eyes as the tears began to slide down my cheeks. "Stop it, I can't take it anymore!" And he fell back on the floor as he swung one last punch into Patricks' face.

As soon as Patrick regained himself from the punches of a young teenager, he went straight at Tony. Swinging down the belt harder than before. I could here the slapping of the leather onto the skin as he cried out so loud he broke a vocal cord, which to this very day, made is voice sound rough and distorted.

"Stop it!" I cried from the doorway, as I couldn't watch them beat my brother any longer.

Patrick saw me. "Boy if you don't mind your business, I'm gonna have to do you too."

I began to walk backward tripping on the carpet. That's when my brother found his chance. He ran out of the room knocking Patrick to the ground as he jumped out, then yanked me by the collar and dragged me into our room. We locked the doors tightly. It would be a barricade. We pushed the bed against the door so he couldn't get in. Tony began to fill his backpack up with clothes. I watched him in fear; I was only a boy and didn't know what he was going to do. He worked fast as the pounding of the door was going on outside the room. Patrick was ranting and raving that if he didn't open the door, he would kill him.

Tony didn't care. After his bag was filled with some clothes, a few pictures, and a couple of his comics, he got down on his knees next to the drawer. He slipped his hand underneath pulling out a small tin box. He opened it up and it was filled with money. He looked at me with a serious expression as I was in the corner of the room, on my knees crying. "This is my one chance to escape little buddy. I wanted to wait until I had enough money but if he gets through that door he'll kill me. I don't have enough to get us out of here. I promise little brother, I will come and get you soon." He put out his hand to me. I grabbed it as he helped me up. "Best buds?" He said.

"Best buds," cried the frightened boy. And he gave me the biggest bear hug.

He ran to the window. "I'm out of here, see you soon." And he was gone. I was alone and crying back in my corner where I wouldn't move for several days. Patrick had put an axe through the door asking me where the *little son of a bitch* was. I just cried afraid he would kill me instead.

For six months I heard nothing about Tony. I knew then, I would never see my brother again. I was left alone, with *these* parents of the devil. I became more and more quiet not wanting to speak with teachers or friends, and especially them. There was that day when all my troubles were over. My parents were having money problems and it just so happened that my Uncle Michael from California called to see how they were doing. A week later he offered to take care of me while they get situated. I was more than thankful.

Tony had saved up money that he earned washing peoples cars and steeling bits of money from Patrick when they weren't looking, letting Patrick blame it on my mother. He took the money he had, bought a ticket to California and stayed with my uncle. He told my uncle of what happened to him and we were saved. But in the end, the freedom we had was ruined by our own hands. Tony ran away. And I had trouble with my friends.

A year back with my folks was strange. They were quiet around me. As they noticed that I was able to talk back and understand it went back to normal. I was once the slave, I had prayed I would never be again. Patrick must have tried not to hit me, but he just couldn't be something he wasn't.

I came home late one night from a party at the wrong time. He was drunk as I walked through the door. That night I had the beating of my life. It was almost as bad as when Tony was beaten when he ran away.

There were no longer tears in my eyes only the remains of stains on my face. How could I have been so blind, as to not see them for what they really were? How come they got off so easily?

"Alex, I'm gonna get ready so is we can take yah to dinner." Called my mother.

"Alright," I called from the attic. "I'll be up here getting my things together." I took every picture that had their faces on them, and burned them just like the others. The only remaining ones were of my brother and I. Still in those pictures, we bore no smiles, if you looked closely in a few of them; there were bruises on our bodies.

It was something I blocked out. It didn't plague me as much as being loved from the most beautiful girl in the world then had my heart trampled on. They never had love. So it was never taken away.

I went downstairs where Patrick sat on the couch with a beer laughing at the TV. He saw me then smiled. "Sit down boy, it'll be a while afor your mother gets out of the bath tub. She likes to be just so." He laughed. "Get you a beer."

"I'm okay." I said as I sat down. On the wooden coffee table were some magazines, which I picked up to look through. "So where are we eating?" I asked. "I'm pretty hungry."

"Do you want to go to the country buffet? I hear they got some good steaks out there." He said with enthusiasm.

"Sure, that sounds real good. And I'm pretty fuck'n hungry."

"Even rich folks got some good taste." Under his breath he said, "not like them runaway losers."

"What's that?"

"Nothan." He leaned back on the couch. "Oh I wish yah'd stay. We could have lots of fun. Yous gonna miss out of the town fair."

I slammed my fist down into his head as he stared at the TV. He looked at me in surprise. I stood up with my arms out. "You know, I wasn't going to do this but I think my brother and I owe you a lot more than you realize." I said.

"Damn right you owe me your fuck'n lives." He growled as he put his beer down. "Get the fuck out of my house boy. You don't ever raise your hands to me."

I came closer to him as he backed away almost like the frightened kid *I* was. "You shouldn't have beaten us like you did you white trash mother fucker. You must have thought we were never going to grow up."

He swung at me with this blow that could've knocked me out but all that time I heard my brothers cries in my head. I flew back onto the floor. I got up and rammed him down to the ground next to the wall. "You son of bitch," I cried. I smacked his head over and over punching him with every bit of my strength I had. I used everything. There was blood coming out of his nose and he was wailing for me to stop. He was almost out.

I got off of him. "You're nothing." I said. I walked out while the man tried to regain himself. I came back in with a butcher's knife from the kitchen. "You see this. It's your future." I laughed. I began to chop him up while he struggled for life. The living room was covered in blood. He saw the shadows that followed with every death I committed.

Upstairs was the woman who sat there and cheered him on to beat her own kids. I opened the door to her room. She was wrapped up in her bathroom towel just getting out. I came up from behind her putting my arms around her.

"Hi mother." I said to her in a very awkward tone. She saw the blood on my arms.

"Alex what happened?" She cried with worry. She turned around to see me covered in blood. "What happened to you?"

I sucked on one of my fingers tasting the blood. "Oh, it's just Patrick. You want to taste it." I put my finger out. She looked at me strangely.

"Is this some kid of a joke?"

"No joke Cassandra. I got rid of him. You didn't need him."

"Cut it out!" She demanded. "What's wrong with you?"

"Payback."

She turned to run into the bathroom. As she clasped onto the door handle, I flung the butchers knife into her back. She let go of the doorknob stretching her arm to touch the blade. I walked up to her and yanked it out as blood gushed out of the wound. She fell to the floor in silence. I was going to start with the chopping but she was dead. I let her bleed to death until I didn't hear her heart beating.

It took some doing, but I cleaned the house from top to bottom. I didn't want any of my prints in that house at all. I put the two of them into the closet so they could be hand in hand once more. The plane was already gone but I didn't care. I could come back any time. However I did try that country buffet days later after I was all done and it was very good, even if an old hillbilly did pick it out.

I sat there staring at the telephone, which was ringing this horrible dinging noise in my ears. I did not want to move at all but it could be my brother or that special someone I long to hear from.

"Hello," I said in my most non-energetic tone.

"Hey Alex, are you coming back to work? I know you arrived back from your trip not too long ago. You don't have to come in, I mean, it's not an emergency. Look, we got some new cars and we've been getting some calls from some foreigners. I think they want an assembly line there. They want to set up a meeting with you."

"Alright buddy, I'll be down there soon."

It was Mr. Gale, who was the only one who called me by my first name. I guess they miss my presence. I do go all out for my employees and we pick up lunch for the whole crew.

I was lying naked on the floor, hoping my death was on its way but instead I was forced to make an appearance for all of my seeds. I usually dressed in suits but today I was wearing jeans, a button up long sleeved, and a blazer. My hair was a little messy but I didn't care.

I made it to work just fine in my Camero, which I drove on and off. I ignored everyone as I walked in the building. They said their hellos to me but I blocked everyone out. It's always hard to get back on your feet when you've been off of them for a short while. As soon as I walked into his office, I closed the door for my solitude. I threw my briefcase onto my desk, which flew onto the floor as I slid on.

I went over some of the paperwork that was on my desk, which had yellow slips with messages on them. Everything was simple. Some Germans and a few Danish foreigners wanted to get some of my cars out there to sell on their lots. I had my secretary set up a meeting for me. In the wall behind a picture of my brother and I was my safe. I pulled out twenty thousand dollars. It didn't matter how much I took out of there it was my money.

I took off to my brothers' house after work. I bought a scooter for them each. It was the largest and the coolest looking ones they had at the toy store. When I walked in the house, I had nothing in my arms.

"Hey everybody, Alex is here." Said my sister in law. I gave her a hug as I walked into the living room.

Tony was in the kitchen drinking beer with a couple of his friends. My nephews were sitting in front of the television. They were glued to the TV and I wanted them to see that there was more to life than this fake stuff on TV. I kneeled next to the two on the floor. "Hey, it's Uncle Alex, give me a hug." They hugged me tightly. "I missed you guys." I said to them.

"We missed you too uncle." Said the older one. He sat down; he couldn't miss the part where superman defeated the terrorist. The younger one sat still with me his eyes still on the tube. "I missed you a whole lot."

"Well I have a surprise for the two of you." They looked up and smiled. With me, they knew I was always bringing them something they had wanted. I didn't ever try to out gift Tony, as long as he said it was okay, I would get them what they wanted. I went outside and came back the door popping my head in. "Okay, yah gotta come out here to see it. The two came outside to see my surprise. They jumped up and down in excitement yelling thank you. All that hugging and praising were different from my average killing sprees but it was well worth it.

I pulled them around back so that they could ride them in the backyard. The curtain was open and my brother held up his beer as he watched his sons riding around. "Hey, they wanted those."

"I hope they're okay on those things." Said Jennifer.

"Oh they're big enough. Don't worry about them."

My brother threw a pillow at me as I walked through the sliding door from the back. "Aye, why you touch'n my wife when you're coming up in here?" He laughed. He stood and we gave a smacking on the back, hug. "Later tonight man, we'll toke up. Just wait for my sons to go to sleep." He hardly ever called his sons boys. *Boy* was a term over used in our time.

I could see he was drunk and happy, having a good time. "Could you cut my hair today?"

"You ain't gonna cut that shit. It's already short. It's cool, I'll cut your hair. Like what, cause I don't want to fuck it up since I'll be fucked up?"

"Shave it off."

"Shave it off? That'll look cool. Let me do it right now, while I'm not too messed up."

The two of us went into the bathroom. It was quiet in my mind while Tony held the clippers over my head. I was thinking about the parents I left for dead back at the house that would surely send me insurance papers saying that the house would be fully paid since the owners had died. My brother was going on about what he was up to and how things were at work.

In the midst of everything he was saying, I broke his sentence as I said, "have you heard anything from Uncle Mike?"

He looked at me strangely. "Not lately but he drops by every so often."

"Tony, you're my only brother and my best friend. I need to trust you with something. What do you say, we toke outside and have a serious chat?" He nodded his head not knowing what I had to tell him. But in all honesty, he could be serious and understanding.

My head was shaved, and it looked good. The two of us went outside while Jennifer began to make snacks. We had some joints we already lit one for each of us. I needed my cigarettes for something I would never utter again.

"So what's up little brother?" He asked me. "I want to know what's on my buddies mind."

"Tony, I can say this to you now, I am more thankful to you above anyone in this world for saving me when we were kids." This was a touchy subject that he never talked about since we were reunited in my uncle's home.

"I know that, you don't have to say it." He took a drag of his cigarette looking away which was the signal that told me he did not want to get into this.

"Well I wanted to say it out loud. They were killing me out there." He still would not look at me.

"Well good, I'm glad we both survived." He patted me on the shoulder, flicked his cigarette to the ground, and then turned to walk away.

I grabbed him by the shoulder. "Don't walk away from this conversation Ton! I need you to talk about these things." My voice was serious.

"What's there to talk about man? That you still call them? And go out there to buy them a house and whatever they want. You thank me now about saving you but you must not remember things that they did, but I do." He turned around pointing his finger in my face. "You act like they were good parents and they did something for you when they really just dumped on us. So what do you want from me? What do you want me to say about them? I hope they die! I honestly hope that they are in their graves rotting now, instead their living it up probably beating on each other because it turns them on."

"They are." I said in a low voice.

"What did you say?"

"Nothing. Look I know you think I don't remember anything but I do. I remember when my big brother ran away because he was being beaten with a belt buckle. I remember the blood on your back. I remember you crying. I remember when they locked me outside of the house to sleep in the shed. You think I don't feel anything?" He turned around with his hands at his waist. "I do. And you think that I bought them a house to make them happy. I saw something within myself. I owed you . . . and I owed them."

"Owed them what! What the fuck did they ever do for you, to make you think that you owed them anything in this world? In fact they owed us! There are things locked up in my head," his finger pointed at his right temple, "that I can't let anyone know!" He swung his hand down from his head in anger. "They beat the life out of me and I won't ever want to be reminded of that."

"Oh you think you're the only fuck'n one. You know that in the entire world, I would only give up my life for one person and that my friend is you. My brother. And while you were gone, *I* was beat up, *I* was locked out of the house, *and I* was locked in the closet. And I ruined it all by having to go back. But I'll tell you one thing, I trust you with my life."

My brother put up his hands. "This is fuck'n getting out of hand. What am I doing even talking about this?"

"I'll tell you why I brought this up. But you can not tell a soul." I grabbed his arm really tight, so tight that it must have hurt him because he made this face of pain. "Do you trust me?"

"Come on bro."

"*Do you trust me?*"

"Yeah, yeah. Of course I fuck'n do. I trust only you."

"What I have to say can end my life forever."

"Alright take it easy. What's a matter with you? Hey kid brother don't fuck'n lose it right now."

"Well, it's kind of fucked up but here it goes . . . Mom and Patrick are dead, Tony."

He laughed out loud as he pulled away from me laughing harder than I had seen him laugh. "What's this a joke? You drag all this shit up to make me crack up? What was the point of that?"

I made this face that showed how very disappointed I was. He turned and looked at me with sympathy. "Yeah, okay, you think this is a joke." He had his hand on my arm leaning on me with a smile. "You say you trust me yet you can't even be serious right now."

"Well I was until you said something stupid like this."

"*Tony*, they are dead." I said gritting my teeth with a low voice. "I killed them. I fuck'n beat the shit out of Patrick until he died. I chopped him up."

Tony made this worried face. He shook his head as he put his arm around my head. "Stop it brother. Don't freak yourself out. I don't want to lose you to your insanity."

I began to whimper a little. "I'm not crazy." I began to shake my head then I pulled away pushing him off. "I'm not crazy. I killed them a few days ago. You don't know about it because they haven't been missing yet. They're in their bedroom closet both dead. I did it for you."

"Alex, you're starting to freak me out."

"Alright fine you don't want to believe me, fine, I'm out of here." I started walking to my car.

"Hold up it's a little hard to swallow. It's a crazy story."

"Crazy, huh?" I stood there with tear stains on my cheeks. "Okay, your little brother is telling stories. Like I said, it's all about trust."

"Why would you say that to me, knowing how I feel?" He demanded with anger.

"So you would be relieved of the truth. And so would I. And now that they're gone, I feel a sense of life come back to me." I pulled off my belt and gave it to him with the buckle in my palm. "Here's your proof if you can remember this."

With his mouth open he took the belt slowly shaking. I was afraid he wouldn't ever talk to me again. His eyes squinted in this disapproving look, as if he couldn't believe it was real. "Alex . . . What have you done?"

I started walking to my car. "I released us." I unlocked the door to my car as he stood there staring at the belt. Then he smacked it onto the ground yelling. "Please don't turn me in." I said.

He walked up to me in a power walk. "Turn you in? You are my savior" I saw the tears in his eyes. He held out his arms and we hugged, then laughed, then cried, and let go . . . of everything.

CHAPTER 12

I watched his yuppie scum face laugh out loud in that annoying tone of voice. I had a cigarette in one hand and a glass of whiskey in the other. We were supposed to be having a short meeting in my office. He seemed to be the high light of the day. His face was getting on my nerves. It was the way his nose had a little peak at the end of it making it look like a *dicknose* as I call it.

He was wearing a turtleneck and a blazer of very expensive brand. He was talking on about his business and how well it was doing. I couldn't understand why my rich business associates would send me this guy. He was joking and not getting on with what was important. I found that he was wasting my time. I should thank them later for this useless meeting. I couldn't take it anymore.

"Alright, I think it's time we end this meeting. I'm going to lunch." I said as I put out my cigarette in a very artsy ashtray.

"Well, okay." He stood up, as I was ready to walk him out of my office. "Where do you like to dine?"

"Alone." I looked at him with my eyebrows hanging low over my eyes.

He didn't get the hint. He smiled at me. "Funny." He touched my hand. "But I know this great place that serves spectacular linguini."

I smiled at him leaning forward. "Does anyone know you're here today?"

He moved his head back a little. "Just my secretary."

I moved his hand off of mine. I sat down in my chair then leaned back in my seat. "Well you get on the phone and tell her you've left my office and are on the highway now. You should be there in no time."

He frowned. "Oh, okay."

"Just don't let anyone know of our lunch together because it could be fatal to my reputation. Maybe even yours."

He smiled while he looked down in the carpet then tried to graze his finger over my palm. "Okay, as long as we both understand each other."

"Oh yes we do. How about you follow me to my condo."

He put on his coat as we walked out. I told my secretary to reschedule this yuppie in for another meeting because I had somewhere important to be. He stayed behind as I walked out. I told him to follow my Camero when he reaches the corner store up the block. I made sure that no one saw the two of us coming into the building.

As we walked into my place, he looked around with his mouth opening wide into a smile. "This is great. I love the art, you seem to have good taste don't you."

He sat down on the couch as I stood in the dining room staring at him wondering what he would do or say next. He patted the seat on the couch next to him. "Why don't you sit down."

I had my head down with my eyes looking up at him. I was thinking about something he was far off from believing. I picked up my head trying to smile at the bastard. I walked over to him and planted myself into the seat very uncomfortably. I sat on the edge of my seat not staring at him.

"Did you make the call?" I asked. He nodded his head, as he was about to run his fingers across my hand. I faced him then said, "You want to see my bathroom. I just had it rebuilt the way I like." He smiled at me. I stood up extending my hand out so that he could take it. I knew he was a homosexual. It was up close and in your face but not flaunting. I didn't want to be in a situation where I would be raped by a yuppie.

The voices began to talk in the back of my head, behind my ears as if they were parched right on the rim. They were making my head feel dizzy as they swarmed out lightly in a faded shade. Sometimes I wish they would let me work alone. I stood in the doorway of the bathroom. He looked at the black marble tub with a smile that reached ear to ear.

"Go ahead, try it out."

"Are you sure?" He asked.

He undressed himself in my presence and I thought I could stand there staring at him without smirking or feeling uncomfortable, but I looked away for I wanted to throw up at the sight of a naked man wanting to touch me. He had the water running with bubbles. He then set himself into the water. He looked at me as he lowered himself in. "Are you getting in?"

"Sure." I said nonchalantly. I striped down to nothing as he watched. I carefully placed my clothes onto the chair in the corner of the bathroom. He looked at my body then down at my penis.

"I knew you were something special," he said while he grazed his fingers through the bubbles. He turned off the water. I put my feet in the water. He moved closer so he could kiss me. I backed away. "What's wrong?" He asked.

"I should get some wine. I have some in the kitchen. I'll be right back." As I stood up he was looking down there again. I rolled my eyes. "Did you want this?" I pointed to myself. Like a child wanting a toy, he nodded his head with seriousness.

I grabbed a bottle of wine and two glasses. I handed him a glass as I set myself back in. He held it out as he spoke in that snobby tone. He wanted me to pour the wine into his glass as he spoke about parts of the world where the wine was good and where it was horrible.

I held the bottle tightly as he spoke almost breaking it in my fist. I smacked him in the head as hard as I could. The bottle busted over his head. He tried to get out of the tub but it was slippery and he slid back in. I jumped on him and banged his head on the tub as hard as I could. He began to lose grip. I grabbed him by the neck and held him under water. He kicked and splashed water all over my beautiful tiled floor. I had the tiles special made and put in one at a time.

Blood mixed with the water in the tub. I held down that yuppie as he tried to fight for his life. He stopped kicking as he and death met face to face. Yet death had no face, just empty deception of his own lies.

In the end it was a big mess. I drained the water and the blood from the tub. It took me a long while but I chopped him up into small parts; forearm; calf; torso. What I managed to do was wrap each piece into a plastic bag. Then I would wrap each piece into newspaper like butchers do. After I was done, I put it all in a suitcase. I couldn't leave this mess so I cleaned from crack to cranny. When I was done I took a long shower.

I drove the suitcase out to the Dumpster far from home. Afterward I went out to eat a large bloody steak.

She turned her head to the side in the bright lights that shined all around the area. Cotton candy, hot dogs, and rides. It was a wonder of what makes the world turn. Was it this merry-go-round that spins us to happiness and freedom? Was it the drugs that made us loose all reality? Was it love or hate, death and the living, friend or foe?

I could see how it was different for everyone. It was her that made my world go down and stop spinning. My life stops as they walk passed me. Her long brown hair was soft a luxurious enough to be on a Pantene commercial.

The dress she was wearing reminded me of Kelly Bundy, from, "Married with Children," the spandex only *she* could look good in. Her lips matched the purple of her dress with tones of red like a pedal.

Now tell me . . . how can a girl dress in such a way that attracts the dirtiest men and not get raped? To me she looked like a tramp. She has nothing up here where it counts so to make up for it she shows what she does have. Maybe she just wanted to dress like that one time and I'm catching her at the wrong place. I know that deep down inside, underneath that pretty face, she's nothing but a substitute for the wife that didn't want to come, the girl who picked a fight for no reason.

She was escorted by a tall thin man, very frail, with a large overcoat, and a hat to match. His face was hidden and I couldn't see his features at all. The light shined on her. And as she glanced at me her eyes flashed red. That was not unreal; it was plain and simple that the whore of a devil lies under her panties. I had to meet her.

I didn't plan to come here tonight. I suppose that people have already been picked by the voices and I just do what I am told. I walk through the crowds of families all alone with no one holding my hand. I saw a haunted house, the only ride that really caught my eye. I heard this company made close to the scariest haunted houses. So I had to see for myself.

No one noticed me to be different from the rest. I had on a baseball cap just like any regular Joe here. I was wearing a plain jean jacket and pants. Underneath my cap I had on a blonde wig. I held my head low so no one could see my face and what features lie underneath the alterations.

I looked around the amusement park to see the world revolve around me when two little girls should happen to run into me almost knocking me down and stubbing my foot. I grabbed one of them with the anger of a swollen toe still vibrating in the shoe. I held them still, close to me, so they could see they made me mad. I bent down holding both at one arm.

In my most polite voice, I tried to sound like a decent man. "It may be fun at a carnival kids, but you need to watch where you are going. There are a lot of crazy people out here who might want to hurt children with no parents who are running around bumping into people. Just be glad you didn't run into a serial killer or something." I laughed out loud.

"Oh thank you so much." I heard a woman's voice. I let go of the little girls and stood up. "These girls have been running from me all night. It's not easy being a mother."

I smiled at her in disbelief. She should keep kids like these on a leash. She's right; keeping up with little brats like these is a hard job for such a big mother. There is such a thing as taking control. "Especially since you have two." I tried to break the silence.

"Try five." She smiled.

"Wow, five children."

"Well thank you sir. And god bless you."

"Oh I don't believe in god. But if you believe strong enough in him, he might save you from damnation." I said in a Pastures voice. I found the subject hilarious for I was only a believer in what came to me in my dreams and in my daytime life and whisper in my ears no matter where I was.

I watched the women scurry away with her kids, looking back at me as she did with that face of horror and fright. Her eyes gleamed at me as if God himself had glowed safety in her eyes. I looked away then continued on my direction. On my part as another idiot, I bumped into someone. I looked up and saw it was the red eyes.

"What the fuck is wrong with you?" She asked. The thin man was standing behind her with his head down.

I took off my hat and sort of bowed in apology. "I'm sorry miss." I wanted her to see my face before she said goodbye.

She looked at me with her eyebrows squinting in anger as I put my hat back on. I helped her stand up as she was fixing herself. She brushed off her arms then straightened her dress. She acted like I just dropped her in a puddle of mud. I looked at the thin man. "I'm sorry that I knocked your girlfriend down."

"Oh she'd not my girlfriend." He said strangely.

She came closer to me. "You need to be careful, I might have been hurt." I smiled at her shrugging. "I know you don't I?" She shook her finger at me. "You look familiar." She looked at my face as I was trying to turn away. "I know that face somehow. Are you on TV or something? Did you do a commercial once?"

"You have the wrong guy."

"Well you look like someone from a commercial." She walked passed the tall man and he followed like he was her servant. Still, he hid his face and I found it odd how he walked and tried to be hidden just as I was that night. I saw the demon in her, in her eyes. Everything went silent in my ears but the whole village was chaotic. She called my name. The notion was in my head that I had been sent for her. The pain drifted as I drifted through the crowd like a ghost that no one saw.

My stomach growled and I grabbed a bite to eat at a food stand. Places like this always had good corn dogs. Here I was, wanting to laugh at myself, holding a hot dog in one hand and a soda in the other. As I ate the dog, I looked at the people thinking about how there was nothing in this world that would relate me to them. The only one I ever click with was my brother. And I think he forgave me that day when I told him what I had done.

I washed out my mouth with the Pepsi I held in my hand as I continued on my journey through the crowded *fun park*, though I wasn't having much fun. There were some teenage gang members there. They didn't even know what the meaning of a gangster was. The term gangster, when it was first used, was used on real Mafia members.

I went on a couple of rides that were a little fun, but how do you smile and laugh with when you're all alone? I just kept this half smile, as I was becoming dizzy. The exit was facing the haunted house. There didn't seem to be a line. As a matter a fact, it was closed. But it just leaves me to go in the back doors to the very front of the entrance. It was dark. The sound effects were loud and some of the crying reminded me of the tortured girl who whispers into my ears on occasion. I walked through the cemetery, which had gooey skeletons and bloody bodies popping out of their graves.

I heard a voice that wasn't *hers*. It sounded different. I thought it might be one of the voices calling to me in new tones of laughter. I hid behind a statue of a women with a knife in her throat. I have a visual, I said to myself as if I were in the military with a pair of binoculars.

"How much is it?" Said the man.

"Seventy five dollars." Said the woman.

I got down on my knees to peek over. It took me a little while to spot who was in there secretively talking. It was she, the brown haired girl in the tight dress with the tall man. The tall man had his hat off and I could see his face crystal clear.

They were sitting in one of the carts for the ride. I saw his blue eyes reflecting off of his glasses propped on his large pointed nose. His blonde hair was cut real short almost a flat top, which made him look intimidating. His jacket was opened wide and the girl was sitting next to him in a sexy pose.

He handed her some money. She grabbed it instantly without counting it. She slipped it down her bra then lifted her leg to sit on top of him swinging her hair around as she did. She smiled at him then started kissing him on the face and neck.

"What do you want?"

He began to unzip his pants but she stopped him. She got down on her knees and unzipped his pants with her teeth. I wanted to laugh. Here I was, watching some guy and his hooker get it on. What a predicament. He was grunting as she did what he suggested to her. I sat there on one knee with my elbow resting on my other knee laughing to myself. I turned away for a moment, as he was talking dirty to her. I can only imagine what I would do if I were him.

I was not prepared for what would happen next. It was my imagination that there are things in this world that people despise like your average everyday rude person or snobby or being racist but this night tops everything I ever believed in myself.

"I'm coming!" He moaned. And she began to work harder at it to make him feel like it was the best head he had ever gotten. He was pushing her head down so far I'm sure she couldn't breathe for moments at a time. He held firmly onto her hair, yanked her head back, and then with his left hand; he jabbed a knife into her neck. Cum and blood shot out of her mouth spraying onto the floor. I could hear her gasping for breath.

That wasn't the worst part. As the tall man pulled her and his knife back, above them and around them were shadows swirling around like they were going crazy. The shadows were moaning lightly and stayed close by the hooker. Her blood was spilling out onto the floor. She held her neck gasping for breath falling to the ground fighting for her life. The tall man just crawled out of the cart and cleaned himself off like it was nothing.

He looked at the girl who was now dead and the shadows were gone, tilted his head to the side as he stared at her. "Oh you were such a whore. And I don't like your kind." He laughed.

I knew he might find me. I wanted to hurry out of there but I fell back and my shoe tapped the ground, which echoed in the room. He looked up and scanned the room for me. I began to crawl backward out of there and rushed into the crowd. I know he wasn't far behind me. But I leaped into the rushing families and scrambled to my car.

I sat in my car, thinking about how fast my heart was beating afraid I was going to get caught watching, a fellow similar to me. In ways I can't explain, I let it go and it never bothered me of what I saw. He did what some sane people daydream about their bosses or ex-spouses.

I believe she wasn't as good at head as she pretended to be.

CHAPTER 13

It was one day, one single mistake that changes my decisions from here on out. I can't believe how sloppy and uncontrollable I become once I have done my part. It seems like this mistake might be the end of me. As soon as I had done the unthinkable, I ran home like a child in trouble and locked up every window and door in my condo.

I have to stop the rush in my head. I sit here on the floor trying not to think about what I had done, but it repeats in my head over and over.

There was this girl who wouldn't leave me alone. I was at this bar drinking the night before. A brunet walked up to me with pick up lines like I couldn't believe. She thought I was the hottest thing she had seen in a long time, which is probably just another line. She wouldn't let up. So I left the bar.

Three am I'm walking to my car to go home a little drunk and she walks up to my car asking me if I could give her a ride because her car was messed up. I asked her if she was a hooker and she laughed like it was unheard of. Yes, she was attractive but I didn't want her. So, knowing how I am, one can only assume what I did to her.

My mistake was in the alley near a dumpster. My mistake is giving me pains all over my body making me feel like all my organs are going out. I had her body propped over my shoulder so I could dump her in the large can. I toss her body into the pit of hell with her legs half hanging out. I jump on the side of the can so I could shove her body lower into the filth. A flashlight is shined into my face as I had my arms banging down her body. My heart was in my throat as I tried to see what it was.

"Say, whatcha doing down there buddy?"

"Just getting rid of some trash that was in my car."

"Getting rid of trash at four in the morning? That's a bit strange." He moved the light away from my face and I saw it was a police officer. He was in full uniform with badge, gun, and even the jacket. "I'll tell yah what, you go stand over there for a minute while I see what you're doing out here." He clicked off his flashlight then set it back into his belt. He walked up to me and handcuffed me. I could hear his walkie-talkie going off as we all hear when we get pulled over. I stood where he told me as he stepped to the plate with his flashlight. I knew he would see the girl. I hadn't even had a chance to bury the broad.

He must have been new to the force because he cuffed me in the front. As he tipped down, I knew he saw it, for Christ's sakes her legs were still up in the air. I pulled out my knife, stabbed him in the back, and shoved him in the can. I had to climb the can, with my hands cuffed together. When I jumped in, he had his hand on his back trying to hold back the pain. I saw his face when he was head to head with the dead girl. His eyes were wide like a cartoon and his mouth dropped open. He reached for his gun. I swung down into his back again.

He was no older than twenty-one years old. I saw the fear in his eyes, which will haunt me forever. I had not hurt anyone who didn't deserve it and now I crossed the line. It's hurting me now more than ever. I've been sitting here tearing and drinking, losing my mind over the things I had done in my life and where I ended up. I don't even know if what I saw was real. Were the voices just a mental illness?

It's been dark in my house for days. I haven't eaten, just drank liquor and when I'm sober, water. I can't think of food right now. All I can see was that innocent boy's face when he was dying next to the other girl. I should have just left him alone. I can't change the past. All I can do is move on or dwell on it. I just can't let this one go.

I try to figure out what is making me feel so remorseful and how I could get over it repeatedly in my head but I can't find any way to move forward. I don't deserve to live. No one sees the value of true friendship or love for what it's worth like I do. And that's where my hatred becomes theirs. People want to take and never give. I can't control myself any longer. I'm losing my sanity at times especially times like this one.

I tried before to fit in with the rest of the crowd. I couldn't get involved with the music that's on the radio and MTV but I did try to look as though others shopping at the Gap and Banana Republic but I just can't see myself as others and I quit. My psychiatrist says he's never met anyone like me before. I have the ability to be insane yet I know what reality is. I had never told him about the things I really did. I told him more of the things that hurt.

Until the chance came when I closed my eyes and finally fell asleep, I had lost my head and began to lose all grip of life. I suffered from insomnia on occasion but this has been ridiculous. My eyes had gone completely red with delusion.

There are moments where you can't hear anything and it feels poetic to be so inapt to life that you feel positively free.

Sprinkles float down from the sky with the wind being all that made a noise for miles away. To my left was a house with a roof covered in white snow. The house was surrounded by a brown picket fence looking as though the snow that covered the grass was marshmallow and the picket fence being gingerbread.

My body wasn't cold though I was naked from head to toe with snow sliding down my body like ice melting on a stove. I could barely feel the coldness of the flakes that fell upon my face. Every step I took was crunch; crunch as if I were walking on rice crispies with my feet sinking in with each step.

To my right up ahead was a dark green forest with snow on the ground making me realize that it was like paradise the way the snow quieted the world and just fell upon us like crystals. The forest was nerve racking. My curiosity was to roam the world not caring that I was stripped of all dignity. I held onto the branches of the tress to hold myself up. My body was weak and felt like I had ran ten miles non-stop gasping for air. The trees seemed dead the way they hardly held any color.

In the depths of the trees, losing myself, I stopped in my wondering where there were tombstones surrounded by dead trees. There in the center was a concrete bench where someone was sitting down with their back turned toward me. They wore a black velvet cape with a hood hiding their identity that spread out on the bench like the train of a wedding dress.

I walked around the bench with my arms at my side so I could see this person who sat here in solitude. *She was beautiful.* She had dark black hair that flowed in large smooth waves under her cape. Her eyes were black but sparkled like rubies which were large and round staring at the snow that fell to the ground. Her lips were full, deep red, and rounded perfectly. Her skin was almost as pale as the snow.

She looked up at me and motioned her lips as if she were saying something I couldn't hear. It felt like she was a million miles away from me to touch her. She lifted her frail hand out of her cape and waved me to come closer to her.

I dropped to the floor putting my arms around her waist. She covered us two with her warm cape. That was all I could feel. The snow was not cold, the air wasn't freezing, and I didn't feel anything but her warm touch. There was pain that shot through my body like electric volts running through my veins. I felt like my heart was completely broken but at the same time it felt like I had been saved. Her one touch shocked me, making everything evil and ugly fade out of me. She had my life in her arms. It felt like an angel was holding me making everything that ever hurt me disappear from existence. And for that I would do anything; for her I would do anything. She was a goddess; a beautiful dream.

I let go everything to her crying in her arms, something I had longed to do but it never happened. I didn't even want to touch her intimately just hold her. I squeezed tighter with each tear that I let go of and she embraced me. I felt like we *were* making love. I couldn't think of anything to say so I just forgave myself.

She whispered in my ear, "Don't cry. Love is always feels this good." I tried to let go but it was my only sanctuary. She began to rub my head. "It's okay." Her voice sounded like there were echoes in the woods, three women talking at once in a shattering tone like acid. I didn't understand this feeling that came over me. I felt her love for me the moment her body touched mine.

I heard a crackle in the woods and my head came up out of the cape I was lost in. One dirty hand ceased out of its grave. We stood up in surprise. We watched the hand locked in a trance. A second hand popped out of its grave. They pulled themselves out, as I was too stunned to move. I didn't realize it until the silence was broken by another crack in the woods. It was my first murdered victim. Her body was naked covered in maggots and dirt. She reached her arms out to me.

Another break in the silence and another . . . another. All of them were coming back. I watched them all as I stood there; balls hanging low naked as a jailbird. There was John the guy I killed first of all the people who jumped me. The junkie from the alley. Steve completely naked and fat.

She grabbed my hand pulling me into the woods. Nick was burnt to a crisp. The model, women I had killed trying to get in bed with me. Some of them were crying, some were yelling, moaning, and some were laughing. The cop was naked with a badge attached to his chest. I screamed loudly with fear coming back to me.

They wanted me. All these people no longer existed because of me. They waited for this very moment. She yanked me as I snapped out of my trance. We ran through the forest and suddenly, *life* was real. I felt the coldness of the ground which was numbing my feet. I felt the air shivering my body and I began to grow weak and tired. She had to drag me with her to escape. We made it to the gingerbread house. She climbed over the fence and pulled me with her. It was silent in the house as we walked in. I locked the door looking out the window.

"They're out there!" I cried peeping through the window. I turned around and said, "What are we"—She was gone and the inside reminded me of the trailer I lived in with my parents. It was silent only for a moment, and there he was walking out with a bat.

"I'll teach you a lesson boy." Grunted Patrick as he stomped towards me.

I had my hand on the door. He walked right up to me smacking me in the stomach with the bat and I felt every bit of it. I fell to the ground. As I looked up my mother walked out with blood on her neck as though she wiped it away in one swoop leaving blood to dry. She had my nephews in each arm forcing them to walk up to me.

"See here, your uncle's a loser." My mother had never seen my nephews before and here they were in her arms. "We're gonna rid of you son. You were a big mistake." She laughed.

Patrick brought the bat over my head and clocked me hard. My head hit the floor and I was out. It was black for a moment. I woke up in the sat spot with blood dripping from my head. I got up with my vision blurry. I looked out the window.

Patrick had my nephews and my mother standing there staring at the house smiling. He told little John something and John walked up to the house crying. He dropped a match over a puddle. It flared up in a roar. John ran back to Patrick. I started to scream trying to open the door but it was bolted shut. I began to yell. And that's when I heard the grunting of so many voices. I turned around and the house was filled with my own victims. Lifeless bodies were laughing and walking about as if it were nothing unordinary. I tried to break the window but it was solid like steel. I looked out the window again screaming for them to let me out as the smoke was filling the house and I could see the flames outside spreading like dominos.

Patrick held up John who was crying with his arms out to me. My mother walked up smiling with a knife in her hands. She pressed it up against John's neck sliding it across. I could hear the tearing of the skin from inside of the house as the dead were trying to tear apart my body.

"No!" I screamed out loud, waking up with sweat all over my body and tears streaming down my face. "This has got to stop. I can't go on like this anymore."

I let everything out of my stomach into the toilet. When I looked in the mirror my eyes were red, my facial hair was growing in all directions, and my teeth were sticky. I shaved everything but the goat tee. I took a hot shower trying to wake myself from my dreams. They were continuous.

I went to breakfast and ate like I was stoned. I had realized then, I was in my house losing my mind for seven nights and today on the eighth day I need to get it together. I didn't know what I wanted anymore. After the cop I was lost.

I went to work, which I shouldn't have done until I saw a doctor about what I couldn't conclude on my own what was real and what wasn't. What I felt was real in my dream, what I saw seemed real, and what I heard seemed real.

When I came into the shop they were working on a Chevy truck. I wish I had been there to deal with all of the details. In the corner was a 1936 Ford. The paint was chipping badly, and half of it was covered in rust. They were called Buggy's back in the day.

I was disturbed on the way in with mindless chats here and there.

"Sir where have you been? We left messages on your machine. This place hasn't been the same without you." Said one of the secretaries. "We were kind of worried you were sick or something. Is everything okay with you?"

I paused for a second and tried to look surprised. "Yeah everything seems to be just fine."

She looked at me strangely and handed me a stack of papers. "Okay . . . Here are all of your messages. Some gentleman called about five times and said his name was McKrackin or something. European I think."

"Thanks."

I went into my office. She stood in the doorway with her bushy curly hair poofed out. I looked at her funny then looked at my desk. "Could you get me some coffee please?"

"Right away."

She walked out and I was relived she wasn't hovering over me with this look that made me feel like I was crazy. I looked at a couple of files on my desk when Mr. Gale walked in with my coffee. He placed it in front of me. I removed my reading glasses. I looked at a contract then at him.

"Gale, you make sure all these files here have full report on the condition, cause I don't want you buying a piece of crap for too much. We're not going to make much of a profit if we waste our money."

"I have all the reports in my office. I'll make copies and have your secretary file them in for you."

I took a sip of my coffee looking up at him.

"I want you to know I trust you to make good decisions while I'm not around. In fact you can run this place by yourself." I began to rub my eyes really hard.

"How's it going sir? Are you okay?"

"What do I look like? A fuck'n nut head?"

"I just asked a simple question. Don't snap at me."

"I'm only snapping because everyone is asking me what's the matter; am I okay; where have I been?"

Frank walked in and Mr. Gale quickly walked out the door. He looked back at me. "I can run everything if you need me to but you don't need to fall apart here in the office with people who have been dedicated to you." He kept on as Frank gave him this look of concern.

"Is he okay sir?"

"Oh his just a crazy old fuck. He thinks I've been acting weird lately, I don't see it. Anyway, sit down Frank; talk with me. Tell me what's been going on."

Frank sat down a little uneasy. He gave me a fake smile holding a book tightly in his arms. He sat it flat on his lap. I looked at him up and down with my eyes frowning on his expression. "What's wrong with you? Why are you giving me weird smiles? Don't beat around the bush, I don't have the time."

"*Nothing* sir. Well it just looks like you have a lot of work that will keep you busy. I don't want to take up your time."

"No, no. It's cool. Just sit back and relax." I leaned back in my chair trying to make him feel at ease yet I was very uncomfortable. I looked at his book. "Whatcha got there?" All I saw were these blue swirling colors.

"Oh it's just a school book. I have to do a report on underwater sea creatures."

"I hope work doesn't interfere with school."

"Oh no sir."

"Underwater sea creatures are a fascinating study. I've gone scuba diving quit a bit of times. It's awesome being part of the underwater world. There are things down there you couldn't imagine existed."

"Well it was just a report not a major study."

"So you want to be a smart ass when I wanted to share a bit of information that might have helped you with your *little* report?"

"Oh no sir, I would never do anything of the sort."

I stood up. Nobody talks to me like that, making me feel stupid. I was one with that part of my life. "Get the hell out of here!" I pointed at the door as he had fear in his eyes. "Get the fuck out and don't come back in here until you can show me respect!" I yelled.

He rushed out of my office grasping his book. I looked out of my office door and everyone was staring. I walked towards the door. "Well whatcha staring at? Get back to work!" I slammed my office door heading back to my desk.

Then I realized I was acting like a psycho. What was wrong with me today? I knew right then I couldn't work like this. I was losing my mind. I couldn't take the pressure anymore. I didn't want to be anywhere near my wonderful shop of success. Everything was getting worse. My sleep was constant. I can hardly see things for what they are. The voices are changing speaking to me in devilish groans of madness. My dreams are getting to me almost into my reality.

I did wrong by yelling at the boy for something so trivial as the oceans' beauty.

I went into the shop in front of the receptionist. "Listen up everyone," I called. Everyone stopped what they were doing. "On my behalf, I apologize for my behavior. It was very unprofessional and unacceptable of me. So if you will please forgive me, then it would be greatly appreciated. I'm just a little defensive today and haven't been sleeping too good."

Mr. Gale walked up to me grabbing my arm. "Come on Mr. Dugan let's get some work done." He was acting like he was the caregiver and I was the baby. But I gladly walked back with him. I didn't have a lot of files to look over. As I walked away, everyone smiled and waved at me.

Walking into my office, Mr. Gale was right behind me. That's when I remembered I scared Frank. I turned around. "Mr. Gale, do me a favor and get that guy from make ready, Frank. I'd like to have a word with him.

"Not if you're going to yell at him."

"No. No. I just need to apologize to him. I didn't mean to snap at him." I slapped him softly as if he were a kid.

"Yes sir. Maybe you could calm yourself by looking through your paperwork." He walked out with a look of worry. But I was fine.

"After today, I'm going to give you permission to verify all of these files yourself. You won't need me anymore."

I sat back down. I still had the same file in front of me. I signed it then grabbed another. Hmm. We sold a 1961 Porsche for the price of 32,000 dollars. That sounds about right. He paid by check. That Porsche was hard to sell with a forty thousand-dollar price tag on it. But it had a faster engine than most with all the trimmings. Another file . . . Frank walked in with fear written all over his face. Mr. Gale shut the door behind him.

"Sit down son."

He sat down with empty hands. "Mr. Gale said you wanted to see me."

"Yeah, I sure do." I stood up then he back up in his seat. He looked as though he thought I was going to hit him. "Calm down boy, you're giving me jitters. I just wanted to say," I stood behind him with my hands at his shoulders. "I'm sorry for getting offended. I didn't know what I was thinking. I guess things are a little hectic for me now. I just need to get with the program."

"It's okay sir. Very understandable." He said giving me a smile. "How was your vacation?"

"It was *killer*. And I do mean killer. And you, what's happening in your life? Are you still with that sweet gal?"

"Yeah. She's great. But she can be a nag sometimes."

"Let me tell you something from experience . . . *They're all nags.*" I gave him this crazy look.

"Sir, may I ask why you're not married?"

"If you stay with them too long, they either mess around on you or they nag far too much." I gave him a smile. "If you ask me, I just don't trust women now a days. They're all pretty much sluts."

Frank laughed. "Yeah, that's for sure. But I'm sure you'll find the right girl someday who'll be faithful to you."

CHAPTER 14

As cold as my blood is, I still love my brother and his family. My brother to me is a saint if I ever believed in one. He'd do anything for me. I sure would for him. He's a real man. I know he sometimes smokes weed but he can change all that in a second. He won't overdose on my nephews. If I stuck around for them to see me as I really am, they might turn out as insane as me. I would never want them like that. My brother will show them the right way to go.

My brother has his own life story. He sticks by me like no other friend.

Friends don't mean anything. We stab each other in the back and expect everything to be okay. I remember when friends actually meant something. Being true to each other was something I looked for in a friend. If they slipped, we'd be there to catch them. When they stopped being true, so did I. I should have just left. I should have never looked their way.

I don't know exactly how my brother feels about what I did to our parents but I know he's not mad at me for what I had done. He might be glad they're gone from all hope they might hurt us again. I shall never forget my stepfathers' face when I knocked him over the head. He was frightened of me that time, not a scared little boy as he always thought me to be.

"Hey Alex, come in." Said my sister in Law.

My nephews were riding on their bikes and my brother was smoking a cigarette while cooking over the grill. I gave Jennifer a hug then a large bag of chips and a twenty-four pack of beer.

"Thanks." She put the food down where everyone was sitting. Mostly her family. I had met them many times before on visitations. There were no Dugan's there. Just my uncle, from my father's family.

"Hey uncle Mike." I said.

He shook my hand. "I haven't seen you for the longest time. What have you been up to?" He asked as he took a drink of his beer.

"Just working."

"Yeah, heard your company was expanding." He smiled as he took another drink.

Anyway . . .

I stood there for a moment waiting for him to say something I was desperately waiting to hear.

"I'm sorry about your mother getting kill-, *passing* away." He said with the can halfway to his mouth not knowing how one was supposed to feel grief for such a prudent bitch.

"Thanks Mike." There was nothing I could say to keep a wound open that had been closed the moment they hit the floor.

"Come here, Alex." Said my brother. I walked over to him and gave him a bear hug. I could smell his good cooking. He had leg quarters and sausage laid out on the grill covered in his secret sauce. The food gave me flashes of human flesh for a moment. I'm sick but not that sick as to where I'd cook um and eat them.

"How about a cig, Tony?"

"Yeah, right there. Go ahead and grab one."

I pulled out my Zippo lighting one for each of us. "Food smells good."

"Fuck yeah. You know what's up."

"So who's that guy with the beard. Never seen him before?"

"Just her uncle. But like I give a shit. He's cool." He smacked me on the chest and said, "Aye, that guys a professional tattoo artist. He can cut us a sweet deal. I've seen his work before. Let's get a tattoo tonight. Something that symbolizes brotherhood. Cause . . . I'm proud of what you did."

When he said those words, the sounds of the outside became silent. It made me drift into the beautiful images when I was chopping apart Patrick. I wanted to tear up because it was the most emotional murder I had ever committed but he didn't know that.

"I have to say, I didn't know it was truly real, until I got the call from Texas. And I laughed so hard I almost choked."

"I didn't know what you were going to think or how you would react. I did it for you and I." I said.

I pulled out my wallet and started counting cash.

"What's up little brother?" Asked Tony. I handed him about thirty-five hundred dollars. "What the fuck is this for?"

"Well buy yourselves something nice for all of you."

"You know I can't except this."

"Yes you can. Because if I get caught for what I did, I wanted to at least have given you something before I was caught. Please keep it Tony. You can save it for the boy's college or you can make a payment on your house. Just keep it."

"Alright. But I don't know why you do this all the time. And you won't get caught, I'll be your alibi."

"I still can't stop thinking about what you did. It was very brave of you to take on the world before you could drive." He nodded his head.

"I'm afraid I might have to make a run for it. This is probably our last visit for a while. Besides I've been wanting to get away."

"What the fuck are you talking about?" He asked as he flipped over some ribs.

"I don't think I can talk about all of my problems with you."

"So who yah gonna talk to about them if not me?"

"I'm not what you thought I was."

"Tell you what brother, let's eat a massive dinner and then when I've gotten you drunk enough, you can talk with me in your car so no one will hear us, okay."

"Alright."

I had a large bowl of corn chowder, which was the best I've ever tasted. The TV was on the music was loud. Everyone was talking and drinking beer. In the midst of thinking that my brother was my only family, I created an idea for a tattoo. It would resemble what I had pictured.

I swallowed the corn chowder and headed outside where the food was done cooking. My brother was putting the last of the meat in the tray. On the picnic table there was macaroni salad, beans, chips, and mashed potatoes. The table was in line like a cafeteria. We stood there one by one filling our plates to the very rim trying to get the tallest plate possible.

My brother and I sat inside eating while everyone was chaotic outside.

"I've got an idea for a tattoo." Tony looked at me with a bar-b-queue-sauced face. "Three gargoyles right." He looked at me. "Okay but two of the gargoyles are killing one, which would represent Patrick and the others, us. It will be the same picture on each of us but at different aspects of the fight."

"Sounds cool. I like that idea."

The night died down soon. My nephews went off to bed and I read them a story making sure I could instill myself into their memories. I want to always be there for them. The light went out and I knew things would never be the same.

People left the house soon saying their good-byes and making arrangements to call one another around a certain date just so it wouldn't be awkward just walking out of the door with no actual gratefulness that they had been invited. It was always routine saying goodbye in a certain fashion.

Jennifers' uncle began to draw the picture we had described while we smoked out for a while. It was fun. It took him three hours to detail well and get in everything I want. On Tony it was another three and he didn't finish until three in the morning. It was well worth it. Since it was such harsh hellish hours, I paid him a fifteen dollars for both. He was thankful he made that much in a short period of time. I had mine on my chest and Tony had his on his back.

When it was all said and done, Tony went out to my car with me and we sat inside. It went silent within that very second. The only sound was of our clothes rubbing against the leather as we sat down. I rolled down the windows so we could smoke out. I held a beer in my hand drinking it every so often.

"So brother, what's going on?"

"I'm a little crazy and I don't want you to get me locked away or ignore me."

"Alright then, I make a vow here and now, forever that whatever you utter, I won't think less of you nor will it ever come out of my mouth."

I took a deep breath. These were things I had been holding in but couldn't let out. And now I can finally be relieved. "Alright Tony. I killed my friends back home." He went silent and looked at me strangely. His eyes were wide but looked at the ground. Then he looked back at me.

"Okay. So were these the ones who jumped you?"

"Yeah."

"Okay. Is that what's bothering you? You're feeling guilty? Is that *all* you've done?" He was sarcastic. He wasn't ready for the fifteen year murder spree I was about to lay on him.

"No." He looked at me with his eyes asking what was next. "I took out some sluts . . . and some more . . ." His mouth dropped. "And some more."

"Alex, what the fuck are you doing?"

"I knew you would think I was crazy."

"Hey this is all fine and dandy with getting rid of some jerk ass parents and some kids who screwed you over back in the day but strangers? I do have a right to respond to your shortcomings. What the fuck is going on in your head?!"

"Hey, I didn't want to tell you but you wanted to know."

"Oh yeah, I'm thinking that you were getting sick because of what you did but now I see where this is going. And you have got to calm down. What the fuck did you do that for?" He yelled.

"Because they were sluts. They didn't deserve to live. Some were cheating on their men and I didn't think that was fair."

"What fucked up in your head brother."

"You know what, I gotta go. Tell everyone I love them but I've made some mistakes in my life, and I can't turn back."

Tony closed his eyes almost in tears. He grabbed my hand real hard as if he wanted to crush my hand. "Don't do this." He lowered his head. "Don't leave. You didn't leave any evidence did you?"

"Maybe, I don't know. I have to go. There are things that I can't understand. And I would rather sort them out on my own instead of being put into a psychiatric ward or something. I want to change things and I can't stop but I can't ever go back."

"We can get you a lawyer."

"It won't work out. I promise it won't be forever that I'll be away."

"At least stay the week so you can spend serious time with us. I'll drop all of my plans for the week and we'll go camping or something. Maybe it'll give me a chance to change your mind. But you have to if you ever cared about me as a brother."

So I stayed. I let Tony know that the company was his. There won't be any money for another month because I left enough to pay bills and employees. It usually took me a month to get all my earnings back in a second. I had good consultants and we would never lose out until the day people stop making movies with older fast cars or the day when we don't drive anymore. It was a long ways away from that happening.

That week we had a good time. We took a lot of pictures and spent a lot of time talking and hanging out. It was the best week of my life. I didn't have people to talk to but him and when you hold in too long, your glad to finally let it out. He didn't ask for details but I did let him know I was a whore hunter and at first he found it hard to look into my eyes but then he forgave me enough to keep me in his life.

The way home was taken through downtown after I said my good-byes to my brother and his family. I sometimes think that things can go back to normal but my mistakes have taken over the best of me and I can't see or think straight. Maybe if I just get away for a short while, I can become myself again and get away from the voices. The voices I left out of my story to my brother.

I waited at a stoplight while my car purred like a kitten. At a bus stop next to the light stood a young girl wearing a tight dress held up by spaghetti straps. Her body and shape was showing in all forms. She looked like a slut but didn't know it. The men at the bus stop were staring at her as if they hadn't seen women in years. What made it worse was the fact that the youth of the girl was noticeable. She had plump cheeks with very horrid acne. Her eyes were round and blue. In the middle of her nose was a bump. The only thing in her hands was a purse and in her right hand she was puffing on a cigarette.

I pulled into the lane closest to where she stood just to look at her. My hands gripped onto the wheel as I tried to tell myself, "don't do it Alex. Fight it! Fight it and we can be free! It will be over if you just get help." And I told the voices in my head, I wouldn't take her life. I began to dig my nails into the palm of my hands as I held tightly to the wheel. But they came with such a rush of pain telling me it would never stop. And I was shot with a blurry furring migraine that started to make the left ear bleed a little.

The window rolled down but I didn't roll it down. I saw the voices swerve around in my car and then into my mouth. And my body froze within that very second. All I could do was look and not speak or move. They took away everything from me and I was no longer whole.

"Hey miss, do you need a ride?"

"Yeah, I could use a ride to my house, I've been stuck here forever. It's about ten miles up."

"Hop in." They opened the door for her. I yelled out, "please run!" But she never heard me. They had full control. And because I fought them, they put me in deep pain.

She got in crossing her legs. We drove off. I couldn't stop staring at her. And the more I tried to stare the more I thought her acne was horrendous. It was disgusting me. They convinced me then, I was doing what I really want to do. I tried to close my eyes and not look at her. I felt their cold hands force me to stare at her. "So what's your name?" They asked her.

"Cindy."

"Nice to meet you *Cindy*. My name is Al." Why had they taken over? How long did they have this power over me? "Where are you headed?"

"Not too far. Just stay on this road. I went to a party last night. After this guy and me hooked up, he didn't want to give me a ride home. I was sort of stuck there. But it wasn't too bad."

"How old are you?"

"I just turned seventeen a couple of months ago."

And in the million of voices all at once they told me she slept with several guys. They had passed her around like a toy. They opened my head and made me see the things she was doing the night before.

"Why? How old are you?"

"Too old for a girl your age." They smiled at her. All the while I tried to show in my eyes there was something very wrong. But it was all made into a sensitive look where she must have thought I wanted her. Their voices were moaning now with ten different female voices all at once crying and wailing. It felt like my eyes were being plucked out of my head. I couldn't squirm nor cry. Just smiled at the girl.

She put her hand on my thigh. They smiled with my eyebrows crushing down over my eyes. She started to message my leg moving deeper. They grabbed her by the arm and yanked her head down. She let out a yelp crying. I tried to stop them but they just growled at me, making the demons hold me down in my head.

"Listen you little bitch! I don't fuck whores especially kids!" Said the voices, only this time; she heard what I was hearing. They showed themselves to her. Her mouth dropped when she saw the visual of them sitting in my place with burning red eyes. Then out came a shrieking scream that made her pass out.

They brought her back to *my house* while yanking her by the hair. As soon as we got in, I locked the door then threw her onto the chair. I tied her up then covered her mouth with electric tape. They left her sitting there, trying to yelp while I grabbed my suitcase. I pushed them out of me convincing them I would kill her. So they let go. And they stayed there next to her while she cried staring at them. I knew what she was feeling because they scared me too.

I tossed my suitcase on the bed. I packed up half of my clothes. She kept trying to jump up and down; I walked up to her and smacked her lightly across the face.

"Shut up or they'll hear you!"

I had to get out. This was never going to work. There was nothing that could take this away. The voices were coming after me. I wanted to ditch them, but they lived in me, they lived off of me, feeding off of my hate and death. I untied Cindy from the chair. I hit her over the head to knock her out. I then tore the tape off of her mouth. She passed out.

I ran downstairs. I knew I was halfway safe taking the stairs, because people in this building with this lifestyle, no one ever took the stairs. I threw everything in the trunk of my Camero. Underneath my seat was a gun and a few knives. I had everything I needed. I drove out as fast as I could. I knew the most perfect place to leave her. It was along the way.

I stopped at an abandoned warehouse which was surrounded by acres of weeds and dead grass. When I got out of the car I heard kicking and screaming. I knew she had a trick in mind. If I were in her shoes, I'd use anything I could to beat me with.

I held out the gun towards her as I opened the trunk. I had my blade in my pocket. Sure enough, she had a wrench in her hands and jumped out. I had my gun at her forehead before she could swing. She let go and put up her hands.

"That's a good girl." She looked at me funny because the voice she heard before was completely different. We turned around and headed into the old building. I stood there with the gun in my hands shaking because I prayed for god to let it end. I put the gun to my head then said; "Run . . ." She turned around shivering with fright and saw me with the gun to my head. "Please go before the voices come back," I cried.

She did as she was told, trying to get out of the building. And just as I was going to pull the trigger, they screamed, "NO!" loudly in my head. They jumped into me and swung the gun towards her back. And I tried to stop it all but it was too late. The blast of the gun sent my reality back and I was in darkness for a long time.

There were walls everywhere but I couldn't see. I was blind or in darkness for a while. When I came to, I was hovering over her with a knife in my hands. Blood was on my wrists and dripping off of my fingertips as I stood up. When my eyes opened, I saw what they had done. They shot her and she died. Then they cut the skin off of her face. I could hear them laughing as they drifted off.

I screamed, and then began to cry out. What have I done to this girl? There was blood everywhere. I felt sickness all over me. I wanted to vomit and it almost came up, but disgustingly enough, I swallowed it down. With my luck they would probably analyze my vomit sample.

What have I done? What have they done? The gun was cleanly back in the car. I walked out of that building crying like a baby. They left me when I didn't want to wake up anymore. They left me to clean up their mess. I wanted to know then, was this the actual devil or was it the demons he sent doing this to me?

CHAPTER 15

Robert Miller had been working for homicide for about ten years. For the past two months he had been working on three unsolved murders; a body found in a dump sight; a girl killed in the haunted house from a city fair; and girl found behind the dumpster of some restaurant. A blade of some sort killed all, yet nothing matched together. The body found in the dumpster is missing body parts. The parts were wrapped in packages and thrown into the sight in several different places. The head has not yet been found, so the body cannot be identified.

The girl killed was not chopped apart like the first victim, but rather a quick stab to the neck. She was found covered in male semen. She was thrown into a graveyard of the dead plastic bodies that were props in a haunted house. It took a week to realize it wasn't a statue just set so that the maggots seemed real. The stench was really pushing the customers away.

And last there had been a murder in Sunnyvale, where a girl had been stabbed in the throat as the other girl had been; yet it didn't seem like it was the same killer. There was something a bit uneasy about the way the girls face was wrapped in a bag and hands tied behind her back.

"Three deaths," thought Sergeant Miller. Three deaths that take no part in each other, or do they? There was a murder a few years back where a woman was killed in her own home. She was very beautiful. They found her stabbed to death in her bedroom. She was in there for a week and the people from her job were calling around asking about her. Miller had ended up working on the crime to find a connection, but there was nothing. No finger prints, no footprints. There wasn't a trace. The death of the girl reminded Miller of that case for some odd reason. *And* there was no connection with the death of the chopped up human with no head but there seemed to be a passion. They eventually threw some new assignments onto his desk and had him move on. But it plagues him now, as did it before.

He was always at the crime scene more than the other detectives. He sat there trying to picture what happened and how to find his killer. He had tracked down quite a few of the more sloppy ones, but the others who didn't seem to have any pattern or instrument at all seemed to be harder than the rest. Maybe that was the connection. There was no connection between any of them and the gut feeling within Detective Miller was accurate.

The door flew open and Detective Heller swayed into the door hanging on the rim of the wall. He tossed a yellow folder on the desk of the confused detective with a tired look on his face. "There's another one for yah. This just happened two days ago. They found the body last night. You might want to rethink this one."

Miller snapped out of his train of thought. He had his arm propped on the desk with his hand hanging a little. He just looked at Heller with uncertainty. "What's this?"

"It's a tough one. Try to read through it and tell the captain what yah think."

"Alright, could you bring me a cup of coffee please?"

"Sure thing, you probably need it for this one."

Miller looked at the folder kind of peeking at it not wanting to open it up. He tossed the cover open with dismay. He didn't want to know what was in that folder. But it was tossed open with force. He read the file through to the end. The page would turn and he would sicken.

Cindy Ramos only seventeen years old, was last seen by her parents when they dropped her off at school Friday morning. They expected her home any minute but she never returned. Her body was discovered two days later in a warehouse outside of highway 101. She was shot in the back three times and the skin was sliced from her face, her nose removed, her eyes gouged out. The room where they found her was covered in blood.

Miller could not understand why people could do these things and walk around the everyday life as though it were just a normal day. His reason for being on the force was to get rid of the killers, child rapists, and children abusers of the world. He had a wife and a thirteen-year-old daughter who could be this very same girl.

He sat there with his eyes closed trying to imagine what other spots he could look to find a clue to the girl killed in the fair and the girl who had been stabbed in the throat. This new death was not slain like the others but there was some hatred in this new death.

I read the newspaper today and saw a photograph of the girl *they* killed. I can't take the pain of what I have become. This proves more and more around civilized people, I will begin to show. I don't want to be hauled away. They chopped off her nose, stabbed in her eyes, and sliced the skin off of her face. I threw up on myself as I drove out. The smell of the blood, the sent of the girl; it was all on me at that very moment.

If I am correct, it should only be seven hours till I hit Los Angeles from my home. I know now why I must leave. I cannot control myself. Now that I want out, the voices are thrashing at my brain. That one hope that I might have changed my mind to stay is all lost when they opened the door and let her in.

Things are going to be spur of the moment from now on. There is no more of this planning out the deaths of others nor where I plan to be in the near future. I won't even care how I live, as long as I'm far away from here and the voices. I don't ever recall feeling remorseful but with the passed couple of things I have done, I can't feel anything but remorse.

The things I didn't do intentionally are all that's eating me inside. I was forced to do something I didn't want to do. Everything I had ever done in this life had meaning. Everything I once believed in isn't the same and now I'm completely lost.

It was time for me to collect my assets and book out of here. Now if they'll just cooperate with me, this will go quick and smooth.

"Hi, how can I help you today?" Asked the customer service bank representative.

I paused for a moment in my own thoughts.

"Sir?" She asked.

"Oh I'm sorry. I'd like to close my account with this firm today."

"Well sorry to hear we're losing your business. I just need your account number."

I leaned back in my chair with full memorization of the number. I would never forget the number that lead to the wealth of the family. I slowly called out the numbers to her as she tapped them into her computer.

"I need you to fill out this paperwork here, I'll need your ID, and I'll be with you in a moment to get you your money."

I sat there quiet and still. I became absent-minded dreaming of nothing I would become. I sat there staring at the coffee cup on her desk for about ten minutes. She came back placing sheets in front of me.

"I need you to sign where all the X's are here to implicate you closing your bank account."

I took the pen from her hand and scribbled my name on all of the lines marked x. I handed her the papers and she gave me the check. She started mumbling about the bank services and filling out paperwork. They started to whisper to me.

"No, no," I said quietly. "Go away."

"Excuse me."

"Oh nothing." I said as I looked over my check. The whispering got louder and my head began to burst. I grabbed my head shaking dramatically. She looked over at me. I fell to the floor holding onto my head weeping.

"Sir are you okay?" She asked.

My ears began to bleed. I was gone once again. They swept into me and I could see them making all decisions for me. I pulled myself up with a handgun in my hand. I grabbed onto the desk. "I want cash," they said in unison. Her eyes sank staring at the gun and she could hear the voices growling within my voice. She put her hands on the desk. I knew my life was over now. "Did you hear me?" They asked her. "I want it all in cash."

"Oh my, that's a gun." She tightened her grip on the pen in her hand. I knew she believed that in this very moment, the fright of the gun made her think my voice was altered and it was just fright, but reality was set in with the two of us and I was really a demon.

"Yes, now if you don't want your pretty little head blown off, I suggest you cash this check in for some real money."

"Sir, that's 3.4 million dollars. That'll leave us with barely anything. We don't keep that kind of cash in hand for just one client."

They pointed at her with the gun. "Move," growled the demons in their most horrifying voices.

"Yes sir," she cried.

She turned around and stood up. "Come here doll face, I change my mind." She walked to me trembling. They grabbed her by her jacket. I put my gun to her head. She began to cry even more thinking that it wasn't a smart move to work in a bank. Their voice came out as one, and it was in my own tone. "Everyone listen up or I'm going to blow her fuck'n head off!"

Everyone began to scream and run in panic. They fired the gun into the air. "Now that I have your attention, I want everyone to get down on the ground." They pushed the gun to her head harder. She was whimpering all the way through. "Keep quiet before I put one in your head. Let's over walk to the entrance."

The two of us walked sideways to the door. "I'm not stealing anyone's money here at all. Not even the banks. But I've got so much cash here and they just want to give me a check. You know how long that will take to process? A fuck'n long time. So I don't give two shits when you give me *my* money, you might be low on cash. I have 3.4 million in my account and if you don't give it to me in approximately one minute, I will put a bullet through this ladies skull . . . *Go!*"

I felt a sharp pain in my arm. I turned to my side and fired straight into the guard that was standing in the doorway. He fell to the floor, blood gushing out of his head. Everyone began to scream. They weren't going to let go of the woman so they held her by her hair.

"No more bullshit! Five . . . Four . . . Three . . . two . . . wo"—The manager walked up to me with a large bag then opened it up to show me it was all there. *They* grabbed the bag and the woman. *They* ran to my car yanking the woman along. *They* threw the gun and the bag in the car. The demons growled again. "Has anyone ever told you, you whine too much?" She was staring at me with tears in her eyes.

All at once the voices flung out of my mouth like ghosts who possessed my body but screamed like demons as they fled. She saw it all because she stared directly at them screaming. I could hear my heart pounding and life came back to me. It was painful when they left my body. And when reality kicked in, I looked at the clerk and she stared at me crying. "Oh god, help me!" I cried. She started to scream. I backhanded her and she fell to the floor unconscious.

I jumped into my car crying, punching the wheel, and crushing the gas pedal with my foot. I knew they have a clear description of my car. They did it once more, leaving my body when it was all a mess. I punched the wheel so hard I began to bleed on the knuckles. I didn't care. Why did I run? I should just let them take me in.

I had a very ingenious idea that might work. I couldn't let my car go. They might have the license plate number, make, and model. I've had this car for a very long time. My idea was ridiculous and would take up a lot of time but that didn't matter to me at all. There was no such thing as time as far as I'm concerned. My arm was bleeding badly and I knew what it was from. The officer had shot me in the arm. There was blood on my sleeve.

I pulled into the garage of a hotel after speeding down the highway for twenty minutes. I grabbed a black long sleeved shirt from my suitcase then rushed to the public bathroom and cleaned myself up. I tied a towel tightly around my arm to slow the bleeding. Then crushed my bloody shirt underneath the garbage in the can next to the door. It was covered with trash, mostly paper towels.

I felt really drowsy walking out of the hotel. I went through with my harebrained scheme. I switched my license plates with another Camero but a old Camero to throw them off. I took my car to a paint and body I had seen up the road. It was a ridiculous thing to do, but I asked them to paint my car dark maroon. I asked them what was the fastest they could get it back to me, it would take two days max and that's if I paid extra. I took a taxi along with my suitcase and duffle bag of money to a semi nice hotel.

I looked at the wound and saw that it would not stop. I went out and bought some pliers, a small sewing kit, alcohol, and bandages. As soon as I got back to my room I sat in front of a mirror and ripped that bullet out. It was a very excruciating pain but it had to be done. The alcohol burned when I rubbed it down. With my left hand I took some thread and sewed the wound very crookedly together. It would have to do. I took a shower to wash the smell of fear off of me. When I came out I rubbed tripple anit-biotic ointment on the wound and dressed it as best with a left hand as I could.

I slept the whole day.

So far, pieces on the murders weren't going so well. It was getting the point where he knew his captain would take him off the fair grounds murder and have him work on something petty. Deep down, Miller felt a connection with these murders but there were no prints and no witnesses.

He switched on the news and saw the bank that had been robbed in a small city early that day. The *assumed* robber was closing his account and then had a mental breakdown killing an officer and beat a bank teller. There was no clue as to where this gentleman was but the news reporters said to be on the look out for an old 1969 black Chevy Camero. They showed part of the security camera.

He's bald, five feet ten inches, green eyes, and was shot in the arm. He goes by the name Alex Dugan but it could be an impersonation of Alex Dugan. Alex Dugan seems to be a very successful business owner and has no past psychological problems whom is a very respected man.

Miller hardly paid attention to the very infinite details being that he was far from that jurisdiction and he was a homicide detective. He sat there thinking about his wife and how much he missed spending time with her. She was worried about him constantly with his line of work. She was a kindergarten teacher.

Miller opened the file on the two females who seemed to be connected. He took a magnified glass and looked over the pictures of the rooms and the bodies to find a clue to help him find this guy. He looked over measurements of shoe prints from the abandoned building sight and the haunted house.

The haunted house shoe print was a size twelve and the one from the barn was a size ten.

He sat back crossing his arms holding onto the magnified glass. He decided to get back to the scene of the crime to look in places that seemed distant to the case.

The sound of the door clanking in such a hard and rough tone was not what I wanted to wake up to. The room was so black I could barely see my hands in front of my face. The hard knock was pounding slowly with the voice of, "Mr. Dugan? Open up!"

I sat up on the bed. All I could see was the light from under the door. I dragged myself to the door. I unlocked the door and turned the knob thinking, *Mr. Dugan?* I used a different name, the name Jacob Thompson, from my perfectly made fake ID. But it was too late to turn back. There were officers standing there with their badges out ready to apprehend me.

"Mr. Alex Dugan, we're placing you under arrest for the killing of an officer early today at the Franklin National Bank."

I grunted loudly jumping up out of sleep. It was dark and I heard the door clanking. I sat up quietly ready to flee the scene of a bad dream that could come true. I stood by the door with my ear on the wood and my hand on the lock. "Who is it?"

"Room service would like to know if you wanted to order any food before the kitchen closes. We tried to call but your phone isn't working. Would you like to make an order?" Said the lady.

I grabbed my gun holding it with my left hand; the barrel on the door. I opened the door ready to fire. The service attendant was wearing a white uniform with a menu. She smiled at me as I realized how paranoid I was. I let the gun low but she couldn't see it.

"Would you like to look through our menu?"

"Got any shrimp?" I asked smiling a little.

"Sure, fried shrimp with a baked potatoes."

"Is there any way possible you could grill that? I'll pay extra. And can you put a couple of slices of lemon and a cup of warm butter on the side?"

"I'm sure we can work out something. Anything to drink?"

"The biggest Dr. Pepper yah got." Being shot really builds up an appetite.

CHAPTER 16

I bought myself a new suitcase with a lock for the money. I left everything at my hotel room in a secret hiding place. The maid might be nosey and I'd have to kill her for my own hard earned money. I showed up at the paint and body shop early that day. They were putting on a second coat of clear coat on the Camero. I smiled wanting to laugh at the gay color I had picked. It looked good but I had never anticipated a maroon Camero. They were usually black or red. But this was okay. My plates were clean and I don't think the person I stole them from would notice.

I waited around for an hour and a half. I paid them and went on my merry way. I got rid of all things that lead to the name Alex Dugan. All I had were my Jacob identifications. My brother was probably worried. But I couldn't contact him. They were probably harassing him now or soon would be.

I went back to the hotel and got my belongings. I headed out clean as a whistle. A couple of hours and I would be in Los Angeles. I was ready to get out of this world and hoped there might be a future for me out there. I might want to see a doctor over there.

It was late when I headed out. By the time I was almost out of the city, I was drowsy. I couldn't keep my eyes open and wanted to fall asleep. I stopped off at a rest area on the side of the highway. It had a snack machine and restrooms. I locked up the doors and slept in my seat. The only sound you could hear was the crickets in harmony.

I awoke when I heard a car drive up. The lights shined bright on the restroom reflecting into my eyes. I sat up pulling my seat with me. I looked to my side at the vehicle. The car looked familiar. It was a 1973 impala. It looked just like the one my mother used to have. I stared at it for a while then noticed the two boys sitting in the back seat of the car. They were play fighting with each other.

There was a tap on my window and I flinched. I looked up at the person. "Mom?" She looked young and beautiful. She was thin. I rolled down my window.

"Can you help me sir? My tire went out on the highway. I'm not very strong when it comes to lifting. At the same time my boys are gett'n out of hand. We're trying to get to Dallas."

Dallas? That's where we used to go. I hated Dallas. Doesn't she know who I am? Maybe she just *really* looked like my mother. I got out to fix her flat.

"Here, let me open my trunk and help you out with the tire." She said pulling the keys out of the ignition. I guess it wasn't my mother, just a big resemblance of her. Not that I even remotely want to remember the *bitch*.

On her way towards the back of the car, she popped her head through the window facing the back. "Alex, Tony, you two better behave or I'm going to ring both of you. We're leav'n in a minute. Keep quiet."

She walked over to where I stood behind the car. She opened the trunk and I helped her with the little spare and rolled it to the front of the car. I began to unscrew the lugs on the rim while she stood there smoking a cigarette.

"Would you like one?"

"No thank you." I replied.

"So," she blew out smoke, "what's your name?"

"Um, Jacob."

"Jacob huh? My name's Cassandra."

I dropped the wrench. I sort of choked on my own saliva. Her name's Cassandra; the boys in the back seat are Tony and Alex; the car is the same make and model as my mothers who used to live in Dallas.

I looked to my side. Behind the restrooms were tall bushes and acreage that stood out twenty feet. Something caught my eye in an instant. There was a glimmering reflection of eyes and a shadow standing behind the trees. They were staring straight at my *mother* and me.

"There's someone out there. You stay here Cassy. I think someone's trying to spy on us." I handed her the wrench and began walking towards the figure slowly.

"Cassy? My husband is the only one who calls me Cassy. Boys you stay in the car." She threw her cigarette onto he floor and got inside of her car. She rolled up all of the windows and locked the doors.

The figure backed away when it saw me coming towards it. "Aye, come back here!" I yelled as the figure run off into the woods. I ran after the eyes in the bushes. The thorns began to prick and stab me on the arms. I could see the dark shadow running through the bushes. I chased him to the very end; when I came out, night had fallen completely out of existence and I was standing behind a fence.

"Stop following me!" I yelled at them.

The night change to day. It was bright white, not sunshine yellow, but bright blue skies with the whitest clouds. Beyond the fence was a playground where children were running around on black pavement. It was an elementary school. There was white paint on the ground that was meant for games to be played at like four square and duck, duck goose.

I stayed along the fence against the bushes. I walked around very slowly. All the little girls were wearing white ruffled dresses and black buckled shoes. Each girl looked the same with all of them wearing their hair in pigtails. Three girls were playing jump rope and singing songs. Some boys and girls were playing hopscotch. There was a circle of girls holding hands, singing a song, with something in the middle of their circle. I moved closer to see what it was.

I couldn't understand what made children act the way they did. Was the joke in the whole situation differed from the justification on the eyeballs popping out of a dog's head? The teachers did nothing to stop this and I felt I were in the twilight zone. The dogs tongue was hanging out of its mouth surrounded by blood. There was the stench of rotten flesh. The girl's giggled for what reason I don't know.

"You cry baby!" Was the sudden noise that rushed straight out of nowhere and I felt as though someone was talking to me.

"Alex pees in his pants!"

"He's a retarded defect." One girl laughed.

They began to push a small boy. "Stop!" He cried. They pushed him again.

I couldn't stand it. I walked over to the group of children and was about to push them away from him but when I reached out, my flesh was nonexistent. A woman about the age of forty grabbed Alex by the shirt and yanked him into the building. "I'm calling your mother!" She growled. When she yanked him up the stairs, his hat flew off of his head.

I stood there watching the mean little kids run off and laugh. Did that really happen? Was I treated this badly in first grade? I didn't remember any of this. There was something odd about the whole situation where it differed with the teacher placing me in trouble and not the other kids, especially the ones who were playing with the dead dog.

I walked into the building. Down the hall it was quiet and I looked through every room as I passed by. I saw Alex sitting on a chair in a small office. The old woman was in there with her scowled old face frowning into unhappiness. I kneeled next to Alex.

"What's wrong?" I asked him.

But there was no reply.

"Are the mean kids upsetting you?" But I didn't exist to him either. I turned to my side when I heard the old lady's voice.

"Mrs. Dugan, your son has been causing some problems with the other kids. I think Alex is in bad shape. That's twice I had to call on you this week. Is there a problem in the home? Oh I see . . . And his father? . . . I'm sorry to hear that . . . Well if I were you, I would take him to see a councilor. Now you have two choices. Either pick him up or he can sit in the office with me all day . . . Good day Madame. I'll see you soon." She stuck her head out the door. "Alex," she called.

He lifted his head, and then stared straight into my eyes. I guess he could see me but he didn't want to talk. We kept eye contact for a while until she called on him again.

"I don't want to go in there."

"Why not?" I asked.

"She's mean to me." He looked down. "They all are."

"You don't have to go in. I can help you."

"No you can't. No one can. I'm damned for life."

"*Alex*! Get in here now!"

He stood up then walked right through me. *Right through my body!* What was going on? I followed him. He stood in front of her desk staring at her.

"Alex, your mom is coming to pick you up. I'm sorry to say, she's taking you out of this school and putting you in another school. A special school for children like yourself. Children who need special attention. You can sit in here until she arrives."

"Can I get my hat from the playground?" He asked.

"Hurry up. I get your bag from the classroom."

He turned around and walked out of the office. I followed him into the hall. It was very silent. All I could hear were his shoes tapping on the tiled floor. He walked slowly down the hall, as if he had all the time in the world; running his fingers against the walls as he walked on; very careless and quiet.

We stepped outside and it was raining. Not one child outside made a single movement or sound as if we were frozen through time. They were all on the ground. The little girls in frilly dresses were covered in blood. The rain that came down smeared the blood all over the playground. Every child was dead.

I ran out to check everyone of them. There were no souls left. The whole playground was a blood bath. I heard a cry behind me. I turned around. Little Alex was crying. Then his face changed. He began to laugh at all of the dead bodies. I was in complete shock. He was laughing like a psychopath . . . He picked up an axe from the floor, ran his finger across the blade, checked the sharpness of the blade, then licked his thumb. He tasted the blood and smiled.

Lights shined brightly in my eyes and I opened them to see the bathrooms covered in headlights. It's happening again. I looked around and saw two squad cars parked a couple of spaces from me. I hope they weren't here for me. The good thing was they weren't in sight.

I pulled my seat forward and turned on the car. I drove out towards the freeway hoping everything was going to be okay. I began to think about the dream I had. It was funny how people can step outside of themselves and see the past. I'm so glad it was a dream. But I do remember where it all came from. When I was a child, I remember imagining that was what happened when I walked outside; that they were all dead. They teased me pretty bad in school. The only way to get passed it all, for me, was to imagine they were dead.

I drove the close to the speed limit not wanting to point myself out. I put my hands in the back seat to feel my suitcase with the money, which was safely still there. I kept my eyes on the road. It began to slowly rain. Then it became heavy and loud. I could see someone's emergence lights blinking. They were standing next to their car in a red Patton leather jacket with an umbrella over their head.

I thought about all of the crazy people in the world like me and I thought of the movie, *The Hitcher*. I wouldn't want to pick up someone like that, but it might be my destiny. As I slowed to see them, I saw her. I pulled over, further up the road then ran back to where she was.

"Do you need help miss?" I asked while covering my head with my jacket.

"My car died. It's the starter, I've been meaning to replace it but I guess I waited too long." She tried to look at my face to see if I were trustworthy. "Can you drive me to the nearest payphone so I can call someone?"

"No problem miss."

We ran to my car and I unlocked the door for her on the passenger side. I got in the drivers seat. It became silent when the door shut. I could hear the rain coming down heavily onto the car.

"My name is Jacob," I said putting out my hand.

"Karen, nice to meet you."

Her blonde hair was wet and dripping on her face then landed on her red jacket making this tapping sound. Her hair was wavy and her face was tan. Her lips were red like her jacket. Her eyes were light brown almost hazel. Her make up from her eyes was running down her cheeks. She'd be pretty underneath the crude.

As I stared at her observing everything of the stranger she looked at me as if to say, *let's go*. I turned on the car driving out into the rainy night.

"Do you mind if I turn on the radio?"

"No. Go right ahead."

I pulled out a cigarette lit it with one hand on the wheel. The cigarette was hanging off of my lip.

"I'm glad you stopped. I don't know what I would've done if you hadn't showed up. I know there's nothing around for at least a couple of miles." She looked at me. "So where are you headed?"

"I was going out of state to visit some friends."

"Oh." She smiled. "And where's that? If you don't mind me asking."

"It's far; near the boarder of Arizona."

"Oh . . . that's nice."

The next exit wasn't far off. I took her to the payphone of a gas station. She got out making her call. I watched her from inside of the car. She was out there for about ten minutes and on occasion she would look at the car. She got back in.

"So are you okay for now? What happened?"

"Well a friend of mine who could tow my car isn't around until tomorrow morning. I'll have to wait or call tomorrow."

"Well, I'm heading to a hotel to rest near by. If you want to get your own room, you're more than welcome."

"That would be really nice of you."

The closest motel I found was a motel 6. I pulled in. As we entered the office, I pretended I didn't know her and stood behind her in line as if I were just another customer. I was in room 12 and she was in 23.

I felt good walking into the room. It was clean and quiet. I threw myself onto the bed. I kicked off my shoes, then like a child I laid back watching TV. A horror movie was on. After a while the rain fell harder. It was pouring outside the window with flashes of lightening and roars of thunder. The television turned off. I looked out the window and waited for the power to click back on.

There was a knock on my door about two hours later. I sat there not wanting to open the door. It knocked again . . . I got up and opened the door.

There stood Karen with a blanket wrapped around her. Now why did she have to go and do this? I wanted her to be good; and with that comes death. I can't help it. They call when evil comes. They do not punish the innocent.

"It's scary in there all by myself. Lightening and thunder scares me." She said with a sad expression.

"I stuck my head out the door to see if anyone was around; but there was no one. I opened the door wider to let her in. It was completely dark in the room.

"Sit down." I said.

She sat on the bed. I sat on the opposite side. It was quiet for a minute or two. Then she spoke. "I hate this weather. It frightens me."

"I just want my TV to turn back on."

It switched on. I leaned back to watch the tube. I didn't want to look at her. I hope she was really scared and if she wasn't, she will be. I hope she was innocent. At the end of the movie I was tired. It was still thundering. Karen was watching TV. It turned off again. I hated these electrical problems. But when I turned to my side, she had been the one who turned it off with the channel selector.

She crawled over to me. *Here we go.* She began to unbutton my pants slowly. I wished this wasn't happening. Was I a slut magnet? She had me in her mouth. My body was up for the occasion but I wasn't. Her mouth was wet.

She undressed me. It was process. If a woman was going to do this, I may as well help her out a little bit. She sat on me kissing my neck. I helped her with her clothes. I sucked on her chest as the foreplay process goes. She moaned as they all do. And in my head, I heard the voices of every woman I ever made love to, call out through her voice. It seemed to be very passionate.

The penetration was great. Some woman seemed to be so used up that I didn't even want them. There was always something that was never quite complete with the sex I've had. It felt good when we moved, but when making love with no love, I don't care for it.

How could she just get into bed with me? She just met me a few hours ago. Maybe she was horny. What did I say to her to make her want me? It was slow and good I must admit. Even if it is always in the presence of the damned. And I wanted to let go so bad. But we kept moving. I grabbed her face and kissed her lips. I couldn't help it anymore. It was over.

We lay in bed. She fell asleep in my arms. I stayed awake for reasons of my own. For an hour I sat there thinking about where I needed to go and how much more time I had to finish.

I looked at her naked body. I was disgusted. I dressed myself in clean clothing. I headed towards the door to escape from the girl. She made a bad decision doing it with me, but I guess these girls can't let up. Before I walked out the door, they called to me. They struck my head with lightening. They told me to kill her but I didn't want to. I wanted to leave her alone.

But the beast inside of me knew who she really was. I was put on this planet for one reason and it wasn't to be a success. I jumped on top of her, wrapped my hands around her neck, and then squeezed. She woke up instantly. She started kicking then dug her nails into my hands.

She was far from stronger than me. She couldn't get me off of her. I squeezed her so tight, the veins in her eyes popped. Tears were running down the sides of her face. She stopped struggling when I felt a crack in her trachea. She released her hands from mine. Blood came out of her mouth flowing down her chin. Her eyes lost life with emptiness.

I threw her off of the bed. I took the sheets; rolled up the sheets and the blankets; grabbed all of by belongings; and walked out of the door. I threw the blankets into the back seat of my car. I wanted her to be a good person and now she was.

"I'm sorry sir; I can't find any records on this gentleman." Said police officer James Conely. "Are there any states that this person used to live in that we could look up on?"

Robert shook his head. "I'm just going to interrogate this guy." Robert stood up putting his jacket on. He pushed in his chair, grabbed a file folder off of his desk, and walked out of his office. He walked down to interrogation where there stood two suits, one of which was captain Leblings. All had their arms crossed staring through a two-way mirror.

"The lady who pointed him out?" Asked Miller.

"She's in my office having some coffee trying to relax." Said Detective Caroso.

"So what's this guy's name?" Asked Robert.

"John Doe for now. I have some people working on his prints as we speak. I can see how he frightened this girl and why she hadn't come forward for a long time." Said Leblings.

"Well I'm going to speak with him. You guys watch my back."

They watched through the two way mirror as their officer sat adjacent from the suspect setting his file onto the table. The man they brought in was six feet three inches. He had brown hair that hung down his cheeks like string. He was very thin wearing a black long sleeved shirt and black slacks. His eyes were sunk in as if he hadn't slept in a week.

It was quiet for a moment then Miller said, "Would you like some water or coffee?" The man just looked forward. He slouched more so into his chair then smacked his lips nonchalantly. "Well I have a couple of questions I have to ask you. You may not answer me but the easier you can answer me, the easier we might release you."

"What's your name?" Asked Miller. The man was silent still. "Alright I have a few pictures of women who were killed. Someone had pointed you out as the killer." Robert tossed out the pictures of the girl from the carnival. The man didn't look at the pictures. Miller picked it up and shoved it in his face. "You better start answering me or else you will be charged with four counts," Miller put up his fingers, "Four counts of murder. And I *will* find your prints and more people to speak up. So far we have two witnesses on you." Miller was frustrated.

The door opened and in walked one of the officers. "Miller I need you out here."

Miller slid the pictures sprawled out on the table as he stood up. He walked over to the door while the officer was calling him out with his hand gesture. Miller shut the door. "What's going on?"

"There's been a murder out in Los Angeles with prints that were faxed to us."

"Why us?"

"Someone out there suggested we get out there. There's a flight leaving in an hour and a half. You and Ramos get out there. We want to see what this is all about."

"I have a lead right now with the witness and this gentleman here," said Robert.

"Don't worry, the guy's not going anywhere. I know people who'll give me extended time for three days with this guy. We get some more of these hookers talking, we get a charge."

Miller and Ramos flew down and made it there in forty minutes. They met up with homicide detective Edward Felding. He was a real young cop but very professional. He greeted the detectives courteously. They took a squad car out to the scene that had not been moved since it only was found five hours ago.

Felding sat in the passenger seat while a uniformed officer drove out. Miller and Ramos sat in the back looking around at the scenery. Felding looked back at the two. Miller made this face that was unsure of why they were there.

"I can tell what's going through your head." The two nodded their heads. "Well I keep up with murders from all over. In your sight there had spontaneous murders between Modesto, San Jose, Sacramento, Oakland, and San Francisco. I have only been in homicide for about four years but I'm good. Don't let my age fool you; I didn't just land this job by stupidity. Anyways, back three years ago there was a murder in Gilroy. A girl was strangled to death out in the streets behind a trashcan. She was a stripper. Okay." Miller nodded his head. "*A* year before that there was a woman stabbed to death in a hotel not too far from the strip club she worked at. A few girls reported a man about six feet to six two in a long black trench coat and a rounded hat. In the same area where the girl who was killed three years ago, there was a murder where a woman was stabbed to death out on the streets a few blocks away. She was also a stripper and the doorman reported seeing her outside talking with a man of same description. Thing is, that was six years ago. Oh this is all in your area, am I right?"

"Pretty much. San Jose's a little ways off; we sometimes go there but not too often."

"Well the hotel we're about to pull up to, is where this next victim is. She was strangled to death. There are two connections. The choke on this girl's neck was so forceful I swear this guy's gotta be huge. But anyway, the choke was so hard he crushed the trachea in this girl's neck. The woman who was killed three years ago had her neck crushed in the same fashion. A few other women that I have lists of from the passed nine years, about six of them have had their necks crushed. I can go through my paperwork in the office and make you copies. Not only that but the gentleman seen last night was about six feet and was wearing a long black trench coat. This guy has probably never been arrested because he doesn't seem to kill in the same fashion for them all. I have reports on woman that are killed with quick death and others who were tortured from your area. Not only that but he doesn't leave prints nor does he kill in close cities and not even within six months of each other, which might mean the cases are closed by then."

"That's really good."

"We heard just recently while we were waiting for you, that the clerk just realized he has security cams from last night in the lobby."

The car pulled in. The four men in the car opened their doors before the car was fully stopped. They rushed up the stairs where all the police officers and specialists were running in and out. Felding led the way.

"Most of these girls were not raped but had intercourse with the killer willingly."

"Any Semen?"

"None, this guy's good."

They walked through the door with the chaotic sounds of conversations, pictures being taken, and walkie-talkies going off. Miller walked up to the woman. He put on pair of gloves to examine her all the way. She was on the floor next to the bed completely naked. He saw and felt where the neck was crushed. He believed Felding to just have helped him with cases he was working on. A few of the officers spoke with Miller and Ramos about what they found.

Felding walked up to Miller and Ramos. "We got the tape set up for you in the security office. Hope you might have something on this guy out there."

"Well we just caught this tall weirdo up in Frisco. A prostitute stepped forward after it's been a month and pointed him out as picking up a *co-worker* and then she ended up dead. Thing is, if this happened last night and we caught him this morning, that's cutting it pretty close to time periods."

"Manson did make his trips out of state over nights too. It might just be him."

They stood in front of the security monitors while thanking the rent-a-cop for finding it on his videos. The clerk stood with the detectives so he could point out who was who. The video was a little blurry.

"This is the lady that was in room 23. Her name is Karen Ross. In room 12 where she was found is this gentleman here," pointed the clerk. "And his name is," the clerk flipped through his papers. "*Robert Palmer?*" Everyone looked at each other knowing Robert Palmer is a music artist from the 1980's and 1990's. Everyone looked closely at the monitor. Karen was wearing a red coat. Behind her stood the man in the black coat. His face was somewhat visible.

The TV was on next to the security monitors. "If you come by and see us at one of our three locations at Dugan's Oldies, we guarantee"-

"Hey could you shut that TV off?" Said Felding.

Miller glanced at the silent TV for a second. His eyes widened as the commercial ended. "Can you turn that back on? Did any of you see that?"

"What?"

"Did not that gentleman on the commercial look like that guy there on the monitor?" Said Miller pointing.

The security guard turned in his spinning chair. "That was the classic car commercial."

"Do you know who that actor was?" Asked Miller.

"Yeah, that was Alex Dugan sir. Lives up in Northern California. He's a millionaire. *Aye*! Didn't someone steal his money from his account?" He asked.

"Ah I'm not sure that's not my department so I haven't been following." One of the detectives rushed in. "I've got prints gentleman!"

Everyone was working together on this one. It came down to ten years of murder and seventy different murders that were never solved were now being dug up from the basement files. Felding put out an APB on Alex Dugan with descriptions and three possible vehicles registered under his name. Ramos was going to call the car company he owned and also speaking with some officers over the phone about where to look for Alex Dugan.

Miller spoke with some of the officers involved in the robbery. They hadn't gotten hold of Alex Dugan to find out if someone was trying to impersonate him. And the woman who had a concussion was in the hospital not wanting to speak with anyone. Robert got through the doors of her room with extreme force.

She had a bandage wrapped around her head. The bruise that was supposed to be covered somewhat ran down her cheek in little purple spots. She was eating breakfast as Miller walked in. He smiled at her.

"Oh continue please. I didn't mean to interrupt. I'm detective Robert Miller. I just have a few questions for you."

"How did you get in here? I specifically didn't want to see anyone."

"I'm sorry miss but this is a matter of life and death."

"Alright."

Miller sat down. "Do you remember what the man who claimed to be Alex Dugan, look like?"

"My mind is joggled."

"Did his ID match perfectly with him? Was there a slight difference in appearance?"

"I didn't really look at the picture fully. He had a social security card, Id, bankcard number, and secret code to an account that large. I can only assume it was him. He had everything he needed."

"So exactly what happened?"

"He closed his account. 3.4 million dollars." Miller's eyes widened. "He grabbed his head and fell onto the floor. When he got back up he pulled out a gun and demanded cash from me. But if we cashed in his million-dollar check, we would have run out of money. He put the gun to my head." She began to whine. "And, and."

"It's alright miss."

She wiped the tears away from being sucked into her nose. "He ah . . . We waited by the entrance. Our security officer fired at his arm and the robber shot him in the head. When he got his money he dragged me out with him. He then began to beat me over the head." She started to cry while holding onto her head.

"Do you remember what he was driving?"

"I'm not really good with cars all I can say is that it was an old black car."

Miller handed her a tissue. "Well there's not much more I can ask of you but if you remember anything else, anything at all, please call me." He handed her his card.

He said goodbye and rushed out of the hospital. She did remember something. He was blurry to her. His voice was distorted making him sound like a monster. She didn't want to mention any of what she *thought* she saw. They might put her in a mental hospital.

Robert rushed back to Feldings' office. The floor was busier than he could ever imagine. People were running around with files in their hands, talking on the phone, and rushing across the room with information. Leblings desk was covered in files. He was on the phone but on hold.

"The prints are in." Felding said with his mouth away from the phone.

"Dugan's?"

"Yep." Felding looked down. "I'm on the phone waiting for the manager of his company." Miller began to rummage through the files Felding pointed to in the box on the floor. "Yeah. Hi. My name is Detective Albert Felding. I'm with the Los Angeles police department. I was looking for the owner, Alex Dugan but the receptionist says he's not in."

"Yes, he's not working here today. Um pretty much I'll be in charge, is there anything *I* can do for you?" Asked Stan.

"I would like to ask you some questions about Mr. Dugan."

"If I can help I will but I am not at liberty to say where he lives or anything personal because I don't know who you are and not only that, that is classified information."

"Were you informed that Mr. Dugan had robbed a bank a few days ago?" Stan laughed horrendously on the other line.

"*Right!* Alex is this you? This has got to be a joke."

"Why do you say that sir?"

"Because Mr. Dugan is rich, not only that but he is a very well respected person. I don't believe this is a real phone call. So if it's you Alex, let me know, if not, I *am* hanging up right now."

"Sir! *Sir!*" Felding put the phone down. "He hung up." He shook his head. "He thought it was a joke. But anyway, we have his address and we're sending a swat team out to his house right now. I have them on monitor so we can see what's going on. There are also going to be some undercover agents from your department who are going to look for him at the car lot." Felding lifted a file off of his desk. "Oh, and right now, Ramos is leading a team with a warrant to raid his brothers house for his where abouts. He has an uncle who lives in Sunnyvale."

"Technically, he never robbed the bank, he only shot an officer."

"Which are grounds of killing a uniformed officer?"

"Parents?"

Felding shook his head. "We haven't heard anything yet but we'll find out soon. Right now, we were going to sweep the area at hotels and strip clubs. We're going to send out a couple of squad cars out to the boarder of Mexico to see if he might possibly be on his way out."

Tony was playing video games with his sons in the living room while Jennifer was cooking in the kitchen. There was a knock at the door. Tony was about to get up. As he lifted his son half way Jennifer walked out with a towel in her hand.

"Oh no honey, don't get up. Just keep playing with the boys." Said Jennifer as she walked towards the door. Tony smiled at her then continued playing video games. Jennifer opened the door. Before her stood a stranger in a business suit and a tan trench coat. As she focused on the stranger, she saw that he was surrounded by a swat team fully loaded with weapons and headgear.

"Is there an Alex or an Anthony Dugan here?" Asked the man.

"Honey . . ." her voice shrilled.

Tony's' smile was half way when he looked over and saw how she was frightened. He lifted his son setting him on the floor. As he walked up to the door he had a questionable expression on his face. He looked at the stranger then the SWAT team. "What's going on?" He asked.

The stranger held out a white form with writing on it in front of his face. "Are you Alex or Anthony Dugan?"

"I'm Anthony, yes."

"I'm detective Ramos with the San Francisco police department. We have a warrant to search the premises. Sign here and we'll be going through everything. You can read it all in the forms." Ramos was about the walk into the house. Anthony stood in his way. The Swat team in the background held up their guns.

"Wait a minute gentleman, I would like to read through this completely and I would also like to see your badges." Ramos held it out so he could see it from every detail. Anthony began to read through. Without turning to his wife he said, "Jen, take the boys outside to the swing set while I handle this."

"Honey what's going on?"

"Please baby, I'll let you know once I find out what's going on."

She took their boys to the back. Tony signed the paper and held it in his hand. "Before you fuck'n rush through my home, I expect you to be polite with my belongings. It says here that anything damaged will be your responsibility and I worked hard for everything we have. So don't go fucking it up cause I'll come looking for you."

"Threatening an officer?" Asked Ramos.

"No, defending my home while you savages come onto private property. Now you want to tell me what this is all about before I have to knock in some heads single handedly."

"Aggressive I see."

"No defending my home."

Ramos gave an okay to the detective to go through the home while the SWAT team made sure Alex was not on the premises. Tony followed them through the door. "Aye watch the stuff guys!" Ramos stood next to Tony in the living room. Tony turned and looked down at the detective. "What's up with you? Are you gonna talk or what?"

"I have a couple of questions to ask you about your brother Alex. Could we sit down to talk?"

"Sit down? No, I don't think so. We'll stand here just fine if you can stay on your feet detective Ramos."

"Alright, have it your way. When's the last time you seen your brother?"

"Over a week ago. We went camping."

"Do you know that he robbed a bank two days ago?"

Tony smirked than laughed as he spoke. "Are we talking about the same Alex Dugan, cause ah, my brother's rich. He don't need to rob no one."

"Well technically he didn't *rob* the bank but an officer shot him in the arm as Mr. Dugan demanded his account of over three million dollars in cash with a gun pointed to an employee just outside of Los Angeles. Mr. Dugan then turned and fired into an officer's head killing him."

"Nah! Nah, you got the wrong guy. My brother ain't crazy. What the hell is this?"

"Sir, with all do respect can you tell me anywhere he might be? Anywhere you know of he might be hanging out at?"

"No I wouldn't. All the man does is work and on occasion visit with me."

"We believe Mr. Dugan had some sort of a laps or psychotic episode which caused him to do these things. If your brother steps forward and we find that there is some sort of psychological problem, he won't be sentenced to death for the killing of an officer."

"First of all there is no way I will believe this story."

"Is there any mental history you remember from his passed?"

"Mental? No!" But he then remembered when Alex was put into a mental institute for a few months on account of some drugs and psychotic episodes that he believed his *parents* had done to him.

"We have prints on him sir. I'm very sorry to break it to you like this but"-

"*Break it to me like this!* You're invading my fuck'n house; scaring my family with this bullshit."

"Prints don't lie sir."

"What the hell yah got? Prints on what?"

"Well I didn't want to tell you this now, but he's a suspect for murdering a female persons in a hotel in Los Angeles. His prints were on the lamp and in the bathroom. There is no doubt that he committed these crimes. We will take him in and prosecute him. There are other connections but not solid ones that date back from the past ten years." Tony went silent. He knew some of the things his brother did. He was waiting for the detective to say, *we found prints on the killing of his mother and stepfather.*

Tony lowered his voice and stood closer to Ramos. "Look, whatever this story is that you're coming up with, could you keep it down. My family out there and *I* think the world of this guy. Now whatever this is about, I can't in good judgment believe this but if you want to ransack my home for what ever it is you are looking for, then hurry up and do so, but my family will *always* believe my brother is a good person."

"Are your parents close by?"

Tony backed away turning his head to hide the secrecy he would never utter. "No they are not."

"Where can I reach them if I needed to?"

Tony turned around as if he were offended. "In the Floresville Cemetery in Texas."

"Oh I'm sorry."

"Yeah. Well, it's not like you knew."

One of the officers walked out. "Sir, there's no one here and the only thing we found was this hand gun and a small bag of marijuana." He had the evidence in his hand.

Tony lowered his head. "I have every right to carry that gun, I have a license and I have the gun registered under my name."

"And the weed?" Smiled the detective.

"What can I say? I'm one of the millions of people in this state that smoke weed."

"Well we're going to confiscate this marijuana but I won't take you in on that, but if you're hiding your brother anywhere, we'll get you for accessory to murder. You have a good day sir. And thank you for the cooperation." Ramos looked at the SWAT team who stood in the living room. "Come on boys."

"Yeah, sure."

The team filed out of Tony's' home. Ramos stood in the doorway. "Don't forget, if you hear anything at all, you'll give me a call."

"Oh yeah." Tony said half smiling.

CHAPTER 17

I made it through the boarder of Mexico. I waited a long time in line. I stopped to get something to eat. I had this feeling that I was going to get caught. I wore the thickest glasses possible so that my eyes were hard to see. On my head, I wore a red wig for a male, with a baseball cap over it. I had to look completely different.

I was one car away from being discovered. There were police cars driving up, as I was the next in line. They were searching through everyone's cars inside and out. I could see people pulling out their Id's. In each officers hand they held a paper with a picture of someone. I could only assume it was me. My eyes were locked.

I jumped at the sound of a honk. "Hey move it! I ain't got all day!" Yelled a man from the vehicle behind mine. I drove up.

"You visiting up there?" Asked the man in the booth.

"Yeah." I could see in his hands also he held a picture of me. But there wasn't any resemblance with my face now.

"ID and social security card."

I pulled out my wallet and gave it to him. I kept looking around, hoping the cops wouldn't come near and ask for me to step out. If I had to, I would shoot every cop I could to get away. I just need to cross the line.

"Okay now Mr. Thompson, just remember that if you want to cross the second boarder out there, it'll cost some money to get your car through."

"Oh okay." I tried to sound like a nerd.

"Go ahead sir, and have a nice day."

"Oh thank you sir."

I looked around as I drove through. A police officer was about to check my car but I made it through clearance. I was home free. I was afraid I would be caught. My heart was pumping fast as I drove down the road.

The slate was clean in this new country with different cultures. I'm proud to be here since my real father had decedents from here. I think it was my great great grand father who was half-Mexican.

The day was dry and hot. I could see the heat rising off of the road. I had some miles to drive before I reached the next city or town. All I wanted to do was relax. I wanted to let it sink into my head that I was far away from my troubles.

I want to lose the voices here. I won't reply to them nor answer to them when they call. I decided when they come; I might just handcuff myself so I won't hurt anyone. Their voices changed though. They used to be pleasantly calm. It was pleasing to ones ears to hear the melody of them in harmony. Now they sound like tortured demons and souls crying out and screaming.

I rolled down my window to breath in the fresh air. The sun was shinning down on the maroon Camero. As I made it to the first town, there wasn't much room to drive through. I decided to park and get some rest. I wanted to get into deep Mexico. I wanted to explore. I have the freedom to do what I will.

I parked the vehicle behind a small building locking it down with the club and set the alarm. My car was one of the most precious possessions to me now. My money would be in there. There wasn't anyway it could be stolen. I hid the suitcase in a secret compartment in my trunk. Even if they did break in, they wouldn't find it.

I knew very little Spanish. How would I communicate with these people? I didn't want to be a snazzy rich boy here. I'm not the type of rich person, which likes to flaunt it. I hated yuppies and deep down, I was one for a while. No one is beneath me but drug addicts and whores. I have to get that out of my head too. I will not dwell on things I hated once before.

I passed a few food stands down the crowded streets. I noticed a Caucasian woman. She had blonde hair with large round eyes making her image look a bit British. Her eyes were a very light blue and looked as though they were crystal. She stood behind a food stand in a long white dress.

"Excuse me miss, but do you know where I can find a decent hotel around here?"

"Perdonane, pero yo no saro ingle," she said.

"What?" I said to myself. I thought she was white.

A gentleman from the stand next to hers leaned her way and looked at me. He was flipping a tortilla between his hands. "Don't underestimate the people in Mehico. We all look black, white, or brown . . . but we're all still Mexican."

"You mean, this lady here," I pointed. "Is Mexican."

"Oh for chure man. Whatch you want anyway?"

"I was just looking for a good hotel."

"Jew walk up the street up the corner there and jew find a places called Jose's' Inn. You'll enjoy it there. Many of the Americans go to stay there."

"What kind of food you got?" I asked.

"Mexican." He looked at me like I was dumb.

"Obviously. What's your specialty? Tacos, enchiladas?"

"I have the best chalupas and tacos here. You know what a chalupa is?"

"Yeah." I was going to say, *like the tostadas at taco bell*. I didn't want to offend him. "I'll take one of them."

He began to work his hands fast. I turned around to watch the people around me while he finished up. I felt a tug on my slacks then looked down to see what it was.

"Can you spare a dollar mister? I'm hungry." Was the tiny voice.

My heart sank into a sad reality of these people. I looked into the child's' eyes. She was no older than four years old.

"I'll get you something." I turned to the man. "Can I get ten tacos please?"

"Chure."

I paid him. He hand me a large tray of food. I took my food off of the tray then helped her sit down at a table with her food. Then I stuffed a one hundred dollar bill into her pocket.

As I walked away the rest of her family sat down next to her to share the food. I wish I could give her more. I knew there was a family around waiting to see what she would get.

I ate my food while walking back to my car. It was nice to see that there were only people looking at the car and not touching it. Everything was where it should have been. I had to drive slowly through the streets because people were walking everywhere.

The sun was going down but still bright outside. I saw the sign of Joses' Inn. It looked okay. I was afraid there were people looking at me awkward. I parked in the front near the entrance. I walked into the building with my suitcases. I rang at the desk. A woman with light brown hair walked out from behind the counter.

"May I help you senior?" She asked.

"I'd like to get a room for tonight."

"And jew name?"

"Jacob Thompson."

"It's fourty-five dollars a night here." I paid her as she handed me the key. "Your room number is 109 and Antony will show you the way. Enjoy you stay." She smiled.

A boy came out. He was wearing some old brown slacks and a tan colored shirt. He took my bags from me. We walked through the building as I watched him with my bags like a hawk. He had *my* money.

"Here you are sir." He unlocked the door for me. He opened it up and handed me the bags. "If you need anything just press one on you phone and we will answer."

I grabbed my bags and tipped him ten dollars. I went into the quiet alone. I switched on the lights. I locked the door very suspiciously. The room had a full sized bed with pink, orange, and black striped blankets. The colors clashed but that was the least of my worries.

I took a long hot shower. I went straight to the bed. Sleep was all I wanted. I needed to rest up for whatever would come next.

It's when you sleep that everything comes back to haunt you. It's in your sleep that everything is settled into your mind to realize all the things you have done. I am seeing things more clearly. I reminisce about all the things I had accomplished and all the things I would like to do. I can imagine myself settled down living in a nice house with a devoted wife and a son to carry on my father's name. But imagination can only take you so far. When you wake up, real life takes in effect; you become sadder than you had been before you lay down.

I can't imagine a pure woman who could love me. For I myself am not pure. I see the hurt, pain, agony . . . blood. I wanted to end it all. Killing myself was never an issue. I always have this thought in the back of my head that tells me, *something* will happen, *something* will change.

The blur of my own wishes faded away and I was in deep sleep.

I found myself on the bus in the cold sun rising morning. I put change in the machine taking an empty seat near on old lady and a child. I sat next to the window staring outside to get a view of where I was. In the front of the bus sat a woman in a white uniform like in one of those church cafeteria outfits. She was having conversations about her life with the bus driver, which he didn't mind. There sat a couple of men in ragged clothing who sat in the center talking about their boss at a construction sight.

Across from me was a teenage boy with his head down. Observing his clothing, as I had with the others, I noticed the image he held with the ripped jeans and converse sneakers. He wore a black t-shirt and over it he wore am army green jacket. The jacket had drawings of skulls and band names all over it. From his jean pocket hung a shiny silver chain. His hair was jet black spiked all over. Besides him was a skateboard which he held close to him and a red back pack done up just as his jacket.

The bus went over a bump waking him up instantly. I saw his green eyes look up giving an evil, *I hate the world*, stare. It occurred to me then, *it was me.* I couldn't take my eyes off of him. He turned to his side trying not to make eye contact with me.

The bus came to a stop and in walked 20 teenagers with their backpacks propped on themselves like little hunchback people. Most of them were in baggy clothing like rappers trying to sag. And the girls were dressed like sluts with short skirts, tight shirts, and ten tons of make up.

Alex lifted his bag from the seat to offer Nick a place to sit. I can't believe this. Why Nick? Nick deceived me. I hated him! Nick had bright red hair that looked as though he never washed it. He wore black leather pants with biker boots overlapping the ankles. He wore a dirty shirt with rips all over. His leather jacket was covered in spikes, chains, and patches.

They began to have a conversation. I hated watching the two together. I wanted to shout out to myself that he was a horrible friend and back then I was so anxious to be liked, that I didn't see it. I told myself that he was dead now. He can't hurt me anymore.

The bus stopped in front of the high school. All at once they emptied the bus to about three people. I looked out the window to see my old high school. I had forgotten all the things I used to do at this age; I followed. Most of them went up the path for school. Some went their separate ways.

Nick and Alex went across the street next to Stop N' Go. They walked to where no one would see them. There sat David the pot head, Andrew the storyteller, and Nick's girlfriend Terry. I hated her. She tried to sleep with me during high school but I thought she was nasty. She was five seven in height, taller than the average girl here. She had dark skin with patches of fair complexion make up trying to cover her true color. She was kind of chubby around the stomach. Her butt was completely flat but it didn't stop her from wearing tight clothes. Her chest was so large that in a tight shirt her breast looked like a giant marshmallow. She had safety pins all over her clothes. She thought she was the *queen* of punk rock. She would tell me, "You're just a skater trying to be punk rock. You'll be gone in a month." She talked like a valley girl. And after all that talk about *punk for life* she was gone in two years.

It wasn't the size of her waist not the color of her skin; it was how she presented herself. For one she was Nick's girl for a long time. It was the fact that she smelled a little bad and the way she tried to cover up everything.

Nick walked up to her putting his arm around her shoulder. He took off his jacket wrapping it around her as if it were their sacred robe. She was an ideal type of woman I hated with a passion. She slept with so many guys. When she met me, she tried to make me look stupid by preaching about her way of life (punk). I told her I didn't care about anything she had to say. I wasn't a punk rocker. I was a skateboarder interested in listening to that kind of music when I skated. After my brush off, I guess it turned her on so she tried every which way she could to get with me. When I continued to ignore her, she told people that I tried to rape her. And Nick still thought the world of her.

I stood behind everyone, not saying a word. I might have not existed.

"Hey!" I yelled. Not even a flinch.

Alex sat down while Nick cuddled up with Terry.

"So what's going on?" Alex asked.

"Nothing. I know David's got some herbal refreshment," said Terry.

Everyone looked at David. David put up his hands. "Okay. Okay. I've got a one hitter bong so I guess we'll smoke." He stuck his hands in his pocket and pulled out a bag of weed. He loaded up the bong, took a hit, and then passed it to Andrew. It went around the circle.

"Roll a joint or something. It's mush easier that way." Said Alex.

"Yeah, David." Said Terry. I hated the sound of her voice.

David rolled a joint in no time. He lit up. The group of friends smoked until their eyes were red and they were laughing at stupid things. They squinted their eyes at each other.

The bell rang for school across the street. They grabbed their bags as they stretched to get to class.

"I say we just go back to my house." Said David.

"Cool," said Alex.

"Nah man, I have to go to class." Said Andrew.

"Come on Andrew, don't be such a puss." Terry smiled. She gave him this sensual smile, as if she wanted him. She loved flirting. I was her past-time.

"I guess." He didn't want to go with them but her smile made him think he was really wanted.

They headed down n the street into a neighborhood. It was only a few blocks. David lived next to the school. I followed him into the house. David walked towards the back. "I'm going to fill the bong with some water then we'll get real high."

They went into his room to hang out. Young Alex sat on a crate very quiet as if he wasn't comfortable with the group. Most of them took place on the bed. David walked into his room with the bong in his hand. "You ready to get high?" He asked as he walked over to his stereo. He turned the music up really loud. He pulled out a tray dumping weed on it. He filled the bowl as much as he could. They smoked once more.

"Let's go outside. I can't be cooped up in here." Said Nick as he paced the room.

They left their belongings in the room then they went into the backyard. The sun was shinning high and becoming unbearable. Everyone sat at the wooden picnic bench that was next to the patio.

"We should have stayed in school." Said Alex.

"Hey Alex, I have something to tell you," said Nick. Terry moved closer to Nick with that face that knew what this was about. She smiled at Alex.

"What's up," I asked. I could tell I was high by they way my eyes shrunk into redness.

"I know you tried to mess with Terry. She told me about the time you two were alone and you tried to fuck her."

"*No fuck'n way in hell,* would I sleep with that slut? I wouldn't ever touch her. Besides that, she's your chic." He turned away. Under his breath he said, "if that's what you call her?"

"Well, she *is* with me. And I think that shows you aren't a loyal friend. And I think I ought to do something about it."

Alex smiled a little. "Well why don't you believe me? She's lying whatever she told you. She just wants you to pick a fight with me because I don't want her."

"I don't think so pal. She wouldn't do that."

"Well if you're going to make such accusations on my ass, then I suggest you don't call me pal. And if you have to do something about it, then here I am. Do something *hero*." Said young Alex with balls I had never seen before.

Nick smiled as he glanced at David then Andrew, as they were waiting for the action. Alex just looked at Terry and smiled. He knew what she was up to, *the little whore*. She was a troublemaker from hell.

"Thank you so much Terry," said Alex as he looked at her.

She blew a kiss to Alex. Nick broke a bottle over Alex's' head. He fell on the floor. They began to beat him; punching and kicking in his face and stomach. While all was happening to him, all I could do was watch in anger. I wished for something to stop all of this hellishness. And it did . . .

Alex jumped up. He held a hatchet in his hand that he yanked out of his jacket. He swung it across Andrews' face. Andrew flew back. Blood shot out with the hatchets' swing. David tried to grab him but he shoved the hatchet into his stomach and yanked up into his chest until it smacked him in the chin knocking him down. Nick had fear in his eyes as he backed up. He put up his hands so Alex would come near him. Nick grabbed a shovel that was behind him and swung it at Alex. Alex smiled as he moved back. Alex moved forward as if her were marching. He slashed the hatchet down into the little boy. He hit him over and over. There was blood everywhere.

And as for Terry, he smacked her in the head. She fell to the ground cursing. He smiled at her. Then he grabbed her by the hair as she was on the ground. He yanked her into the bathroom. He threw her into the tub and just chopped her up.

A deep breath and it was over. I couldn't believe these things are still haunting me. Although, I hadn't dreamt of Lila. It was just a wish I had when I was a kid and they beat me up. I sat up listening to the air. There was loud fiesta music playing. I had to get out and relax for it was over.

I brushed my teeth and got dressed. I knew I'd let myself have fun. It would cure all ugly dreams. I locked up hiding my money where no one would look, locking up as I went out. The same lady was sitting behind the front desk smiling at me as she walked out.

"Excuse me, what's going on outside?" I asked.

"Is the noise bothering you?"

"No, I just wanted to know what was here."

"Well they have a fiesta here every week for the tourists. And tonight just happens to be the night."

I walked out to see what was out there. When I walked out, people were dancing to mariachi music. Some men were drinking. Many people were walking around looking for something to do.

I sat down at a table just outside a little restaurant. I pulled out a cigarette. A woman with a big fluffy colorful dress walked up to my table. She put down a basket of chips and salsa.

"Como te puedo ayudar?"

"No speak Espanola." I said.

"Okay then, how can I help you?" She smiled.

"Um, I'll take a plate of chicken enchiladas and a beer." I closed my menu.

"Sure."

There were so many poor people walking around with their children. I felt bad. They had no food or shelter. What was I supposed to do? I had my own problems. I sound like an asshole. Most of the people were dancing having a good time. Some were drunk and loud. And then I spotted her . . .

She smiled at me with her long lushes lips. Her hair was long and dark tied up in a bun. Her skin was tan. Her eyes were round. She wore a tight black dress. She stood near all the drunken men.

"Here you are." Said the waitress. "Enjoy."

I looked down and saw the delicious plate of enchiladas, beans, and rice with some flour tortillas. I began to scarf down the food. It was good. It didn't taste anything like American Mexican food. It was awesome. After I finished, I left a tip and paid. I wanted to look around for any gimmicks that might interest me. Most of the items were cheaply made. I stayed near where they danced. I stood in line at the bar. I ordered a beer sitting down. Women stood waiting for a dance partner at the edge of the dance floor.

I too wanted to dance. I began to scan each woman to see if any caught my eye. Some of them noticed me staring at them and tried to make themselves pretty. I decided on the woman who passed by me earlier, the only who put their thin body in my face. She sat next to me crossing her legs then turned to me.

"Obla espanol?" She asked. I shook my head. "*Oh*, so you are American."

"How did yah guess?"

"Naturally most Americans come here for vacation or to visit." She said. She had a beautiful accent.

"Would you like a drink?" I asked her.

"Sure. Some tequila if you can handle it?" She laughed.

"I can drink anything you want me to."

We took a shot together. She grabbed my arm pulling me on the dance floor. She showed me how to dance to the music they played. After the song was over, we sat down taking more shots, then two more, and two more. I looked at her with lazy eyes.

"Why did you want to talk to me?" I asked.

"Well, I saw you staring at me and thought maybe you could use some company. Anyway, it's only thirty dollars."

"You mean, you're a hooker."

She laughed. "You didn't know? This doesn't come free you know. Most of the girls out here are working."

"But we haven't done anything."

"Yet." She laughed.

What! Of all the insidious things! What a whore. I hate prostitutes and felt I would lose my nerve. I hate teases. I hate cheaters. *Damn it! Damn it! Damn it!* Calm down, I told myself. I'm a little drunk. I knew she was some sort of a slut whether it was for free or it had a price. I just didn't realize she was a hooker.

"You want to dance?" She asked.

She grabbed my hand. We walked out there. She looked at me tripping over something on the floor. She brought me down with her. She started laughing. I helped her up as I stood trying to revive myself.

"Let's just forget the dancing." I smiled.

We continued to walk around. I had no idea where we were going. She stopped in front of a cheap motel.

"What are we doing here?" I asked.

"Do you have money to pay for the room?"

"Yeah, why?"

She put out her hand for the money and I gave her twenty dollars. I was sure this place was between ten and twenty. I watched her walk into the motel office. It seemed like forever waiting for her. I thought it was because I was drunk. I fell asleep against the wall. When I awoke she still was not there. I thought this was all a dream by then.

I walked over to the office to see what was going on but there was no one there. She walked out of some door in the office. She ran out with the key. We went to room 15. It seemed like she was the one in charge. I didn't like that. I stood in front of the bed dazing in the darkness. I felt her push me onto the bed. I turned around. She lay there staring at me.

She slipped down her black dress. She was wearing lace panties under her dress. She got on top of me. She began to kiss my neck. She pulled off my shirt while kissing my chest. I was too drunk to pay attention. She unbuttoned my pants with her teeth, along with my boxers. She put her mouth over me.

She took down her panties. I smelled something awful that made me almost throw up. It smelled as though she had been passed around several guys before me. She was about to get on me. *I stopped.* Who knew what kind of diseases this woman had.

"Wait."

"What?"

"I want you to kiss me."

She smiled moving towards my face. She began to kiss my lips but I barely kissed back. I ran my hands through her hair. With my right hand I searched for my Knife in my pants pocket. I felt the blade and grabbed it.

I pulled her head back by yanking her hair. I sliced through her neck. Her eyes rolled back. She let go holding onto her neck. I got up quickly. I threw her to the side of the bed. I wiped as much as I could onto the blanket. I went into the restroom washing all the blood away from my body. I dressed myself. As I walked out I didn't see anyone around but a man getting into his car. I waited until he was gone. I walked out into the empty night.

CHAPTER 18

"So, you think he went across the boarder, huh?" Asked Detective Miller.

The police officer standing there said, yes. He looked around at all of the officers that had been standing behind him. "All of us searched his house, his brother's, and his shop. We have an APB out on him. We checked the train stations, buses, and plans. There's no sign of him anywhere. His uncle didn't believe anything we told him but we checked his place also." The officer got quiet then put his head down.

"Go ahead officer." Said Detective Steels.

"I don't have the authority to say what happens next." He looked down once more.

"Well, there's nothing wrong with new ideas." Robert put his seat back. "We need all the help and ideas as possible. Go ahead and say what you want to say."

"I don't know." He looked around while cracking his knuckles. "Well, we know he's got to be in Mexico. There's no where else he could be because of the fact that we checked all of the airports and showed his a picture to every single employee, which took a hell of a lot of time." He looked at Miller.

"Well you know the law officer Riggens. He committed his crimes here. That's a whole other country." Robert pointed outward as to make an example of *the whole other country.* "You can be kicked off the force if the FBI gets on this. And trust me, they will be. His crimes date back to ten years of unsolved murders all across California. He robbed his own money, so this must mean he snapped. All we can do is ask Mexico to cooperate with us."

"It was just a thought to go after him. He killed the mother of two children and who knows how much more damage he can do out there."

"Looks like you fellas got some homework to do. Tell you what, you guys continue to send out his pictures all over America as wanted for murder. Send it on the Internet for any information at all on finding this guy. I'm going to see what I can do on the television. As for you," he pointed to Riggens; "I want to talk with you on a few procedures."

He looked frightened. It sounded as though he might get the third degree. The other officers walked out with their own files and things they need to do to catch this guy. As soon as they walked out of the office to the loud room of phone calls and criminal investigations, Miller shut the door. It went dead silent.

He lit a cigarette and then sat down.

"Don't be afraid." Riggens took off his patrol cap that he was sweating in underneath. He wiped his brow with his sleeve, widened his eyes, and looked up. "Don't feel nervous. Just relax. I didn't hold you back so I can yell at you." Robert stood up. He looked at all of the other officers out the window. "I feel as though you do. This prick motherfucker is running around cutting the faces off of women and there's nothing we can do about it."

There was a tapping at Miller's door. Detective Felding popped his head through the door. "Is this not a good time?" He asked.

"Oh no, we were just speaking about Mr. Dugan. Come in. You got anything?"

"Oh yeah I got something. I looked into Alex's past and found where his parents reside. We found that Alex's parents were dead. His brother had mentioned his parents had unfortunately passed away, he just didn't say how or when. This information was from Ramos, correct?"

"Yeah, sure."

"Speaking of which, is he in?"

"No I don't think so."

"So anyways, I called up the Texas department of records on deaths and found that it was most recent they had died." The other two detectives were staring at him in an unconscious way, knowing the end result. "They were murdered. And I don't just mean killed over a wallet or robbery, they were hacked into pieces." Miller moved forward in his desk. "The detective I just spoke to said there was nothing that resembled a break in. Not only that, but there was not one single finger print in the whole house."

"The killers?"

"No ones'. Not even the parents. The house was spic and span. Some of the employees got curious as to why Alexs' step father hadn't shown up to work in a week. They stopped by noticing a horrid smell. When the police finally got in, the house was clean. Clean as can be. No traces of blood that had drained from the head of the stepfather. Their body parts were in the closet.

They called up Alex and his brother to let them know what happened. They never came down for the funeral nor did any of them claim the house.

"Alright we're going to get this fucker. And I want a tight watch on this guys' brother. What's his name . . . Anthony Dugan. You find him and you question him again, only this time, ask about his parents and if he had anything to do with their murder. Let him know he can be locked up for life, away from his family, and they could lose everything, if he doesn't speak up."

"Are we leaving now?" Asked Felding.

"You bet your sweet ass."

Riggens took another officer out to Anthonys' home, where it was surrounded by several watchdogs. He dressed in normal attire to make it seem as though he wasn't just a petty street cop. He had called the officers on duty to let them know he was heading inside.

Anthony was looking outside of the widow staring at the two vans parked on each side of his house across the street. He was ready to go out there with a crowbar and shoe them off. Jennifer looked at him as he looked through the Venetian binds pacing and talking to himself. Jennifer followed him back and forth within his steps almost crying.

"What's going on Tony? Why are all of these cops here? And where's Alex?" She demanded.

"*I don't know!* These guys are making up stories about my brother. Don't believe them." He looked away from the window. "I can't even live my life in peace without these assholes haunting me. What the fuck is going on?!"

"I don't know! I don't know!" She cried.

"Baby, don't think I'm mad at you. I'm worried about my brother. What am I going to do for him if he gets thrown in jail?"

"What *can* you do Tony? What can you do?" She put out her hands to him. "There's nothing you can do or say but just wait. So come lay down with me in the room. The boys are doing their homework and we can relax for one moment."

"One moment? Jennifer, I can't sit here relaxing if my brother's going to jail and I might be going with him."

"Why would you be going with him?"

"*Because!* Because, I don't know." Tony threw himself on the recliner clicking on the TV. The news was on and that's just what he wanted to see.

The news cast was speaking of an earthquake in Sacramento a couple of days ago. The lady speaking had the same voice as all the women who were news broadcasters. She was dressed in a spiffy business suit. She gathered together her stack of papers and began. "In other news . . ." She went on to say that there was a series of murders all over California. "And here in person we have detective Robert Miller."

Live in front of the police department stood the detective. "I'm detective Miller and we wanted to alert the people of this man here," he held up a picture and the camera closed up, "Alex Dugan is responsible for a series of murders across California. It is solid evidence that Mr. Dugan did in fact murder these victims. His prints and seaman were found at the scene of several murder sights. If you have any information, please call the station here."

Tony clicked off the television off. "Son of a bitch!"

"What the hell was that?"

"I don't know! This is all fucked up."

"Do you know something?"

"Babe, come on. You don't believe this crap they're saying about my brother. He's a fuck'n saint for Christ's sakes. I love him and I won't believe this bullshit. He just got so rich that someone's trying to fuck up his career."

"Then where is he Tony? Where's Alex if this is all false."

"Babe-," there was a subtle tap on the front door. Tony put his finger to his lips. "Shh." He crept over to the door. "Who is it this time?" The voice was muffled by the door. It was an officer and he wanted to speak with Anthony Dugan. Tony looked at Jennifer, "go watch the boys, love."

"In a minute."

Tony opened the door. "What's going on?"

Ramos and Riggens were standing there with their heads down. "We need you to come downtown to answer a few questions." Said Ramos.

"Like what?"

"We can talk about this downtown Mr. Dugan."

"I ain't going. You'll have to arrest me." Jennifer stepped forward ready to cry.

"If we have to we will. Now come with us sir."

Tony looked back at Jennifer. "Can you believe this shit!"

"You're under arrest for accessory to murder, place your hands behind your back . . ."

Tony watched Jennifer's face as they hauled him away like he was dirt. He looked at her with a sad smile as if he would go to jail to hide secret he never told her. He would not say one word no matter what.

When they had him in the interrogation room, with his hands cuffed, he sat there wondering if his brother was caught. In walked the two detectives and the captain of the police department. They sat down laying their files on the table.

"I want my lawyer." Said Tony.

"Well, where are you going to get the money at this hour for a lawyer?"

"First of all, it's none of your business and secondly I have every right. So get me to a phone to call my wife, so I can call my *fuck'n* lawyer!"

"Ooo. A lot of tension built up. Maybe we were after the wrong guy."

"I'm not dangerous but I know my fuck'n rights you piece of shit cop. Now if you don't get me to a phone right now, I will sue this whole department for falsely arresting a person who has nothing to do with any of the shit you guys are concocting."

The captain wanted to put an end to this scuffle so he got him a phone. Tony had Jennifer call Alexs' lawyer who had won him a case in property ownership. Even though that was all he had done for him, he was one of the best defense attorneys in Northern California. She got hold of him letting him know they would pay him in full as soon as the matter was taken care of.

When the lawyer named Richard Talice showed up, Tony was relieved. He had them take the cuffs off of Tony. Richard heard both sides and smiled abruptly at the officers. "You told him he was being arrested for accessory to murder, yet you have not one hint of proof. You better let my client go now, or we'll sue the department."

"Tell us about the murder of your parents!" Yelled out Riggens.

Richard leaned over, "Tony, you don't have to answer that. It's none of their business. If need be, when they find your brother, you can answer them in court."

"What the hell does this have to do with my parents?"

"We know all about it Tony. Your parents were hacked up by either you or your brother. We'll find out."

"You son of a bitch!" Yelled Tony as he jumped across the table grabbing Riggens by the collar trying to hit him. "My fuck'n parents were murdered and you accuse me!" Everyone became hysterical as they pried Tony off if the man. "My parents fuck'n died you piece of shit! You think I haven't suffered enough!"

"Come on Tony, before they *can* charge you with something." Said Richard as he pulled Tony by the arm. Tony pulled back with one of the same killer faces Alex made before.

"You better fuck'n stay away from my family. I have nothing to do with this shit or my parents' death. And neither does my brother. I'll get you in court for this one."

Miller, Felding, Samuel Gonzales, Tom Alberts, and Brian Walsh met up in the streets of where his footprints once walked. They followed within every instinct they had to get him. All were officers of different ranks and lifestyles, but all had the moral to step outside of their universe to bring in Alex Dugan.

The men decided upon separating to look for any trace of Alex Dugan. It wasn't the end until it was the end of him. Sam went looking on the eastern side of the town, Tom went to the west, Brian went to the south, and Miller and Felding went to the North. Miller was the only one who didn't know a word of Spanish.

Felding was on his toes. He kept his eyes wired and his ears cleared of all nonsense that would come through. If he were successful in his attempt to help the officers find Dugan, there would certainly be a higher position for him in the force and a pay raise. He loved his job but wanted to work on cases like the one they were working on, more often. It was only a hobby now.

A respectable looking woman walking down the street passed by Miller and Felding. She was wearing a long designed skirt that waved in the wind. She wore a wrap around top with the same beautiful colors exenterating her figure. Felding touched her arm trying to make her feel as though he wasn't after her, but he was not successful. She swung around her purse yelling at him in Spanish.

In her foreign tongue, Felding said, "Sorry miss, I only needed some help finding someone. Can you please help me? I'm looking for someone who might be a threat in Mexico."

She pulled away trying to gather her thoughts together. "Give me a moment to collect myself," she said in this passionate Spanish accent. She pulled her purse close to her shoulder and then brushed her hair back with her fingers. "Okay mister, what can I help you with that you had to be so rude as to grab me."

"I'm looking for a man."

"Money."

"What?"

"If I have to answer any questions at all, I want some money. Say . . . twenty dollars."

"Twenty-dollars? Alright."

Miller stood there watching the two in wonder. Why was his partner giving this lady money? What was he asking her? He observed quietly though waiting patiently for the end result. Felding grabbed the picture of Alex Dugan from Millers arms and held it in front of her face.

"This man here is a serial killer from California. I need to find out if you have seen him or if there have been any murders within the last two days. Would you know *anyone* who might be able to help me?"

She took the copied print of Alexs' face into her hands staring at the handsome man for a moment or two trying to recognize him. She had known many people who lived in Laredo and would recognize a foreigner in an instant. "The white man I have not seen. But yes, there has been a murder at this cheap motel two nights ago. I think it was a prostitute."

"Do you know where that was?"

"I think it was at . . . Juan's Place just five miles east."

"Thank you so much miss." She walked away with a smile. Felding tapped Miller on the back. "Come on let's go."

"What happened?"

"There's been a murder at some motel east of here."

It took them forty minutes to find the scene of the crime that Dugans' hands last touched. It was in both of their minds that they were on the right track. Sam was also there looking around the scene of the crime but the Mexican police told them to keep their distance. They began to ask questions about whether they knew what was going on or not.

Sam was standing by a few other people who were trying to get a good look when someone said, "poor woman." A voice with a deep Spanish accent spoke while they pulled the body out of the room.

"Did you know her," asked Sam.

"Everyone knew her. Easy Rosalyn is what they called her. She slept with everyone. I'm married so I never touched her. Not that I wanted to. Beautiful senorita. But it would've happened sooner or later."

"What do you mean?"

"Come on, there's a lot of people in dah world. I'm chure that who ever she was doing, caught her doing what she does."

"And what's that?"

"She brings these guys to this motel, tells them to give her money for the room, and instead of paying for it, she sleeps with the owner for the room."

"And so you think the man she could've been with caught her?"

The man turned to face the voice he had been talking to for a while. He put his hands in his pockets. "I'm saying, I saw her with the man she was with the other night." He began to walk away.

"Wait! Wait!" Yelled Sam. He grabbed the man by the shoulder. "I'm sorry. Look, I'm an officer from California and I'm looking for a man who has been committing a series of murders all over the place." He flashed his badge.

"What the hell are you doing here? You can get into big trouble being here with those intensions."

"I know, but he could be hurting your people. We need to stop this guy." He put his badge away pulling out a picture of Alex. "Is this the man?" He held a picture in front of the man.

The mans' face lit up, as if it *were* him. "I don't think so. The guy with her was bald."

"Are you sure?"

"Get the fuck away from me! You'll get me killed." The man walked away.

Sam smiled at the man as he walked away. He waved at him saying, "Thank you very much sir! You were very helpful." He ran into the other officers who were combing the area. "It's Alex Dugan alright. Some guy identified him from the other night."

"I figured as much. Let's hook up with the others and find a trail." Said Miller thinking he was in charge of this expedition.

I had been awake since the moment I laid my hands on that woman. No sleep in my life ruins everything I do. I can hardly concentrate and now, with this on my conscious, I don't know where I'm heading.

News travels slow around here. I expected to hear about the death of that prostitute in the daily paper. I had someone translate it for me. There was nothing. The time here moves slowly and I think my life can come to a stop so I can think things out. My new goal is to escape from their dreaded haunting in my head. I'm all-alone here. It's all been a lie; everything they told me was just what I wanted to hear.

I hung around near the second boarder. In the drivers seat of my car, I slowly close my eyes but then my head pops back up into the reality that I might be taken away or someone would rob me. It's six in the morning and I'm pretty hungry. I can see from where I lay a small restaurant that seems to be open.

There was a man siting on the floor talking nonsense to himself as I walked up to the door of the café. He was laughing at something while he held me close to his face. He was drugged up or something.

"Excuse me," I asked. "Do you speak English?"

The man looked up at me with these large filtered pupils. He looked as though he were going to cry. He grabbed my hand putting something into it. I felt the weakness of his hands as he stared at me for one last moment. His eyes looked up at the sky as if he were, right then and there, asking God for forgiveness of all his sins he committed and then he was on the ground like he took a toll.

I was discouraged about staying in a place where people just die right in front of others in the middle of the street. Maybe I should kick some dirt over him; say a prayer. But you know me; I don't do much of that. So I just walked on in with the same hole in my stomach of emptiness. I sat down at the counter in a spinning stool that had lost its spin. One man sat a few seats away from me. The rest of the place was empty.

The waitress walked up to me in a little apron. She spoke in Spanish as they all did. I felt dumb because I always had to find someone to translate for me. One can only assume she asked me what I wanted.

"Coffee por favor." Please was the only word I knew in Spanish so far. Then I pointed to a picture of eggs and ham with all the Mexican accents on it and she nodded her head. As soon as she walked away, I opened my hand to see what he left me. He gave me the last precious thing in life to him. It was wrapped in foil. I opened it up to find a few slices of mushrooms. My coffee was placed in front of me. He most likely died from eating the shroom. This might be a destiny. Taking a deadly drug to get me out of this life. It was well worth the effort. Life was meaningless to me everyday. I took half the bag of shrooms which is not half as bad as people describe. I drowned my mouth with hot coffee to kill the taste.

"Handale senoira, cambie el canal television." Said the man sitting next to me.

I sat there staring at the wall. She nodded her head to him walking over to the television hanging against the wall. She turned the volume louder. I could smell my breakfast heating up in the kitchen.

"Es el, en el television!" Yelled the man. "The killer el assino!"

The man pointed to me while I was trying to figure out why the hell he was yelling. Behind him I saw a sketch of my face on the television. I understood why he was going crazy. *SHIT!* The waitress stood there with her eyes closed almost like a prey thinking if it closed its eyes, the predator will disappear. The man wouldn't stop yelling so I lost control. I grabbed my knife and flung it into the man's chest. He fell to the floor holding onto his chest. He grabbed onto the stool trying to hold him self up.

I looked at the woman who had her eyes closed while she held a container of tortillas. I pulled my knife out of the mans' chest wiping the blood on his shirt. I ran out without even looking back. I knew they were on to me. I jumped into my car and headed for the boarder. The mushroom was taking over my mind and there was nothing I could do about it.

"I say we grab something to eat before we continue on." Said Tom over the walkie-talkie.

They were driving around, just the two, looking for Dugan in any of the alleys and hotels. He was here somewhere. The men parked their cars in front of a café that had the early morning sign up for customers. It said twenty-four hours in Spanish.

"We really don't have time," said Felding looking at his watch.

Brian and Tom walked into the restaurant. The two were talking amongst themselves as they walked into the scene of an imperfect crime. The waitress was standing there crying still holding up a plate of tortillas. A customer was bleeding to death on the floor still holding onto the stool.

"Senoir! Senoir, the white man, he killed him!" Yelled the lady crying and wailing.

They stopped smiling as the two looked at the bloody man on the floor. Tom checked his pulse after he let go of the stool but he was already dead. Brian ran out to the truck that Miller was sitting. Felding was smoking a cigarette by the other vehicle talking with Sam. The others were wondering what was going on. Tom ran out trying to tell the others what was going on, while Brian yelled for Miller to start the truck and *haul ass*.

The others began to load up in the Jeep. But from where they sat now, Miller and Brian had already shot off into the morning darkness.

"I saw him!" Said Brian.

"What do you mean you saw him?" Asked Miller not knowing where he was going.

"Let's just get this fucker!"

They saw nothing coming as they drove. It was as if he just disappeared into nothing. They traveled down a long empty road. As they drove up to an intersection, they saw him coming to a crossing.

"There he is! He's at the intersection!"

Miller stepped on the gas making them feel as if they were on a roller coaster ride. They headed straight for Alexs' beautiful Camero. They yelled, as they were about to collide with the killer. The truck smashed right into the passenger side of the Camero sort of smashing Alex. The moment they hit, it went dead silent. Alex began to bleed from his arm where he was recently shot in the arm.

The silence was broken when Alex stuck his head out the window and began to fire his gun towards the drivers' side of the vehicle. He saw no passenger. Brian got out of the car. He fired back.

"Okay! Okay." Yelled Alex calmly. "I give up."

"Show me your hands Alex Dugan!" Yelled Brian. Brian believed this was his moment of glory. He would be the hero of his little escapade. Brian would definitely get his prize.

"How do I know you're not going to shoot me?"

"I promise it to you Mr. Dugan. I can give you my word." Brian was raising just a little out the truck to see where he was.

Alex peeked again. Before Brian could duck away, Alex shot him in the left eye. The only sound from there was the gun dropping and his body hitting the floor. The maroon Camero drove off peeling out. The engine was fine but the body was crushed in on one side.

The jeep pulled up five minutes after the Camero drove off. They hurried out of the car to see what happened to their partners. Brian was on the ground dead. Miller was knocked out with his head smacked against the broken window.

"Shit! That motherfucker! I'm gonna kill this guy!" Yelled Felding. He checked Miller. He had a pulse but was unconscious. Felding and the other men pulled him out of the truck, laid him on the ground, and covered him with a blanket. Felding then wrapped a wet towel over the gash on Millers' head. "You guys get on the road! Don't dare let this guy go!"

Sam and Tom were the only ones left. They checked their armor as they were driving away. They were armed with pistol grip twelve gage shotguns fully loaded. They had shells at their waste. While Sam was driving the vehicle, Tom put on his bulletproof vest. It would be one of the *most* exciting missions they had ever been on.

I thought that was the mushroom crashing me into the other vehicle. I saw things that would send me straight into the pit of insanity. The car looked like a giant ghoul. When I heard the shots fired back, I knew the reality was beyond my comprehension. So I closed my eyes for a moment to see the truth in it all. There were neither flashing lights nor sirens.

I saw one man when he stuck his head out of the car. I killed him. I saw more of the ghouls coming to me; I saw more of these cars. They had something to do with where I was from because they knew my name. Out of the wilderness from my escape. I saw a lonely house in a field just off the road. It looked as though it had been abandoned for a few years. I hid on the second floor of the barn.

I'll try to kill them all if they come near me. If they should get me then so be it. But in the midst of the whole crisis, I knew I had to move forward no matter what. I had gone too far out to find salvation to give up now.

Shhh! I heard a car roll up pealing to a stop. The lights were bright then went dark ruining my vision from the sudden salvation. If it stays quiet enough I can hear them talking or moving.

"Yeah, that's the car. Different plates but that's it." Whispered one.

"Check the barn, I'll be in the house."

"Don't stop to apprehend him, just get rid of him."

It was silent again. I was nervous. I couldn't hear them anymore. They weren't Mexican officers. There was only American accents. It was illegal to come here for me. I can only hope they weren't the best of the best, because I was no pro. Only psycho.

The crunch on the floor down below gave away the person who was trying to sneak up on me at this very moment. I moved back a little. I held tightly to my knife. I had my gun but I wanted this to be silent deadly. I guessed there were three.

The rattling of the hay was too loud for anyone not to notice. Maybe he was scared of me as much as I feared the faceless man. I heard him cock his gun. It wasn't a handgun. It sounded like a shotgun. Maybe they were just family members of victims. I looked over the side to see him walk into the open. He was covered in what looked like a full on SWAT uniform. He had his gun pointed parallel to his shoulders.

"Looks like no one's here," he yelled out. He took a look around the barn to see if he missed anything. "What the hell?" He found the ladder I tried to cover up with hay. "He might be up there." He said to himself.

I moved back quietly, tightly gripping my knife. My heart was pounding making me feel as though I would go into shock. Butterflies were around me like clusters of pain and fear. I heard each footstep he made with those army boots. I knew he would have my head in no time if I were not careful. I realized I was in serious trouble. I was sweating like a racehorse finding it hard to breathe. I watched him through the cracks of hay. There was no way out.

He came to where I was hiding on the opposite side of my haystack. I moved the other side as he was coming to mine. I was behind *him* now. I pressed my blade tightly to his neck. His hands went into the air with the gun over his head.

"Quietly, drop the gun the ground." I whispered. He followed instructions accordingly. "Why can't you people just leave me alone? I'm done with it all. I just want to get on with my life." I asked him while pushing deeper against the skin of his neck.

"You killed many innocent people." He tried to speak. "Give it up. I'm only doing what's right." His voice was distorted and cracked.

When he spoke, it got to me. I was feeling something of his righteousness, to bring my rage against the world to an end. He wanted to avenge against the lives he knew nothing about. Even the whores out on the streets I just put away for them. My mind was joggled with guilt. I had to do something. At my most remorseful moment of repent, he pulled some fighting tactic on me and knocked me to the ground. His gun was hidden under the hay somewhere so he just pounded me in.

I couldn't feel it though. I should have just knocked out then and there, but the drugs where all over my body and I felt nothing. I took the punches. Those thrusts should have knocked me out. Blood gushed out of my nose and I was done for. I laughed because it was all too predictable. My knife, I never dropped, nor would I have used it on him. It was over when I shot it into, *I don't know where.* I just heard him grunt and fall over.

I lay there in the hay trying to recover. But I was so beat up that I couldn't move. I felt nothing, yet physically my body didn't want to function. He must have broken something or injured me somehow. So I lay there for ten minutes. I pushed up as I thought about the others who could do away with me. It was a loss of blood that made me so weak.

The body next to me on he floor was still breathing. He was staring at me. I felt remorse all over again. He looked like he was in shock from death. Life was leaving his body. *Life!* I took his life and I realized how much fear I put into all those people.

The gun was still in my pocket, fully loaded. It was silent as I walked out of the barn. The sounds of the crickets were everywhere. I won't ever forget this moment for as long as I live.

Still, I know not why I entered that house. It was a blood bath as before in my days. The lights were off downstairs but not upstairs. Footsteps were creaking the floorboards and I knew exactly where he was. He would come down soon. Then there were lights from outside. I was surrounded, as of this moment, with more people of vengeance. Before I could escape through the front door, another man walked in. He too was fully loaded.

"Sam! Tom!" Called the stranger. I hid underneath the stairs as he called out to his companions.

"I'm up here!" Called one.

As the stranger walked up the stairs slowly, he swung his gun slowly back and forth to make sure I wasn't going to lunge out of nowhere. He disappeared upstairs. They were speaking in muffled tones that I could not understand. It was my chance to get myself out of troubles I started. I headed for the door.

A sudden rumbling of footsteps came down the stairs and I was discovered by one of the men. He had his gun to me and he was sure I was over. But you know me; I don't stop to think anymore. As soon as I heard the steps I had already turned around with my gun to him. We fired almost simultaneously into the night. Though he had better shots of me, my handgun landed a hole right into his face. I just saw blood splat all over the stairway and he tumbled to the ground. *Fuck!*

How come it was not I dead on the ground?!!! But as I looked down, there was blood gushing out of the arm that had already been wounded quite a few times and my foot was probably missing the toes. I didn't care. All I could do was cry as I hobbled out the door.

"Sam!" The other footsteps came running along! I was already at the door of my car. "Sam!" He cried from inside. I was on the passenger side of the car. I had to get to the other side as I was bleeding to death.

I felt hands grab my shirt and yank me out of the car onto the ground. I was crying. He was yelling. "Think you're so fuck'n though, huh!" He yelled at me. He, like the other one, was pounding the life out of me. I had lost it completely. I was ready to let go. I was ready to let death come and take me with the others to suffer. The shock was coming onto me as my life was leaving *my* body. I cried out, "thank god, let it end!"

He stepped back for a moment as I wailed, knowing I was at bitter end. But it didn't come. I cried out. "Please kill me!" He stood there looking at the mess I had become. *They* won't release me. They never will. So in bitter end, when I was ready completely for salvation. They came to my rescue.

Out they came like swarming demons crying into the night. I thought they were coming for my soul to take me to hell. They yelled out in so many voices. And that's when the stranger stepped back from my body away from three swarming shadows.

He saw them too. They were chasing him away from my lifeless body.

Never letting me go. I was in hell. There was nowhere I could go to escape these demons. They came back to me, took over as before. But they were weak. They lunged my blade into the chest of the man. He fell back. They pushed me out of myself. It was them who took me to highway. I was safe in the darkness where they left me. I felt no more pain. I figured it was over. They would probably send me over the nearest cliff.

CHAPTER 19

I woke up again. I cried as I saw the light of day. The leather seats were covered in blood. I was at a rest stop on the highway that never ended. Crying was something that I couldn't stop doing for the next few hours. There was nothing real anymore. I was out of control and I had no one. I was ready to go home and see a doctor. Let them lock me up in a straight jacket, at least they might cure me. In my life now, there is no death. If I am caught, they'll rid of me, but then the voices will come and take me where I don't want to be. I have to be strong. I can't lose my mind completely.

Conveniently, there was a restroom right near me. I gathered some of my black long sleeved shirts. It was time to see what I had become. The lights were flashing a little as I walked in. The mirror was filthy full of rust spots on all corners. Starting with my face, I had eyes so swollen I looked like a blowfish. They were purple covered in dried blood and I could barely see. In-between there somewhere, there were gashes that the men had punched ripping the skin apart. My mouth was swollen making me look like Pamela Anderson with inflated lips from the circus. My neck was covered in bruises.

I pulled off my shirt to find many bruises on my back, chest, and stomach. My right arm was good compared to the mess of my left. This however, was not a savoir. I could barely move my fingers. There was a shot in my arm the size of a dime, which did not go all the way through. It was bleeding a little but the bullet stopped the blood from gushing out. The bullet wound from before was ripped open again from the man in the barn. My legs were okay, nothing much but a few scratches and bruises. But my foot had lost two of the middle toes. My shoe, on the right foot was open like the mouth of a frog. The toes, I could not find. They were bleeding still. I was almost drained.

Knowing me, I was prepared. I had my first aid kit. The first to do was stop the bleeding in my foot. I wrapped up my foot so tight, but my foot was numb so I felt nothing. I pulled out the bullet from my forearm with pliers. Blood shot out like a rocket. I was losing consciousness. I sewed quickly with one hand, plugged it up with gauze, and then wrapped it firmly. I had to re-sew my old wound. My left arm was numb and I feared I would lose it all. I used elastic to cut off circulation in my arm at the very top where the artery began.

The last to do was clean up last minute gashes putting stitches here and there. I ended up with about twenty stitches on my face. It was so utterly ridiculous. But I had to do it. I was close.

My clothes were covered in blood. Blood from the others and me. I tossed them into the trash not caring if anyone found them there. I washed off what I could in the sink. The covered my body in a long sleeved black shirt and slacks. I covered it off with a pair of dark sunglasses that just about hid the bruises in my face. I could barely walk.

I had to drive with my left foot, which was so very difficult. I found a very large shopping center in the next town. There I brought face make up to hide what was showing outside of the glasses. People were looking at me strangely as I limped around like a crazy person. I also acquired a cane to help me walk in this sudden old age. I ate as much as I could but my body could hardly hold anything. I needed strength though. I drank lots of water. I drove on to get across the boarder. It was not a long drive. I could make it through as long as I don't get caught.

I knew I was not okay. I was dieing. I could not keep my eyes from rolling over. I saw the trees covering the brightness of the sun looking out the window of my car. I closed my eyes. In an instant they opened. Then again it repeated.

The thump of the car woke me up as the sound of a loud horn roaring at me, woke me up. I grabbed the wheel again flying onto the side of the opposite road almost crashing into a huge truck. He never stopped just kept on going. And so was I, falling into the pit of trees. My breaks were in tune with me and we screeched to a halt at the end of a smack.

Robert woke up in loudness of a strange hospital. There were people everywhere. Kids crying with sickness, people wailing in the halls, few doctors not knowing what to do. Robert was woozy with pain. He had a concussion. He was lying on a hospital bed in the middle of the hall.

He sat up in bed to see if there was anyone around who could tell him what was going on. As soon as he leaned forward, he fell back. All the feeling in the back of his head struck pain from his head down his back. He grabbed his head trying to get hold of himself. A nurse walked by him and he pulled her arm as he was lying there.

"Where am I?" He asked. In a language he couldn't understand, she said she didn't understand him. She would get someone who could. "No wait miss!" He called as she walked passed him in the hall. He stared at the people around him in fear. He had heard stories that Mexico had the worst hospitals to go to. Some had said they would rather die then go there.

He pulled the covers off his body. He was afraid to even graze his shoulders against anyone as he was crawling out of there. There was some people screaming in the halls. The doctors and nurses completely ignored them. He grabbed a jacket that hung next to the nurses' station covering himself with it. In one of the rooms, a patient was bleeding to death, going into convulsions. Miller found his chance. He searched through everything they had until he found his belongings. He rushed out hoping they wouldn't stop him.

Outside it was silent. He had no car and no money. Everything he had in his wallet was missing. He didn't know where he was. He stood near the intersection of traffic and saw a yellow Volkswagen with a sign on top. Miller chased it down.

"Can you take me to the boarder?"

"You want to try and get out of this place or what?" Asked the driver.

"I want to get to the other side of Mexico."

"I can drop you off there but I won't go passed there."

"Fine whatever."

"That'll be forty dollars *cringo*."

Miller pulled out his gun from the bag. "I ain't got it. Now drive on."

"Pinche way!"

The driver drove off as instructed. Miller began to dress in the back seat. The man started watching him in the rearview mirror. He smiled at Miller. Miller looked up as he was zipping his pants together. He saw the driver watching him. The driver blew a kiss in the mirror laughing.

"You sick fuck'n bastard."

"You know whitie, you'll never get across with no money. That gun won't help you either. They have guns bigger than yours. This place is corrupt. They dump you body into the river without a care in the world."

"Listen here Jose, I have got to get there. This guy"—Miller looked to his side, seeing flashing lights. There was a house surrounded by police cars. The bug came to a slow to see what was going on. There were dead bodies being pulled out. He saw both of their vehicles there. He punched the seat in front of him. "Shit! Shit! Mother fucker!"

"There were three guys killed here. Some shit happened where they were slaughtered. Crazy. Shit like this happens all the time."

"This shit didn't just happen. This is a serial killer. This sick mother fucker is gonna pay. Do you know if there were any survivors?"

"So far, none."

"Let's just get there."

The driver laughed again. He got off to Millers anger. *Anything you want*, he said to himself. Robert was upset that he was losing. He wouldn't stop now. He didn't think about his wife and child at home who might be worried about him at this very moment.

"If you get me across, if you take me there, I'll make it worth your while."

As the driver came up to the line, he was about to let out the detective. He looked in the rearview mirror."

"What's your beef with this guy?"

"He's killed several people all over California and now he's just killed five peace officers. Men with wives, family . . . children."

The driver pulled the car into the lanes that would take a good half hour to reach the checkpoint. Robert just had to play like normal. He had to get across. That son of a bitch was just on the other side, he could feel it.

He was nervous and anxious at the same time. He wanted to find Alex Dugan and crush *his* trachea. All his friends were dead. He did want to stop at the sight where the barn was but then he would lose his driver and possibly get caught by the police. He didn't want to stop now. There was nothing between him and the killer.

Robert held onto his head and closed his eyes. His head was hurting from the collision. In his mind he pictured his daughters laughing as he pushed her on the swings. She was staring at him with a smile, her missing teeth showed her pink tongue as she laughed.

"Daddy!" She laughed. "Daddy not so high your making my stomach tickle."

"Well, then how about I spin you." He said as he was about to spin her.

The car went over a speed bump and snapped him out of his thoughts. It was hot and it was making him dizzy. He held the gun loosely for a moment until he saw the driver watching him to catch him off guard.

Robert sat up in his seat trying to act like he had his shit together. He saw that they were getting close in the line. He crawled the front passenger seat. He looked around very paranoid then sat back. He put his gun down his pant pocket holding it in his hand.

"Here's the deal Pedro, when we pull up, you act all normal like you and I are pals and were just going down to visit. Before you do any sudden eye jesters and head nudges, just so you know, if they pull a gun on me or catch me, you're the first one getting a bullet to the head, you got it?"

"Got it."

"Just get us through, dump me at the closest town and we're home free."

"Fuck'n asshole." Said the driver under his breathe.

But he did as he was instructed. They got through the boarder and Robert was on his way to the nearest town to hunt down his suspect.

Still there was no sign of light . . . I couldn't see but I could hear. There was a light rumble of a few voices in the back of my head. At first I thought it was just me dreaming after I hit my car into the tree. But as I looked around myself, it didn't feel like I was sitting in the front seat of my car.

"Hello!" I called.

But there was no reply. I got up from the ground still not able to see a thing before my own face. I reached out feeling for the walls. I felt cold and naked all over my body.

"Hello!" I called again.

I heard a grumble way at the other end of whatever room I was in. It was deep and angry. I tried to see.

"Hello?" I whispered as I stood there shivering from fear.

Suddenly, there came a dim red glow coming from the other end. He came out slow standing on two legs. He must have been seven feet, a mouth like a dog with a long muzzle with no hair, his mouth was filled with fangs, his eyes were burning red, he had two horns coming from the top of his head, he had a chest and arms like a man but his legs were like a goat.

I began to whimper as he slowly approached me. He was breathing heavily at my face. Tears began to flow down my face and sweat was pouring out my skin.

"Please." I whispered as I quivered. "Please, I don't want to kill any more."

"You will," he spoke in unison with other demons at once.

He grabbed me by the neck and squeezed lifting me into the air.

"You can never escape." They said.

I shook my head as I cried. He flung me across the room and I slammed right into the wall. I grabbed my back trying to put pressure on the pain. I sat sternal trying to regain myself. As I sat there trying to breathe again, I saw the shadows, the images of demons and men began to fill the room. Their images reflected off of the devil himself.

"I can't do this anymore." I whimpered.

The demons came towards me. Their hands reached out for me, tearing me apart. Tearing apart my insides. My screams sounded the way it felt. The sounds of my cries echoed in my head until my eyes met with the morning sun.

A person can only beat them self until it's just too damn pathetic. I lay on the floor just mumbling to myself while the noises stayed alive. Hours passed like weeks. If my mind is gone, that bright light coming through isn't real. The light was so white I couldn't open my eyes. A shadow came over the light standing before me. He threw water into my face. There, I could see a dark skinned man.

"Quitet de mi propiedad!" He yelled.

I stood up quickly. I grabbed my bag and ran as fast as I could. It's over. These dreams I have won't let me escape. Dreams like this will make a man never want to sleep. But you can't stop sleep from coming. The difference between my dreams and others, is that I feel every ounce of pain inflicted on me. Dreams aren't supposed to be real. Unfortunately, mine are.

I felt weak as I tried to run through the heat with my heavy bag. I felt like I was running from them, trying not to fall, leaping over bushes, nothing can stop me now. I looked back at the dark man who was yelling at me in Spanish. I called out to him saying sorry. I made it to the road where few cars passed. I just kept walking along side it hoping it would take me to a town. I had never before, but my body was weak, stuck out my thumb for a ride. No one stopped. I moved slower with each step. I had morning breath and dry mouth. I needed water and was close to fainting.

Just then a blue pick up truck pulled next to me. There was a very heavy set female inside. She was chunky all around, short, yet her face was pretty.

"Would you like a ride, you look like you're going to pass out?" Asked the lady.

I opened the door trying to smile at her, but my body was weak. I sat in the truck holding my bag between my legs. "Could you drop me at the nearest town?"

"Sure, no problem."

We drove away in silence. I grazed my fingers across my bag thinking about the new life I would start. I am retiring from everything with this money. This was not a bad place to spend the end of my days.

"So, how long have you been in town?" She asked.

"Oh not long." I realized then that I was filthy and smelled sweaty. "I barely got here. I wanted to see what deep Mexico looked like. I've never been here. So I'm pretty much blind."

"I've lived here for a while. I just came back from visiting a friend in Los Angeles. I know this town well, if you need directions."

"If you don't mind me asking, how did you know I wasn't from around here?"

"I saw your picture in the paper. You're wanted for some murders up in California."

"What?" I freaked out. I stared directly at her. She's going to turn me in! She smiled while she spoke.

"And then I saw the suitcase, so it was pretty much obvious."

"Yeah." My expression was at a loss. I must have imagined this.

"Well, I'm sure I'll do fine in this country." I patted my bag.

"So, whatcha got in the bag? Money?"

I closed my eyes. When I opened them again, it seemed as though she never said anything. She just smiled while she drove. My pores were releasing all over my forehead. She leaned her big fat face at me and smiled. Her teeth were a little green. "You can tell me *stud*. Come on baby, what do you say we hop in the back and fuck for a while." I slid against the door away from her. Sweat was dripping down my face. "Are you okay sir, you look a little pale?"

I held my bag. I wiped my face with my stinking arm. "Sure," my voice was cracked and high pitched. I wanted to get out.

"So where did you want me to jerk you off?"

"Huh?"

"Where did you want me to drop you off?" Her voice was slow and loud as if she were speaking to an old person. "I know most of the good spots around here." I felt as though I were a special Ed student. Then she winked at me.

"A restaurant would be nice. I'm pretty hungry."

"I'll drop you at the best restaurant in town."

"Where's that?"

"My panties!" My eyes widened. "Oh just up the street."

When she dropped me off I was as white as a sheet. The restaurant was quite disturbed with my appearance as I stepped in. I stayed in the bathroom a while to clean off the smell that followed me with a green mist. People stared at me as I ate scooting their chairs away as if I were a dirty criminal. I didn't care. I ate my food happily and drank down three cups of coffee to make sure I didn't pass out somewhere unexpected.

As I walked the streets people begged me for money left and right. I had to push them away from me. Some were glad to get away once they smelled how horribly disgusting I was. I knew it was terrible because I could smell myself and wanted to throw up. The smell of old blood can stain the hairs from your nostrils if not cleaned early enough.

The sun was going down as I walked the streets; bag in hand like some scared child who wouldn't let go of their most favorite toy. As it grew darker the people from the streets began to move into the alleys. I felt alone as I had all my life. But this was a new beginning. This time I might start afresh, meeting people without having to kill them. Was I so pathetic that the only precious commodities in my life were in this very bag, which I would not let go of? It was all I had left in the world. I could not go back.

As I imagined what kind of new life I could be living, I saw a man standing against the wall staring at me as if he knew me. The rage he wore in his eyes could only know what I held in my hands or an old friend, which I could not place. Yet there was no one in my life that I could forget. His eyes burned red with hate. I glanced at the man but kept walking; staring at the closed down buildings around me.

Footsteps were now behind me. They echoed in my steps as if they were mocking me. As I moved faster, so did the clacking of the person behind me. My heart never skipped a beat. I lost fear and felt my blood run cold with death.

I turned at the next alley. The footsteps still with me. I pulled my gun out ready to shoot but as I turned the man had already lunged a kick straight to my head. The sudden whiplash sent my gun to the ground almost in failure as I heard the sound of the heavy metal smack to the ground in a slide. I fell back trying to react but he jumped on my body pounding my head with his fist harder than ever I could. My back was in utter pain as hit the ground. He not letting go of my shirt. My arms got free reaching for my boot. As I clasped onto the blade I was almost unconscious and in my last fit of glory I stabbed him in the arm. He fell over while I tried to recover. My vision was blurry, I was almost out cold. Blood was all over my face.

I pushed him off and stood my ground. I began to kick him in the face and stomach though I could barely see. He was reaching just as I in the last moments of savior. I jumped on top of him so he couldn't aim, grabbing both of his arms. He fired into the air while we struggled to break free. I pulled the knife from his arm then stab him in the stomach as many times as I could.

I sat there watching him as he coughed out blood from his mouth. He forced the gun towards me aiming for my chest. His eyes began to close but he got one out on me. In my shoulder he could've killed me.

Who was he? I could barely hold myself up. I reached into his pockets looking for his wallet. As soon as I flicked on my lighter with the wallet in my hand, I saw the shiny badge. Detective Robert Miller. Santa Clara police.

CHAPTER 20

People here don't care what happens out on the streets, as long as you can pay them. I was in the hospital for three weeks. The doctor was glad that I could pay him off well. He fixed me up nicely. I lost a lot of blood and a transfusion was done at once. I paid the doctor extra to make sure it was clean blood. It would be a while before I could really move my arm well but it's better than having it amputated.

My fast ride is over which I am not sorry to say. My reward was nothing as I thought it should be. I had become loyal to my own head injuries and I can say now, I will lock myself up if I hear them again. Sometimes I think I should have let that man kill me. I deserved it yet here I am.

I got a street map of Mexico at my hotel. My retirement has come early and I have no problems to deal with. I've always wanted to live by the beach. People said Cancun is really popular where many people go during vacation. I took a bus out there dressed up almost looking like a drug lord.

The city was beautiful. There were people everywhere many foreigners and Americans. It was not like the other little town that looked almost run down. I asked a man who worked at the bus station, where there were nice quiet houses to buy along the beach. I didn't want to be too near the crowds. He told me there were private parts on the beach that no one was allowed to enter unless they were the owners, which was perfect.

I replaced my smelly old bag with a new one and clung to that one as if it were the same. The beach was beautiful where I stood. The sun was hitting the end of the water where it was about to go down. The water reflected so much light it could blind a man. I rolled up my pants letting the water that rolled on, touch my toes making my feet sink into the sand as if the floor were moving and not the water.

I sat down and just took in all the beauty that surrounded me. Down at the other end there were some beach parties; some people were swimming and some walking around. I didn't want to deal with another hotel so I slept right there in the sand.

I felt wetness in my face and I felt as cold as I did back in San Francisco. I opened my eyes to the morning with mid light but no sunshine. A shaggy dog was licking my face as if I were an ass. I backed away trying to get to my feet.

"Oh, sorry senoir." Said a man running along the beach. He called to his dog and they jogged off together.

I grabbed my bag which had my head print in it. I wanted to meet my new town. I walked around looking at all of the shops. I bought a pair of jeans and a t-shirt. I had all sorts of bags with me hurting my shoulder.

I found a perfect house on the beach. It was beautiful, almost secluded. There stood a large rocky mountain near about sixty or seventy feet away. The water came in low where the ocean touched the land. The sand was white almost like snow.

The house had three bedrooms, a large kitchen, dinning room, two bathrooms, a huge living room, and a patio that lead out onto the beach. The house was cheap compared to where I came from. I almost cracked up when the salesman told me the price. I brought in a decorator to set up everything. I wanted plain and simple. The furniture was cheap in price but not in quality. *Nothing flowery.*

Everything was quiet. Everyday I take a walk on the beach. I think of my brother often. I wish he were with me now, enjoying the view with my handsome nephews. Now is not the time to write to him. The police are probably waiting for something from me. If they met my psychiatrist then they know for sure to stick by my brother.

Before I felt alone. Now I feel really alone. When your born into family, no one ever tells you that someday, all you have is yourself. And it's your arms alone that will have to comfort you in despair. Quiet is too frightening to my ears.

Every time I go anywhere, to a grocery store or in town to walk around, my world seems so quiet. Everything moves, the world turns, but in my little world there is only silence and my heartbeat is all I can hear now. The sounds in a distance don't even rupture into my life, yet it could be a foot away from me.

The months go by all alone. I'm learning their language as respect for the country. And even though I can hold a small conversation in Spanish there's no one to talk to. I decided then to take up drinking. And everyday I hold in my comfort the joy of a new bottle. Out on the porch with myself. And when I'm near the end, I find myself in a world full of friends and many things to do. Alcoholism is something unintentional, but for me it is my quick death for a mistake I thought was my salvation. I always start when the sun is going down, when it hides right behind the ocean. Sometimes I'll read and other times I watch what fun people are having down below.

One day, close to a year here, I stood up and knew what might fancy me. I went out and bought me a sailboat. Not too grand but quite a beauty. I called her Freya, the goddess of beauty. Even though I never stopped the drink at my side, I cut back to feel the wind rush against my face as I chased the end of the water. The dolphins swim near you. I fish and catch large appetizing creatures. Sometimes, if I catch a lot of grand fish, I sell them at the market, with a cigar in my teeth and a fisherman's hat over my head with a Hawaiian shirt wide open just like a shmuck.

The tide rolls along the shore whilst the air held a tune that I heard ringing from the other end. The sun has already given its last glance at the ocean as I held tightly in my possession a friend of mine, Mr. Daniels. We too can spend passionate nights alone together watching the wind move the waves in rapturous splashes.

The parties on the other end have not stopped for the past few nights. It occurred to me that I made myself a little promise the night I was shot in the shoulder. I had to become more associative with the fellow man. I stood up stretching my arms. My Hawaiian shirt was wide open, my kaki slacks flapped in the wind as I began to walk down the beach in my flip-flops with sand in-between each step. I was already drunk before the night began. The closer I got to the party, the louder the band was screaming in my head. I wore a smile, which I couldn't let go of ever since I bought my sweet Freya.

There was a bikini contest on the stage with rappers jumping up and down, talking into their microphones in beats of Dr. Sues, and swinging their arms near their crotches. I had never been amused by this kind of behavior but I did come to mingle and plan to enjoy the sexy bods on stage that I plan to never strangle to death.

There were calls from all sides of me in words such as, "Hi what's your name; I'm staying at such and such hotel; would you like to go with me for a swim;" and so on. One of the hosts that stood near a camera and on her microphone, which said, in fashionable letters *MTV,* began checking me out. She asked me if I wanted to be in the male body contest. I gave her a side smile, saying *no way!* Very persistent were these little ladies in tight bikinis but I had to get away. This was not the fun I was looking for.

It grew dark but the party was still going. I was well on my way of passing out. The rap groups on stage, switched to some R&B group of girls in tight little outfits. They jumped out swinging their arms just like the men while they leaned over cursing to the crowd and the crowd cheered on. I was just there. I had already tossed the bottle. Not often had I drank down a bottle and had to stand on the ground. I walked around for reasons I don't know. Girls would stop me on my way but I pushed them off. I finally fell which I knew was coming.

Here I was, in the middle of everyone's spring break, and I was getting drunk with these shit eating dogs whom I've spent my life hating. I decided to just lie on my back and catch my breath. I found my way to the bar after long moments of hard breathing. The bartender didn't look cheery as the crowd but more involved with continuing his duties.

"What can I get you buddy?"

"Got any hot coffee?" I said rubbing my brows.

"You know, I keep some on the heat for myself, but I'll hook you up. Do you want it as it sits or would you like me to add in anything?"

"No more liquor for me. Black is just fine."

I sat there with my blurred vision staring at my coffee. I sipped on it as best I could. I began to doze away dreaming of a life I shall never have. Then my head fell between my hands. I was out for a few minutes but was awakened by someone grabbing the ashtray next to my head. I looked up for a moment.

"I'm sorry, excuse me," said she who caught my eye. Her voice was raspy like Kathleen Turner. It was deep and sexy. I hadn't usually been attracted to blondes but this one was different. I looked at her and smiled as best I could.

"Sorry I was in the way. I must have been drinking too much." I passed it to her. "There you go."

She took it between her thumb and index finger as if she tried not to touch it. She tossed it in front of herself. In her left hand she held a cigarette between her index and middle finger. I looked at her in astonishment. She impressed me in those insignificant seconds of life. She looked upset or board. She put the cigarette to her lips, sucked in lightly, then blew out the smoke while her elbows rested on the counter and her cigarette was up in the air.

She looked at me because I was staring at her. She blew smoke into my face, which didn't bother me at all. And in that beautiful Kathleen Turner voice she said, "Something on your mind bud?"

I smiled like an idiot, not knowing what to say for the very first time in my life. She was sexy. She had soft shiny blonde hair that reached down her back arching with her curves with light brown tints here and there. Her complexion was slightly tan but not like the surfers around here. She wore a silver armlet on her bicep that curled up her arm. She was wearing a flowered wrap around skirt that was either silk or satin with a black bikini top. She sat with her legs crossed perfectly. On one ankle she wore a charm anklet. She was sophisticated and snobby almost. I hadn't met a girl like her before. Most of the girls around me threw themselves on my lap like whores.

"I'm sorry. I just . . ." I couldn't find the words to start a conversation with her without sounding like a jerk.

She turned her head back to the bartender. "I'll take a beer." She stared right at the wall where the liquor was. "You know, all these people make me sick. I hate all these girls getting drunk and showing their tits to everyone. Very immature. And don't get me started on the men."

I looked at her again. Then in a shy smile with my head looking down I asked her, "Are you talking to me."

She took another drag of her cigarette then a drink of her beer. She turned to me then said, "Yeah, I guess I am." She took another drink of her beer and stared back at the wall as if she were too proud to stare at me. "My friends dragged me out here on our break for school. But I knew I wouldn't like it here. I can't click with this type of crowd."

Before long we were wrapped in conversation. It didn't seem like she liked me at first, but once she got a feel for my intelligence, she seemed more willing to hang out with me. She told me about what she was studying in school. I told her I used to own my own company but I gave it to my brother. She is majoring in business just as I had done.

"Well this is just a coincidence. Not many people jabber on about this stuff. I thought I'd be here with nothing but kids who only went to college so they wouldn't have to start on their own. You know, that mommy and daddy will support me as long as I go to school." Said she of a goddess body.

I gave her one of my side smiles. I stuck a cigarette in my mouth. I lit it and gave her one. She took it then brushed her hair back so she wouldn't burn it while I lit it. She took a drag. "So who are you here with on this vacation?"

"Actually, I live here."

"Really? Why?"

"I'm retired."

"My god, how old are you?"

"Thirty four."

"You are very lucky. So what do you do now?"

"Well it's like being on vacation all day everyday in paradise."

For those few hours we spent talking, the place began to grow quiet and everyone was slowly leaving to their hotels or suits. We were almost alone. She looked around when she realized how quiet it really was.

"I wonder where my friends went. Their probably at the hotel."

She was very intelligent. She seemed a little stuck up but she was cute and she thought I was pretty smart too. At first she thought I wanted to hit on her but that was far from the truth. Right off you must be thinking I'm going to fall in love with her, but I didn't. She was very smart and beautiful. She didn't hit on me, which was what I liked the most. She wasn't a slut. Still I thought she was too sophisticated for me. The way she held her cigarette, the way she sat while she spoke and how she talked of others.

"Well I guess I should head back home. It's really late and I don't want to take up too much of your time." I stood up. I grabbed my cigarettes from the counter. "It was really nice talking to you . . ."

She put out her hand. "Nicole. Nicole Welsh."

I shook her hand politely. And because I was taken by her conversation and her sexual wall between us, I kissed her hand like a gentleman. "It was a pleasure."

I began to walk away. She turned around. "Maybe I'll see you tomorrow."

"Maybe," I replied.

"I didn't get your name."

"Alex."

I thought about her as I walked home. I had the urged to look back and see if she was watching me or gathering her belongings but I had to be that different man. I could imagine what kind of girlfriend she was. Always telling me to hold my hand upright and gesture. She was rich; I could see that a mile away. She probably only had sex in certain positions because other ways made her feel like a slut.

I did show up the next day. I walked around that night drinking a bottle of tequila. I was so drunk, I could hardly walk. Some people had to help me keep my balance. I was having a good time.

"Make sure the maids don't go through my things. If I catch them, I'll have them fired." She turned away from her friend who was walking off. She looked at me. "Wow, didn't think I'd see you here today."

I smiled at her with my lazy eyes. I took a drink of my bottle. She gave me a disapproving look.

"You look like you need to slow down."

"Oh, I'm okay." I said. I didn't realize it until the next day, but I was staring at her with perverted eyes. She was angry with me.

"I thought you were different." She said.

Once she said that, I explained to her that, boring old rich folks need to have fun too. Life's too short to be sober all the time. And after a long conversation with Miss Nicole, she took a few drinks of my liquor.

I passed out. Somehow, I told her where I lived when she asked what part of town I was living in. I guess she wanted to know what part of the food chain I was on. I just pointed down the beach and said, "down that way, on the beach." Then I laughed. With my drunken eyes I pulled out my keys. I read my hand and said, "number five one two three." It went black after that.

Upon my face I felt a hot wet rag. My vision still blurry from the alcohol but I could see the clock on the wall saying two in the morning. I felt a little drunk but not like before. I was in wear down and felt all the collisions that come with it. I saw the shadow of someone standing a few feet away, staring at my credentials. I sat up, the rag falling from my head onto the couch.

"Nice place you got here. And you talk about me being rich."

I looked at Nicole, seeing her now in the dim light that shined in the kitchen. She was viewing my place as if it were a museum. "And what are you doing here might I ask?"

"Well, I helped you home." She looked around herself. "It's just beautiful Alex."

I looked at her funny. "How did you find my place?"

She turned around. "You told me."

"We didn't . . . you know?"

She laughed as if it were impossible for someone like her to make love to someone like me. "Of course not. I'm not like all those bimbos out there who come to fuck their brains out. I have a little bit more self respect than that."

"Thank god." I said as I leaned against the wall.

"What, you don't think I'm good enough?" She asked me, as if I *should* want her.

I lifted my head a little then laughed. "Honey, I don't believe you *haven't* been hit on by every man who passes you by. You got a sting. Trust me, you are the loveliest thing I've seen all my life. And I'll be honest, I've had gorgeous women before, but none have ever been as . . . what's the word?"

"Intelligent."

"Well okay, you can go with that, but I'd like to go with *snazzy*." I threw up my arm in a snap as if I were snazzy.

She stood up. "You have got to be kidding me. I have never bee"-

"Never what, be with a man like me."

"I wasn't talking about that. I'm not what you think. I can't believe how rude you are after I helped you home all drunk. I thought it would be a nice gesture but you are very inconsiderate and very,"

"Handsome." I smiled.

She looked at me funny. "Are you trying to bait me with this horse shit?"

"Baby, aren't you tired of being hit on by every man who comes across you. You are just that sexy. But I bet you; you don't have a man because you're so snobby. And I'll tell you this much, just by our first conversation I could tell you've probably only slept with about three men or less; you're just too confined at the knees."

She slapped me when I said those words. With my head tilted sideways I smiled. "I won't let you piss me off."

"I believe I already did."

I could tell that everything I said about her was true and she was hurt by it.

She grabbed her purse that was on the couch and headed towards the door. "Well, it was very nice meeting you Alex but I have to be going. Maybe next time you could pay your condolences to someone when they help you out." I smiled at her as she put her hand on the doorknob. She closed her eyes. "I can't believe I even helped you."

"You better hurry back or what would your friends think."

"They don't know I'm here."

"How convenient for you." I laughed with my arms crossed.

"You fuck'n asshole." She opened the door but I smacked it closed. "What are you doing?"

"I'm going to show you how good it feels to be bad."

"Let me go. I've had enough of your games."

I grabbed both of her arms with one hand and put my other around her waist. My lips were pressed against her neck. "You can have a little fun. I'll show you." I pushed my body against hers.

"Please, I'm not a whore."

I rubbed my hand over her flat stomach. "You know you could you use it. Stop being such a snobby bitch and I promise I won't tell anyone how bad you really want to be." I whispered in her ear. She closed her eyes then stopped trying to struggle. She loosened her arms then one grabbed my neck pulling me closer to her. I knew now, not to speak or everything else would be ruined. And if she wanted, I would let her go.

I turned her body to face me. I got down on my knees kissing her soft stomach that smelled sweet as wine. It may as well been her first time, in the way that I touched her. I picked up her legs with both over my shoulders. It was easy to rip off her little bikini bottoms. Her fingers rubbed through my hair as I suckled her body in my mouth. She was sweet almost untouched. She began to moan in ways I didn't think were possible.

I picked her up and carried her to my bed. I continued on where we left off. Her hands were grasping the pillows covering her mouth. I kissed her thighs touching them slowly feeling every bit of her. I moved in slowly trying to comfort her as I did. Her body was so tight I could hardly move.

"Wo, oh no,that's too big." She said.

I smiled almost wanting to laugh. "Don't worry." I touched her cheek with my hand. "I'll be gentle with you."

She touched my hand closing her eyes. I made love to her. I moved slowly trying not to hurt her. She was moaning and a woman's voice is extremely sexy when you make love to her. It made me want to move faster. My sheets were drenched with her alone. She was so good and I wanted her more than she wanted me.

She told me not to stop, not to ever stop. Then she began to moan my name. A man's name being moaned without asking for it is such a complement. I could hardly keep going. She put my hands over her chest as we made love. She urged me to lie down. Her long hair flung into my face like silk. I grabbed her cheeks softly pulling her to kiss me. I couldn't hold on anymore because she was rocking back and forth and moaning loudly in my ear. She shivered and closed her eyes.

"Something's happening," she whispered. "I feel so dizzy and hot. Everything is spinning. Ohh!" I looked at her and smiled. "Oh my what's happening?" I held her tight and I too, could not hold on any longer. I pulled her perfect body off of me and she lay there almost immoveable. Her breathing was harsh and she was sweating. It was as if we were both too high to come down. In moments we fell asleep in each others arms.

The best time of the day is to wake up in the afternoon. The sun is already out. No cold morning weather to make you shiver as you stand in front of the mirror to brush your teeth. As soon as I woke up I made myself some of the best-imported coffee from Columbia. I order a box of coffee so I won't have to keep ordering over and over.

I walked out to my porch sipping the hot coffee that I brewed. In the doorway I stood to look at the beauty that I enjoy everyday. The sun burned my eyes that day because of the glimmering in the water. It was almost as though god had sprinkled the water with crystals.

My boat was right out there waiting for another ride. Freya was where I could live if I wanted to. She would be the only other place I would rest my head. The ocean sent gets blown into my face when I ride her. I have to clip myself onto the boat when the water is rushing hard.

Some people need synthetics to fall asleep to this. For me, I leave the back door open and I can hear the ocean bubbling in the tide. Sometimes I would take a blanket to the sand and sleep right under the stars, on the soft sand, with the world moving around me. In the morning the seagulls flap around searching for crabs or something to eat. People jog right along the water and in the end they swim after their run. I wanted to share this with someone.

Nicole left in the morning. She asked me not to tell anyone about her and I. That was fine by me, but I didn't know anyone so who would I tell. I just let her know, I knew what she had at stake and I wouldn't take away her rich stuck up name. I gave my word.

When she left I said a long goodbye, which I had never done. I kissed her soft lips long and gentle. I held her tightly in my arms and she drifted back to her hotel hoping to slip in without anyone noticing. She had not tired to be with me at all, which made me want her. Her voice was addicting. I think I'll call her V.I Walschalskie. Thank god for women like Kathleen Turner.

I stayed in today. I didn't want to go back to the crowd. I wanted to cut back on my drinking since I found a new passion in the waters. I wanted to play houseman for the day by doing all my shopping at the market. Some stuff I special order, you never can tell what's in the food down here. I treated myself to a nice lunch outside at one of my favorite restaurants.

I planted some bushes in the front of my house today. At the market they had the roots in a bag, so it was easy to just drop them into the ground. I had one on each side of my walkway. Some rose bushes might be nice for the next plants.

I stayed in for the rest of the day. I made myself shrimp pasta. The seafood here was easy to get and very fresh. I wanted to try crabbing and shrimping on my boat, even though it wasn't made for that, I could still try.

I fell asleep early that night. My bed was so soft and comfortable it was hard not to just pass out. My comforters were so soft and heavy. There were no lights on around the house. I kept the back door open as usual to hear the world. I was in deep sleep. I was dreaming of soft hands touching my body and I grew aroused. I felt wet and thought I was sweating. I believed I was letting myself get really turned on. I felt soft wet penetration. I realized I needed to wake up.

I sat up in bed. There was Nicole. She was wearing a string bikini just lying there in my bed. She had me in her mouth. I touched her soft hair never once forcing her mouth like I had done to so many others. Like her body it had hardly been touched. The only thing that was in that mouth was criticism or demands. I watched her in ecstasy. I could tell she was having a little bit of trouble.

She did something that I did not expect at all. She took off her bikini, with her eyes closed, and began touching herself. She rubbed her hands all over her breasts. No one in the world could see this in her. I moved towards her. I pulled her next to me and started to kiss her face.

In a soft, sweet, tender voice that no woman would or ever did hear out of my mouth, I said, "Nicole, do you want me to make love to you?" With others it was demanding just as a mockery of themselves. I asked her what she wanted. And she would be the only one I asked in that voice.

She held my hands, caressing them and kissing them. She grazed my fingers over her soft flawless face. She was so strange. This is history in the making. Now if I could make it with all snobby women in the world, it might be a better place.

She kissed my face holding it in her hands. She looked right into my eyes. She said in a low voice, "I want you in my body Alex."

And I did what she wanted. But it wasn't like the first time. This was more passionate and meaningful to us two. We didn't get into any crazy positions, we just made slow love and still it was just as good. I loved her mind and her body. She must have thought the same for she looked at me in the same way. This was not love at first sight. I didn't believe in that anymore. But I did like this girl.

After it was over, I made her some of my imported coffee. She and I had a blanket wrapped around ourselves as we watched the sunrise together. She rested her head on my shoulder. As I handed her the coffee, I sipped on my own,

She took a drink. "Mmm. I know this coffee from somewhere."

"I'm sure you do."

"What's that supposed to mean?" She asked with a smile. She wanted to know what my sarcasm was for. I smiled back at her as if it were nothing at all. "My parents buy this coffee. It's French, no?"

"No. English."

"I really don't understand you at all."

"Why, whatever do you mean?" I asked as I sipped my coffee.

"Well you moved out here for a different life I suppose." She leaned back as she stared at the water. "Yet you still live the life with all this expensive effigy. You can't sit here and tell me that all of this furniture and things weren't specially ordered or made."

"Excuse me Miss Nicole but I just want to intervene this whole lifestyle. You merely lived off of your rich parents all your life. And you still do. I know that you plan to become a success without them but I had to do it all alone. My dad worked the same lousy job with low income all his life. And my mother still works to this day. I had to earn scholarships and work backbreaking jobs to pay for my clothes and food. The scholarships were just enough to pay tuition and books. I was lucky. Now, because I'm rich, you chose to throw it in my face for wanting the finer things in life."

"Geese. I didn't know you were so touchy about it. I'm sorry. But I don't want to talk about my parents. They're . . ."

"Yuppies."

"Yeah."

I kissed her forehead. "It's okay. I'm sorry too. I didn't mean to make you feel bad. I just don't want to talk about any of my past. I didn't mean to put it in such a way. You're really hard to deal with."

"Am I that bad?"

I touched her hand, which rested, in my lap. "Baby, you make a priest want to sin." She laughed. "But you are a little"-

"Stuck up?"

I gave her this agreeing look but I wasn't happy to agree with her. And she forgave me with the expression on her face. I just smiled as I put my arm around her. We looked out onto the ocean together. It was silent for a long while. We fell asleep in each other's arms. After I woke, I kissed her soft lips. She opened her eyes and looked at me.

"Why are you here?" I asked her.

"I don't know. You have sparked something in me. I can say goodbye but I'll miss you. I'd like to spend some time with you before I go tomorrow morning. I'm not going to take pictures or make a big deal but I do like you Mr. Alex." She touched my face.

I smiled at her touching her hand. "I like you too. I didn't think I would but you are so sophisticated and smart. And I gotta tell yah, I like the sound of your voice." She laughed. "How about I take you on my boat today?"

"You have a boat?"

"Right out there."

"Wow, I thought that was your neighbors."

"Well? I'll catch you a great dinner and make a suflay."

"Alright, let's go."

It took me an hour to put all that I needed on the boat. I had bought some crabbing and shrimping gear. I was going to try it all out. I got out all of my best filleting knives and some swimming gear.

She went through about three feet of water before she reached the boat. As she climbed on, I unhooked the boat from the ground and the boat already began to float away. I sat back in the drivers' seat, which I made all nice and cozy for me, then stirred her out into the sea. We drifted out pretty far and I pulled up the sail. We were moving fast with the wind blowing hard today.

She was having a good time. When it seemed as though we were out in the middle of nowhere, I pulled out a little anchor and the two of us went swimming. Both naked, kissing in the water. The sun was high; it was barely two in the afternoon when we stopped to swim. I put out two heavyset rods with large chunks of meat. I didn't know much about crabbing but I set out the nets as deep as I could get them.

We sat back, just the two of us. She had a towel wrapped around her head as she sat at the end of the boat washing herself off with soap. Naked there taking a bath in the salt water. I sat there with my wine and just watched her bathe. She jumped up laughing.

"Baby, a dolphin just rubbed against my feet!" She yelped.

I rushed over to her with a smile. I looked down at her feet but nothing was there but soapy water. We both looked out as we saw the dolphin splashing along in the water. He took off quick. She grabbed my hand laughing. She was released from her snobby self.

One of the rods began to tug. I grabbed it quickly reeling it in. Unfortunately it was a stingray.

"Oh my god, what are you going to do with it?"

"Well let it go. But I'll need you to hold the rod. If I get him the wrong way he smack me." I stepped on its body near the tail. I tried not to rip it up as I pulled out the hook. Now I had to grab it. I felt bad doing it, but I pitched it over the edge. "That's it for now. How about more wine. I don't think it's so bad if we get a little drunk."

"Three in the afternoon is not so bad."

Still naked and covered in soap, she began to turn me on. She took off her towel so it wouldn't touch the blood from he stingray as she continued bathing. Nicole took a sip of her wine. She had bubbles all over her body and the sun was right on her. I licked my lips tasting the wine believing I was in heaven. She dunked her self in the water quickly with a scream. When she got out, she seemed frightened to see me standing right in her face. I had a heavy thick towel ready for her.

I pulled her out of the water pressing her body up against mine. "You look real good, *baby*." She laughed out loud. "That's what you called me."

"Yeah, I guess I did."

I smacked her ass. "Get dressed, I'm going to check my bag-o-shrimp." I cranked my wheel bringing in the meat. Funny thing was, there wasn't much in there, but a few small crabs and tiny shrimps. She laughed at me as I stared at the bag in dismay.

"Maybe we should have brought some food in case."

"Why Nicole, I believe you're doubting my capabilities."

"Well I am a little hungry."

I smiled with my teeth grinding. Why hadn't I just killed the bitch? I wouldn't, I'm done. "Hold on baby, I'll get you a buffet!" I said as I walked across to the other side of the boat. She was freaking out on how fast I brought in the anchor and began to roll out my sail. She fell back a little as the wind began to take us on. She went down below to put on some clothes.

When she came back up I had her hold the wheel steady. I brought the sail down a little. Then I slowly began to wheel in one of my rods. There hung a nice large two-foot fish flapping away its fins. Her mouth dropped. I pulled in the other rod with a smile but there hung another *stingray*. She laughed.

"You gonna start cooking sailor?" She asked as I hung the fish up for a second.

"No baby I gotta check my crabs." And as luck would have it as I tried to impress this rich woman of the age twenty-five, there were gigantic shrimp and crabs stuck in my net. I told her to sit out on the deck while I stayed in cooking on a great stove that came with this boat. I had my ingredients ready and my knives nice and sharp. When I came up, I set out a fold out table. On it there were large crab legs, fried and basted jumbo shrimps, and the fillet of fish with secret ingredients. She laughed out loud when she saw what I prepared for her.

"Alex, you really are special. This looks great. If I got stuck with you, I'd probably end up fat."

"Oh, no way baby, I'll make sure I broil all the goodies and they'll taste just as good."

Nine at night, when her belly hung out like a drunken wino, I took her back to the shore. It made me happy to see her eating all the food. I really didn't mind her tiny belly. Women are too anorexic these days. I walked her to her hotel. She gave me a hug and kiss goodbye telling me this was the best time of her life, and she'll never forget it. I let go thinking it was the best time in my life also.

The whole day nearly blew me away. I haven't even made a dent in my funds. I'm as happy as a king. In the middle of the night as the clock ticked and tocked on my wall most annoyingly, I thought about what was next in my life. Who will I meet in the future?

I had waited for this moment to happen for a long time. I lived in a very nice house with furnishings people around here could hardly afford unless they were rich themselves. The rest were utterly poor, whom I'd rather mingle with than with others. Here the rich get richer, the poor get poorer.

I knew someone would break into my house sooner or later. It was easy anyway since I didn't lock the back door but left it open. I heard the steps on the porch, then into my living room quietly creeping as if I were deaf. I knew I would have to give them a beating, so I grabbed my bat that was next to my bed. Their shadow was there in the doorway and for some reason it reminded me of the ones I saw long ago when the voices wanted to scare me in the dark. But oh no, this wasn't a voice in my head. They reached over and grabbed something from my nightstand. I saw him lean in closer and as he did I knocked him in the head really hard. I felt I could've broken the bat.

I laughed out loud like a psycho giggling to them self. I clicked on the light saying, "How dare you try to break into my house!" What I saw was a shock. My Nicole was on the ground screeching, barely breathing. "Nicole!" I yelled. I screamed. Her head was gushing blood. I grabbed a towel from the bathroom wrapping it around her head where I must have busted something.

She grabbed my hand putting something in it. "Don't you fuck'n die on me! Don't you die one me! Oh baby please don't die!" I yelled out. Tears began to welt out of my eyes. Hers were beginning to close. I shook her. "Don't you close your eyes? You stay awake! Keep those eyes open!"

She could barely breathe. I heard it in my own heart. How blind could I be? This was not supposed to happen. Keep those fuck'n eyes open and don't go to sleep, I thought.

CHAPTER 21

When someone you care about is dieing everything comes to a complete slow down. You can't hear anything anymore but the heartbeat of the one who is drifting out of life. I can hardly hear her breathing. Rushing in the hospital hallways, holding her hand, and I can't see anything but her. And so the other rooms and halls become black until you must do something quicker to save the one you care about.

I slammed my hand on the counter. "Doctor Frank Martinez now!" I yelled. The blood was rushing out of her head but the towel was tightly holding everything together. The nurse who was smoking behind the counter smiled at me rudely.

"He's with a patient down stairs, I can find you another doctor." Smoke blew in my face.

"I don't want to get rude, but if you don't get Martinez up here now, your head will look like hers in about five seconds. Now hurry up!" She went over the intercom while some nurses rushed Nicole into a room. They began to take her temperature and pulse. I couldn't hear anything all over again as I stared at her from the doorway.

"Sir, we need you to step out." Said one nurse. She tried to push me out but I was as solid as a rock.

"Touch me again and you won't live to regret it." She looked at me frightened. "Where is my doctor?"

"I'm right here," says Martinez from the doorway right behind me. He was looking over his clipboard slowly. I turned around and as soon as he saw my face, he lit up. "Alex, what's going on, my favorite patient?"

"Doctor, this girl is very special. I'll take care of everything just as last time just get her healthy again please." He saw me almost begging.

He patted me on the shoulder where I had been shot. "You may not be my kind but you know I'll take care of you. Just step out and I'll be out in a moment."

I clenched my fingers into a fist then released myself in utter dismay. I sat next to the door in a chair waiting to see if she could survive without becoming a nut. At five in the morning the nurses walked out quietly talking to each other. I lifted my head as the doctor stood next to me. He waved for me to come into the room shutting the door behind me.

"Alex, she's almost lucky to be near you in this country."

"I think not doctor, I'm the reason she's this way." He looked at me strangely. "She snuck into my house in the middle of the night and I thought she was a thief! I smacked her on the head with a bat."

"Yes, I see. Well we've stopped the bleeding, but she has lost more blood than you did before. We'll need a transfusion."

"I'll give all that I have."

"I knew you would, so I sent the nurses to get the equipment." He held out his hand. "Sit down next to the bed. Roll up your sleeve."

"Is there trauma? Will she be retarded?"

"It's not safe to say yet, but we'll do a cat scan when she's better."

I gave her as much blood as I could, then passing out next to her. She barely awoke at eight in the evening. She called her friends, telling them not to worry and to leave without her. She's not far behind. After that she was out like a light. She stared at me as she laid back. I couldn't tell whether she was angry with me or not but either way, I just wanted her to get better.

They did the cat scan on her head late the next day. She seemed to be okay for now but there might be some long-term damage, which can affect her years later. Medicines and therapy might help if she works on it well enough. I promised her I'd pay for that until the day I died. She told me later not to worry about it. Her parents would make sure she didn't become mentally ill. I prayed nothing would catch up to her *in the end.*

A week later I took her to the airport so she could get back home to New York. She gave me her address but knew it was hard for us to ever keep in touch.

It was windy the day I walked her out to the plane. Everyone was boarding the plane walking up the stairs. I held her bags. She stopped before she walked onto the stairs turning to face me.

"I know I said I didn't want to make it hard when I left but you didn't have to hit me." She said touching her head.

I closed my eyes. "Nicky, you know it was an accident. I didn't"-

"I know." She touched my lips with her fingers. "And I thank you for taking care of me the way you did. I've heard of what kind of hospitals they have out here and you made sure I used your blood and your doctors'."

"Don't worry my blood is clean. I got it from the doctor." She looked at me funny. "It's a long story. Just have a safe trip and a good life. Don't go back to your snobby self, Nicky. Just be that girl who was naked, swimming with the dolphins."

"Nicky?"

"Sorry, you don't like it."

"No, I do." She was quiet for a moment not wanting to say a word and then she said, "I'll miss you." She hugged me tightly and then she was in and out of my life like she never existed.

As I walked out of there I tried not to think of her at all. But it was hard. On the bus ride through town I wanted to pat myself on the back for not killing her, even though I almost did. She didn't deserve it. I felt bad for what I had done to her but there's nothing more I can do now.

A rapping suddenly woke me up as I was sleeping on my chair out in the patio. I snorted as I sat up hearing the noise.

"Alex, what are you doing, sleeping back there?" Said Eric through the door. It then sounded as though he put his mouth to the door muffling his voice on purpose. "Al . . . ex!" He called. "Open the door or I'm going to go in there and steal all your shit."

"Alright! Alright." I said as I opened the door.

He smacked my hand. "What's up dude? You heading up to the bar tonight?"

"Nah, I might just go fishing or something."

"Dude you never want to do shit. Come on down and we'll get all fucked up."

"It sounds fun, it really does, but I just have some shit on my mind."

"What do you possibly have on your mind? You don't work, you don't have to take care of any one, and you're home free. What is it? Are you thinking about that girl again? What was her name, Natalie?"

"Nicole. And no, I'm not thinking of her. I was just thinking about taking a trip out of town. Maybe in Europe."

"Man you rich fucks get to just get up and go. What's say we go down to the docks and grab a couple of beers."

"Alright we'll go."

Erick was a guy who ended up here by mistake. I met him shortly after Nicole departed. He was from Oregon and came down for vacation. He ended up becoming a bartender at one of the most popular bars in town. He saw how depressed I was one night. After several drinks he and I had a long talk and found we had a lot in common. I needed a buddy.

We hung out on the pier, ate some shrimp from one of the food stands and drank down some beers. He had other friends he hung out with but I hardly mingled with them. They were different from me and thought I was strange. We were talking about businesses in the states and what made some fail and what made some shoot high. He didn't know who I was.

By midnight we were slightly drunk and heading back to the bar where he worked. He had several girlfriends and wanted me to meet some of the women that came in there. I didn't really care about that anymore but it wouldn't be too bad if I were dancing with a nice girl.

It was pitch black out with a few streetlights on. Three men were walking our way. I could see them from far off. They kept their heads low and were very quiet. I pulled on Eric's sleeve.

"Say man hang back." I said in a low pitch.

As the three men walked passed us. Two of the men pushed into Eric and I moved out of the way. They got on top of Eric trying to take his wallet. The other guy tried to grab hold of my arms until the others were done. I grabbed him from the back and swung him down over my shoulder. He lay there curling into a little ball slowly. I took hold of one of the men who was looking through Eric's pockets. I slammed him up against the wall and started pound his head with my fist.

"Hey, get off of him!" Yelled the other one in Spanish. He let go of Erick. He grabbed a broken piece of wood from the floor and smacked me across the back. Erick regained himself and saw the other guy hitting me in the face. He yanked him off and knocked him a good one in the face. I grabbed the other guy and hit him over and over.

"You think we're fuck'n stupid." I yelled in Spanish. "Don't ever fuck with me again!"

"Woh! Woh! Alex let go of him, you're gonna fuck'n kill him." Erick yanked me off. The three men ran off.

I was trying to catch my breath. "You fuck'n let them go!"

"Yeah, you were about to finish them off. That was freaky. I had no idea you rich folks knew how to defend yourselves."

"Oh shut up."

From that moment on he believed I was a little psychotic but he liked me like that. It made me more human than I seemed to be. My emotions seemed to be non-existent. But they didn't know me from the bar. I came in there, got drunk on occasion, and sometimes I would buy drinks around the house when I was really happy. Instead of being an alcoholic alone, I had the disease to share with others.

My headaches still persisted when I let them get to me. I had an economy pack of Excedrin, which seemed to be my only savoir. I had to take three pills to stop my headache as I went fishing. I seemed to be catching the drift of crabbing and shrimping. I had caught a small shark, which I was proud of. I had left my equipment on the boat so all I needed was some chicken to catch the ocean scavengers and some worms to catch my fish.

For some reason, the rides weren't as fun as they once had been. I was out in the middle of nowhere. I had wine in my system keeping me at ease as I sat at the end of the boat watching the waves; smelling the breeze. The only sound was the creaking of the boat as it swayed with the waves. She was out there by the water, naked, beautiful. I smiled at her as she rubbed the soap on her body. The boat shook a little as a school of dolphins swam by.

"Oh my god, it touched my feet!"

Her voice drifted with them as they swam out farther than my eyes could see. I felt the yanking on my boat and pulled in a fish. It was small. He seemed to be laughing at me. I took him off, throwing him back into the water. I played my symphony loudly as I sat there motionless. I wanted to relax as I always do, but I seemed to be tense.

I took a gulp of my wine. I chuckled for a second almost mocking my own laugh. Who needs women, I thought. I stood up trying to make the mood for all things around me. I took off my clothes and jumped in the water even though it was getting pretty dark. It wasn't as fun as it should have been. I grabbed my underwater flashlight from the boat. I ducked myself underwater with the light pointing down looking at the fish, the salty seawater for what it really was, and trying so very hard to see the bottom. It was magnificent.

Later I pulled in a large amount of my all shapes and sizes shrimp and crab. I also caught myself one lobster, which was a little small, but if I kept him alive for a short while, he would be quite a dish.

These things as good as they seemed were not for me. I took half of these things to the poor on weekly bases so they would have something to eat. It lasted long for some. For the greedy, it lasted two days. The other half, I took to the market and sold to the snazzy restaurants and snazzy townsfolk. My funds were usually spent on beer and liquor. It was a life.

That night I came home with a migraine that Excedrin couldn't cure by a mile. I laid in bed, in the dark, trying to make it go away. I tried to sleep it off. I took a cold shower, which helped on occasion. This was one that hurt like before. I had to get out. I walked the streets in the middle of the night.

There I was, barely able to move, in the middle of town. I wanted the outside environment to take it all away. I passed by the bar but never went inside. I could see people dancing and having a good time through the window. I kept my hands in my pockets and kept moving. Down near the pier, I sat down on a bench just thinking of what could make me well.

"Hi stranger, you look like you could use a friend right about now." Said a woman from behind me. She spoke Spanish smoothly. She came around and sat next to me.

I replied in her own tongue, "I'm okay, I just feel sick."

"Maybe there's something I can do to make you feel better." She put her hand on my chest scooting closer to me. She was wearing this maroon tight dress with designs all over it. She looked like a crack addict and began to get on my nerves. "Since no one is around with the hour so late, I could help you feel really good." She touched my crotch, then trying to grab at it. "Only twenty dollars." Said she.

"Miss please don't do that."

But she wouldn't stop. My head began to pound. I was feeling dizzy, irritated, and ready to explode. It was a feeling I knew all too well. They were coming back. It seemed as though they just thundered through my head loudly. Then clawing at my brain crying, "kill her! You must kill her." All demons coming from every direction! She was unzipping my pants as the voices were tearing me apart inside. I smacked her hand away saying, "No I don't want you." She was persistent. Demon heads were showing me blood and death. I couldn't take it anymore. If this is what I have to do to get rid of this pain, *then so be it!*

I grabbed her by the neck and began to squeeze. I looked at her face as I was almost taking her life. She was gasping for air trying to get me off. My hands almost crushed her neck when I let go. As soon as my hands left her body, I could see the demons yelling at me. It was as if I killed them when I let go. She fell back on the floor holding onto her neck with one hand, coughing.

"Oh my god, I'm sorry!" I said in Spanish. I jumped up as she flinched back. "Forgive me miss, I didn't mean to." I began to walk backwards. "Please, I'm sorry." I laid out a fifty-dollar bill in front of her. "Forgive me," I said again as I ran away as fast as I could.

As I ran home, I felt them chasing after me. The shadows were jumping around behind me. I feared them worse than anything in this world. If they got hold of me, I'd be stuck in their world. In pain, in death.

The bar was right there. They couldn't do anything to me if I was surrounded by people. I went inside. The bar was still packed with people. I saw Eric sitting at a one of the round velvet couches with a few ladies and his friends. He smiled at me as I walked in. But he saw something horrible in me. I was pale. My face was covered in sweat as if I had been on a marathon. I was nervous and looking around. He took his arms away from the girls rushing to me.

"Alex what's going on? You look horrible. Are you okay buddy?"

I looked out the window. They were gone. "I'm just sick that's all."

"Well what are you doing here?" He put his arm around me walking me to the bar. I tried to relax as I moved in with the crowd.

"I ah, can't be alone at home. I'm having problems being in that house right now. But I'm hoping that some whiskey might help me sweat this out."

"Hey no problems. Why don't we drink a little and I'll come stay with you until you get a little better."

"You would do that?"

"Hey, you saved my life the other day. I think I can help you around the house for a little while."

He grabbed me a glass with ice, and then poured in the whiskey. We sat down with his friends. I was still looking around for them. As I was about to drink the last of the whiskey, I looked in the bottom of my cup as I was bringing it to my mouth, and I saw one of the demons. "We'll get you." It whispered. I jumped back throwing the cup to the ground. All of Eric's friends were looking at me. I looked at them, and then said, "I'm sorry, I felt like I was going to throw up with that last drink."

Good old Eric took me home. He was drunk but we walked well into the night. He laid me in bed leaving the door open just incase I needed anything. He slept in one of the spare bedrooms.

For days I was ill. I had a headache, a fever, and a bad cough. He wanted me to see a doctor but I didn't want to be caught for any mental illness I had. I was popping pills. I ate nothing but soup and juice. I tried my best to get well with cold alcohol baths. It stayed that way for a week. And Eric sat through it all like a good friend. I dreamt of the Demons on occasion. He would wake up to me screaming in the night.

Slowly calming myself down by the sea. I had my lawn chair right in the wet part of the sand. I was sipping down a nice cold glass of tea. My shades were on as the sun was setting apart from the sky. My head tilted back with no headache at all. I could hear on the other end of the beach, some reggae music that had me shifting my head from side to side with the rhythm. It was a good day.

"Is the tea cold enough for you my love?"

I looked behind myself where Nicole stood in her little wrap around skirt and bikini top. I touched her hand, which rested on my shoulder. "Everything is great. And I just wanted to say I missed you while you were away in the kitchen. What were you doing?"

"I was making some sauce for our roast later." She came around the chair sitting in my lap. She put her head on my shoulder. I put my hand around her waist. "Let's say we take a hike together. I feel like getting up and doing something."

"Whatever you want gorgeous, just as long as I have you."

"But you don't have me." I looked at her strangely. Before the sun faded out, the water turned red as blood. The sky became dark. Clouds began to rush in making the tide splash higher than I've ever seen it. "You don't have me," she cried. A hand came out of the water, taking her from my lap. She was pulled to the center of the water. "Help me Alex, I need you."

I stood up looking out at the demon who came from the water still grasping her in his hands. Its voice was deep; laughing at the same time. "If you can reach her, you can have her."

I jumped in the bloody water swimming out as far as I could. I thought there must have been a lot of fish in the water but when I looked around myself it was filled with dead bodies. They were reaching for me pulling me under. The Demon held her over my head.

"If you can reach her, you can have her." I tried to swim to the top of the water but they wouldn't let go of my legs. I could see above the water, even though my vision was cloudy with blood. "Do you love her?" He whispered. I tried to talk but the water was filling my mouth. I tried to hold my breath but it was going away. I was forced to breathe water and began to cough underneath. I could taste the blood in my mouth.

"I do love her!" I screamed out trying to breathe.

Erick ran into the room. He swung in holding onto the seal of the door. "What's going on bro? Are you alright?" I could tell he was sleeping himself and I had awoken him again for the tenth time this week. I threw the blankets off of my legs and stepped out of bed. "Wow, that's the first time I've seen you get up all week."

I went straight into my closet pulling out a duffle bag. "I've got to go." I started stuffing clothes into the bag.

"Where are you going? You're a little sick man."

"I've got to find her and tell her how I feel about her."

"About who?"

"*Nicole.* I'm in love with her dude. It's taken me this long to realize it." I was rushing around the house with him following me. "I tried to tell myself it wasn't love at first sight, but it was. I've wasted too much of my life waiting for that perfect somebody and I let her walk out of my life." I was in the kitchen now. I opened the refrigerator drinking down a bottle of water.

"Alex, you realize it's been about over a year since you last saw her?"

"And?"

"*And,* she may have started over and forgot about you. I mean, it was her spring break and you might have just been a fling."

"No." I shook my head as I was cramming food supplies into another bag. "This is real. I have to know if this is my one chance for sharing my life with somebody. Maybe it's not the life that you choose but I'm in my thirties and I haven't had a girlfriend since the ninth grade."

"Alright then, I'll drive you to the airport."

"I'm taking my boat."

"Your boat? Alex have you gone crazy? You don't know how to sail that far. You'll end up lost in the Mediterranean. Why can't you take a plane?"

"It's better this way."

"Well I can't stop you but if you want, I can give you a little herb to help you relax when you're lost in the middle of no where."

"Cool." I looked around the house. "Now take me to the docks."

I took everything I needed. First aid kit, perfect fake identification cards, food, clothes, hygiene, fishing gear, maps, tools, ect. I had to get to her. I never realized it then but I do now. She is who I want to be with. I should have never let her leave my grasp.

Eric was right. I had no idea what I was doing. I thought if I kept along the coast of the main land I wouldn't get lost but I was sent off in deep waters when I was off the coast of Florida. I had got trapped in a storm. I called for help but no one could hear me. The tides were rapid almost knocking the boat over. I was afraid I would die out there in the waters. My boat was damaged. I was lost. It pushed me away from my destination.

I was knocked unconscious when my stereo came down crashing over my head. I awoke two days later. There was no more storm, but my sail was gone and I couldn't get anywhere from here. I began to call out for the coast guards over and over. Still nothing. I threw out my anchor so I wouldn't drift outward anymore.

Eric was right. When the moment was right, I lit up a blunt and got myself high as a kite. I should have thought to buy a cell phone or something. In my mistakes, I can laugh at them here with my joint. I sat there shortly two hours, as high as can be expected when drifting out alone.

Over my head I heard a loud engine. I was stoned and didn't move quickly enough. I grabbed my flare gun and shot into the air. I had believed it passed me by, so I went back to smoking. Twenty minutes later the plane was over me again.

I yanked on my radio almost breaking it apart. "May-day! May-day!" I was stoned. "Can anyone hear me? I'm stuck out here!" I looked around myself. "In god knows where. Can you hear me?"

"We can hear you copy."

"Oh! Oh! Get me out of here! I don't know where the fuck I am." I looked up seeing the plane whiz by me again. "Is that you above me, in the orange plane?" I cried.

"That's a roger. We're going to send a rescue team out here for you. Just give us about an hour or two."

"Oh thank you."

I laughed to myself, then threw my body back onto what used to be a great sailors chair. I took the blunt from the floor then relit it again. It was probably two weeks already and I had gotten nowhere. I put together in my bag, the most important of my belongings, identification and money. I also had the note that Nicole left me with her address on it.

Less than two hours later they showed up in a helicopter. I felt I should be in one of those rescue TV shows. They lowered in a gentleman who looked around the boat wondering what had happened to my boat.

"Is it worth fixing?"

"Like hell."

He helped me onto the ladder and we flew away. I was very thankful to them for saving me. I had been caught in a storm for two days and it brought me out about sixty miles from Georgia. My boat was wrecked and there was no use. They told me if I was heading out for far distances, not to use a small sailboat. I felt really ridiculous.

I set myself in a small hotel. From the weeks of sickness and the days spent on the boat, I had acquired myself a fully rounded beard, which I had never seen on myself. I kept it just in case. My hair had gotten a bit long since Nicole had seen me. It had grown down to my neck and I looked as though I were a biker of some sort.

The easiest thing for me to do now was to buy a ticket on a train and just ride out there like a normal human being. It would take me three more days to reach my love. She was all that was on my mind.

Since I was here and no one could trace me from California, before I left on the train. I made a very special call.

"Dugan's oldies, how may I direct your call."

"Anthony Dugan please."

"I'm sorry but," and I was afraid he didn't want my business or he was in jail because of me or, "he's not in today. He doesn't come in on Saturdays, would you like to leave a message?"

"No." I dialed to his old number but I got the tone of low to high pitches, *we're sorry but the number you have dialed is no longer in service* . . . I put the phone down. I had one more idea. I dialed my old house number.

"Hello." A woman's voice.

I cleared my throat trying to make the voice of a stranger. "Ah yes could I speak with Anthony please."

"I'm sorry but he's a little busy, could you call back in a n hour or two."

My voice sounded like an old pathetic car salesman. "Well miss, it's very important. It's a matter of life and death."

"Give me a minute."

I could hear the phone moving around. "Yeah."

"I'm very sorry to disturb you, but is this line secure and free from all legal aspects?"

"What? Who is this?"

"Don't ask questions. Is the line okay?"

"Probably not."

"Call me back. Is the number on your caller Id?"

"Well it says location."

"Good enough. Find out the number and get back to me." As I hung up the phone, I thought he wouldn't call me back. But he did thirty minutes later. I picked up the phone.

"Who is this?" He asked.

"It's the person you took care of when you were little."

"*Alex?*" I grunted to let him know it was me. "Holy shit where the fuck are you. They have my house phone tapped, or your house phone tapped. I didn't bother changing the number."

"Lucky for me."

"Are you okay? What the hell went on? I know it's gotta be true with you taking off like that."

"Everything is true. But I called to tell you that I'm okay. Is this line secure?"

"Oh yeah, it's Jennifer's mothers cell phone. Just recently bought."

"Good." I took a deep breath. "I live in Mexico now. I ah, well recently I fell in love and I'm on my way to see her. See, she went back home to the states and I didn't realize I was in love with her. Was that Jennifer who answered the phone?"

"Yeah, we were in the middle of making love but for now this is way more important. The police have you on the ten most wanted list. It's a five million dollar reward to bring in your head. But I wouldn't trade you for anything."

"And the boys?"

"Going to a really good school. That money and everything you left us made us just as you left off, successful. But how could you leave me like this? I didn't know what to say to the police. They went through everything in my house."

"I can't stay on the phone for long, I have to catch a bus out of here. If you give me some safe address to write to, I'll send you information and pictures, the whole nine. I wanted you to know it had nothing to do with you. Tell the boys I love them very much and I can't wait to see them."

"I'm being watched like a hawk brother. But you can send the letters to my mother in law's house. Just be careful out there. And I love you."

He gave me her address, which I wrote on the letter she had given me. Now it was time to set things the way they should be, in each other's arms.

CHAPTER 22

Speaking to my brother was very reassuring. I had missed him since I left but had to keep my distance. If they catch me now, because of that one phone call, it was worth it. And so is she. I sat here in the dinning cart dressed normal like any other Joe. People stare at me strangely because of my hippy look with the beard. It was smart to stay like this. I ordered myself an *all American* burger. The ones in Mexico tasted like shit. But even in this dinning cart they brought me a good thick burger with all the junk; cheese; bacon; veggies.

I sat there with the newspaper reading up on new murders and robbers of the US. Americans have this idea that if they come up with a good plan, then they can rob people blind. In Mexico it's different. They just come out and rob with no plans at all. They might be eating at the same restaurant as you, then decided right then and there they want to rob you. Not thought out well but it works.

When arriving in the city I had to find a replacement boat. Luckily there was a convention all week at one of the large coliseums. I purchased a small yacht, which I was instructed on thoroughly.

I was ready to see her again. Her home was exactly what I expected. The butler informed me she was at her graduation. I called around looking for the right location of the graduation. She was going to be a master of business I thought. I was proud of her.

It was crowded in the auditorium. I looked around for her but there were too many people. They made their announcements and began to call upon every graduate one by one. It had been two hours and still they did not call her name. Her name was Welsh, which would be one of the last. I fell asleep until her name was called. In my dream it awakened me. I saw her walk on that stage with a beautiful smile. I looked around seeing a group of people standing up before the rest to cheer her on. I stood up clapping for her myself. I was so proud of her. When I saw her walk on that stage, I felt my heart pumping faster. I was nervous just from the sight of her. I missed her for so long and could not admit it to myself.

When the ceremony was over, everyone was gathering around with their families talking loudly, hugging each other. I walked through the crowd looking for my one and only. There she was standing by the stage smiling. I stood still, not wanting to move because the sight of her took my breath away. I could have been happy with just taking a look at her. Her family was talking with her. There was a young man with his arms wrapped around her with his own cap and gown on. He kissed her putting his hands on her face. I began to walk closer reaching out my hand to call her. I was stopped halfway there as I watched them taking pictures together.

I turned around trying to push myself to leave, asking myself why I was there. I wanted to take her and never let her go. She was so different from every woman I ever laid my eyes on.

I left. This was not my place to be. I stayed by her apartment building waiting for them to come home. Her parents were back around eleven o'clock; dropped off by a limo. I was upset that when they saw me standing there, they moved around to stir clear. I felt almost like my heart was breaking the farther away I was from her. She came home at two in the morning, dropped off by a BMW.

I was leaning against the wall watching, as they were drunk, loud, and saying their good byes. As he kissed her I felt almost like I could kill again. They drove away before she walked into the building. I grabbed her from behind covering her mouth with my hand. I didn't want to be noticed, so I did the unthinkable to my love, I knocked her out with chloroform. I took her back to my yacht. I laid her on the bed in the room. There was no way she could escape from there. I stayed up waiting for her. She was asleep several hours.

Nine in the morning came around. I was half awake, half asleep. I heard her taking a deep breath as she was waking up. I sat up firmly waiting for her to come out. As she walked out of the room, I could tell she was not fully awake. She stood in the doorway when she finally noticed the strange man sitting on the couch. She moved back looking around herself. Maybe she was looking for something to bash me with.

"Good morning beautiful." I said calmly.

"Who the fuck are you?" She demanded.

"You don't recognize me?"

"You're that bum I keep seeing. What am I doing here? What do you think you're going to do to me? If you had any idea who I was you'd realize you'll be spending a long time in jail."

I stood up with my arms opened as I talked. "Nicole, you look real good. I have to say; I liked the blonde hair better. But this is still just as good." She tilted her head sideways trying to recollect. "I missed you and I had to come and see you." She looked closer at me. "I thought I wasn't just a fling."

"Alex?" She almost whispered.

"Yeah, it's me. Don't like the beard and long hair, huh?"

She covered her mouth. I stepped closer to her. She pushed herself towards me and we hugged. "I can't believe you're here. I thought I'd never see you again." She pulled away to look at me. "What are you doing here? Why were you stalking me?"

"Well, I wasn't sure if I should talk with you. But you were the only reason I came here."

"Really?"

"Nicole, I have to say honestly, ever since you left, I tried to push you out of my head. I thought maybe I was thinking about you because of the accident. But just a few weeks ago, while I was suffering from a violent fever, I woke up realizing that I was in love with you. I tried my best to get here sooner but I ran into some trouble with my boat." She looked around the new boat. "This is my new baby. Do you like it?

"It's beautiful." She backed away. As she began to speak, her eyes were on the ground. "Alex, I have my life here. I've started all over with a new person. I think it's sweet that you came for me but things are different since, what, almost a year ago."

"Marry me Nicole, I swear I'll spend my days making you the happiest person alive. Please, be my wife."

She turned away from me. I touched her hand that was resting on the counter. "Alex, you never called or wrote to me." She turned around to look at me. "I'm sorry but I really have to start my life and it won't be with you."

"Is it the other guy? Do you love him?" She didn't answer me. "You can't love him. He won't be as good to you. Nicole, I can take care of you. I'll give you whatever you want. But most of all, I'll love you more than any man ever could in this lifetime. Just tell me if you love him."

"I don't know. I don't know what to think. You can't just walk into my life after so long and expect me to just marry you all of a sudden." She touched my hand when I let go of hers. "What we shared together was beautiful and special and I'll never forget that, but you have to let it go." She turned around. "I'll admit, I thought about you. I thought about what we did together, even wishing this would happen someday, but that was a long time ago."

"Go ahead and leave." She began to walk up the steps. "Nicole, I can't go sailing without seeing the vision of you laying on my boat. I can't sit out on my porch watching the sunrise without imagining you there in my arms. And I wanted to do that for the rest of my life." She stood there quiet for a moment, and then she was gone.

"Is everything okay Nicole? You seem a little distraught." Nicole was looking at the floor while she and Charlie were eating lunch. "Nothing. I'm okay."

"Good. Because I was trying to tell you about this interview I was on just early this morning." Nicole yawned as she looked at him. "Anyways, as I was saying, he asked me what my best qualities were and I went on to say . . ." As he spoke she began to look away again, lost in her own thoughts. After seeing Alex, even the way he was, brought back the sweetest memories of her whole life. "Nicole, was that not funny," laughed Charlie in a fake deep tone. "Nicole? Nicole?" She looked up at him again. Seeing Alex's face she smiled at him, but the voice of Charlie brought back his own. "What is with you today? I'm not getting any of your attention at all."

"I'm sorry, I just have my mind on a couple of things."

"Like what? You can tell me."

She just looked at him strangely as he smiled like a schmuck resting his elbows on the table. "Well I'm not up to talking right now."

"Well, fine by me. I have another interview with this law firm downtown tomorrow."

Nicole looked at him almost with her mouth open. He was very uninterested in her or her problems. Whether or not she wanted to tell him anything was irrelevant, the fact that he didn't care upset her. "Look Charlie, I've got to get going. I'll see you later."

"Later?" He smiled. "Why, where are you going?"

"I just have some things to do."

"Do you need a lift?"

She stood up collecting her belongings. "It's okay. I don't want you to rush through your lunch."

"Well thank you. I'll call you okay."

Nicole kissed Charlie on the cheek. She rushed out to the street to grab a taxi. As soon as she sat down in the car, she took a deep breath. She headed to a spa for the rest of the day to sort out all of the odds and ends of her feelings. She had made a decision and it might not be what she wanted.

I saw her boyfriend at the tennis courts with some other gay boy just like him. These were the type of rich boys I used to eat up in the old days. I followed him into the sauna. Five other men were in there just relaxing with their towels wrapped around their waists. I was sitting in the corner watching them talk. The only thing they had to talk about were lower class citizens, people they knew from high school who ended up in small time jobs, and welfare debate. I just stared at him with my evil eyes hating every bit of the man who won my Nicole's heart.

"Well I've got to head back to the office but I'll call you later." Said a few of the yuppies as he was walking out.

The rest of the men slowly left until it was us two. Lightly in my head were old faint sounds of whispering. I was not going to resist. I would go with them this time. I walked over to the door as he had his eyes closed. I locked the two of us in.

I grabbed that jerk with my hand on his throat choking the air out of him. His eyes opened instantly. His voice was trying to cry out but I had grip of him good. I stood him up without letting go. He tried to get my hand off of him by hitting my wrist with his fist. He only earned himself a hard blow to the face, breaking his nose.

"You stole my love. Now you're going to die."

"Please don't kill me he screeched."

I looked at him as he began to cry like a woman. I heard dripping. I looked at the ground where a puddle had formed down the side of his leg. My head tilted sideways in amazement. Of all the men I killed, none of them looked this pathetic, not even the gay yuppie I killed in my apartment. My face turned red with anger as I began to squeeze the life out of him. His face was turning purple.

I dropped him to the ground. He grabbed his neck coughing loudly trying to catch some air but it was hurting his chest. I stepped back, staring at him like I was hurt and angry at the same time. He looked at me as he held onto the bench. I stepped backwards then was out the door.

His life was in my hands like so many others, yet I could not do it. Not like this. He had never wronged me nor was he hurting Nicole. Maybe I should just step out of her life and find a new life for me. She is in my mind always.

Nicole had not been with Charlie since they had lunch, which had been two days ago. He had tried to call her two times but she was not up to talking with him. She would think about all the things they did together and ask herself if he even made her happy. She could not stop thinking about what was so exciting about Alex.

It was the middle of the night. She couldn't go to sleep. She played solitaire on her computer while the late night TV shows were on. They were having a special on crime all over America. She had her mind off both men as she was playing her game.

"The ten most wanted list has now been changed so if you see or know of any of these men call us at the number on the screen."

Nicole glanced at the television for a second then back at her game. She saw something that caught her eye. She looked back quickly. As she did, for the split second they showed the pictures, she swore one of them looked like Alex. The pictures disappeared as they changed the topic of the show. She waited to see if they would show them again but there was nothing.

Quickly, she signed on-line searching for America's most wanted list. There were many articles through each page she went to. It finally had a tiny picture where it said; click here for photos of most wanted criminals. She clicked on. The pictures were blurry and small. She looked through each one trying to make sure but the pictures were so small. There was one that looked like Alex. She closed her eyes as she clicked on the face. Sure enough, on the top of the screen it said, Alex Dugan. She read pages on most of the murders committed. It wasn't even a jail photo; it was a nice picture of him in a suit. She read how he owned a very popular car lot, which his brother now owns. The more she read, the more she cried. She slept with a serial killer. A man who murdered women all over California. A man who dismembered people so bad, others couldn't recognize them.

Each story she read on these women, each detailed death, she pictured her own face on those women. Covered in blood, strangled, stabbed, skinless, choked. It could have been her when she was with him. She touched her head where he had hit her. But he cried when he did. He screamed for her to stay with him. This could not be the same person. She couldn't believe that, that intelligent, sensitive, romantic man was a serial killer, mass murderer.

There was a sign that said, click here if you have any information on this person. She wanted to click it, but it could be someone else. *It had to be.* The stories he once told her about his masters' degree and his car lot, were a match to the story on the computer. She would hide out for the next couple of days.

I had to see her one last time. I had to tell her how much I would miss her when I'm leaving. I miss her now. Three days after I almost killed her boyfriend, I waited for her at her home. I didn't want to scare her like last time, so I decided to go to the door and ask for her. The butler answered as usual. He let me in telling me to sit in the waiting room.

In there, there were fancy couches that looked as though no one ever sat on them. There was a long white piano that looked silent and never touched. The room seemed to be a showroom or where the woman of the house had her little tea parties. I waited five minutes.

She came into the room striking back as she saw me. She moved away looking around as if she were in danger. She grabbed a poker from the fireplace.

"Nicole, what's the matter with you?" I asked as I stood up.

"Move back! I know who you are. I want you to leave before I call the police."

"What are you talking about?"

"Don't act so innocent with me. Who are you?!" She demanded. "Who are you really? What's your real name?"

"Alex."

"Alex Dugan?"

I tried not to make an expression as if it were true. She must have looked me up some how. "Look, I only came to say goodbye. I'm leaving in the morning."

"*Don't* try to change the subject, are you Alex Dugan the killer?" I kind of laughed as she spoke like a child. She was so cute trying to be defensive. I walked towards her. "Come any closer and I'll scream!"

"If it makes you feel better, I'll sit back down and you may stay as far as you like. Now what's this all about? Come on Nicole, you know me."

"Oh yeah! Then what's your name huh?"

"Alex Stevenson."

"I don't think so. Now get out of my house."

I stood up walking towards the door. With my hand on the knob, I looked back at her then said, "I only came because I'm in love with you. I would never in this lifetime, ever hurt you. All I want is for you to be happy. That's all." I opened the door taking a step.

She put down the poker with her eyebrows up trying to be sympathetic. "Alex." She called softly. I stopped and turned around. "If you're really in love with me and would risk anything to be with me, then tell me the truth."

I put my head down thinking for a moment if she was worth it. In a moment I knew. "Yes I am Alex Dugan. And not a day goes by where I don't wish I could take it back." She touched the poker again. "You know where I'm at. You know when I'm leaving. If you want to turn me in, you have all my information." I walked out of the waiting room then out of her life forever.

Whether or not she testified against me, I would not see her face again. This is the life I made for myself. I won't point the blame at my abusing parents or back stabbing friends. This is me; this is who I've come to be. The voices might be real; the shadows might be a hallucination. If she was to be the death of me, then all that I have done will come back to me.

I waited on my boat. I waited to be surrounded by New York's finest in fully loaded swat uniforms. There would be police sirens crying out into the night that I was finally caught. While I waited, I decided to drink myself pretty deep. I picked up a little weed on my way back to my boat. I was drunk and high as I laid in bed. My back room was small. Almost perfect the way the TV was right at my feet. The whole boat was rocking me to sleep as I watched TV. I hadn't really veged out like this in a while. I ordered a pizza. On your last days in *the world*, you want to do as much as you can. In this very moment some men might be calling the best call girls in town to show them a good time. The only girl I wanted in my bed, was the very one who is turning me in.

I fell asleep dreaming of Demons this night. I wanted to dream of something pleasant before morning came. But I woke up screaming at nine in the morning. My boat was still rocking softly. It was coldest waking up this close to the water. I put my hand on the door thinking that when it opened there would be a gun in my face.

There was nothing. I made myself some coffee. Stepping out of the boat I expected the same thing. There would be hundreds of officers with their shotguns at me. But it was a cold morning with the other fishermen or sailors walking around with their equipment. I stepped out onto the docks with my coffee walking over to the Dock Security Officer. We talked about the weather for the next few days. He told me there wasn't anything expected yet but to keep my radio nice and loud. If I should here of any storms at all, pull into the nearest docks and take a break.

I went into the convenient store they had on the docks and bought some food, first aid, water, whatever I needed. I headed back to my boat trying to carry all my bags. I looked around as I got on the boat. No one was around. I began to unpack putting some things into the small refrigerator I had in my little kitchen.

Before taking off, I took a quick shower and then ate breakfast. It was time to leave. It was ten thirty. I put my radio loud in my captains' room. I turned on the motor for the first time by myself. She sounded beautiful. It made me forget all of my problems. I made sure everything was as it should be. I walked out taking my rope away from the pier. I felt like a king as I stood behind the wheel.

I pushed the gas handle with my hand just pulling out.

"Alex!" I heard lightly. "Alex wait!" That did not sound like the police, I thought. I looked back expecting to see a few officers there. I was going to rush out of there. I never let go of the gas. But it wasn't police that I saw, it was Nicole. She stood there waving at me. I pulled back on the gas and sat there for a moment.

I pulled back in then climbed my way to the back where she stood. "What are you doing here?" I asked her.

"Taking a chance with a killer." She smiled. "Take me with you. If I can't be with you, I'll never get you out of my head."

"Be careful or you might lose yours." Her smile was gone in an instant and she frowned. "I'm kidding." I smiled at her. "I'm kidding. What I said to you I meant. Will you come with me, be my wife?"

She looked down then back at the world she thought about leaving behind. "Yeah, I'm coming." She handed me her bag. Then I carried her on board with me.

We drove out together, she in my arms helping me stir my way back to the Mexican coast.

CHAPTER 23

The ride back home took us quit a while. I can't remember how long I was lost at sea in my sale boat but it was just as long getting back. I could tell through the ride she tried to relax around me but there was this uneasiness about the way she looked afraid of me. I tried my best to comfort her but I have to earn her trust in a big way.

There were times where she felt like it was us all over again. While I was behind the wheel, she would come up from behind me and wrap her arms around me. When it was hot she would lay out on the deck in her bikini. At nights I would rub her shoulders. We did not become intimate with each other at all. We kissed but I kept my hands to myself along with a distance to let her know I was not going to hurt her. I let her sleep in the bedroom while I slept on the couch. Sometimes I would find her squeezing in with me on the couch in the morning.

In the moments that we shared alone on the boat, it was enough for me to have spent a lifetime with her. I can't keep her from her dreams. Just as we were off the coast of Florida, I had to tell her what I felt.

"Nicole, I can turn back right now and take you home." I was standing behind the wheel. She just walked in from sitting on the edge of the boat with her feet grazing the water.

"What do you mean?" She asked.

"Look, I know this is a big step for you. I can be satisfied with having seen you all this time. You won't ever have to worry about me trying to hurt you at all. You'll fulfill your dreams back home."

"No." She shook her head. "No. I want to be with you. If I wasn't sure, I would not have stepped foot on this boat. It will take me some time, but I will be comfortable with you just as we were before."

I smiled at her and never brought it up again.

"Rise and shine my love." I crawled next to her on the bed. I had her mocha Swiss coffee ready and hot. I made her Swedish pancakes topped with strawberry butter and fresh strawberries. "Wake up sweetie."

She opened her eyes looked up at me. I put my face to hers and kissed her nose. I had never acted in such a way but I felt like mush around her. Her eyes squinted from the sunshine as she tried to sit up in bed. I put the tray over her lap. "Oh thank you Alex, you have really got to stop making me breakfast in bed. I'll never get a chance to cook breakfast for you."

"I love doing this for you. So, what do you want to do today?"

"What haven't we done?"

"How about you fish with me and we sell at the market."

"Like those people off of the harbor back home?"

"Yeah," I smiled. I could tell she thought it was a little tacky. I knew it would be strange for her to do things like this but she didn't know how fun it was. "Just try it today."

She had strawberry butter on her lips. "But I'll stink of fish forever. And people will think we're vagrants or something. I've never worked a job like that before."

"Oh it's okay. You don't need to impress anyone but me. We'll spend the day together and come back to sell in the market."

She took another bite of her food with a smile. "Okay, if it means that much to you."

"Yes it does." I said. I looked at her with no expression not even knowing it. I saw how she feared me right there and then. I didn't know what to do so I kissed her on her forehead and walked away.

We took out the boat with all of our supplies. Back in New York I found some good scuba gear. I figured we could go down to the bottom and find some lobster. Out there along the coast in the hot sun, we had four strong rods out along the side of the boat. She caught one large fish and we stored it in the freezer. I sat still on the deck with a glass of beer in hand. She had a frozen Pena Kolata. I stared at her looking overboard at the water. She was wearing a Hawaiian wrap around skirt and a tank top. Her hair was pulled back out of her face. Her brown hair was growing back blonde and the sun began to dye the tips of her hair. She turned to look at me with her sunglasses hiding her eyes.

"When can we go scuba diving?"

"If you want, we can go now." I sat up in my chair. "Have you gone before?"

"Once a long time ago. It was beautiful. Do we have an underwater camera? I'd love to take pictures of the bottom."

"No but we can get one soon." I stood up drinking the last of my beer. "Alright, let's go now."

In the bottom the world is beautiful. In the bottom there is no rape, murder, cheating, all what's left back at the large continents of life. All you hear is quiet beauty. The water seems dark on the end with fish everywhere. I saw her smiling as we held hands under water. We searched the bottom to find large crab and lobster, some small, some grand. When we had about ten of each, we went back ashore a little ways from the boat. I pulled her up on the boat, both of us dripping heavily.

"Oh my god, that was incredible!" She said trying to catch her breath.

The two of us looked at the lobster and crabs we had collected in the net. They moved like crazy. We laughed dropping them into a tin tank I had brought along for them to swim in. We dressed ourselves. We wheeled in many more fish together. She was smiling all day long. And as the sun went down and the sky was red, we rested together out on the deck listening to the ocean.

"This might be a strange question because we don't know too much about each other but, do you have any pot on board?" She asked me with one eye squinting at me. I laughed as I looked at her rubbing lotion on her legs.

"*Do I have pot?*" I laughed as I spoke. "Do I have pot? Lady, you're looking at *the* pot head of the century." I went inside and pulled out a large bag of weed. She laughed loudly as if it were just too funny. We smoked a couple of joints and drank some more. We were both feeling pretty messed up. I continued on catching more fish and storing them away. We had all kinds of beautiful fish.

"So honestly, what did you do back home? Did you really rob a bank and that's why you have all this money?" She pulled out a cigarette and handed me one as she lit her own.

I took a drag. "Honestly, I don't know what the papers were trying to say, but I was a millionaire in California. All that money was mine. I just lost it in the bank when they refused to give it all to me in cash. It was all my money. I had my own car lot. Dugan's Classics."

"Oh, I've heard of that place."

"Yeah. It was all mine. I was poor when I started a long time ago. And if you're wondering, I *did* earn my Masters Degree. It wasn't a lie."

And in the sudden quietness that came with my finishing words, she broke it with a question I dare not ever answer her. "Alex, why did you kill all those women? Who were they? What was it like?"

I stood up baffled by the question. I walked over to the rods waiting for a bite but there was none to change what she just asked me. I could no longer look at her. She would never look at me again if I old her what I have done. *A bite!* I pulled the rod and turned the reel. It was nothing but a small fish, not even size enough to eat.

She stood up then went below. As she did I closed my eyes in horror of what I was. I didn't want it to be like this. I knew one day she would demand to know the horror of my past. I looked over at the dark black sky with the moon changing the water to a deep blue. I was in paradise and for a moment it didn't feel like it.

She came up from behind me kissing my neck. "You hungry?" I turned around facing her and she had two large subs made all nice and neat with a salad on the side. We sat on the deck floor, it being our favorite place and ate quietly.

She loved when we went to the market. We purchased our own spot where others were selling what they could. We sold all the lobster and crabs for a cheap price. I didn't care. She had a great time and the people who came to us were very nice. She took a little spending money and shopped around the market while I sold what was left. I found her by a bookstore at the very end of the market when I was leaving. And still my fondness for her never faded.

I put my arms around her as we walked home late at night. There were some children in the streets of the town we walked through. We gave them all the money we made so they could have something to eat. As we made it to the doorstep of the house I stopped to look at my flowers, which had been blooming just nicely. I picked one on the biggest brightest flowers. She stared at me smiling as I put it in her hair.

"Nicole, would you do me the honor of making me the luckiest man in the world?" I looked in her eyes.

"I thought I did."

"Will you marry me?"

It was silent for a while. It was a long shot but she was here with me now. It didn't hurt to ask. She looked around at everything. The sky, the beach below, the house, me, and it came clear she wanted it as much as I did. She wrapped her arms around me whispering yes.

I picked her up taking her inside. I laid her on the bed as we kissed. I touched her body like I had since I saw her a long time ago. She was moaning as I suckled her body. "Kill her." A whisper came in with the wind from outside. I sat up looking around. She looked at me strangely. It seemed to be my imagination. I kissed her neck and she held tightly onto me. "Kill her!" Screamed those demon voices. My head began to pound. I sat up staring at her. As she was asking me if I were okay, her face changed from gorgeous to a demon and her voice changed into the many that called out.

"No!" I cried as I grabbed onto my head. I got out of bed and rushed outside where I threw up all the fiesta food we ate earlier. "Go away!" I cried. "Please go away." And slowly they began to fade. I was in the sand on my knees when Nicole came rushing out.

"What is it? Are you hurt?" She touched my shoulders.

"I'm sorry. I have migraines that could make you want to kill yourself. And I hadn't gotten one until today. It was a long time since I had one."

It was strange for me to fight this off. I had to keep my head straight; keep the demons from trying to make me kill my one true love.

With the excitement of the wedding, she shopped for decorations everywhere. She said she wanted to ceremony on the boat so she had a wedding planner come on the boat to see what they could do. She ordered the cake and sent out invitations to our friends from the bar. She wanted to have seafood, so we spent lots of time shrimping, crabbing, and fishing for the best dinner.

I had to make the call. "Is your line safe?" I asked.

"Call me back at this number." Tony gave me a number to a payphone just around the corner from the house.

I called him back in ten minutes. "Tony?"

"Alex?"

"Yes it's me. How are you?"

"I'm great. How is everything?"

"I'm getting married!"

"No shit!"

"Yes. I want you to come down. Is it safe for you to leave?"

"Well, I'm not sure. I can pretend I'm leaving to work on a normal day, and then we can take a cab to the airport. Yeah, I can get around them if they're still out there. Who is this girl? A Mexican gal?"

"No, she's American. I met her last year when she came down for spring break." I gave him all the details and we decided what day he would be here. He was going to tell work to cover for him and if anyone calls he was in a meeting or out to lunch or already left for the day.

Everything was all set. My brother would be in for a few weeks. My bride was having a bridal wrap around skirt made. It was all so perfect. They toasted us at the bar for our engagement party. That night I was a little drunk and so was she. We came back home ready to fall asleep.

I kicked off my shoes and undressed into my shorts, yet she was out on the beach sitting on the sand. I waited for her about fifteen minutes until I found her out there. In the dark. All alone. I came out there to see what was the matter and she just looked at me.

"Baby what's wrong."

"I can't marry you." Her voice was low almost in a cry.

"Why not."

"I need to know, Alex. I need to know what you did."

"And if I tell you, you'll runaway. I'm not proud of any of it. But I would never hurt you."

"But if we're to be married, you need to be honest with me."

I began to gather wood and sticks together so I could make a fire. I had to get comfortable and there was no way I could. She sat there waiting for me to speak. I lit a cigarette and sat back down.

"So what do you want to know first?"

"Who were all these people?"

"Mostly hookers, stripers, that sort. But some were old enemies."

"Old enemies?"

"Yeah, my friends thought it was a good idea to jump me and make up lies about me until they stole the only girlfriend I ever had. They wanted to humiliate me. And I sure felt like it. I got them back."

"What did you do to them?"

We spent all night and until morning about what I had done. I told her about Nick and the others. An easy way to say what I had done getting around the torture details. I told her about a few women I killed but the less grotesque stories. She was shaking a little. I let her know I had been seeing a doctor out here for a year and that I was doing just fine. When it was mostly said and done, I told her that if she felt uncomfortable, there was money in the house and she could leave now if she wanted. I kissed her head and went to sleep. What she thought now was something I didn't want to ask just yet.

We didn't talk much after that. I slept the whole day in. She must have gone out because I didn't hear anything all day. She might have left. I put money on the table as I came inside to ensure her now, she could leave if she wanted. I told her things that no one should ever know about things I had done.

At night when I could hear the waves splashing, I woke up alone. There were no lights on in the house. I walked out onto the porch, still no sign of my love. She was gone, so was the money. Instead of crying because I expected this, I sat down on the chair in the patio watching the tide roll in.

Headlights pulled in from the front reflecting off of the house. I felt the beams behind me. I stood up to see who it was. Nicole came out. I ran inside as she unlocked the front door with many bags in her hands. She was breathing deep as she smiled.

She took one deep breath and said, "you'll never guess what I found at the market?" She pulled out some things from the bag. "I picked up some good wine and dinner for us. I didn't feel like cooking, so I picked up some chicken. Sound okay to you?"

I just looked at her with my puppy dog eyes, quiet as a bird. She walked up to me looking at my face. "I thought I'd lost you." I put my arms around her tightly. Afterwards, we ate dinner, drank our wine, then sat out on the beach. I let her bury me under the sand while we talked.

"Alex, I don't know how to react to what you have done. I'm trying really hard. And any person in their right mind would leave and turn you in. But for some reason, I can't do that. I have this feeling that you won't hurt me. And I can't believe I'm sitting here talking with you. You are known all over the US for dozens of murders. I'm marrying some one famous."

"Oh my god!" Said Tony as he got off of the plane. "Son of a bitch." He laughed as he walked up to me giving me death hug. We both laughed as we saw each other. From behind him came Jennifer and the boys. She gave me a hug. I squeezed my nephews tighter than ever. "Look at where we're at honey. So where's this beautiful woman you've been raving about, that you're going to marry?"

Nicole walked out from behind me. I put my arm around her waist. "This is Nicole. Nicole," I faced her, "this is my brother, my best friend, and the only man I can trust."

Tony put out his hand and shook hers. "An honor for someone with your courage." He laughed.

We walked out together. Nicole and Jennifer began to chat a little as she got acquainted with my family. I asked him if he were followed and he was sure there was no one trailing behind. He snuck out of work in one of the cars disguised and they hitched a plane out of there.

We decided to take them for a stroll around town. I spoke to both of my nephews as we walked around at all the sights. My brother and I were wearing Acapulco shirts and khakis. The girls were wearing summer Hawaiian dresses. It was a nice day.

By nightfall, Tony was talking with Nicole as they stood at the end of the pier. "My brother and I went through some rough times together. I know him more than anyone else. I promise you, you'll be safe and happy with him."

"Do you know what he did to all of those women?" She asked him.

"Of course." He nodded his head. "Yeah, I know. And I fought every inch not to believe it all. They still keep tabs on me at home. I live in his old penthouse and I run his shop now. It's even more popular than ever. I guess America loves a good killer celebrity. But it's over. He's okay now. And he's a good person. One day, when you find the time, he might tell you how it came to be so. I'll hint to you, our parents could have messed with his head. It was rough. Not to many words can explain what we went through in the house of my mother and stepfather."

"Are you serious? We haven't spoke about our past too much. Except for what he did. I have to admit, I do get really scared. But now that I've met you and your family, it seems pretty normal."

"Gosh you are very beautiful. My brother deserves a woman. Can you believe he hasn't had a girlfriend since high school?" She looked at him strangely. "I mean, everywhere we went, women would throw themselves at him. But he wanted nothing to do with them. I guess that's where all *this* came in. And I'll tell you this much, if you every need anything, Jennifer and I will be right here for both of you. If you think he's acting different and not for the better, I promise you, I will come right out to see what's going on. I would not let him harm you if you felt something was going to happen."

"Thank you." She whispered as she hugged him tightly.

My day has come. I had the best chef in town prepare all the food we caught. Shrimp, lobster, crab legs, fish of all kinds. I could smell the food tasting so wonderful. She wanted her parents there but she knew it wouldn't go too well. My brother walked her down to me. We had a very close friend who was a minister, perform the ceremony. There were about thirty people all dressed beautifully on the boat. It was sunny out. We moved out to sea.

As she walked out from the bottom, I was afraid. But when I turned around to look at her, I was in shock. She had the most beautiful dress made. Her skirt was a long white wrap around, like what they wear on the beach. It trailed down about four feet behind her. She wore almost like a bikini top, all white with the pearls and embroidery all over her top and her skirt. Her blond hair was pulled back halfway with some sort of a beaded crown winding through her hair. She was gorgeous.

It was down hill from there. We said our vows, I promising to never harm her. We ate a wonderful dinner with everyone. We had music and dancing. It was wonderful. The boat stayed out until one in the morning. We headed back dropping everyone off at my own pier near the house. My brother said he'd wait the weakened and when we came back he'd be there.

She and I stayed out at sea for the weekend. We made love more passionate than ever before.

A year has gone by. My brother has come by two times since then. We've been happy. Tony's wife is pregnant with her first child. I was happy for him. For now, I try to steer clear of children. I want her to be comfortable with me. It's a great life for us too. We fish and sell the food in the market, then give the money to the poor as we decided a long time ago. She's been happy. We've gone to Hawaii and to England for a few trips away from home. She's taking up painting. Nicole sits outside staring at the world then practices painting. She's getting better. She told me some about her childhood, I had a hard time talking about mine but she's my wife. I have to open up to her.

"Honey, I thought I could make some Italian tonight." Called Nicole from the kitchen.

I walked out from behind her as she was cutting vegetables on the counter. "Oh, you think you can cook Italian." I kissed her neck and tickled her a little.

"Hey, you'll mess me up. And yes I *can* cook Italian. You just don't let me cook."

I backed away. "Have all the space you need to cook your Italian." She looked at me with a smile as I backed away. "I'm gonna take a shower."

"Alright."

She new I loved Beethoven. I walked over to the stereo and turned the music loud. I set up the water in the shower just nice and hot. Life was different for me this way. But it's better. There's no more hurt. I took one peak at her as she was mixing her sauce. I smiled at her thinking how much I loved her.

In the water I was beginning to think I was ready for a child with her. We'd be even more complete. All my dreams and wishes are finally coming true. I have a smart, beautiful girl who's wholesome just the way I always wanted. Now I can complete this life if she wants to. We can have child. I can be normal. I can finally be happy.

I felt a strike of pain in the head. I heard the voices slightly in my head. I kept hearing them talking amongst themselves. When I turned off the water, it was gone. I smiled to myself. It was only the water making me think it was something else.

I stepped out of the shower. The air was filled with steam, I could hardly see. When my eyes adjusted to the foggy room I saw Nicole standing there.

She looked frightened and angry. But it was too late. She broke my heart right there. It was the end for me. I chose not to strike back nor stop the stabs she thrust into my chest. I fell back onto the ground with tears in my eyes. I could hear her screaming.

"The voices! They're everywhere! They're in my head! They won't stop!" She was screaming so loud as she cried. And then I saw the demons, which forced her to me.

Blood everywhere. I could hardly move. My eyes rolled back, staring at Nicole. Echoing onto death was her cries, Beethoven's *Midnight Sonnet* playing on the piano, and my heart fading away, all because I wanted to get away from the voices. They found a way to get back at me through her beautiful innocent hands.

And darkness falls on a broken heart. The demons were right.

Women . . .